THE Lost Rose

VICTORIA LYNN

THE Lost Rose

g.w.
press

To all the ones who needed rescuing. The Knight already came, and He'll never leave you.

Beach
illias pass
mines/caves
Wood River
Niran
Docks
Woodriver tributary
Wood River Village
Kingsman Training Outpost
Valhaven
watchtower of amardeep
Raintamount Forest
ELIRA
Violets
Padsley
N
W
E
S
PAVLIN

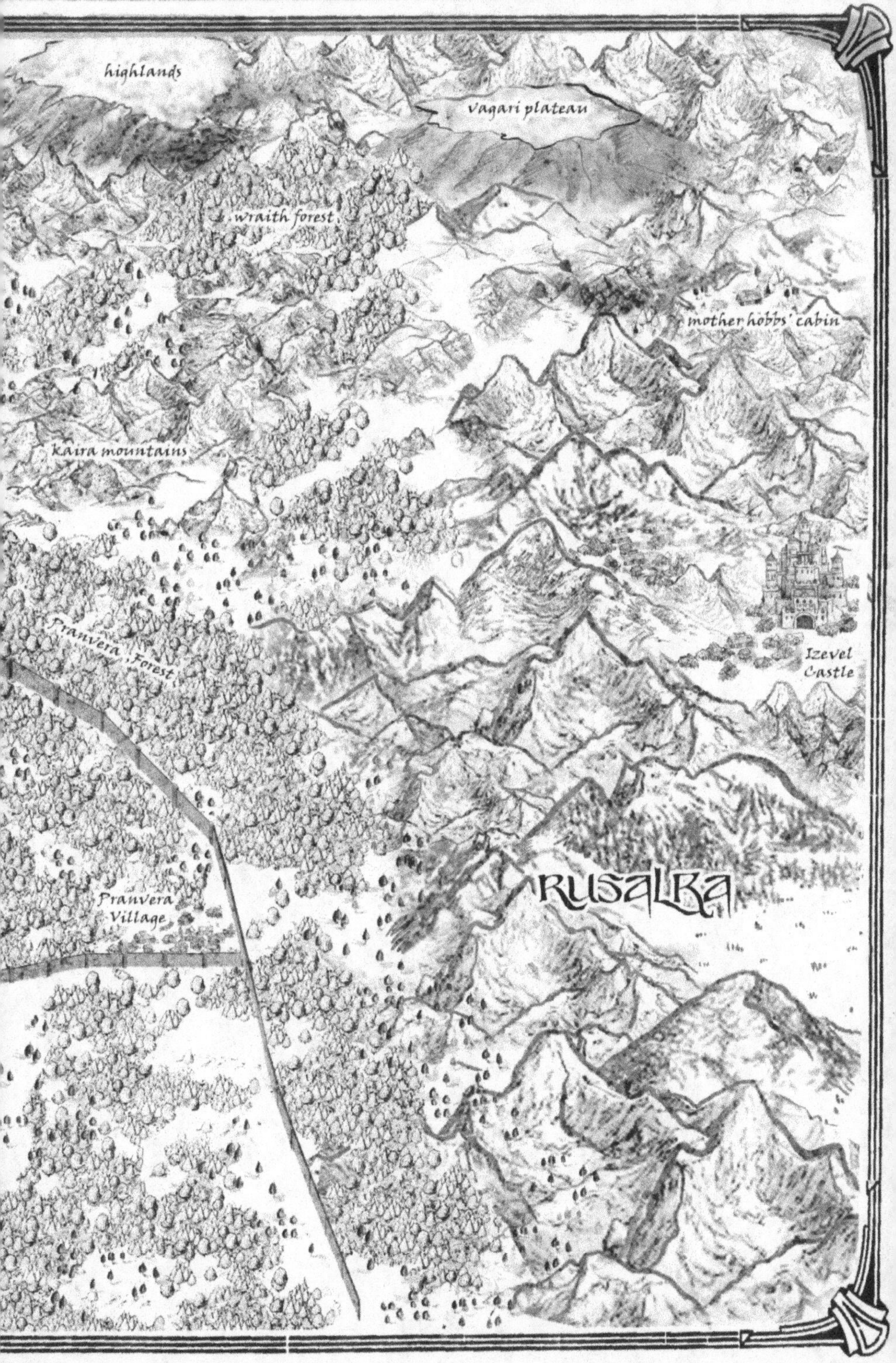

highlands
vagari plateau
wraith forest
mother hobbs' cabin
kaira mountains
Izevel Castle
Pranvera Forest
RUSALKA
Pranvera Village
vagari plateau
wraith forest

TABLE OF CONTENTS

$\mathcal{P}$rologue

A HEART OF COURAGE

VIOLET'S HEART BEAT fast in her chest, and the extra flutter beneath it made her grip her bow harder in her left hand. The danger they feared was upon them, and like the last time it had come knocking on her door, she was fully prepared for what it would bring.

The cries of her handmaids drew her attention away from the large wooden door shuddering with every pound of the battering ram against the steel-barred beams. The women were cloistered on the dais behind her, faces lined with panic.

"Hold fast. Even in this, the Lord has not forsaken us!" Violet's sharp call rose above the clamor, and the maids muffled their cries of panic. She pulled an arrow from the quiver hanging at her side, grasped moments ago in too much of a hurry to place over her shoulder properly. "Gather your weapons, ladies. Every man who comes through that door will feel the wrath of a warrior of the king." Her voice did not waver. Her pulse thudded in her ears with the rush of energy before the attack, sharpening her sight.

The loyal kingsmen who guarded the door were too few. The two faces that looked back at her were ones of stalwart loyalty, eyes rimmed with sorrow.

They knew, as she did, that their defense would not stand against the onslaught of unfaithful kingsmen and Rusalkan warriors who had formed alliances and were now attempting to break down the door. The entry to the throne room of Elira, while built to be a defense against a battle, could not hold back the very gates of hell.

She nodded to them with an accepting and sorrowful look of her own. More than likely, these men would not return to their families. She knew them both. Saw them in her daily passage of the halls. They were her personal guards; Baird had a daughter barely two, and Stephen had a set of twins just born at home. Their poor wives.

Her poor husband.

Elgon was away on a trip through the lands of Pavlin to visit the lords there and ensure that the treaty they had agreed upon was signed. After a ruthless attack from Rusalka, the normally untroubled land of Pavlin had come running to Elira for protection and help, seeking asylum with the king of a peaceful country over settling with the Rusalkan mountain king, Zuko, who was known far and wide for his tyranny and bloodthirst. Violet and Elgon had long debated his departure, and she bitterly regretted her support of the decision now. At the last, she had bid him to leave sooner than later, that he might return in time for the birth of their child. The heir of Elira.

She shook with the pain of anguish as another thud of the battering ram set the stone walls to quaking.

Now Elgon may never see his firstborn nor look into the face of his wife once more.

"Lord, be with him. Comfort him. Make a way for the future of Elira, the future of freedom, and the protection of your children. Do not let this nation fall. Steady my hand that it may do service to your reign. Do not let my husband falter." Her voice broke and tears welled in her eyes.

Blinking them hastily away, she straightened her shoulders as the doors began to crack, metal bolts flying, clanging against the stone floor of the throne room.

For God and king.

She raised her bow and placed the arrow against the string, feeling its bite against her fingers. "Ready!"

The doors creaked beneath the weight of the pressure from without, and one of the steel reinforcements fell from its position.

"Aim!" A deep breath filled her lungs as she drew back steadily on the bow, her swollen stomach fluttering in distraction as her child turned over within her.

"Fire!" The doors burst open, falling from their hinges, and she released the arrow as others, from her maids, whizzed past her head toward their foe. The clang of blade against blade filled her senses and sent shivers down her spine. Her voice tremored with her strength as a roar issued forth from deep within her.

"FOR GOD AND KING!"

One

O'ER HILL AND VALE

FOURTEEN YEARS LATER...

IT WAS PITCH BLACK. Darkness lay over the land like a heavy cloak, smothering the world in its inky blackness. The light spilling from the few windows in the peasant huts scattered a small yellow glow upon the village street. But the miniscule lights, cast by candles or a fire on the hearth, were no match for the darkness that devoured the valley.

A hooded figure took careful, but quick steps, his feet silent upon the grass and the dirt alike. No pebble moved as he stepped over them, his thin leather boots allowing him to walk as a deer.

Swiftly and silently.

He drew in a breath and let it out again with only a soft whoosh of air, every muscle taut, every tendon screaming with vigilance. This mission was more important than all the others and arguably the most dangerous.

He sped from shadow to shadow, making his way toward the craggy castle that towered above the valley like the dangerous face of a mountain that could give way to an avalanche at any moment. Any stateliness of the building that looked to be nearly one with the dark mountain it sat upon was lost in the ugliness of its structure.

He paused and took a moment to glance up at the castle, his eyes following the towers up, up, and toward the sky. His neck ached with the effort, but he strained to catch a glimpse of the tallest spire. A soft light could be detected from around the shutters that barred a treasure within. It was that treasure he sought to retrieve.

Pain throbbed at the back of his head, reminding him of his fear. He drew a shuddering breath to relieve it. If it weren't for him, this rescue mission would not have needed to be undertaken in the first place. It was the most important thing he had done in his life, given the circumstances and years of turmoil that had placed this moment at last within his grasp. He again expanded his lungs, letting the air out slowly to the count of ten. *Lord, let it be as the spy has said. Do not let the king be disappointed again.*

Stepping out from behind the hut where a family shared bread over their crude wooden table, he resumed his stealthy trek.

Onward and upward. For Lord and King.

The shuttle of the spinning wheel clacked as it spun round and round, the girl's foot growing weary as she used it to work the pedal. Her thin, callused hands strung the wool and flax over the wheel, slipping just the right amount through her fingers.

A rough piece of wool caught one of her calluses and sliced into her finger with its pull. Catching her breath, she grabbed the spinning wheel, halting her foot at the same time to stop the movement. Clutching her finger, she squeezed it below the cut, thin but painful, as a drop of blood squeezed through the slice in the skin. She lifted it to her mouth and sucked away the droplet, doing her best to eliminate the chances that it would stain the rest of the wool that lay in her lap or the flax fibers that filled the basket at her feet.

Standing, Rosalie placed her hands under her arms, pulling her woven shawl closer around her as a blast of frigid air shuddered under the wooden door of her home—her cell, her place of captivity. The stones always made the air taste and feel dank, damp, and oh, so cold.

She longed for the fresh air of the chalet, the moments of freedom, and the sound of laughter from the shepherd children which occasionally drifted on the wind. What had she done to be subject to a life stuck within these walls? Why was she locked away while all without these heavy wooden doors and stone walls moved freely?

She shut her eyes. If she tried hard enough, she could remember her mother's face. Her memories were faded and the features hard to discern, but they were there nonetheless. She remembered the long, waist-length, curly blonde hair, shocks of silver threading through the gold like a fiber through a tapestry, and the undertones of cool brown that looked like silver and gold twined together. Two metals she had seen little of, but her mother's hair had been far prettier than any metal. If she concentrated, she could sometimes see those eyes. Dark green like the ivy climbing the tower walls was colored for a few short months before it turned brown and dead from the cold, the leaves shriveling in the temperatures of the mountain air.

The soft yellow rays of the sun as it approached its setting were just spilling over the cliffs to the west. Surrounded on all sides by mountaintops, this chalet was cut into a depression in the midst of them. Legend had it that centuries ago, the king of the dark realm had once mined these mountains, creating the cavity the castle and surrounding village now rested in like a fortress within a fortress. The sun set earlier for them than the rest of the world as the towering peaks cut off the light from the sun like a barricade as it sank toward the horizon.

Rosalie could hear sheep bleating in a nearby pasture, their bells ringing. Shouts from their shepherds and shepherdesses sounded over the chalet as they called them in for the night. The maid who brought her food always told of the wolves that prowled at night; the maid's family were shepherds in service to the king and needed to cloister their flock inside or else risk losing them…or even a shepherd if not careful.

Evil things skulked about in the darkness, and it was wise to stay indoors. One never knew if they were human or cursed spirits, but while inky blackness sat heavy on their valley at day's end, the mountains echoed with noises that sounded otherworldly. They might have been from animals, but no one was ever truly sure.

Rosalie swept back a lock of her brown hair, the long curls messy as she pulled closed her wooden shutters the rest of the way to stay the wind and perhaps allow her to sleep a bit longer when morning came—should her guards not jerk her from her sleep. Slumber was the only thing that helped the days go by faster. Sleep and her spinning wheel. She rubbed her callused hands together. They were showing the wear of her work but, they were also growing far too timid and cold for use. Sleep would be just the thing.

If only she could wake up one day and be able to spread her wings like the eagles in the book her mother's old maid, Zehra, had encouraged her to memorize. Or like the hinds' feet, God could make her run on high places. He said so. If only she could have a taste of the freedom in real life that He had promised she would experience if she trusted in Him.

She sighed. Maybe someday.

Rosalie tried not to think about what freedom from this cell would mean. She knew that if nothing changed, the king's plan for her would be to join his courtesans—women who were nice enough but whom she also knew lived their lives to please the king…no matter what it entailed. She shuddered. Surely there was more for her in this life than that. To be another trophy to a man who needed no such accolades and who took no delight in what he did have, only seeking more at every turn. One woman seemed more than enough to her. She couldn't understand how a man could have use for more.

She left her kirtle on. The wind that whistled through the cracks in the stone and up the stairwell was too cold to resort to a night shift. Pulling the heavy wool curtains closed over the window, she drew a breath, her heart beating hard in her chest. Gathering the poker in her hand, she stoked the fire, blowing through pursed lips upon the coals and watching them glow deeper orange as she did so before throwing another log upon them. She continued blowing until the bark she had placed on the underside caught a slow flame, flickering against the red of the coals. The open fireplace seemed to let out most of its heat in the chimney, but it did help a bit.

Pulling her wool blanket from the cot that rested against the wall, she tried not to look at the empty space beside the bed, curling up into a place upon the animal skin rug that rested on the ground before the fire. The fur was soft beneath her rough fingers and she wrapped the blanket around her shoulders. Zehra had shared this room with her 'til the winter she had grown sick, the cold biting deep into the woman's bones and setting her to coughing late into each night.

Rosalie's one companion—the one who had raised her, had kept her mother's memory alive, and had given her the beautiful glimpse of scripture that she now held within her heart—had succumbed to the cold a handful of years ago. Long were the years without the soft and beautiful heart that cared for her like a sister. The woman's flaxen hair, grown silver before its time, had fallen about Rosalie's face as she had sat upon Zehra's crossed legs before the fire each night.

Zehra's arms had been a shelter as she had rocked them both back and forth, hymns filling the cold, dark corners of the room with light. It was as if the room still echoed with those songs and words.

Rosalie clutched the blanket harder in her fists and scooted closer to the fire, her own legs crossed as she leaned her elbows against them.

Adding another log to the now blazing fire, she started quoting her favorite psalm out loud to fill the silence of the room that was punctuated by the wind howling around her cylindrical tower.

"The Lord is my shepherd, I shall not want. He maketh me lie down in green pastures, He leads me beside still waters."

She closed her eyes, the warmth of the fire on her face as she pictured the green pastures that the sheep roamed, wishing beyond anything she had ever hoped before to lie back in that grass and feel every blade as it bent and danced in the wind. To touch the still waters with her fingers, letting the cool ripples drown her spirit in their peaceful depths.

"He restoreth my soul. He leadeth me in paths of righteousness for His name's sake."

A soul restored. Zehra had often told her of the restoration her mother experienced when she went to heaven. The perfect body and soul that she had been given. White and pure garments. A heart pouring out in worship in every second to the King of Kings as He sat upon His throne.

She could hear a wolf howling in the distance, even through the thick shutters and wool curtains. "Yea though I walk through the valley of the shadow of death, I will fear no evil, for thou art with me. Thy rod and thy staff they comfort me."

He was the shepherd that kept the wolves at bay, that drew her through the valley and was with her in every circumstance. Every time the king came to see her. Every time the guards thought to have fun using her as their drunken amusement. Every time the wind whistled and she shivered through the night and the wolves howled outside.

"Thou preparest a table before me in the presence of mine enemies: thou anointest my head with oil; my cup runneth over."

One day, she would be seated at a feast table and would be the one that sat at Jesus' feet, His hand anointing her with oil as He called her His own.

"Surely goodness and mercy shall follow me all the days of my life: and I will dwell in the house of the Lord for ever." She would one day live in a house of a new Lord. Not the lord who called her his property and kept her 'til the day when she would be disposed to join his court. No. Not a cruel lord, not a man, but her King. She would dwell in His house with her mother and a heart filled with peace and protection.

And she would live there…forever.

A thud slammed into the shutters, and she started, her blanket slipping from her shoulder. The sound reverberated through her room, her stomach instantly in knots and her heart beating heavily in her chest.

What on earth had that been? Nothing had ever struck her shutters before.

Open them.

Her breath quickened. Everything within her fought the urge to open those shutters, but her spirit drew her bare feet across the room and to the window. Was the castle under siege? Under attack? The guards always said no one would ever reach the castle; it was far too strong a fortress and the mountains far too impassable.

She swallowed hard against the panic that sought to rise within her and, instead, followed the little voice within her heart. Pulling back a curtain, she gripped the shutter and pushed, opening it a crack.

The head of an arrow met her gaze, its point embedded into the shutter that was still closed, a rope disappearing into the night from the end and a piece of parchment wrapped around its shaft. She drew a breath. Dare she reach for it? What if another one flying through the darkness found its mark in her hand? Her vision blurred with the heavy pounding of her heart.

Take it.

Two

DESPERATE HOPES

MALCOLM WAITED SILENTLY in the shadows of the castle walls. Though his pulse raged, his trained ears could hear everything. The flutter of an owl's wings in the stillness of the night, the crickets that cried out from the corners of the buildings as they lay hidden in the grass. The shutter opened a mere three inches, and his eyes caught the strip of light in the crack. Nothing more.

Take it. He prayed silently, his every nerve on edge. *Please be there.*

He jumped at the sound of a metal door slamming, followed by raucous and drunk voices. The images of the moment when this entire journey had started fourteen years ago gathered around him like a tidal wave about to break, and he nearly ducked, trying to hold it at bay. The evil memories could resurface at another time.

A hand darted out between the shutters, and his straining eyes rejoiced as the arrow was drawn inside. He felt the slight tug against the slack rope that rested in a coil in his hand.

Read the note. Tie the rope. Three tugs.

It was simple. All she had to do was follow the instructions…assuming she knew how to read. His heart ricocheted faster at the thought that his plan might not work after all. He could scale the wall, but that would take too long, and he didn't want to make her feel threatened. A strange, bearded, and travel-crusted man entering her bedchamber would be frightening enough, even if she knew who he was, and he didn't want to risk her encountering him without that foreknowledge.

The note would take care of that.

He had spent much time trying to think of just the right amount of words to use to convey his feeling, keep it short, and still give clear direction. He knew it would not fully put her mind at ease, but it would have to do.

It had to work.

More slack pulled from his loose hand, but he remained still. Quiet. He couldn't betray his presence. Not yet.

Three tugs.

Good girl.

He waited a hair's breadth, then, satisfied that there were no soldiers about, darted across the space between where he now stood and the adjoining tower.

His feet made no noise upon the stone, then the dirt-packed ground, as he ran in the shadows of the wall across the courtyard of the castle, taking up slack in the rope as he went.

A second door slammed and more voices met his ear, and he flung himself against the wall and further into the shadows. *God, don't let them see me.* He struggled to hear over the deafening sound of his own heartbeat as it exploded over and again in his ear drums.

The raucous joking and clatter of their drunken feet upon the stonework set his mind at ease. Intoxicated soldiers rarely knew what they were about, let alone were cognizant enough to be on the lookout for someone with his skills of reconnaissance and secrecy. He was dressed just like them in clothes he had been able to procure through back-channels and which, to their drunken eyes, would allow him to remain unseen, even if he was detected.

Or so he hoped.

They staggered down the alleyway and into another outbuilding, one he knew to be the soldiers' barracks. The Rusalk warriors were deadly when encountered on the battlefield or when receiving the full force of their strength on the other end of their curved scimitars.

He drew a breath, the tightness around his chest still remaining. Though the danger was past for the moment, more could be just around the corner. He gripped the pommel of his borrowed scimitar, hating the way it curved away from his body in its sheath. He much preferred the broadsword of his home country and couldn't wait until he could use it again. His steps pattered softly against the ground as he continued to loop the rope in his other hand, running swiftly against the wall and up to the base of the tower.

Looking both ways over and again, he wrapped the rope behind his back, looped it beneath a leg, and pulled up the coil of slack on his right side, again shoving the weapon at his belt behind him and out of the way. He dropped the coil of rope, testing out the feel of it in his hand, gripping it and then letting it loose before he tossed the excess over his shoulder. Taking a deep breath, he shook out his hands at the wrist, and with one last look around and a prayer for protection, he reached up, gripped a crevice in the stone, found a foothold, and propelled himself upward.

Hide me from prying eyes, Father. Keep me hidden.

Rosalie paced in her room in front of the fire, her arms folded around her, gripping her wool shawl tight. The subtle embroidering on the hem she had been working on for the last few months caught her eye, and she rubbed the raised stitches between her thumb and forefinger. She had gathered dyed threads from her weaving and saved them for this project, bringing some life and light to her rather drab gray clothing. The trees and purple violets that danced across the hem comforted her and helped her to feel that her mother was close, at least in spirit if not in life.

The note from the arrow was clutched in her other hand, the paper crumpling with her movement and setting her nerves on edge whenever it crackled beneath her grip. Her breath came hard and fast, and her legs shook beneath the strain of her worry that was punctuated by prayer. She walked to the doorway and tested the chair that rested under the door handle. It wouldn't hold anyone back for long, but it would be enough to give her at least a moment to hide the rope or get rid of any evidence of the visitor who was on his way—the one who had written the note.

She didn't know what to think. Had she just made the biggest mistake of her life? How was she to know that the person who had written this note had her best interests at heart? That he was sent by the Lord or that he was there to keep her safe as his letter had stipulated?

I am friend, not foe. Tie the rope to something that can bear the weight of a man and give three tugs upon it once done.

A violet had been crudely drawn in the corner, and her heart had stopped when she'd seen it. A flower she had never seen in real life but that Zehra had made sure to teach her about. It held so much symbolism and memory alive for her that she had no ability to remember. That one symbol was tied to so many things she had wished she'd known. Zehra had been a young servant girl who had grown up in the castle of the Rusalkan enemy, Elira. She had shared with her the story of how Violet and Zehra had been as sisters and captured at the same time.

A scrape against the stone outside sent her hands to fluttering, and she clutched them against her chest, drawing the note with them as she shrank against the wall. A soft grunt reached her ears, and her shaking fingers reached for the fire poker. *Lord, protect me if this man means me harm.*

I am friend, not foe.

She drew a deep breath.

A hand reached up over the windowsill. She knew it was coming, yet it still startled her beyond what she had expected. She drew the poker behind her to keep it out of sight so he wouldn't see it coming if she needed to use it.

A head rose over the sill.

Brown hair, dripping with sweat even in the chill of the mountain night air. Brown eyes that sought her immediately and a face that grimaced in effort as he pulled himself up farther, swinging his leg over the windowsill and climbing in. His height seemed to dwarf her room, and the windows that she had seen as massive all her life now seemed small behind him. His gaze ran around the room, hesitating for a swift second on the hand she had tucked behind her back, then to her face once more before he turned, pulling the rope up and looping it around his arm and shoulder so quickly it seemed as though she blinked and he was done.

She still couldn't breathe as he pulled the shutters closed and spun to face her. A bow was strung over his shoulder, a quiver of arrows beside it, but he was dressed like a Rusalk, and her heart stutter-stepped as she took in his uniform and tried to swallow against the rock that was in her throat.

Who was this man?

He took a step toward her, and she raised the poker over her head, trembling and holding it like a weapon to be brandished, her eyes never leaving the scimitar that hung from his belt at his left hip.

He lifted his hands slowly, palm out, and stepped back again, his feet nearly colliding with the base of her window seat.

"I'm not here to hurt you, child." The gentleness in his voice could just be a trick, but she felt herself swaying to the power of kindness immediately. "As I said, I am friend, not foe."

The familiar words were a refrain in her spirit, and she clutched the poker in both hands now, though it lowered slightly. It was awfully heavy in her shaking grip. "Why are you here?" Her voice shook nearly as badly as her hands.

He didn't move, and her arms lowered another fraction.

"I'm not here to hurt you. I'm here to…to rescue you."

Her mind went blank, and her arms dropped completely. All these years. Her entire life in this tower, her heart always longing for outside and now…suddenly a stranger climbs through her window and proclaims rescue? The rescue she had been praying and asking for from her very earliest recollection?

Tears started into her eyes, but she blinked them back. Her heart didn't want to believe that this could be true. How could rescue have come? She licked her dry lips and rested the end of the poker on the floor, her arms too weak to carry it any longer.

"How can this be?"

He stayed where he was, his hands still raised as if to offer her comfort. "I am not a Rusalkan, though I may look like one."

She kept a steady gaze on his face. "No. You do not look like them." His face was lighter and less angular than that of the Rusalks. His eyes were not as dark; instead there was a lightness to him. Not just in looks, but also in movement. He was graceful and had a gentle demeanor about him. Something that was in stark contrast to the rough movements of the Rusalkans and the heaviness of the spirits they carried.

He reached inside his shirt and pulled a small medallion from around his neck where it hung by a leather cord. His movements were slow and steady, his eyes never leaving her face as he moved with the smoothness of a cat slinking in the shadows so as not to disturb its quarry. She shuddered at the thought, wishing it hadn't come to mind. She always did hate cats.

"Do you know what this is?" He held it out to face her, the embossed gold reflecting and casting light at odd angles in the flickering flames of the fire.

She squinted to get a better look, trying to make out the image on the palm-sized piece of metal. Her eyes widened. A lion, a crown of thorns… She had never seen it before but Zehra had told her of it. Reminded her often of how to recognize it. She had long since given up hope that she would ever be returned to the kingdom that had been her mother's home… But here stood a man who bore the mark of her homeland.

"It is…the seal of my people."

He stood straighter, confused by the way that she had hesitantly phrased her answer. Instead of focusing on it, he focused on setting her at ease. He glanced around the room. The large windows he had climbed through were the only entrance to the outside world. The door that led into the hallway he knew had no portal outside except at the bottom of the tower. He had done his due diligence while scouting. Her small tick cot rested against the brick wall on the other side of the room. A spinning wheel and basket with a small number of belongings along with the piles of flax and wool rested to his left beside the door.

The fire to his right was ablaze, barely taking the chill out of the room, and he now shivered with the damp cold that pervaded the space and seeped from the very stones themselves. He swallowed. Might as well out with it.

"Will you come with me?"

He saw her gulp and search his face, fear written in her every feature—but there was hesitant interest as well.

"How do I know that you do not wish me harm?" She couldn't hide her quick glance at the weapons he carried.

"I understand your worries, but there is little time, and is risking your freedom with me more dangerous than staying here?"

She bit her lip and twisted her hands together.

The door at the base of the tower thudded open, and his blood ran cold as footsteps clambered up the staircase, echoing up into her room and off the stone walls.

Rosalie's eyes widened, and with a sudden movement, she surprised him by rushing forward, grabbing his arm. "Quick, this way."

Three

CURRENT PAIN AND PAST MEMORIES

ROSALIE CAUGHT HER breath, acting on impulse as she grasped the stranger's arm, her mind focusing on—of all things—the fact that she didn't know his name as she drew him toward the wardrobe against the wall beside the window. "You must hide! If they catch you, any chance of escape is lost!" Pulling the door open, she removed a basket and pushed him in front of her.

He clambered awkwardly inside as she shut the door carefully behind him, her heart hammering in her ears and in tandem with the steps that thundered up the stairs. She could hear them now. Laughing, jesting, probably drunk beyond reason. Panic squeezed her chest, and she untied the rope with shaking hands from the only beam she could reach from atop her bed since the roof slanted at the edges of the room. Coiling the remainder of the rope as she went, she gathered the arrow that had sent it flying into her shutter nearly an hour ago. She grunted beneath the weight and opened the wardrobe, shoving it all in after the stranger and slamming the door behind it.

Her last few breaths of air were spent dashing to her place on the rug beside the fireplace where she pulled her shawl around her. The scraping of the key turning in the lock sent a shiver down her spine as the door was thrown open with a solid kick and another laugh from one of the guards.

Merlin and Talon. The night guards. The ones she feared the most.

"What're you doing up so late, me leddie?" sneered Merlin. The gray Rusalkan uniform cloaked his broad shoulders, a dragon emblem in black and lighter gray woven in relief on the front of his tunic.

"I've simply been about my weaving and am now about to retire." Her voice was shaking, but she couldn't seem to help it.

"Oh really…and what is that?"

She froze. What did he see? Had she forgotten to hide something?

He stepped toward her with his mocking and splotchy red face. The ale on his breath was enough to knock her backward as he leaned in and plucked a tuft of flax from her hair. Then blew it from his fingers and into her face. Could one faint from the stench? But then he suddenly gripped her face within his strong fingers and gave her chin a shake.

"You're turning into a pretty thing, ain'tcha?"

"Unhand me." She grasped his wrist, trying to pull it from her face, then winced as he clenched harder.

"Don't argue with me, wench." He growled, his voice low and threatening, his eyes glinting in the flame from the fire as he squinted.

"Merlin! Let 'er go afore you get us in more trouble! You know the king has given specific orders not to touch 'er." Talon strode over to his mate with a slightly tottering step and pulled at his arm, dragging Rosalie across the floor in the man's unshakeable grip.

"I'll do as I please!" Merlin bellowed, his eyes losing focus as he stumbled back a step, still tugging Rosalie with him. She whimpered, clutching at his hand to lift some of her weight from his solid grip on her chin.

"You won't if the commandant sees us and then reports us directly to the king. You know what happened to the last man 'at threatened the wench." Talon was clearly not as inebriated as his mate and was doing his best to rescue him—and perhaps himself—from future trouble. All Rosalie knew of the matter was that she had never seen Revin again after he had roughed her up for not being quick enough to mop her floor.

She was the king's, and everyone knew it. And if they forgot to act as though they knew it, she never heard from them again.

"Please, let me go." Her voice rasped from her restricted throat.

The slap came hard, fast, and heavy, flinging her to the side like she was a rag doll. She fell into her cot, the post knocking her hip before she tumbled to the ground.

"I'll do as I please, and I'll not be rushed about it!" Merlin's voice was even more slurred than before, and he didn't make another move toward Rosalie except to trip over his own feet and right himself against the wall near her cot.

She cowered anyway, though it didn't put her out of danger from getting a kick to the ribs where it wouldn't show and would leave her gimping about for a week or more.

Talon gripped Merlin's shoulders between his hands, directing him toward the door. "You know the king has other uses for her, and if you dare touch her, there will be hell to pay. Now, get a move on, you lazy lout, and get to the barracks before the commandant hears us and comes to investigate. She must be delivered to the king on her fifteenth birthday without a mark upon her, and you know that."

The door slammed on Merlin's drunken arguments, and she heard them singing when they finally exited the tower below. Her heart still hammered.

The wooden door of the wardrobe creaked open, and she jumped, then relaxed as the stranger exited the small alcove, unfolding his long frame from the upright wooden box, kicking his rope out before him.

His eyes made her hesitate and draw back again; they were ablaze, his shoulders tense as he came toward her.

She lifted an arm to shield herself, and he stopped instantly.

"I'm not going to harm you." His voice was deep but gentle, annunciating each word so that she could not miss his intent.

She looked around her arm, shaking still from head to toe. With a shiver, she pulled her kirtle skirt down over her feet, wrapping them in the wool and reaching across the floor for her shawl that had fallen from her shoulders.

His eyes flashed again as he took in her face. "Did they hurt you, child?"

She shook her head quickly, knowing that any complaint was sure to get her another bruise to add to her collection. "Not badly." She reached up and shoved the hair that had fallen from her braid behind her ear.

"You do not have to pretend with me. I know what manner of scum your captors are, and I want you to know right now that I will never do anything that would harm you. I have sworn an oath to the King of Elira to protect you with my very life."

His eyes were steady, their brown depths reminding her of the wooden beams, sturdy and reliable, holding up the walls and ceilings of her little room.

"The king..." she breathed, her voice small and barely heard above the crackling of the fire. Fear rose in her heart again, and she drew back. "What use does the king have with a lowly servant girl?"

The man hesitated. "My child. Do you not know who you are?"

"I am Rosalie, servant to Zuko, king of the mountain."

He shook his head, his eyes filled with wonder and confusion and backed by that ever-burning fire as he stood to his full height and looked down at her, his bearing regal and so much more graceful than those of the Rusalks.

"I am Malcolm, first knight to King Elgon Indulf of Elira, and I am here to rescue his daughter, the princess."

Malcolm watched his princess, the heir to the throne of Elira and his sole responsibility. She was the answer to every prayer and hope prayed in his country and from his heart for the last fourteen years. She cowered away from him, shock on her face as her eyes were wide, her mouth hanging open.

"Surely you jest. I am no princess. I am simply a servant girl. My mother was a servant in the palace. So Zehra told me."

Pain shafted through Malcolm's chest. Her mother, the queen. Zehra, her maid. It must have been a story they had told her to keep her safe. To protect her from the harsh realities of what her life in captivity would be. If she didn't know who she was, her mind could rest easier in this tower hidden away in the mountains, unaware of the full import of her having gone missing.

Years had been spent in the search for her. Years of prayer and hope upon hope until even those grew faint and dim. Spies had been sent forth, their ambition of finding the queen their one prayer. His heart caught and stammered in his chest at the pain and sorrow of a king who not only lost the love of his life but the child of their love all in the same day.

Every year, a pyre full of violets was set out upon the Sirene sea, their fragrance coating the breeze and mixing with the smell and taste of salt, until one flaming arrow was launched, lighting it aflame. A day of fasting and prayer for the return of their queen and the solidification of her memory into the hearts and minds of her people.

For Violet Indulf was not just a queen. She was a maiden from their very borderlands. A peasant with a story of strength and courage in weakness, of loyalty in the face of betrayal, and of forgiveness when restitution seemed impossible. She brought their king closer to the people, and instead of further setting the castle upon the metaphorical mountain, far from their reach, their hearts trusted one of themselves who now not only had the king's ear, but his heart.

The fire in Malcolm burned hotter. So much injustice upon a young woman and now her daughter. Fourteen years of searching, of praying, of hoping, and now that she was finally within his reach, he hoped that not all would be lost on the treacherous and dangerous journey back to Elira. It had taken him nearly a month just to travel all this distance undetected… How much longer with a child in tow? And one that had never set foot in the real world?

"May I?" he asked, reaching out his hand and stooping down to her height.

She blinked, her eyes still glazed over in shock as she stared up at him from her place upon the floor. But then she made a move that made his heart leap with the meaning of it. She reached out a hand. A small, tentative paw that he took in his large, callused, battleworn one. He held it gently, not wanting to frighten her or make her feel as though she were unsafe in his presence. She had to know, had to trust, had to understand that his loyalty would never waver…even if it sent him to an early grave.

"Your father is the King of Elira. He has been looking for your mother for the last fourteen years, and we only heard of your existence just in the last few months. He didn't know if you had survived the perilous journey as your mother was near her time to give birth when she was taken. This is not your home." He gestured to the room with his free hand, then leaned in just a bit more, his eyes never leaving hers, those emerald green depths making the tears clutch around the back of his throat. Of course she had the queen's eyes. "Your home is with the king, your father, Elira's ruler, and he has sent me to bring you to him. My child." His voice grew husky of its own accord, and he swallowed, trying to clear it as her eyes seemed transfixed on his face, the flicker of hope just starting to dawn on her thin features. "I have sworn loyalty to your father. I will bring you back at any cost to myself. It is my life for yours, and upon the word I have sworn and upon the name of my earthly lord and the Heavenly King whom I have chosen to serve, I will gladly give my life for yours if it is required of me."

He hesitated for a breath more. Praying, he begged the Lord to move on her heart and instill in it a trust in him. He did not doubt he would be called upon to prove his trustworthiness many times over on this journey that would be theirs together for the next weeks and possibly months.

Rosalie paused, looking around at the room that had been her prison for the entirety of her life, and then slowly stood. She gave him a deep, searching look, her eyes seeming to grow in size as she stared deep into his gaze. Then they closed, the lashes fluttering as she caught a deep, shuddering breath.

They opened again, and she returned his grip on her hand with a gentle squeeze.

She bowed her head in the motion of a bow or curtsy. "Let it be to me as you have said."

The formality of her speech was not lost on him. He knew that tradition trained the maids of a kingdom to speak with reverence for their master, and by her acknowledgement of his request, she had, in very formal, but meaningful terms, given herself into his trust.

And he would not betray that trust. Not again.

He rested his hands gently beneath her elbows, lifting her upright again as she met his gaze. "Do you trust me?"

Those eyes drilled him again, but there was no reservation in them this time.

"Yes."

Four

A DANGEROUS ESCAPE

ROSALIE FELT THE bite of the rope against her ribs, her shawl tied tight around one shoulder and under her opposite arm so that it would not be lost in the descent. She had grown used to the height of her tower. Had never thought to question it. But now that she was about to be dangled out of the window, merely supported by a seemingly thin rope and one man's strength, her stomach churned.

"You sure you're all right?" Sir Malcolm, her new protector, finished tying off the knots that held her, the rope tied about her to form a seat beneath her legs and then looped around her waist for security.

She nodded, swallowing back the dryness in her throat that she simply could not speak around.

"You will be perfectly fine. Just walk your legs down the wall, and I will hold your weight. I will not let you plummet. Do you understand what you will do?"

"Rest my feet upon the wall and climb down while holding onto the rope above my head."

He nodded. "Good. Now, you must be as silent as possible. Even if you are sorely tempted, you must not, under any circumstance, scream or cry out. Do you understand?"

She swallowed hard, clamping her jaw shut tight, and nodded back.

"All right. Let us commence."

He wrapped the slack over one shoulder, behind him, and around his waist, having already wrapped it also around the bed frame for an anchor. Securing the rope fast in one hand, he helped her climb the windowsill, gripping her hand and slowly letting her down until he transferred her hand to the windowsill. She felt the rope take her weight beneath her legs and around her waist as he took up any slack.

She knew that she needed to grip the rope, not the windowsill, but as her knuckles strained, her fingertips digging into the stone, Rosalie swallowed back the panic at the idea of trusting her weight to the rope and the rope alone.

"Shhh… Now, let go, grip the rope, and lean back."

The pounding of her heart threatened to drown out his words, and she wondered how on earth he had been so calm about scaling these walls a mere hour ago. Her fingers grew sore with their grip on the windowsill, and she started to pant. She wouldn't be able to hold on much longer. Her insides heaved.

"Rosalie. You must let go. You can trust me. I've got you." His whisper was sharp in the darkness, and it did nothing to quell the thundering in her ears.

Let go. Trust me.

Taking a deep, shuddering breath, she let go and reached for the rope, stifling a gasp as she twisted and bumped into the stones until she was able to get her feet under her and against the wall. Awkwardly hanging from her arms, desperately bent and clutching the rope to give her some modicum of safety, she didn't know how to move.

"Lean farther back, and let the rope around your waist and legs take the weight. I'll begin lowering you down now." Sir Malcolm's whisper met her ear softly, too quiet to be heard by any but herself.

Her breathing shallow, she tried to loosen her arms and felt herself spinning backward. She bit her lip, hard, so she'd not make a sound when all she wanted to do was flail and let out a yelp. *We mustn't be heard*, she encouraged herself, trying to take a deep breath into her restricted lungs.

The rope grew taut around her as she leaned farther into it, allowing it to carry her downward with Sir Malcolm's guidance, her feet barely keeping up with her descent as they slapped against the stones. She could be brave; she was almost there and would be on the ground shortly. It took longer than she had anticipated, but her feet finally touched the ground, and the rope stopped biting her waist and legs long enough for her to start working on the knots. A few moments later and Sir Malcolm was descending himself, his plummet down the rope looking far more graceful, sure, silent, and swift than hers had been. She watched him in awe.

He gathered up the rope, twirling it with ease into a coil that he hung from his shoulder. Taking her hand in his, he drew her close to his side, his cloak falling over her shoulder, shrouding her in the darkness of the shadow of the courtyard wall. "Quickly," he breathed, too quiet to be called a whisper.

Rosalie did her best to keep up with his large steps as they slunk from one end of the wall to the other, gathering near the door in a pause as he looked around the frame, waited a breath, then drew her through after him.

A night owl hooted in the distance, and she jumped. Malcolm's hand on her shoulder soothed her, and she tried to catch her breath. They had barely made it across one courtyard and were halfway across another and she was already battling for air.

He grabbed her arm, stopping her short and pulling her further into the shadows of a guard tower. His arm scooped her against the wall beside him, protective yet alert. Voices made her skin crawl, and she held her breath. Guards. They must be at the gate. Footsteps on the cobblestone streets and walkways sounded, followed by a few laughs and more growling conversation.

Stepping softly back the way they had come, Sir Malcolm drew her with him. She tried to ignore the feeling of her head growing hot as she didn't dare to breathe.

She stumbled on a stone, and he caught her, nearly lifting her completely off her feet, his muscles tense as he held her around the waist. Her hands gripped his forearms around the leather bracers he wore. They waited until only silence met their ears.

"Breathe." His breath whispered against her ear, and she drew in the precious, cool night air, realizing as stars danced in her vision that she had been holding her breath this whole time. The flaming orbs finally held still in their places in the sky after a moment of deep breaths, and then Malcolm drew her onward, avoiding the pools of moonlight that illuminated the pathway in splotches as if it were some silver version of daytime.

"We'll have to go over again. The gate is too heavily guarded." His words seemed to rest upon the night air, only traveling as far as her ear instead of cutting through the courtyard.

She swallowed. Another descent.

Malcolm cupped her elbow with his large hand. "This wall is higher yet, and it's more likely that we could be spotted by the nightly patrol. If that is the case, I am going to let you down quickly and you must run and hide yourself in the heather on the hills amongst the sheep."

She was shaking her head already, her heart dropping into her stomach at the idea of having to make it on her own without her guide.

His hands felt heavy on her thin shoulders, but his fingers were gentle. "You can do this. I promise. The Lord will give you strength, *if* it is needed. Now, lift your arms."

She swallowed hard as she obeyed, her breaths coming fast and shallow.

"Shh," he soothed as he wrapped the rope around her waist again, tying it off and creating a loop that he slipped behind her knees. "Breathe deep, from your belly and slow." He drew out the last word, glancing over his shoulder in both directions as he looped the remainder of the rope over his shoulder and head. Drawing her into the shadows once more, he rested his hand on her head. "Stay in the dark."

He turned, gripping the stone far above his head, and pulled himself up, not a grunt or noise slipping from his lips. His feet followed suit, and soon he was propelling himself up the stone wall, his fingers searching for cracks and crevices to grip and aid him in his ascent. His movements reminded her of the sheep that seemed so sure of their footing on the mountain rocks around the castle and surrounding structures. Many in the village that surrounded the castle were mountain dwellers, their only resource being that of raising sheep and goats, the only livestock that survived in the rocky mountain passes of the Izevel mountains.

She tried to focus on her breathing, just like he had directed, and felt her heart rate slowing as she breathed deeply in and out, filling her stomach with the air and letting it reach the bottom of her diaphragm instead of just her lungs.

Suddenly there was a tug on the rope around her waist, and she looked up again. Malcolm was crouched low on the top of the wall. He stooped to one knee and leaned back, the rope growing taught around her ribs and biting with a pain that was now familiar as she lifted her feet, sinking back against the rope that rested beneath her legs, allowing it to carry her aloft. Reaching upward for a rock, she gripped it, climbing up the wall, her actions almost effortless as Sir Malcolm pulled on the rope, carrying almost her entire weight. Her fingers missed a hold in her hurry, her breath coming thick and fast now, the air feeling thin. The scuffing sound it made set her blood to running cold in her veins as she froze, her limbs shaking as Sir Malcolm paused in drawing her upward.

Voices in the distance sounded, and she felt the panic rise in her chest, tightening around her ribs as fiercely as the rope.

The sound of a cooing turtle dove broke through her thoughts. It was far too late in the night for a mourning dove. Her limbs shaking, she looked up and saw Sir Malcolm give her a nod, the rope wrapped securely in his hands.

Lord, give me strength. Comfort blanketed her, drowning out the pulse that roared in her ears. She reached for another stone, using her feet to prop her against the wall and then another. The rope pulled, her ribs stinging, but she ignored it, pushing through the pain and using it to propel her upward.

No sooner had Sir Malcolm pulled her upon the top of the wall beside him, her stomach flat against the stones, than he was already guiding her legs over the other side and letting her down again.

She was never so glad as when her feet touched the heather that coated the steep hillside on the outside of the wall. Rustling in the bush startled her, and a soft bleat from a nearby sheep sent her heart hammering hard again.

With shaking fingers, she untied herself, fighting against the knots that had grown tighter since carrying her weight. Sir Malcolm was by her side in an instant, his breath coming thick and fast as he sucked in air to fill his lungs. His fingers fumbled next to hers, helping her with the knots and then winding his rope over his head and shoulder again before drawing her away into the heather, the branches whistling in the wind and the dry twigs crackling beneath their feet. The soft leather shoes that she wore were no match for the rocky and rubble-encrusted hillside as they half slid, half walked down the steep face of the foothill.

They paused at the bottom, shrinking back into the shadows the heather cast. Rosalie gasped for breath. Her feet were stinging, but she could barely feel them after all of the pounding they had endured on the short trek down the hill.

"Are you all right, little one?" Malcolm's voice was soft in her ear as he handed her a small leather waterskin, its contents barely enough to soothe her dry, choking throat.

She nodded, ignoring her feet. Ignoring the ache. Ignoring the pain around her ribs even as she attempted to slow her breathing.

"I know you aren't used to it, but we will have to move fast. Just keep breathing as I showed you, and it will help tremendously. I will pause as often as I can. I'm so sorry." He whispered at the last and the compassion and sorrow in his voice pricked her eyes with tears.

"'Tis not your doing. I shall keep up. I must."

He nodded, his hand a comfort on her shoulder again. "Now that we are out, it may be a short while until they notice you are gone. Does someone usually check your rooms between dusk and dawn?"

She shook her head, still loathe to speak as she fought to simply breathe. Frustration burned that they were scarcely a stone's throw from her prison and she was already exhausted.

But then it struck her. She was out. Outside the walls that had held her in her entire life. Outside the company of those that abhorred her and whom she abhorred. Outside the life that she had seen no end to. Outside the pain that plagued her and the memories that felt empty and repetitive.

Adventure was at her doorstep if only she were strong enough to take it on. Adventure and a family she thought she had lost forever.

Father, I'm coming.

A goat's bell rang off the mountain side, echoing in the evening stillness. Rosalie spun. A set of bony shoulders stood out amongst the shadows. Those, and the widest eyes beneath the darkest thatch of hair…

A shepherd boy stared at them, his eyes blurry from sleep and his cloak falling from his shoulder where it must have been wrapped as he had slept in the heather.

Five

WEIGHTY DECISIONS

ELGON, FIFTEEN YEARS AGO...

The world was closing in. Now he knew what Violet meant when she had explained to him the feeling of her beloved forest that, once a comfort to her as a child, suddenly felt like a monster seeking to devour her. The walls of his castle, the very borders of his land, were pressing in from every side, each attack feeling like a dagger severing another heart string.

Elgon strode purposefully through the castle hallways, his heart aching with the news he had just received. Violet had been ill the last few days, and the doctor had advised she rest in her chambers until it passed.

He never ceased to marvel at the way his wife was attune to the spirit realm and all that took place in the world of Elira, even if she had no idea what it was. Her illness, the pain in her ribs and the inability to catch her breath, may have been a bit more than simply pain from the growth of their child. He couldn't help but smile, even as he carried the ill-tidings in his heart. Their child was due to be born in just a few months' time, and the idea of a little child running about the castle brought with it a hope and light at the songs and laughter that would soon echo off these walls.

As he drew near to the door of her chamber, he heard her sweet voice, thin with the lack of space to breathe, singing a lullaby in the stillness of her room.

Be still, my love,
Don't fret, nor fear.
For as surely as your heart beats,
The King is ever near.
Be still, my love,
Hush the pain and woe,
For every tear you shed,
Is held in precious store.
Be still, my love,
Still your aching heart,
For pain endures the night
But joy will come at dawn.

He stopped and leaned against the doorframe, tears starting to his eyes as he leaned his forehead against the rough wood. Her voice soothed his own soul even as his heart ached for the loss over the border.

Be still, my love,
Close your weary eyes,
You needn't watch and wait,

The storm that's on the rise.
Be still, my love,
Let the King your battles fight,
For as you rest and sing His praise,
He'll bring on brighter skies.
Be still, my love,
Rest your heavy head,
For as you sleep,
The King will win again.

He stepped into the room, holding the door open as Zehra curtsied slightly before him. With one look at his face, she stepped past him into the hall, and Elgon softly closed the door behind her.

Violet half reclined on the large window bed, the sounds of the tossing sea making its way into the room on the salty breeze that drifted through the half-open window. Her hair was spilling down over her shoulder, the ribbon that held it doing little to keep it back from her face, the long blonde curls trailing the bed beside her as she toyed with a lock of it over her swollen midsection. The red velvet blanket that rested across her lap was strewn with yarn and the rippling fabric and threads of the article of clothing she was making for their child. Her song died on her lips when her green eyes caught his gaze, the restful, serene look replaced by one of instant concern.

"Elgon? What is it, my love?"

He drew a deep breath, the ache now in his own ribs as she started up into an attempt at a sitting position, adjusting her blossoming girth with a wince.

He hurried to kneel beside her, laying his hand softly on her shoulder, and prompting her to relax against the pillows again. "Hush, love. Don't exert yourself." He couldn't meet her eyes as he fussed over the positioning of the blanket.

She gripped his hand in hers to keep him from fidgeting and cupped her finger under his chin, drawing his gaze up to hers. "I'm not exactly weak and sickly, Elgon. Just a little worn down. What is it that has the worry lines so deep?" She brushed her fingertip over his furrowed brow.

He swallowed the bitter taste in his mouth. "Rusalka attacked Pavlin today. It was an organized strike, and their army took severe casualties, though they were able to hold them off for now, by the grace of God."

Her gasp coincided with the goosebumps that rose on her arm, and he rubbed her hand and arm to bring some warmth back to it. He wished he hadn't been the bearer of the news that filled those soulful eyes with tears. She winced and pressed a hand into one side of her abdomen.

"Are you all right?" The worry that rose in him was tempestuous at best. None of her reassurances stilled the overwhelming sense and desire to protect her and their child at all costs.

"She kicked a little hard, that's all." Her breathless reply made him tilt his head.

"She?"

"Marcus said as much, did he not?"

He shook his head. "And you're taking it as fact?" A subtle smile drew at the corner of his mouth. Wasn't that just the way of life? The joys mixed with the sorrows? One coming close upon the other as the heart beats in an attempt to keep up with it all.

She gave him a glare as she used his arm to adjust herself on the cushions. "Have you known him to be wrong?"

Elgon shook his head. "Not that I can say."

"Exactly. Now, what is to be done about Pavlin? Can we spare the kingsmen to help them?"

"They have not asked it of us." His tone wavered as if he wanted to continue.

"Yet, you mean?"

He nodded. Elgon was unsure if Pavlin would come to him for help, but he preferred it to them giving in to Rusalka. If Zuko won Pavlin for himself, it would mean that he would border Elira on both the east and the south, would most likely open trade routes over the sea, and Elira would be his next target. Pavlin could be made to fight Elira with the Rusalkans, and it would be a frightening reality if that assumption was carried to completion.

Elira had risen a century ago and cemented its footing as a country to be set apart when Zuko's and Elgon's ancestors disagreed on the way their lives were to be lived. The Rusalkans had stood for their own way above all else, and Elgon's predecessors fought against the idea, declaring that freedom was more valuable than the sacrifice of one's morals and the pursuit of Christ and His justice worth dying for. The countries had split, but Elira had won, keeping the capital city, the ocean ports, and the valuable land as the Rusalkans fled into the mountains to the east.

Elgon sighed. Pavlin had always attempted to remain neutral, to stay out of the fight and remain intact, be it siding with one country or another on given issues, rallying with those they would gain the most from. Elira usually won their support, due to its rich land and the farming community that often kept Pavlin from starvation. Their land was dry, the rains of the forests and the mountains of Elira rarely making it that far south, and their crops were subject to the whims of the weather. Their seaside cliffs were too rocky to build wharves, and their commerce was inhibited by the need to travel to Niran to trade supplies.

But this time, Zuko may have gone too far. "It's anyone's bet if they come to us for help. I wouldn't be surprised if they do. Zuko has little to offer them other than slavery and pain."

Violet frowned. "Their farmers need help. They know not what they are doing in the south."

Elgon tried not to chuckle at her indignant superiority. "They do, but one cannot bemoan a lot that God has set for them."

She shrugged. "'Tis true, but if they do ask for help, perhaps we can help them construct waterways so they can grow their own food."

He smiled as her eyes lit up.

"Perhaps we could divert a waterway from the Raintamount River south to their lands! It would take some doing and probably months of work, but if it helped them create a sustainable crop..." She gestured as she spoke, as if the motions would further explain the idea.

He stilled her hands. "We don't even know if they are going to ask us for help yet."

She sighed, the nervous energy rippling off of her slowing and the sad look returning to her eyes before it was replaced by a furrow of anger in between her brows. "What did Zuko do to them?" Her words were clipped, as if trying to keep the anger controlled.

His own shoulders slumped as he relaxed at her side again. "Their army has been depleted, though they put up enough of a fight for the Rusalk soldiers to retreat. Not for long, I'd wager, and not without grave cost to Pavlin's militia."

She sighed, her words quiet. "How many?" She twirled the loose yarn in her lap tighter around her finger.

"Five hundred."

"Dead?" she squeaked, her face paling.

He nodded.

"Lord, rest their souls and comfort their families," she breathed, her eyes filled with tears that tumbled down her cheeks.

MALCOLM, PRESENT DAY...

Malcolm's heart leaped wildly at the sight of the shepherd boy. How had he missed this small boy sleeping in the heather? In Elira, the shepherds and sheep were shut up at night to keep them safe from predators, but in the mountains and what he had seen of villages, many barely had shelter for themselves, let alone for their animals.

He gripped Rosalie's hand in his and whisked her behind him, the shape of his cloak covering her in the darkness. He hoped that the little boy who was rubbing sleep from his eyes would think this all a dream and forget about it in the morning—or simply not tell anyone.

But the news that was about to sweep the country of Rusalka would give Malcolm and Rosalie little choice. Their freedom would be gone before it had even arrived if this was not dealt with now and tactfully. The little boy had seen Rosalie, seen his face, and most likely noticed their departure from the castle. It wasn't commonplace to see a man and a young girl rappelling off the castle walls instead of using the gate.

"Are—are you the witch they keep locked up in the tower?" The boy looked right past Malcolm at the young girl peeking around his shoulder with curious but terrified eyes.

"A—a witch?" she breathed, incredulity written all over her features and in the notes of her voice.

An idea formed in Malcolm's mind. *Father, forgive me.* "She'll cast a spell upon you if you so much as speak a word of this to anyone," he hissed through clenched teeth. If there was anything he had learned about Rusalka up until now, it was that the ghost stories and superstitious folklore ran deep, and without the truth of Christ to combat it, many lived in fear of a spiritual battle that either did not exist or had a sure way of defeat if they only knew the truth.

The little boy's wide eyes grew even wider beneath the thatch of his tousled jet-black hair. "P-please, m'lord, don't let the lady curse me. Our family barely 'as enough to eat as 'tis." He raised his hands in the air, palms out, his shepherds crook in one as he stepped back.

"Then keep this between us and her spell will not be spoken. But if she finds out through her second sight that you have told a soul, she'll cast it, do you hear me?"

"I won't tell a soul. I promise." The harsh whisper had a tremble in it.

It was all Malcolm could wait for at this time. They needed to put a great deal of distance between them and this pile of stinking rocks before the sun rose and revealed their path to the captors who would surely find out their ward was missing. And the hellfire and terror that would befall the villagers would be enough to make this timid boy talk, he had no doubt. Even with the threat of a spell hanging over his head.

If there was one thing Malcolm knew by experience, it was that the fear of death held far more sway over a mortal than the threat of a lost meal or a simple curse.

He gripped Rosalie's hand in his, gathered up the bundle he had previously buried in the heather, and pulled her after him into the night. An owl's mournful call sent shivers down his spine. Or perhaps it was the sense of dread that he could not shake no matter how brave he was or how far he tread. One did not forget a fatal mistake. It hounded them for the rest of their days. And his was nipping at his heels.

Six

THE LAST DASH

ROSALIE, PRESENT DAY...

Her feet ached beyond belief but it was the pressure on her lungs that scared her more. Still she kept on, her hand gripped in Sir Malcolm's, his fingers pressing into her flesh with urgency. The stitch in her side had long since grown to make her feel as though her insides were about to split open and spill out.

Her feet gave way, and she fell to her knees, Sir Malcolm's momentum dragging her a stride or two farther, her knees skinning on jagged rocks before he noticed the weight and stopped. Her stomach rid itself of its contents on the ground before her.

She wasn't sure if the stars she were seeing were those of the night sky or that of her exhaustion.

A soft cloth dabbed at her lips with a tenderness she had never experienced, then a cupped hand filled with chill water came to her mouth. She let some of it cool her heated face, and the rest trickled into her sour mouth and down her burning throat. The words softly whispered could barely be heard over the roar of her own ears.

"I'm so sorry, m'lady. I can't help but spur us on quickly, lest we are caught, but I should have paid closer attention to your flagging energy. Here, I shall carry you a spell."

A harsh wind whistled over the rocks, sending the pebbles to dancing on the path and the cloak he had fastened around her shoulders whipping within its current.

"I—cannot—let—" Her words were broken by gasps for air that never quite seemed to fill her lungs.

"Hush, save your strength." He gave her another sip of the water, using the rest to bathe her face before he knelt before her, pulling her hands over his shoulders, then lifting her legs to rest on his hips. "Grip here." He patted her knee, and she wrapped her trembling legs around his middle, and they were off again.

His easy lope was soothing, just below a trot and over a walk, his long stride taking them farther than she ever thought possible. Her thudding heart slowed from constant thunder in her veins to a matching cadence of his steps as she drew deep breaths of the mountain air into her lungs.

Now that she had a moment to rest, she was able to take stock of the scenery as they passed through. They skirted the edge of the village that surrounded the castle. The huts were less beautiful up close than she had expected. From her window in the castle, they had looked like tiny, sharp little dwellings. Now she was able to take in the squalor and poor upkeep. The thatched walls and roofs had shingles missing, the pine slats looking dark and rough in the moonlight. The yards smelled foul, as if her chamberpot had been emptied upon them. The distant sound of cattle bells occasionally rang in the background, be it from one side or another. The local shepherds stayed out with their animals all night, trading watch so that the flock was looked after at every waking moment. She had observed how they roamed the hills freely, only being herded into the village upon occasion to be shorn or butchered. They were thin, lanky things, but she had always wished to be out among them.

Her highest desire had been to be a shepherdess, to taste the fresh air and feel the sparse grass and heather beneath her feet, to be able to run about and chase the wind like the goats, sheep, and cows upon the hills. These lowly animals had more freedom than she ever did.

She could hear Malcolm's breath start to come heavier and faster as the terrain moved uphill again. Her body had started to relax, and though her legs and side still throbbed in pain, she had caught her breath and her eyelids started to droop. She jerked her head up when she caught herself resting her forehead on Sir Malcolm's back and sucked in a gasp of crisp, mountain air.

"Are you rested, m'lady?" he asked, his feet still moving, his voice barely making its way back to her ears upon the wind.

"Yes."

He paused long enough to set her down, taking a drink from the leather bottle he carried. Giving her a swallow, he gripped her hand and pulled her along. His feet still moved swiftly, and she took two steps to his one, drawing deep breaths of air to stay her lungs from spasming. She stumbled at first, her ankles and feet quite sore from the previous trek.

As they stepped from the shelter and shadows of the village, sneaking around the last, low pony wall that fenced in the huts and yards of mud and rock, the wide expanse of mountains made her reel in awe with their stature and sprawling views. The world was so much bigger than she had ever realized.

MALCOLM, PRESENT DAY...

Sir Malcolm gathered himself. This run, while taxing, was one he had trained for ever since he was a young lad welcomed into the castle and trained alongside the prince. He smiled sadly, remembering the times when he had bested young Elgon at the foot races they had been forced to run over long distances. He had always been faster and more suited with stamina for the long exercises. Their one attempt to run from the impassable peaks east of Niran all the way around the wall, fording the rivers and tributaries on their way into or beneath the city and making it to the cliffside overlooking the ocean by nightfall, had been adventurous to say the least. Elgon had barely made it as the moon peaked the horizon, casting its milky light over the tossing ocean. Malcolm had stayed his speed, choosing to remain with his friend and ensure that they both arrived at their destination rather than best him. He could have passed the test hours before if he had given it his all.

Elgon had been on shaky ground there. Life without his mother starting to take shape as a young teen and his father growing quite ill. He had been a different man then, too young to know the consequences of his actions, but too old in spirit to handle them as a child should. Perhaps Malcolm had failed him there as well.

"It's beautiful." Rosalie's whisper met his ears, and he gripped her hand tighter. He may not have been able to protect her father or mother, but he would sacrifice everything within him to protect Elgon's daughter.

"Beautiful, but dangerous," he whispered back, giving her a swallow from the waterskin again before taking a sip himself. He turned, arranging her cloak over her head and tucking her dark locks into its depths. He drew her to a brush of heather, helped her hunker down, and manipulated the cloak over her to conceal her presence as best as possible. "Stay here. I need to refill our water."

With a few easy steps, he sprang over the wall and into the village. The well near the gate should be close. He squinted into the darkness until he caught sight of the round of stones that protected the well from muddy water and rainflow. Using the shadows to his advantage, he made his way across the courtyard, darting from one splotch of darkness to the other. As he was dipping his skin into the bucket of clear spring water he had pulled up, the sound of a door opening and grating laughter fell upon his ears like a thunderclap. He held his breath as he steadied the bucket he'd nearly dropped so that it did not plummet into the depths below.

The voices came closer, and he set the bucket on the ground outside of the well, cursing under his breath and praying that it did not seem too strange for it to be outside instead of in the well. He moved like a snake making for shelter, crouching low, hugging the brick wall of the well, pulling his hood closer over his head and slinking around to hide on the other side.

A loose stone in the well rattled against his back, and he sought for it with trembling fingers to stop the noise.

"Did you hear that?"

"Do shut up. I'm far too sleepy to care."

"We *are* the village guards. We oughta keep an eye out."

"Didn't you drink enough tonight, you clod? Nothing of note ever happens here. Save the sense of duty for when you get sent over the wall into Elira. That's when you'll need your fighting sword. Them Kingsmen don't take kindly to invaders, and they'd sooner chop your head off than let you best them in a fight." The words were slurred as if too much had been drunk, and Malcolm prayed it was so even as he gripped the hilt of the scimitar that Vieggo had given him to complete his outfit.

Lord willing, they were drunk enough to simply turn away, and if not, then he hoped they would not question his story of being a new Rusalk recruit just coming in from the highlands to join Zuko's guard.

"I just need a drink of water before we head to the barracks. I'm exhausted."

Lord please, keep them away. Do not let us be revealed.

Seven

SORROWFUL NEWS

MALCOLM, PRESENT DAY...

The footsteps that came nearer sent his heart flying into this throat, and he took a breath through his nose. His grip tightened on his scimitar, and he slowly and silently drew a deep breath, filling his lungs, poised to strike.

The guard tripped over the bucket and let a despicable curse fly from his lips. Malcolm heard the man stumble, heard his hand grip the stones and his clothing rustle as he complained loudly.

"Filthy women, not putting their bucket where it belongs." Picking up the bucket, the guard hurled it. But he overshot the well's opening, and the bucket struck Malcolm on the head, the heavy blow knocking him away from his hiding place against the well. He rolled, catching himself on his feet in a defensive position, not pulling his scimitar just yet as he did his best to blink the stars from his eyes.

"What 'ave we here! Fall asleep by the well tonight, did ya? Have a bit too much to drink? Wretched sod." The guard choked out a laugh, his voice gravely before he cleared his throat with an ugly hawk and spit into the dirt at Malcolm's feet.

Cover me. Pain still sprung across his temple where the bucket had clipped it, but he swayed slightly as if intoxicated, catching himself dramatically against the stones of the well. "I guess I did," he slurred, giving his best imitation of the drunken idiot opposite him.

"I haven't seen you around here before." The man, though drunk beyond walking steadily, still had enough faculties about him to recognize—or rather *not* recognize—Malcolm.

The last thing Malcolm wanted was to use violence to get away. Not only was it not his first choice of action, it would surely rouse suspicion that would more than eliminate their head start.

Despite his attempt to appear unsteady and sleepy, Malcolm's muscles tightened and coiled beneath the heavy weight of his cloak, readying to spring if needed. He lifted his hand slowly to the hilt of his dagger beneath his cloak, swaying on his feet, praying he wouldn't have to use it.

"New recruit, eh?"

Malcolm fought the urge to breathe a sigh of relief. "Does the training get any easier? It's killing me," he grumbled, still slurring his speech and rubbing his shoulder as if it was sore.

He was hoping that the camaraderie of his tone would be enough to send the Rusalk fighter on his way.

The man snorted in response. "Can't say as it does. The ale helps, but don't drink too much. If a superior finds you out cold like you just were, you'll thank him to take your life rather than live through the punishment you would get. The training is brutal. Better take it back to the barracks afore they find out you're missing."

Malcolm nodded, stumbling over his feet and turning it into a bow. "P'raps you're right." He stepped away from the well, heading in the direction that he knew the barracks existed from his reconnaissance and that of the spies who had passed information to him.

The heavy weight on his shoulders and the prickling sensation that crawled up his spine stayed with him for a moment more. He could feel the gaze of the other soldier on him, and he tried to swallow the shaking twitch that tempted him to pull his blade and run the man through in self-defense.

"Going the wrong way, ain't ya?"

Malcolm stilled. Had his intel been bad? Was he truly headed in the wrong direction?

"Just teasing you, mate." The drunken fighter guffawed, and Malcolm felt a rush of air fill his lungs. "Sure got you though. You should see the look on your face. It's common to make life hard on the new recruits. See you around, fighter." He slapped Malcolm on the back and headed off to gather up his crumpled partner from the roadway and drag him toward the barracks.

Malcolm waited a moment, holding his breath as he slunk into the shadows again in the direction of the barracks but went no farther once he was hidden. That had been far too close for comfort.

Once back on the other side of the wall, he found Rosalie, her head cradled in her arm and fast asleep in the nest of heather he had left her in. A small smile came to his lips but quickly disappeared at the thought of all that she had been through and what Violet had sacrificed to keep her daughter safe. He saw the queen in the tilt of the girl's lips, the freckles across her pale face, and the curl in her long brown locks. Her mother had been more a woman of internal strength than of stunning beauty, but somehow it had colored her features, painting them in gorgeous tones of loyalty, joy, and light. It was he who had failed her and this little precious bundle who looked just like her but also bore a striking resemblance to the sharp nose and strong chin of her royal father. She would set the nation of Elira back on her feet and give the people a hope they had prayed for.

If only they could make it to safety—and beyond, to the nation that had birthed this heir.

He hated to wake her, but the sooner they put distance between themselves and this ugly place, the sooner they could be in a safe place for the night.

ROSALIE: PRESENT DAY...

Rosalie's feet had ceased to ache and instead were numb. Perhaps that was why she kept stumbling over them.

"We must create a story to explain our journey together. To ensure our safety within Izevel, I was a Rusalkan fighter, newly entered into training. But now that we are outside of the village, we need to have a story that will be plausible to get us across the entirety of this country and to our own."

She tried to catch her breath, but no words came out as she simply nodded, huffing as she reached up and grabbed the edge of a boulder to pull herself higher on the path. She had never thought she would walk something so steep in all of her life.

"I'm a mountain dweller, and you are my daughter. I have no idea what may occur, but unless I tell you that it is safe to do so, we must not separate for any reason. If you are cornered on your own, you must pretend that you either don't understand or are simply looking for me. Don't answer if you don't know the answer to a question. Don't make anything up. It may be easier to be tripped up in the details of our story if we do."

He gripped her hand tighter, and she looked up into his face. By the light of the moon, his jaw was clenched, his close-trimmed beard doing little to hide the stress upon his face. "We are from the north east. If anyone asks any other questions, do not answer. It's best if you refrain from talking with strangers if at all possible." The seriousness of his tone let a note of fear spring into her heart.

He paused, his chest heaving with the exertion as he swung the leather water-pouch off his shoulder and pulled the cork, holding it for her to drink. She swallowed greedily, the cool water soothing her dry and scratchy throat. She wiped her chin and pulled her cloak tighter around her arms, fending off the night chill that grew colder the higher they climbed.

Sir Malcolm quenched his own thirst, but instead of taking her hand and continuing up the path, he placed his hands on her shoulder, the weight of them heavy yet comforting. "Rosalie, you must understand. I do not know the full extent of what you were exposed to in that tower, but unless I acknowledge them as a safe person, you must assume that anyone we come in contact with is either a danger to you or to me. Elirans are not welcome here, and I have done my best to fit in. News of your escape will be out much sooner than we'd like, and I have no doubt that a bounty will be set. Your position in Elira is strictly coveted, and Zuko will stop at nothing to get you back." He paused, his face close to hers, the steam from his breath creating puffs between them as his words rumbled from his chest.

Sweat started to her face.

"I don't want to scare you, but I do need you to be aware. Zuko will have no qualms about your safety if it means he may remain in control of the Eliran line or sever it completely from existence. Your life will surely matter less to him than losing, and he likely will not pause to allow you to keep it."

Rosalie trembled beneath his hands.

"This is why I ask that you do as I say the instant that I say it. I know you have very little reason to trust me; you know nothing of me aside from the sign that I carry. But I ask that you trust me. I follow the one true King who rules not on this earth and I will do all in my power to keep you safe, regardless of the cost. Do you understand?" His tone was gentle, his hands more of a support than a weight and his eyes ones of intense compassion and determination as she stared deep into them.

Rosalie's heart, though frightened at the possible consequences of their actions, was filled with trust and faith in this man. But more importantly in their God. She nodded, blinking back the tears that started to her eyes. They were not of fear but of a strong emotion that she had not felt since Zehra had passed in her youth. "I trust you because I trust God, and I know that He has sent you to me. 'But the salvation of the righteous is of the Lord: he is their strength in the time of trouble.' Zehra spoke often of the salvation of the King for His people, and I trust that He will be our strength." She reached up and slid her hand into his, squeezing it within her fingers as she kept her gaze on his. "I never thought I would see this day, but you are an answer to the verses Zehra made me quote 'til I knew them as I do my own heart."

His eyes seemed to grow misty—perhaps it was only the mist in her own—before he nodded, cleared his throat, and stood once more, his hand clasping hers in return and pulling her up the mountain to resume their trek.

"We will reach shelter by nightfall tomorrow, but we must keep moving. We will rest off the path during noonday."

ELGON, FOURTEEN YEARS AGO...

"They have come!" Kenton, once a squire boy, now a knight in training, ran into the library, his brown eyes alight with excitement and his hair, always a mess, bouncing in the wake of the wind he created in his run. Kenton rarely walked anywhere and instead let his feet carry him swiftly.

Elgon drew a breath. He had waited for this day and was loath to see it come, even though he knew what his response would be, what his course of action was, and where he would be going. He swallowed hard, setting his shoulders and tilting his head to the side to stretch one of the tight muscles in his neck. They had grown more tense since the news of Pavlin's hard-earned, though temporary, win over Rusalka in the recent battle. It had been over a week since the news had come, but a council had finally arrived. Perhaps it was time to ally with Pavlin, once and for all. He had been thinking on Violet's words and her insinuation that some things could be done to make Pavlin more independent. But perhaps independence was not what they needed so much as an alliance with a kingdom that could not only defend them, but also offer them occupation and assistance in growing their country into more than dry and arid plains with little to no resources.

He had never sought to conquer Pavlin; conquering was never much his or his father's desire. Everyone deserved an opportunity to make the most of themselves without being stolen from by an ambitious neighbor, but perhaps an alliance would benefit them both. It would broaden their territory and draw them into a relationship with Elira that would not only reciprocate assistance but would also bring Christ to their fallow lands.

"Who is it?" he asked, picking up his royal cloak from the chair and draping it over his shoulder, pinning it beneath his pauldron and flipping it back over his other shoulder.

"An envoy. They bear the flag and the sign of Pavlin!"

Elgon tried not to grimace at the excitement in Kenton's voice. He had yet to fight a battle, and the elation in the lad's voice made Elgon wince at the idea of what the envoy from Pavlin signified—their desperation and dire need for help.

He laid a hand on Kenton's shoulder as he moved to precede him out of the doorway. He could feel the boy's energy coiling in the taut and trembling muscles beneath his hand. "Tread lightly, lad, and consider the loss they have endured to get here and the loss that could be ours if we stand with them to fight. I am not against standing with them in the gap, but be mindful of how much and what they have lost that has prompted their journey here."

Kenton sobered. "Of course, your majesty. Forgive me." He bobbed in a subtle bow, his face growing red beneath the gaze of his king.

"No apology necessary; just know that your excitement is misplaced. There is nothing wrong with looking forward to putting your hard-won skills to good use, but do not do so at the detriment to your awareness and compassion for those you will fight with and against. Loss is not a possibility of war; it is an unfortunate and heartbreaking surety."

Kenton nodded, his pronounced Adam's apple bobbing and the red in his blond hair glinting in the sunlight that was thrown through the stained glass and leaded windows of Elgon's study.

"Fetch Malcolm. I'll want him there when they make their way into the throne room."

Kenton scurried off in the opposite direction as Elgon strode through the decorative marble halls of the castle that was his home. Ever since the return of his memory, it had been a conundrum of the highest order that he felt just as at home amongst the cold stone and marble of the castle and the living, breathing archways of the forest. Violet had given him that, and he thanked God for her and the life he had been forced to live when his mind had forsaken him. It had not only given him the opportunity to truly understand the heavenly King his father had served, but also to understand the hearts and minds of the people in his kingdom. They were not simply peasants to be ruled but people to be served in the manner of Christ Jesus—protecting, providing for, and honoring them as friends and brothers, not as somehow beneath him.

His heart was heavy for the loss of those who had come to seek his help and it was at the forefront of his mind as he turned the corner of the hall and met his wife, her hands cupped beneath her swollen middle as she swayed from one foot to the other on the threshold of the throne room.

"Darling, should you be walking so far in your condition?" He stepped to her side quickly, his hands reaching out to steady her elbow.

"Elgon, for heaven's sake. Babies are a natural part of life. God made me this way. Not to say it's not a smidge uncomfortable…" She shifted, stretching her back with a slight wince. "But not something I wasn't made for." There was a twinkle in her eye as she stole a kiss from his lips and stood on tiptoe as he bent down so she could kiss the furrows from his brow. "Go with God, my husband. May your words be His and your heart move in time with His."

He squeezed her hand in his and leaned forward, drawing her close to him, their little one pressing between them as he soaked in her presence, his lips claiming hers in a long kiss that filled his mind with a peace and steadiness that had not been there a moment before.

A throat being cleared at the other end of the hall interrupted their tranquil moment. Elgon turned to catch sight of Kenton, who was blushing and had his eyes roaming anywhere but to his monarchs, and Malcolm, who stood with his arms folded and a look of slight amusement creasing the serious stoicism of his face. "You called for me, your majesty?"

Elgon smirked and wrapped his arm around her waist, pulling her close to him and feeling the warmth of her body against his. She rested her head on his shoulder, and the smell of wild violets that permeated her velvet gown soothed his senses.

"I did. Kenton, have the kingsmen bring in the envoy from Pavlin. Malcolm, will you stand with me to hear them out?"

"Aye." Malcolm nodded, his fist to his heart, then bowed to Violet as she strode past him after kissing her husband's cheek, a soft smile on her lips.

Elgon drew a deep breath. The skirmish at the border a few months ago had been a baiting attempt by the hands of Rusalka. He knew then that it would not be the last he would hear of antagonism from the mountain king against his nation or another. Zuko was not one to sit quietly by when he could seek to conquer or better his own standing in the world. Elgon stepped through the large wooden doors that were swung open to receive him, adjusting his cloak and treading to the dais and the throne that sat atop it. Malcolm followed, and their footsteps echoed off of the vast, dark room, the light cascading in from the western windows sending shadows of the pillars across the wooden inlay on the floor, the patterns appearing inconsistent in the alternating light and darkness that spread across the ground.

He took his seat on the ornately carved wooden throne, the seat hard but smoothed from years of use. The smaller and less ostentatious throne that belonged to his wife for ceremonial purposes sat to his right and behind by a small margin.

Malcolm took his position on the dais to Elgon's right, holding his wrist in front of him, his head high and his shoulders set.

After a few short minutes that seemed to stretch into hours as Elgon tried to still the racing of his heart, the distant echo of footsteps echoed through the halls and in through the open doors of the throne room. The group's silence and somber presence seemed to precede them.

Elgon only recognized one by sight. He was much older now, but if Elgon's memory was correct, it was one of the lords of Pavlin, Milton. Kenton led the envoy into the room Their banners were held proudly, but the carriers' shoulders seemed to droop beneath the weight of their own grief.

Elgon felt his heart lurch. Their loss compelled him to act. Even before they had asked, his heart was already at their side. No one should suffer such loss and have to endure it a second time.

As they neared, Elgon noticed some of the lords looked battle worn themselves.

Pavlin's government did not have one ruler, but instead had a counsel of the predominant land-owners, their mission to guide and protect their small country and their tenants with their collective wisdom and decisions. Elgon did not doubt that these lords had fought along with their men, attempting to hold back the tide of Rusalk fighters. Five hundred men was a score so great, Pavlin would take many years to recover. A devastating loss.

The pain of it drew him from his seat, and he strode down from the dais, meeting Milton, who was first in line. Elgon gripped his forearm, compassion choking his throat so no words could come forth. He hoped his face said it all, but the lord's face crumpled just the same, tears making tracks on his face in the dust from their journey.

"I'm so sorry for your loss." Elgon's voice was hoarse, and he pulled the lord into an embrace, their hands still clasped between them.

Milton drew a shuddering breath. His shoulders were set when he pulled back and the tears gone from his eyes, though the trail of one remained. Instead, jaw clenched, his eyes were harsh in the shadow of a pillar he stood in. "Will you help us, your majesty? We have come to offer not just a treaty, but an alliance. We know you owe us nothing, but the Rusalks cannot take from us again, nor can we defend ourselves with—" His voice broke and he cleared his throat, looking past Elgon as he steadied himself with a breath. "With what we have left."

Elgon nodded, still grasping Milton's forearm. "I would be honored to discuss the terms with you, my lord, but know that my heart is to serve your country and hold fast against the evil of Zuko and his fighters that seek to take your land and give nothing but bloodshed in payment for its use. The Lord has given me not only the ability but the heart to do so. But first, won't you rest, wash for the evening meal, and allow me to host your envoy before we get to particulars? Are you safe for the moment? I know your journey here was one of haste."

"Aye. 'Twas. The Rusalks took their own beating, and our men did not fall without a fight." Milton's eyes flashed. In his thirties, he was less than a decade older than Elgon, but had already been taking over for his father years before when Elgon's own had passed. "They will not attack us soon I think, as they will need reinforcements from the mountains and their travel is not easily taken in the mountains of Kaira and Izevel."

"I am grateful. I have already dispatched word by courier that my border patrols are to push into Pavlin and assist in setting up defenses."

Milton's shoulders, indeed those of many in the envoy, seemed to relax at these words. Elgon knew the horror and the fear that existed for those who had wives, children, mothers, fathers, and even livelihoods to protect in their home country. "Thank you, m'lord. You have no idea the relief that is to hear. We are more grateful than we can say for your assistance."

"I think I have some idea, Milton. Come, my men will take you to your quarters and help you prepare for the evening meal. We will stand with you, brothers. Rest now, and tomorrow, we will talk."

Eight

CLEAR AIR AND DARK DISCOVERIES

ROSALIE, PRESENT DAY...

Their journey seemed to spiral toward the heavens, the path growing steeper and the air thinner with every step. When Sir Malcolm led them off the trail when the sun was near its zenith, Rosalie was beyond the point of being out of breath and had nearly forgotten what it was like to breathe easily. He left her at a small stream, and while she was desperately trying to fill her lungs with fresh air, the sun glittering off the surface of the water captured her attention…and her heart.

She had always longed to be free, to find her feet upon the hills, buried in the sparse grass which she had come to realize, upon closer examination, was more rock and heather than actual grass. The shepherds had always intrigued her; their nomadic lives, asleep in nature with heather for their pillow and the moon and stars keeping watch over them during the night filled her with a thrill of longing and joy.

Pulling the leather boots Malcolm had given her before their departure from her feet, Rosalie winced at the sight of the blisters that had not only formed but burst upon her feet and the back of her ankles. She hardly noticed the pain while walking, but now that the blisters were exposed to the air, they burned. Gathering her skirt around her knees, she turned on the rock she was sitting upon to dip her toes into the sparkling water. She hissed in a breath at the frigid temperatures, the water most likely fed by the snow-capped tips of the mountains or the glaciers in the north. The water stung, and red joined the dirt that washed off her feet and floated downstream. She cringed, but as swiftly as the water flowed, the pain ebbed, replaced by the gloriously refreshing cold.

A song bubbled up, and breathlessly, around the gasps for air, the scripture that she had committed to memory by combining it with song floated from her lips.

"The Lord is my shepherd; I shall not want. He maketh me to lie down in green pastures: he leadeth me beside the still waters. He restoreth my soul: he leadeth me in the paths of righteousness for his name's sake. Yea, though I walk through the valley of the shadow of death, I will fear no evil: for thou art with me; thy rod and thy staff they comfort me. Thou preparest a table before me in the presence of mine enemies: thou anointest my head with oil; my cup runneth over. Surely goodness and mercy shall follow me all the days of my life: and I will dwell in the house of the Lord for ever." The lilting, rollicking melody reminded her of the cavorting brook that danced around her feet and the wind that playfully tugged at the hair that had slipped from the confines of her braid.

She had always longed to know what lying in fields felt like. What walking beside a stream would do for her soul. And despite the pain, the deep ache in her side from the walking she was unaccustomed to, her torn up feet and the blisters that would plague her for many a mile more, her cup overflowed with the goodness of the Lord.

She continued singing, the melody repeating itself over and over on her lips, as familiar to her as her own voice and the whispers in her heart. She gently massaged around the blisters, loosening the dirt that had gathered inside her boots and permeated her stockings. She tried not to moan when she accidentally hit a raw patch of skin. She heard Sir Malcolm's footsteps behind her and dove for her stockings, her face heating as she desperately tried to pull them on before he could see.

"Was that your voice I heard?" His tone was soft, his hands full of berries that he must have gathered just off the trail.

She nodded, kneeling beside the riverbed and scooping water with her hands to splash over her face. Then she drank as much as she could.

He sat on the large, flat stone beside her and eyed her carefully as she brushed the hair back from her face and settled back when she had drunk her fill. "Who taught you those words?"

Rosalie reached for her boots and pulled them on over the stained stockings, using her skirt to hide them as best she could. She laced them quickly and avoided his eyes. "Zehra.

She said that no matter what happened to me, the Lord's words would always comfort me, no matter how alone I felt. So I turned them to song to hide them in my heart for when I would need them most."

He held out his large hands to her, cupped and filled with the small red berries he had gathered. "You have a way with the melody."

She dipped her head, her face flushing as she reached for a few of the berries. Putting them in her mouth, she closed her eyes in wonder at the sweet and sour taste, the feel of the seeds grinding against her teeth, and then swallowed. Her stomach grumbled, begging for more. She watched him take a mouthful before dumping the rest into her outstretched hand and reaching for his leather pack as she ate the rest.

He pulled a knife from his belt and unwrapped a wedge of cheese and half a loaf of bread that had been bundled in his pack, slicing off a chunk of each for her, which she ate with relish.

Sir Malcolm polished off his own serving, putting the remainder back in his bag. "We'll rest here for a few hours to avoid being seen. Then we will finish our journey and be at the inn by nightfall."

Her eyes were already drooping, the food in her belly and the miles she had walked taking their toll. Sleep was sneaking up on her like a cloaked assassin, ready to pull her into slumber. Stumbling over her own feet, she tried to follow Malcolm toward the clump of bushes they would conceal themselves behind. Her vision blurred. His hand was suddenly on her elbow, and before she knew what was happening, her head was resting on a slightly scratchy, but soft, cushion of wool. She let her eyes fall shut.

MALCOLM: PRESENT DAY

Malcolm curled up on the ground within the hiding place created by the large bushes around them, roots poking him in the back as he shifted to get comfortable. He smiled softly. The princess had her father's determination and her mother's grit. Having been cooped up in a tower her entire life, it couldn't have been easy to traverse these trails and these distances. They had likely been a harrowing experience for her.

He watched her as she slept, her thin face flushed from the sun and the exertion, sweat still beaded on her brow. He reached out a hand to dab it away but stopped short, not wanting to wake her. Though if he were to hazard a guess, he doubted much of anything would wake her. He had grown used to little sleep, and when one was on the trail, little is what one got. He would keep watch while she rested. He wished he could give her more than a few hours, but getting out of the midday heat was not the only reason they were avoiding the trail.

The Rusalks would surely be aware of her absence by now. And if that was the case, they could be anywhere looking for them. Even the most elaborate cover story would not help them if they were discovered this close to Izevel, even with the distance they had already put between themselves and the castle. A young girl traveling alone with a man was questionable no matter how far they got from the castle. His one protection was that most had no idea what the princess looked like. In his attempts at reconnaissance, many had either not known of her existence or thought her a witch that Zuko kept locked up in a tower for his own amusement, and they only caught a glimpse of her upon occasion from a distance as she stood in a window.

He smiled and let his eyes close to rest them, folding his arms and shifting on the rocky ground again. Little did they know that the thing they feared and thought so ugly and dangerous was actually a petite, weak, beautiful little girl who could no more hurt a small animal, let alone another human being. The stories he had heard of the ghosts and animals that haunted these mountains had only given him a more complete picture of the superstition and fear that those of Rusalka lived under.

Over time, Zuko's line had slowly taken their place as rulers of Rusalka, beating out every lord and lady who had tried to stake their claim in these mountains. The ruins of the castles that sat like lowly, abandoned sentinels throughout the land were said to be filled with the ghosts and demons of the past—witches and devils and the bodies of those Zuko had defeated who had been too cursed to pass into the heavenly realm.

Malcolm reached over and adjusted the cloak he had covered Rosalie with, pulling it up over her shoulder to make sure she did not catch cold after getting overheated on the climb. Malcolm did not doubt that demons clung to this land, holding power over those they could exert their strength upon and using the people's own fear against them. Lands carried the sins of those that made them, and when allowed to stay, the evil was given a right to what should never have been under its authority in the first place.

But he had the weapon that would defeat such spirits, and he was not afraid of their existence, be it rumor or fact.

While he rested his eyes, he did not let his ears close to his surroundings. If someone was coming toward them, he would be the first to hear and have an arrow nocked and pointed in their direction before they could so much as move a branch.

"How did she escape?" The voice was quiet, soft, but it held back fury like a dam built over a torrential waterfall.

"W-we don't know. Her room was undisturbed, and no one was seen entering or exiting the room except..." The Rusalk warrior turned pale and swallowed hard.

Zuko examined the man's face, making the soldier squirm beneath his gaze. "Except what, Talon? Speak or lose your tongue." His voice never once changed in pitch or passion, as smooth and soft as if he were speaking of last night's dinner entertainment.

Talon's eyes drifted left and then back to Zuko. He raised his chin, meeting his lord's gaze. "Merlin and I checked on her last night, sir, as usual. But Merlin..."

Zuko took a step closer, the unspoken pressure making Talon falter, sweat beading on his brow.

"Merlin—he touched her. He was drunk, and I pulled him from the room. That's all."

"That's all?" Zuko's voice trailed off in a whisper as he stepped closer to Talon, now standing over him and forcing the soldier to meet his gaze, a full head above his own.

Talon gulped and nodded.

"And what have I said about entering her chamber? I seem to recall having extremely strict orders for you boys."

Talon swallowed again, his Adam's apple bobbing violently in his stretched neck. "Aye. You do. And I have done my best to follow them."

"Your best doesn't seem to have kept Merlin's hands at bay, though, does it?"

Talon shook his head, his silence and set shoulders indicating defiance.

"Merlin has earned his punishment, but I'll be merciful to you this time. Not because you deserve it, but because I have other plans for you. Send him to Dracul and call the dark knights. The guild is needed."

Talon nodded, bowed, and fled the room on swift feet. Whoever had kidnapped the princess would be expecting an onslaught. But stealth was more to Zuko's liking. Brute force was fine for certain occasions, but when one tried to ruin something as long thought out and secret as this…covertness under the cover of darkness would do more in his favor. He needed the girl back alive, or his plan would never be realized. Brute force could take a nation, but devious and meticulous plotting to steal its legitimacy would keep it.

MALCOLM, PRESENT DAY...

Footsteps crunched in the gravel along the path. With nary a sound, lying with his back flat upon the ground, Malcolm had an arrow notched on his bow, his entire body stiff as he held it close to his chest.

By the sound of the approach, this person was attempting to be quiet. The steps were hesitant, quiet, and calculated. One could discern many things by the way a person walked, and this man was on the prowl. He glanced at Rosalie, still fast asleep, her face flushed and her eyes flickering beneath their lids. He hoped she would stay still and not be woken by whoever it was that approached. He didn't want her to have to see a fight, but he also didn't want any unintentional noise she could make to alert their stalker.

The steps paused, and Malcolm held his breath to listen. They were close. Too close to their hideout and far too near for his comfort. Had he been careful enough to sweep away their footprints? What if there was a depression in the heather that caught their hunter's attention? What if there was something he had left behind? He had let his guard down once before, and it had resulted in the regret he would carry with him until the end of his days.

The footsteps continued, the pace a bit heavier. Malcolm drew a breath, letting his burning lungs expand with the sweet air. He had created a few alternative paths that led away from their hiding spot. He needed to get her to the inn. The tavern would be the safest place for her, and Vieggo would be able to get them on the next leg of their journey without mishap. Just a few more hours and they would be on their way to their next stop: Bevy Tavern and Inn.

Nine

A PLACE TO LAY THEIR HEAD

ROSALIE, PRESENT DAY...

Rosalie held her breath as she took a large step, trying to fill her lungs with enough air to allow them to expand. The sleep had hardly made a dent in her exhaustion, and it had felt like mere moments before Sir Malcolm was waking her up with the sky glowing orange behind him, the light running away from the gathering dusk.

She let out her breath and immediately gasped for another one, turning over another psalm in her head as Sir Malcolm fairly towed her by the hand up the side of the mountain. She was hoping to distract herself from her growling stomach, from the shoes that she was unaccustomed to and to the way they rubbed and pinched her already blistered feet.

She stumbled more often now, and she cursed herself every time, wishing that she could have those hind's feet on high places that David had asked God for. She had hoped to be as sure-footed as the shepherds and their sheep she had watched from her tower all these years, and she was sorely disappointed to find that such was not the case.

"We're almost there. Keep going. I know it's hard, but we'll reach it in just a few more minutes." Sir Malcolm's voice was irritatingly unfazed and as strong as it had been the moment they had started on the journey. As if climbing a mountain was merely all in a day's work for him.

She looked to the sky and huffed another breath. Why would her lungs not fill with enough air to get her up the mountain face?

A cramp seized her leg, and she yelped. Her legs buckled with the pain, and she collapsed, her knees skinning painfully on the rocks that tore holes through her dress.

Sir Malcolm pulled her upright again, but she couldn't seem to get her feet under her. He helped her sit on a rock and handed her the leather pouch filled with water. She took several swallows of its dwindling contents as he took her leg in his hands and rubbed his fist down the tight muscles. She cried out and bit her lip, twisting on the rock in resistance against the pain. "I'm sorry," she whispered breathlessly.

He shook his head. "Do not concern yourself with apologizing for something that is not your doing nor your fault. It takes away from the true repentance one must feel over something actually done wrong and is simply a way of telling another that you cannot own how you feel."

She nodded, biting her tongue.

"I'll carry you the rest of the way. We can make it. It's not long now, I promise." He lifted her hands over his head as he had done the day before, and she clung to his shoulder as he scooped her up under the legs and lifted her aching form. Setting off, he took them at a slightly slower but steady pace up the mountainside. Between the heat radiating off his back and the lengthy exertion of her own limbs, her forehead dripped with sweat. She rested it on Malcolm's shoulder, letting his wool cloak absorb some of the moisture. Rosalie held on tight, the ground sloping heavily beneath them and making her feel as though she could slip off his back at any moment should either of them release their hold.

The shadows of the mountain cliffs pressed in all around them, their jagged edges appearing like teeth in the night, razor sharp as they sawed through the bits of light that slivered across the rocks. She buried her face into his shoulder again, this time to turn away from the darkness. The cliffs, so majestic and breathtaking with their vastness during the day, took on an entire weight of heaviness in the receding light.

She must have dozed off because a jostle by Sir Malcolm as he hefted her higher on his back made her look up and catch sight of lovely golden light spilling out into the darkness. She blinked the blurriness from her eyes and looked more closely at the tavern sign swinging above the doorway, the name 'Bevy' scrawled across the wooden plaque. The building seemed like it had been a part of the cliffside its whole life, with its peaks and gables blending in with the ledges and bulges in the rock wall of the mountain's face. Trees gathered around it, growing out of the dirt and rocks as the tavern reached for the top of the cliff. The inn's walls stretched for some distance before ending where the next house began in the tiny little mountainside village.

"Here at last. You can breathe easily, Rosalie. We'll be safe here. We'll have some vittles and get a good night's rest before we head out tomorrow morning. Vieggo will take good care of us. You can trust him. Don't speak to anyone else about our story, but he knows it all and will keep the secret—and you—safe with his life should he need to."

Rosalie's nerves thrummed to life with the reminder to watch her words and act her part in the tableau her life had become for her safety. She noticed a dove carved into the front of the door and smiled at the light that spilled from the cutout as Sir Malcolm reached for the handle. She lifted a hand and watched the golden shape of the bird in flight rest in her palm before he pushed the door open.

The sound of loud singing and laughing met her ears with the concussive effect of a rockslide, and her sight spun for a moment as he ushered her in, the light snatching the clarity from her eyes until she grew used to it. Men covered in dust sat around the room, tankards in front of them, plates of half-eaten food littering the tables. Some of the men laughed, some shoveled food into their mouths silently, and others argued, slamming their hands on the table, their fists gripping their utensil of choice.

A few women wandered around, their hair tied back in kerchiefs, carrying either pitchers or platters. She even noticed a couple of women in the corner, instruments in their hands, their melodic voices blending into the noise and casting a song over those gathered, like some spell woven amongst the chaos.

She pressed in close to Sir Malcolm, grasping his cloak in her hand and doing her best not to limp as he led her to the bar-top counter that spanned most of the back of the room. The large man saw him coming, and a smile lit his face. It was the first time she had seen a man look so inviting, and it piqued her interest, her heart going out to him immediately, despite the fact that she had never met a man who had truly held her best interests at heart—until Malcolm that was.

His long, dark hair, like the rest of the Rusalkans, was pulled into a tail at the back of his head and tied with a leather cord. Straight whisps had escaped and framed his square face, rugged and cut from the mountain wind like most of the men. His eyes, though dark, were shining and filled with a light that she felt drawn to like a sheep to its shepherd. He stepped up to the counter and gripped Malcolm's free hand. "Leonid, it's so good to see you! And looking so well! Shall I serve you up a plate and pour you an ale? And how about a room, eh?" His booming voice matched the rest of him, and his excitement spilled over, joy sparking from his eyes like embers exploding from a crackling fire.

Rosalie swallowed at the name he had called Malcolm, remembering that they had a cover to keep and that they had never discussed what her name should be. She lifted a hand to her racing heart, trying to will it back into submission.

"Vieggo, good to see you as well, old friend. I will take a plate and cup, but no ale if you please. Perhaps a toddy. And make that two." He reached his hand down and gripped Rosalie's shoulder in a comforting gesture.

She tried to draw air into her lungs, but her stomach was doing flips. What if she said the wrong thing?

Awareness alighted on Vieggo's face and was quickly wiped away as if it had never been there, making Rosalie question its existence at all. His expression remained the same as before, stoically welcoming, stolidly joyful, but there was a brightness to the look he sent Rosalie's way that made her feel as if she was suddenly the only one in the room and he was welcoming her into a place that had been prepared for her all along. "Brought your daughter as well this time. The great-aunt finally let her out of her clutches, eh?" His shoulders were set, and while his face never changed, he now gripped the knife he had been spinning in his left hand, hilt up and blade down, tight in his fist.

She nodded and he grinned at her. "I'll get a plate for you and the little lady! Looks like you both need it and a bed as soon as they can be prepared. Marie! Can you fetch this young lass and her father a plate of the finest dinner that we have left and a warm toddy to help them sleep tonight? We'll have to get them all set up in the available beds in the fourth room." The edges of his eyes took on a few extra lines as he looked between Malcolm and Rosalie. "I'm sorry to say all I have left is a communal room split by curtains. Will that do fine for you folks or…?" He glanced around as if to determine what others were listening to their conversation.

Sir Malcolm took it in stride. "That should be fine. Thank you, Vieggo. I'm sure my daughter and I will sleep well on your comfortable beds, regardless of the accommodations." Rosalie noticed a tightness in his voice, but he still carried on as if it were of no consequence. He led her to an abandoned table in the corner and helped her sit on the wooden bench that he pulled out for her. She felt his observant eye on her as she attempted to sit and not wince at the tightness in her limbs and the pain in her now throbbing feet.

The food one of the maids served them was some of the best Rosalie had ever eaten. The roast meat was tender and juicy, the heat of it immediately warming her insides and flavoring the roasted vegetables that rounded out the plate. She could almost cry from the relief and strength it filled her with. The empty feeling inside dissipated, replaced by the sleepiness that had plagued her the entire journey. Would she never catch up on rest? She tried not to grumble inwardly over how unsuited she was for this journey but, instead, asked the Lord for His strength.

The toddy was spicy and sweet, warm on her tongue and leaving behind a tingly flavor that buzzed in her mouth. While seeming to be a common occurrence to those around her, the food and drink felt like palace food after the bland gruel and dumplings with broth that had been her fare for what she could remember of her life.

But it was the music that held her spellbound. One woman, old with wrinkles on her face and cheeks sunken from the harshness of the winter winds, had a bowl-shaped instrument sitting in her lap; she strummed the strings. Another held a fiddle to her shoulder and bowed back and forth, swaying to the tune that echoed from it with her eyes half closed and a smile on her lips. Still another, her hair done up in a braid that fell long over her shoulder, sat at their feet, her legs crossed and a small instrument in her lap. It looked like a harp with a flat side as she plucked the strings; the sound omitted was plucky and soft but had a melancholy emotion that seemed to dance in Rosalie's ears and resound in her soul.

She was so fascinated by watching them that she almost forgot to finish eating till Malcolm edged her plate closer while talking with Vieggo about commonplace matters she had ceased to listen to.

Silence suddenly cut through the music with a few untuneful plucks to a string as the women stopped the vibrating notes of their instruments with their hands. Vieggo had stepped to the front of the room and clapped his hands loudly. "Comrades and friends, you know that the time has come!"

Thunderous applause burst from every corner of the room, boots stamping the rock floors and shouts and whistles making the room itself shudder.

Wide-eyed, Rosalie waited expectantly for what would come next. Everyone in the room seemed to know what was about to take place—except for her. She glanced at Sir Malcolm and saw the glimmer of a smile in the corner of his mouth as he nodded at her, tipping his brows to get her attention back on Vieggo.

The tavern owner flicked a knife from behind his back and started twirling it in the fingers of one hand, effortlessly and quickly, the speed of the movement making it blur. He grinned at the crowd. "This act has been performed before kings, lords, and ladies, and now before the greatest audience of all, my fellow peasants! May our lives be long, our happiness be deep, and our joy long outlast our rulers!" He shouted throughout the room, his voice rumbling off the wooden rafters.

With a nod to those behind him, the music started again, softer in volume but dancing as the background for his voice.

"Sit down, and hear my tale. Drink your ale, lest ye become frail. For long ago, in times long past, I traveled far, but rarely fast." He gestured to his hulking frame with a grimace and a bouncing eyebrow and the entire crowd laughed uproariously as if this were the first time they had heard the joke. "Brothers in arms, knives in hand, we spun them long, for many a clan. Vagari by day, entertainer by night, we saw many a lord, much to their delight. Wagons by day, throne rooms by night, we ate well and slept all right." He patted his thick, but firm stomach with a grin, licked his lips as the crowd chuckled again, and suddenly there was a knife flying through the air from somewhere in the crowd. Vieggo caught it behind his back with his free hand; now there were two spinning away on fingers as fast as lightning. He told his tale with all of the seasoned experience of a man who tells it every night, but with a sincerity that spoke of a first telling.

"Rensen and Vieggo, Vagari extraordinaire, our knives warned others to beware! For sharp of tongue, of wit, of trade, we were met with many an accolade." Another knife flew through the air, and suddenly there were three, spinning round and round and circling around each other as his arms moved windmill fashion, his eyes still attentive to the crowd as if the spinning was being performed by another person not of his concern. "Brother with brother, we faced down many a foe. Our knives at our side, each other's loyalty more so. 'Til one day, another joined our duo, betrayal beyond compare, as our twosome became a trio." Stage anger flashed across his face and, still spinning the knives, he growled at the children who had gathered at his feet and were staring with wide eyes. They squealed and cowered, their laughter cutting through the applause and chaos of everyone else in the room.

"But, even though their troupe had grown, it was apparent a wife should be on Rensen's throne." Rosalie gasped as another knife spun into his hand and now there were four spinning around him like a whirlwind as he juggled all of them as effortlessly as if it were second nature to him. "But Vieggo's heart was soon to be even more broken, as his partner and brother left with merely a token.

"They left for far off lands, abandoning Vieggo to make his plans. And now, with knives in hand, my tale has come to an end, for despite loss and pain, it all worked together for our gain. He has a wife, I have the inn, and many a tale and knife to spin."

Vieggo threw two more knives into the whirling dervish of a dome he was crafting as the music hit a crescendo, and they spun higher and dangerously fast. Rosalie watched with her jaw hanging open and her hand on her chest. He threw them higher in the air, his tongue between his lips in concentration as the crowd clapped in rhythm to the music to cheer him on. At Vieggo's request, one of the bystanders threw an empty wooden tankard which Vieggo miraculously caught and added to the spinning blades in his hand. The entire room screamed with applause, Rosalie right along with them.

One by one, Vieggo caught the blades, his hands suddenly as empty as they had been when he had started, the knives nowhere to be seen. The empty tankard was all that was left, which he spun around on its handle and set back on the table. He took a bow at the waist, empty hands outspread with a grin on his face that rivaled the brightness of the moon.

Rosalie glanced up at Sir Malcolm and caught a faint smile on his face that softened all the deeply creased lines near the corners of his eyes and mouth. The music resumed, and Rosalie took another drink of the toddy as Vieggo circled the room, checking in with each of his customers.

Her stomach full, the music pulled at her eyelids, dragging them down as the light seemed to fade away from the edges of her vision. The golden light matched the warmth and comfort that she felt as all of the pain seemed to slip away and a contentment entered her heart. Her entire life she had grown to distrust everyone around her even as she longed for companionship of those that should have been hers, and sitting in this room, she was finally experiencing what her heart had longed for all this time.

MALCOLM, PRESENT DAY...

Malcolm felt the weight of the princess as she leaned into him and looked down to catch sight of her head lolling against his arm, her eyes closed and a beatific look on her thin little face. Poor little waif. She looked hardly anything like a princess, and though his heart worried over the long journey that was ahead of them and the many dangers that probably awaited them on it, his heart breathed a sigh of relief and held a tiny sliver of joy. The search of fourteen years was finally at an end, and he had the princess in his possession to prove it. What he wouldn't give to tell the king himself.

Elgon. What must be on his heart these days?

Malcolm had never expected to be away from his Majesty and his closest friend for so long, but he had been at the helm of the spying positions when they had first opened and had asked for volunteers. Elgon had been unable and unwilling to believe that his wife had been killed, and Malcolm owed the success of this mission in no small part to the resolve of his king.

Truth would be unearthed, no matter the cost, as long as hope was fought for with a tenacious grip. Malcolm felt a burning in his throat at the thought of Violet. His best friend's bride, damned to a life imprisoned. The first years of marriage and motherhood that had been stolen from her by the jealousy and evil of another. His eyes grew blurry at the heavy-handed grip that squeezed the air from his throat and lit the fire that burned him from the inside out.

He took a shuddering breath, wheezing past the righteous anger that held him within its chokehold. Vengeance was not his, nor could he let his mind wander to it. It would only sidetrack him from his mission and misplace the fire in his chest. His form of vengeance would be to set broken things right. To restore what had been stolen and to go at least some of the way toward mending a king's shattered life.

He took one last giant swig from his tankard, the toddy tingling and soothing his throat on the way down. He nodded to Vieggo from across the room and gestured up the stairs with a glance of his eyes. Vieggo nodded, drying his hands on the cloth that hung over his shoulders and muscling his way through the crowd gathered around the bar. Malcolm shifted his weight toward the sleeping Rosalie, placing an arm behind her shoulders and the other scooping her up behind her knees. She didn't even move as her head rolled against his shoulder and settled against his neck. He stepped over the bench and headed through the crowd to meet Veiggo at the foot of the stairs.

This child had seen so much already. Given so much of herself to the point of exhaustion, and his heart ached at the missing years his friend had been forced to forfeit. Elgon had never had the chance to hold his own daughter. To watch her grow. To comfort her when she was sad, dry her tears, laugh with her, or chase her around the palace halls. Elgon had never been able to hold his child…and he never would, for now she was on the brink of young-womanhood, already a woman in the ways of her heart and mind. Forced to grow old before her time.

Vieggo had a wooden bucket filled with water and an armful of clothes that he said had been given to him by one of the maids. "I thought you both would like to freshen up before sleep."

Malcolm smiled, putting the melancholy thoughts from his mind. "Do I look that dirty?"

Vieggo grinned and hiked a bulky shoulder. "Let's just say you wouldn't win the heart of any fair lady looking like that, old friend."

Malcolm shook his head, following the large man up the stairs as the music and loud voices died off in the background. Rosalie was hardly a cumbersome weight; the child would need to put on some muscle fast if she were going to survive the long journey ahead. Traversing the mountains of Rusalka was not for the faint of heart, and Vagari were hardy folk by necessity.

Vieggo pulled a key from the ring that hung on his belt, unlocked the door, and let them in. "You'll be safe here. Only you and your room-fellows can enter, and the room locks from the inside. The two cots on the far side of the room are yours, and the water and towels can be refilled if necessary. Let me know if you need anything and I or the maids will be happy to oblige."

Malcolm laid Rosalie on the farthest bed in the small space between his cot and the wall, the port window at the head of the bed casting moonlight over her pale and peaceful face. He adjusted her limbs so she would be more comfortable and unhooked her cloak from around her neck so she didn't wake herself up in the middle of the night by rolling upon it. He glanced around the room to make sure none of the other residents were with them.

"How are the girls doing…and the mission?"

Steel entered Vieggo's gaze, and his hand went to the knife at his belt. "They are doing as well as can be expected. They all heal at their own pace and in their own way, and some can't do that here. I just received word that two were slipped back over the border a few months ago, undetected."

"The way of the Vagari is clear then?"

"Still undiscovered. It's easy to hide in plain sight when you use flashy trappings and glittery acts as your cover."

"'Tis true. I am sure they are more than thankful for what you have done, Vieggo."

Vieggo cleared his throat. "One does not need thanks for doing what is right in a world that makes out wrong to be right." He shuffled his feet, and Malcolm had to hide a smile. Vieggo was not one to expound upon the good he had been able to do for his community and those that he had taken into his charge. For a man who had never had a child of his own, his fatherhood stretched far and wide to many a young person who had received his love and protection.

"I'll leave you to it," Vieggo said. "You both need rest if you are to travel as far as you will need to tomorrow. The coast is clear for tonight, but they will not stay their hands for long, and the farther you can get from here as quickly as possible the better." The tavern owner clapped Malcolm on the shoulder, his large hand heavy enough to make even Malcolm stumble before he disappeared from the room with hardly a sound, light on his feet and stealthy in his movements.

Malcolm shook his head, turning back to Rosalie and untying the boots he had given her, pulling them from her feet. He paused, shocked at the blood that had soaked through the bottom of her stockings. He winced as he gently peeled them off. Rosalie stirred in her sleep, a moan on her lips. He glanced up, a slight frown marring the rest on her face. He dipped one of the cloths from the bedside table in the bucket Vieggo had brought up and held it to her feet, the water soaking the stocking and allowing him to loosen and pull it from her foot.

He swallowed, glancing back at Rosalie and redipping his cloth with a shake of the head. How she had traversed so far on these feet was testament enough to her strength. Ready or not for the journey ahead, if she could manage this without a single complaint, she would be ready for more than he dared hope.

He gently washed and bandaged the blisters on her feet that had formed and then broken, the raw flesh red as fire. Vieggo had one of his maids run up a balm that he applied to the tender skin, wrapping them and then setting them upon the pillow from his bed so that they wouldn't swell overnight.

Rosalie didn't flinch once during the process, her sleep hard-earned and deep.

At least tomorrow they would traverse the mountain pass with some trail companions.

ROSALIE, PRESENT DAY...

Rosalie stirred, her head foggy. Her feet throbbed. She rolled to her side, trying to find a position that was comfortable. Everything hurt, her entire body aching, dragging her like an unwilling victim from the sleep she so desperately needed. The room was dark, the moonlight casting an oblong round shape against the far wall and ceiling. She blinked the grain from her eyes and looked for Sir Maloclm. He rested on the cot next to her, no pillow, his arms folded over his chest and rising and falling softly with his breathing.

A curtain stood between him and the next occupant, whose snoring was loud enough to make his presence known without her being able to see him.

She blinked again and tried to settle against the tick mattress, her bones aching and revolting against her curled up position. The curtain on the far side of Sir Malcolm's bed fluttered for a moment and then moved to the side. She caught her breath, dread in every fiber of her being.

A pair of eyes glistened in the moonlight, staring right back at her.

Ten

TRACKED

ELGON, FOURTEEN YEARS AGO...

Elgon threw his royal cloak on, tossing one edge over his shoulder so that he had the use of his right arm. Violet's hands circled him from behind and held him close, and he wished that his leather armor did not create such a stiff barrier between them. His shoulders were strong, but his heart quavered within him.

"Lord go with you, my husband." She stood on tiptoe to kiss his neck from behind and spun him so she could insert the golden broach in her hand into his royal cloak, pinning the right shoulder back so he had easy use of his dominant hand and could sign a treaty...or pull his weapon if needed.

He turned to her, reaching his hands beneath the bulge that was his child and lifting the weight slightly. She drew a deep breath of relief and settled her head against his chest. "You have no idea how good that feels."

He smiled, letting the sadness retreat to the edges of his mind and allowing himself this moment to soak in the joy of being a father and a husband. "I can't wait to hold it soon."

"As much as I adore that you can hold both of us at the same time right now, I can't wait for you to either. Trust me, I love this wee one, but I feel like I'm the size of a house."

"Just a wee house."

She hit his arm. "How dare you."

"I said small."

She glared at him, a smile taking over her face despite her best efforts, and she stepped even closer, her stomach between them as she leaned forward to steal a kiss from his lips. She reached up, taking his face in her hands, and he rested his chin against her forehead. They both drew in a deep, settling breath, and his nerves felt as though they had retreated at last.

She lifted her head and looked him in the eyes, her hands still on either side of his face. "Stay strong, but hold onto hope. The world may press on your shoulders and try to make you collapse, but hope in the darkest of times will get you through anything. He is hope. Never fear."

He pressed his forehead against hers, eyes welling, and he squeezed them shut against the tears that threatened.

"Don't let go. Not for a second. Not ever."

He nodded. "I promise."

She gripped the collar of his cloak, her eyes suddenly growing cloudy like Raintamount before a storm. "Never, Elgon. Not once. You hold onto hope like your life depends on it."

She didn't say "because it just might," but the grip on his shoulders and the even more intense grip she had on his heart told him that. He laid his hands gently over hers, cupping them in his and looking deep into those eyes. "I promise," he whispered, the curls around her face waving in the wind of his breath.

She let go and pushed him toward the door. "I'll be praying for you."

He nodded, gathered her hand in his, and kissed the back of it before heading through the door and down the hall. He had one last official meeting with the envoy from Pavlin, and then they would most likely be headed off to visit their neighboring country to ascertain all that needed to be done, what defenses to build, and how to defend the small country against its bigger and mutual enemy, Rusalka. Elgon pulled at the cloak around his neck, adjusting his leather armor and settling it more comfortably on his shoulders.

Something felt amiss, and he wasn't sure what. He prayed in tongues under his breath, trying to dispel the feeling of impending doom. Perhaps it was just the thought of what Rusalka had done to Pavlin, the reality that Zuko would most likely attempt the same with Elira at some point in the future. But they had been able to fend off his attacks before. They could do it again.

But why did it feel like they were waiting for him to move? Watching him stand over the border like a crouching wolf, ready to pounce?

ROSALIE, PRESENT DAY...

Rosalie squinted her eyes nearly shut, long adept at feigning sleep to keep herself safe. She allowed one eye to remain open just enough to take in the sight of a fuzzy image of the man across the room. Her every nerve was tight, waiting to determine friend or foe. She kept her breathing slow and restful, though her heart drowned out any other sound in her ears.

The man was wiry, tall, a cloak hood over his head and his movements slow, like a cat or a wolf hunting its prey. He reached a hand into his cloak and pulled something out; a blade glinted in the moonlight.

Lord, what do I do? How do I waken Sir Malcolm? Her muscles screamed against the way they cramped tight, preparing like a snake to uncoil and strike. Her pain was drowned out by the energy surging through her veins. The man stepped around the foot of Sir Malcolm's bed, coming between it and her own.

Rosalie fought to keep her breathing regular and her eyelids from fluttering. He took one more step toward Sir Malcolm, and she dove.

Like a predator leaping from its hiding place, she sprung at the back of his legs, ramming her shoulder into them and sending the man sprawling with a grunt, the knife flying from his hand. She was tangled in his cloak and felt his weight descending on her, and all the air left her lungs. A heavy hit to her ribcage sent stars dancing around the edges of her darkened vision, and the sounds of a scuffle felt as though it were occuring in another room. A muffled groan and a heavy thud sounded beside her. The disguised man's head lolled on the floor next to hers, a bruise already forming on his chin, but his eyes shut and his limp position indicated he had lost consciousness.

Still, no air had refilled her lungs, and the man's face—covered in a thin, sparse beard with a scar creasing the left side of his forehead and disappearing into his greasy hairline—slowly faded from her view. She tried to gasp, but she only convulsed instead, fighting for just the tiniest bit of air.

A hand scooped her off the floor, and the sudden sharp stab of pain let the air come rushing into her lungs. She gasped for it like a drowning person. Her chest constricted again, and she coughed as she tried to drag in another breath.

"Breathe. That's it. Easy does it." Sir Malcolm had set her back on the bed and returned to the man on the floor. Her vision cleared, and she caught sight of him tying the man's arms up with his own belt while the door to their room swung on its hinges and the light of a lantern bobbed into the room.

Vieggo stood at the edge of the curtain, his face holding a thunderstorm in every pinched line and flash of his eyes. "M—Leonid, how did he get in?" The large man's voice was quiet, but sounded like a dam holding back the torrent of the spring rains. He wrinkled his nose at the sight of the man in the dark cloak and gave him a shove with the toe of his boot.

Sir Malcolm shook his head, handing the intruder's knife to Vieggo and searching him for other hidden weapons. "He must have snuck in after one of the guests. I made sure to lock it after you left. It's a wonder his presence didn't alert anyone else. It's not safe. We need to leave."

Vieggo hesitated for a brief moment, then cast his gaze to Rosalie.

She suddenly wanted to hide, but then she saw the kindness in his eyes and relaxed, gripping her arm around her side where the intruder's boot had found its mark.

"Are you hurt, child?"

She shook her head and tried to take in another breath, but it shuddered and ended in a rasping cough. Vieggo's face took on a lightning storm as he stepped toward her.

Malcolm held up his hand, his voice a harsh whisper. "He kicked her in the side. Please, Vieggo, help us get those horses and get out of here. This man is a dark knight."

Vieggo froze, his eyes widening as he glanced down at the man at their feet. "Mój boże." Vieggo's words were a whisper before he spun and marched for the door, his feet swift but nearly silent as he brushed past the two men who were groggy and staring around the curtain that had separated their portion of the room from Sir Malcolm and Rosalie's. "Come, come, go back to sleep." He pulled the curtain, threw Malcolm a nod, and disappeared.

Coughs still rattled Rosalie's lungs, a piercing ache spreading from where the man had kicked her. Her guardian took a step toward her, grabbing her cloak from the foot of the bed and wrapping it around her neck, fastening it beneath her chin. "May I?" he asked, holding his hand out, and she nodded. He laid his palm over her rib cage, pressing softly, and she winced.

He nodded. "'Twill be painful, but it's not broken, thank God. We must leave immediately. Come." He pulled her boots over her stockings and what she now realized were bandages, lacing them up quicker than she would have been able to. Scooping her into his arms, he carried her from the room, past the closed curtain of their room-fellows and down the dimly lit hall and stairway, wrought iron lanterns flickering with low flames.

The inn was nearly silent, unsettling in the difference that it created from the rollicking laughter and light-filled place that it had been a mere few hours before.

Vieggo held the leads of two horses in front of the inn, their breath huffing a fog into the night air and the faint glow from the open doorway. She glanced up at the dove on the sign again, wishing they had been able to make a longer stay of it. The idea that she would never see Vieggo again filled her with sudden loss as if something precious had been handed to her and then stolen from her grasp once again before she could even have a moment to enjoy it.

Sir Malcolm helped her astride a pony, and she gripped the saddle between her legs, holding fast to the wooden pommel that rose in front of her seat.

Vieggo stepped to her side and laid a hand on her knee. His eyes were misty, and his face twitched with feeling. Even from her seat on her pony, his eyes were still level with hers. He laid his other hand over his heart in a fist. "Go with God." Not breaking her gaze, he gave her a nod before turning away and handing her reins to Sir Malcolm, who had swung atop his own horse. "Both of you. Lord save you both."

Malcolm rested a hand on Vieggo's shoulder, cast a glance back, meeting Rosalie's eyes before he kicked his horse's sides gently and they surged forward.

The golden glow of the inn fell so far behind that all Rosalie could see around them was waves of darkness. Her backward glance showed Vieggo, his hulking form sending them off with a wave from his doorway. Sadness rushed her soul, and a sob bit past her tightly pressed lips.

A friend so swiftly found and swiftly taken was a sorrow all its own.

ELGON, FOURTEEN YEARS AGO...

The world seemed to spin around him in slow motion. The bustle and chaos of the envoy gathering their troops, the Pavlin representatives standing at the ready beside their mounts, the shifting movements of bodies and horseflesh jostling into position. His breathing was the loudest sound in his ears, the cacophony so chaotic that it faded to the background of his mind.

Kenton bounced past Elgon, excitement written all over his young face, his blue eyes bright with it and wide with interest, taking in all that was going on around him.

Sigeric stamped his foot, and Elgon felt his animal's muscles shift beneath his left arm where it rested near the horse's withers, Elgon's fingers twined into the long, curly black mane. He gripped it tightly, holding on as if to an anchor in a storm. He felt every bit the tossing boat upon the surface of a swaying sea.

The treaty had been signed. Pavlin had officially formed an alliance with Elira and to honor such a treaty, Elgon would lead two battalions of kingsmen to refresh the foreign army and to help repair any defenses that had been breached. There would be some mending to do in the foreign country that had nearly lost its stance to Rusalka.

But something niggled at the back of Elgon's mind. Like an itch that wouldn't go away, it tormented him day and night. Violet's sleep had been so interrupted of late, he had been up with her in the night, shaking her awake as she cried in her sleep or being startled awake himself by her strangled gasp as she struggled beneath the bulk of their child to sit up, sweat dripping off her face like she had been submerged.

She told him it was nothing. Perhaps it was her impending birth that was keeping her awake at night, worries from her days drifting into her sleep. While her words had some truth to them, they did little to fully reassure him.

A hand to his arm startled him from his dazed state, and he looked into Malcolm's eyes. They were steady, calm, and Elgon found comfort in the face of his first knight. The one whom he could trust above all others.

"The convoy is ready, my lord." Malcolm nodded to him, a strand of hair escaping the confines of the leather tie near the back of his neck and bobbing in the sea breeze that whistled softly through the enclosed brick streets and alleyways of Niran, the capital city.

Elgon drew a deep breath, letting his eyes lift to the window above the alleyway that wound around the castle and into the stables. Blonde hair spun outside the window in the gentle wind, and a hand raised in farewell. He fought the tears that threatened his eyes. Their farewell had been sweet, precious, and a memory he would cherish forever…but he hoped he would not have to hold it only in his memory for long. He laid his hand over his heart in final farewell and mounted Sigeric, who stomped and huffed in excitement, then stood perfectly still like the war-horse that he was.

"Mount up, men!" Elgon shouted above the din that only grew after his command with the creaking of tack and saddle, the stamping of hooves, and the grunts of his envoy. The battalions waited closer to the gate and near the military training grounds. Malcolm adjusted the leather martingale between Sigeric's legs and stepped back to Elgon's side, holding up an arm.

Elgon gripped his friend's forearm, clasping it tight and looking straight into his eyes. "Watch after my wife, old friend."

"With my life," Malcolm responded. He would stay behind in his position as head of security while Elgon was away, a position Elgon knew he took seriously. But his position as friend was one he took even more so. Elgon trusted Malcolm with what was more precious to him than life.

Elgon nodded, swallowing against the lump in his throat, then glanced up at the window again. He could barely make out her face, but he held that image in his mind until it settled in his heart, like a leaf falling from a tree branch and landing softly on the forest floor. He would return to his love, and they would welcome their child together.

"To the King!" he shouted and raised an arm, kicking Sigeric into a trot. He broke through the crowd of mounted guests and kingsmen, leading the way through the maze of city streets downhill to the main gate. He would see this journey through, and he entreated the Lord for guidance on this new alliance, new season, and new danger that threatened their home.

Eleven

FORGING TRUST

MALCOLM, PRESENT DAY...

"What is going to happen to the man who tried to kill you?" Rosalie's voice fell upon Malcolm's ears, disrupting the attuned listening that he was attempting in order to keep them safe. Any twig snap or the slightest breeze across the mountain face made him stiffen and go on high alert.

She had been asking questions every handful of moments—in an attempt to keep herself awake or distracted, he thought. It had been a long night for both of them. She had barely slept, and he knew she had to be overly exhausted.

"Vieggo will take care of him and make sure he can't run back to the castle to tell tales of our escape until we are long gone...if ever. Vieggo has – shall we say – connections that allow him to pass information to either Elira or to Zuko's fortress."

He heard her sharp intake of breath and glanced over his shoulder to catch a sight of her pale face. It was twisted into a grimace of fear. "I hope I never have to hear his name again."

"Had you met him?"

She swallowed hard.

Her pony and his steed shifted their weight to traverse the rocky path up the cliff side. He wanted her closer to him and drew them side by side when the path's width allowed.

"Once or twice that I remember. He always seemed kind, but in the way someone does when they want something and it feels fake. There was always something behind the way he spoke, as if there was a darkness gathered in the back of his throat and behind his eyes that no one could ever really see."

He fell silent, her description a perceptive one and detailed for her age. He had never met Zuko himself, but his reputation preceded him as a stone-cold, calculating, and masterminded ruler. Nothing like the pompous and prideful Enguerrand who had taken over the kingdom of Elira once upon a time. The man had fled to Rusalka himself, and Malcolm had no idea what use a man like Zuko had for someone like Enguerrand.

Their spies had brought back tales of Enguerrand taking over a castle farther to the northeast, cleaning out the cobwebs and settling there as lord of the locale. It was all Malcolm could do to stay his desire to hunt him down and wring his stuck-up neck for all that he had brought upon the kingdom he should have served.

"What does Elira look like? Does it have the same…this?" Rosalie spread her hand, albeit shaky, to the world around them and then sucked in a breath, returning her hand to grip the pommel of her saddle as her pony shifted its weight again in the uphill climb, jostling her farther back in the saddle.

Malcolm smiled softly, his own thoughts wandering to the place he called his home and where his heart rested, no matter where the King sent him. "Not like this. We have mountains, but not the jagged peaks of Izevel. The craggy mountaintops slope downward, rushing to meet the rolling hills and moorlands below. Forests, where it rains often and snows less, fill all of the nooks and crannies of the cliffs. To the south, where your mother was born, the moorland gives way to farmland where most of our crops are produced. It's beautiful country there, and it rains often enough to keep the fields full and the harvests plenty." He reached out a hand to steady her as both of their mounts stutter-stepped over an especially large piece of shale.

He played out the line and allowed her pony to step back behind his as the steep path narrowed once again. She caught her breath, biting her lip, and his heart leapt in remorse and compassion. He knew she must be in pain after the day and night she had just gone through.

"What…" She took another shuddering breath. "What is my father like?"

The wistfulness mixed with trepidation in her voice pulled on his heartstrings something fierce, and he involuntarily swallowed hard against the grip the emotion had over his throat. Lord help him if he ever had little ones of his own bounding about the earth… He might as well give up now, because if it felt anything like this, his heart would fairly burst with the weight of love for them. He thought of a distant blue-eyed lass with freckles dancing a jig across her face and red hair that refused to be confined frizzing about her head in boundless curls. But no, such a life was not for him.

"You have nothing to fear from your father. He is not the evil man that Rusalka makes him out to be. He is, in fact, one of the most honorable and honest men I have ever met, and I am proud to serve under him." The gratitude, pride, and strength that rang from his own voice set his heart to beating harder within his chest, reinvigorated.

Rosalie watched his face from beneath her lashes with an anxious gaze that turned to acceptance. He could tell she was still hesitant to be fully open and artless, as any child who had been subject to the type of abuse she had received from her captors would be. She nodded, and he faced forward again to keep an eye on the path, loosening his reins and allowing his black steed to take the path at his own pace, picking his own footsteps. "If he is anything like you, I am sure I shall be proud to call him my father."

Malcoms felt his insides quiver. How could children imprison you and set your spirit soaring all at the same time with their love and trust?

ROSALIE, PRESENT DAY...

Rosalie held fast to the pommel of her saddle with shaking hands and tried to keep her eyes open as the world hazed around her. She couldn't remember a time when she had been this tired. It wasn't just her mind that was exhausted; her body had seemed to betray her as it shook, twitched, and startled at the mere sound of a pebble tumbling down the cliff face. The path narrowed again, and Malcolm surged ahead of her, his steed taking careful footing over the path jutting out of the sheer cliff face that plummeted into an abyss to her left. Her stomach rose into her throat and her mouth went dry as her heart pounded hard against her bruised ribs. She couldn't see either side of the pathway around her pony, who snorted, tossed his head, and hesitated as it stepped to follow Malcolm.

"Lord, keep me safe," she whispered, unsure if shutting her eyes would make it easier or harder. The silence that fell was fraught with tension as she sensed even Malcolm grow focused from the intensity of the journey. The cloak thrown over his shoulders caught in the mountain breeze and billowed softly out behind him, flicking with a snap that mocked her timidity.

Her horse took another step, her saddle shifting to one side with the animal and throwing her off balance as the pony struggled to find purchase on the loose stones. She gripped the saddle even harder and felt a tear squeeze out of her eye at the mere terror of the moment.

Her pony walked easier, and she opened her eyes, blinking to clear her vision to see that the path had widened once again. Not enough for them to ride side by side, but enough that she could draw a breath of relief. The world seemed to slow, and she was suddenly chilled.

"Hold on, Rosalie. It's not much longer."

She sucked in a deep breath, letting the air flow fill her lungs, and tried to relax her shoulders. She thought of Vieggo and did her best to remember details about last night. She didn't want to forget him. His kindness. His joy. The way he could command a room. She smiled as she felt her pony start swaying under her again. *Lord, bless Vieggo. And if it be your will, let me be able to see him again.*

Rosalie did her best to take her mind off the nerve-wracking climb and instead dreamed about her father, the man whom she would live with once she reached home. Home. What a strange word. So many spoke of home as the place that they resided, but she had felt as though she had never had one. The place she had left was certainly not her home. There was no safety, no love, no comfort found there. And the place she went to was not her own. It was as if it belonged to another and she was merely set in an opening that needed to be filled.

Perhaps she wasn't the right person for the job. Why her? Why a young girl who had known nothing but the round walls of her one-tower room and the throne room of the man who kept her there? What about the young girls who had played instruments at Vieggo's feet? The girls that she had seen dancing about, smiling up at their parents, and laughing at Vieggo's antics? What made her special? What set her apart that she should be a daughter of the king?

Her hands started to shake again at the idea. Would she be forced to be a ruler just like the one she had left? To preside on a throne and hand down judgment and commandments upon the people who lived in her land?

Her pony shifted hard. Her eyes flew open and her heart ricocheted louder as her foot slipped from the right stirrup and she fell sideways, gripping hard against the pommel and pulling herself up again.

"It's narrow here. I'm going to lead the pony across. Hold on and don't look down." Sir Malcolm's voice was calm but tight when she glanced up at him. He had already crossed the ledge in front of her, over which the path narrowed only to allow for one animal at a time. He stood, having dismounted, his cloak resting off his shoulders and his fingers holding the reins that swung between her mount and his. It rested softly in his palms as he tugged gently, urging her pony to step toward him.

She needed to get her foot back in the stirrup. She reached down, but a huff and a head toss from her pony sidelined her movements, and she squeezed her legs and her hands in a desperate attempt to hold on, a whimper dropping from her lips as she fought to keep her gaze ahead of her and not on the jagged rocks stretching beneath her.

Sir Malcolm played the line, coaxing the hesitant pony who nickered and tossed its head again, his eyes wide and his steps halting as if the very idea of crossing the ledge went against his nature.

Slipping farther in her saddle, Rosalie squeezed harder with her legs, every muscle on the very verge of collapse as she fought with everything in her to not fall. With another jolt, the animal took another step, then another, but as a pebble rolled beneath his hoof, she felt his shifting weight heave too far to one side. Her leg slipped and her body edged toward the abyss.

The pony balked, his feet stamping and shoving backward, jerking his head against the rope. With a squeal, his back left foot slid from the ledge, throwing Rosalie's weight as they went down. A scream froze on her lips. The beast screamed and lunged over the side. Rosalie's loose foot flew over its back as she twisted under the beast, still hung by the one stirrup, her hands grasping at thin air. One thought punctured through the panic… Was she never to see the cliffs of her homeland and the face of her father?

Twelve

CLIFFS AND QUESTIONS

ELGON, FOURTEEN YEARS AGO...

Elgon couldn't help but feel uneasy. There was something amiss. He wished he had possessed the time to do a proper shake-down of the kingsmen, but while they had been able to clean out the castle and only allow those whom Malcolm trusted to protect it, it still remained unclear what master the masses of the Eliran army truly served.

With Enguerrand in prison, there had been silence on the matter, but he wasn't sure if it was just his imagination or if he occasionally caught a soldier staring at him with a look that set his blood on edge. But when he would glance back, the look would be gone.

He shook his head. Something was wrong, but he wasn't sure he could put his finger on it. How did one even go about interviewing every soldier in order to determine if they aligned with the kingdom or with the dethroned ruler? And who was to say if they would be honest? He and Violet had spent much time in prayer over it, but the last thing they wanted to do was take rule and start pointing fingers or creating even more upheaval for the people than was necessary. Soldiers served the kingdom, not its monarch…or so it should be.

If only he could calm the chill that seemed to pervade the atmosphere whenever he was around his kingsmen. *His* kingsmen. He shook his head. There was too much at stake for them. Elira was their country too. Instead of going on a witch hunt to find those who were more loyal than others and potentially pit them against each other, he would trust that the Lord would figure it out and that their loyalties and desires to protect their own home would be enough to set them on the right track.

He knew he was new to kingship and he needed to earn the trust of those men, just as his father had before him.

A different pattern of horses' hooves broke through the steady clop of the cavalcade as they made slow work of the wet and muddy King's Highway. Elgon glanced ahead and caught sight of Kenton's fresh green cloak, now covered in mud splatters around the edges; the boy, astride a mount that was nearly too big for him, was trotting toward him, his reddish blonde hair flipping up and down on his head. That ridiculously excited look on his face teased a smile from his king. The boy's enthusiasm was entertaining, if not downright lifting to his spirits.

The boy, who couldn't have been more than fifteen years of age, freshly squired under the Kingsmen's guild and ready to earn the trust of his commander as well as his king, took on every single task with a tenacity as if it were a life or death matter. Elgon himself was encouraged by the young lad's fortitude and desire to prove his loyalty. *If only we all served the Lord with such fervor,* was the thought that always came to mind when dealing with Kenton. His father was a lord with land between Raintamount and the moors, and Kenton was eager to become a knight in employ of the king, rising through the ranks to a position of leadership. But he served well in the little tasks given him, which Elgon recognized as a solid bent toward good stewardship of his role.

"What is it, Kenton?" Elgon asked over the sound of stamping hooves and squelching mud.

With flushed cheeks and a splatter of mud over his eyebrow that the boy probably didn't even know was there, Kenton's blue-gray eyes flashed brightly. "Commander Montcalme asked me to inform you that we are nearing Padsley and should be there by nightfall."

"Thank you. Tell him we should break camp at the outpost on the border so the men and beasts can rest before we proceed into Pavlin on the morrow."

Kenton nodded, doing poorly at hiding his anticipatory grin before kicking his heels into his mount's muddy sides and cantering back to the front of the line.

Elgon grinned and shook his head. He couldn't wait to be a father. Boy or girl, he hoped the Lord gave him and Violet the energy to keep up after young ones should they have as much spirit as Kenton.

Shadows slowly gathered from the peaks of Raintamount's trees, and the drizzle that had been intermittent all day started again. He reached behind him and pulled the hood of his cloak over his head and flicked the right corner back over his shoulder to shield him from the rain. Sigeric pranced out of his normal pace for a moment before resuming his fast but comfortable walk. Elgon could feel his horse's anxious, wound-tight muscles beneath him, and he patted the steed's neck. "Me too, boy. I feel it. But there is nothing for it but to wait 'til the morrow and see what we face."

He shivered and hunched his shoulders beneath the cold rain. Why did he harbor this uneasy feeling? He almost expected something to spook from the woods off to the left. As if some unseen force of darkness was skulking in the shadows, taunting him with its nearness, but refusing to be seen. The leaves shuddered beneath the cold rain, curling inward on themselves to escape it.

Perhaps it was his own fear chasing him. The worry that he was inadequate. That he was not up to the task at hand. And yes, even afraid. He held on tightly to the hope Violet had commanded he never relinquish. Even though it felt weak, like a tiny flicker doing its very best to stay lit in the rain, it burned nevertheless. He might fall. He might make mistakes over the next few days. There might be many a misstep as decisions were made and this new treaty and how to enact and coexist as a larger country were discussed. But he welcomed new countrymen into the fold of Elira and her people. Pavlin's struggles were no longer Pavlin's alone, but were Elira's now too.

The responsibility weighed on him, and with another chill from a burst of cold air that whipped down the road and threw the cold rain into his face, he felt the fear try to take hold. He drew a breath and set his shoulders against it, chasing the shadows in his mind back with prayer that flowed from his tongue in a whisper that only Sigeric's swiveling ears and the Lord's Spirit could hear. While there might be much to worry over, Elgon knew where his comfort and peace lay.

I will be with you. I will never leave you nor forsake you. He gripped his reins tighter, standing straighter instead of hunched against the rain. Be it good or ill, Elgon, at least, was grateful that should he fall or fail, the Lord's hand was there to catch him.

MALCOLM, PRESENT DAY...

Malcolm's breath left his lungs as he watched Rosalie go over the ledge. For a brief moment, she was hidden from his view by the screaming pony that had lost his footing as a result of its panic. In an instant, with one step and a twist, the rope that he had used to guide Rosalie's pony hung between his horse's saddle and the bridle of Rosalie's. The slack that was draped around Malcolm's waist cinched tight, and he lunged toward the cliff's edge, anchoring himself to his sturdy and more trustworthy mount should the weight of the pony or his own momentum take him over the edge.

Rosalie's face had been one of sheer terror in the momentary glimpse he had caught, and that was what flooded his mind as the pony's momentum jerked at his middle, the rope pulling tight beneath his ribs and sucking the air from his lungs. He reached over the edge. He gripped the fabric that met his fingers with one hand as he drew his knife with the other.

Rosalie and the pony thudded against the cliff face. Scrabbling hooves behind Malcolm sought and found purchase to bear the weight as he wrapped his hand around the fabric of Rosalie's dress. The pony's scream tore at his ears as he used the knife to sever the rope below the edge of the cliff, cutting the light weight of the beast from the only thing that tethered it to safety, leaving it to fall to its death. Tossing the knife onto the ledge beside him, Malcolm gripped the cut end of the rope that was wrapped around his waist and tethered to his own mount. Tightening his grasp of her dress with his other, he twisted the fabric around his forearm and pulled, hauling Rosalie up.

His mount huffed again and dug its hooves into the rocks, pulling backward in an awkward and weighted stutter-step. Now more firmly planted on the ground, Malcolm was able to let go of the rope with his hand and use the other to pull Rosalie up. He grabbed her waist, grunting at the rope cutting into his sides and heaved her over the edge, rolling with her away from the abyss below. He pressed his back into the cliff face behind him, holding her tightly in his arms.

Silence reigned except for their heavy breathing and the horse's creaking leather as the beast tossed its head after the strain. An eagle screeched in the distance, and a sob shook Rosalie. Her body trembled in Malcolm's arms, and he held her close, waiting for the shock to subside. He brushed the hair from her face, pushing himself onto his elbow to make sure she was uninjured. A few scrapes from falling shale marred her face with tiny, thin red lines, and her green eyes were massive, her skin even paler than her usual shade.

He gripped her shaking hands in his, holding them tightly. His were still pulsating from the adrenaline and panic of trying to save her from a plummet that would've injured her beyond repair—or killed her.

"The-the pony. Is he…" Her voice shook.

Malcolm didn't let go of her hand as he leaned and looked over the edge. The poor beast lay at the bottom of the ravine, not moving. He hoped for the animal's sake that it was already dead.

"I'm afraid he didn't make it." His own voice was raspy, and he swallowed against his dry throat, ragged from exertion.

Dry sobs wracked her frame, almost convulsing her from the inside, but her face still remained one of shock. She gripped her side with her hands and held on as she struggled to sit up. He placed a hand behind her shoulders to assist her, but she bent nearly double, one palm still at her injured side.

He hated this feeling. Not knowing what to do, how to help her, or how to ease her mental or physical pain. He rubbed small circles into her heaving shoulders, then lifted a hesitant hand to brush back the curly brown locks that had escaped her braid in the fray.

Sudden urgency rose in him, and on instinct, he gripped the hilt of his sword. "I'm so sorry, but we need to keep moving." He kept his voice soft, but it was husky as he glanced behind them up the path, up at the ledge he knew was above them, and in front of them on their continued journey. Lord keep them safe, he needed to get them to Mother Hobbs before they were found—or worse, recognized. And they still had a long way to go.

ROSALIE, PRESENT DAY...

Rosalie was frozen, her limbs heavy, as if they were encased in ice. Sobs wracked her body against her will. She just wanted to rest. To cease all movement, shut her eyes, and forget that any of this had ever happened.

She tried not to think of what the pony looked like, lying at the bottom of the ravine where she had almost met her death. She willed her body to work, to respond to her desire to move, for the cramps that were pervading her midsection and sawing her in two to cease. She couldn't catch her breath. If only air could enter her lungs.

Malcolm scooped her up in his arms again. She slammed her eyes shut, the feeling of being suspended in the air terrifying. Her arms responded, encircling his neck and squeezing for all she was worth. A grunt met her ears, and she tried to imagine that the darkness that met her closed eyes was filled with the light of her castle room. She wasn't swaying in the arms of another over a drop that would kill her in an instant. She was instead safe beneath the quilts of her tick bed, pulled close in front of the fire.

It worked for only a few seconds before she was hoisted up and away from Malcolm's body. A gasp escaped her lips. Her eyes flew open, and a whimper rumbled up from her frozen throat. She gripped harder, and Malcolm paused.

"Please, don't put me b-b-back. I can't ride. Not now." She couldn't look him in the eyes. She was supposed to be brave. Isn't that what princesses were? She should be able to pull herself together and let go of the fear that had her heart in its vice-like grip. But she couldn't. The idea of riding on any horse over these mountain passes, no matter how trustworthy, sent her into a panic so blind, she felt as though she could fight Malcolm herself in protest.

He hesitated. Shifting her in his arms, he drew a breath, and she could hear his heart hammering beside her in his chest. It had scared him too.

That revelation pulled her out of the spiral that was sending her inward, and she looked up into his face. His expression was pained, shock hovering in his eyes along with the varying options and pressing decisions that seemed to be crossing his mind.

Steadfastness returned, and his brown eyes looked straight into hers. She had never been this close to them, and she could see the hazel striations that radiated from his pupil. But mostly, she noticed the kindness in the lines of his face where the circumstances in her life had taught her to expect, at the very least, frustration and, in most cases, utter contempt.

You can trust him. I will protect you.

"I see no other choice, my lady. Your feet are far too sore and your body is far too exhausted to help you climb much farther than a few steps. I will guard you with my life and hold you fast in the saddle. You will finally be able to rest. Just a short while and then we will be off the cliffs."

She could feel as well as hear the rumble of his voice, and something within her snapped a release. Being brave didn't always mean chasing perfection, or showing oneself worthy and capable in the face of fear. Maybe sometimes bravery was gentle rest in another's protection, relying on the person God had placed over you to keep you safe with their courage when yours was failing.

She swallowed against the dryness of her throat and clung to his cloak with a nod. She could rely on his bravery for the moment.

Thirteen

JOURNEY INTO DARKNESS

ROSALIE, PRESENT DAY...

Night had gathered and the darkness rested on her shoulders, heavier than the cloak she wore, lulling her to sleep. Malcolm's arm around her waist held her upright, though her head kept bobbing when the muscles in her neck relaxed enough for her to let it dip. She had to stay awake. Even though they had traversed the rough mountain pass without any more incidents, it had been a trying journey, and they had still yet to reach a resting place for the night.

She shivered when a cold droplet hit her face. With one hand on the reins, Malcolm wrapped her cloak around her tighter, pulling her hood so that it protected her face before wrapping his arm around her again. She tried closing her eyes. They burned from trying to distinguish between shadows and objects in the dim light of the forest, made even dimmer by the inclement weather. Rain was much colder and less inviting than she had imagined from her room in the old tower. She was used to the cold but not used to braving it in the face.

If only her side didn't ache so much from that horrid man who had attacked them at Bevy Inn, the ride wouldn't be so difficult to endure. The rustle of the pine sounded like a low, mournful whimper as the wind touched each branch on its way by. A bird's wings flapped harshly to their left, and she started, shaking like a drenched sheep just in from the moors.

"Hush, little one." Malcolm's tone was warm, and he held her tighter. "We should be far enough away from your captors by now; we'll stop soon for the night, and I'll make us a shelter."

She nodded, but even that seemed to be too hard a task, draining what little energy remained in her.

"Rest now, child." He pressed her against him, and she let her muscles slacken, falling into his solid form and letting her head rest back on his shoulder. He nodded and she let her mind wander to her imaginings of Elira. Better to dream of that than the old tower she hoped would never be her home again.

She felt as though she had hardly gotten comfortable before they suddenly stopped. The jolt startled her awake, her side cramping in a stitch and stealing her breath.

"We'll stay here for the night." Malcolm shifted her forward, threw a leg behind him, and slid from the mount, leaving her clinging to the saddle and swaying with the effort it required. Steadying her with a hand, he caught her gaze, and she could barely see his features between the dusk and the raindrops. The drizzle had continued, the drops growing heavier as they collected and then fell through the pine boughs above them. A copse of several trees was off to her right, ringed together, their branches intermingling, and the ground beneath them almost dry.

Placing his hands around her waist, Malcolm lifted her from the horse. The beast shook his chestnut head and let the shudder travel back over his haunches, water droplets flinging them in the face. "Here." Malcolm pulled a leather water bottle from its place tethered to the saddle and handed it to her. "Drink this and take shelter under the trees while I make us a place to sleep for the night."

Rosalie stumbled, her cloak heavy with water though it remained dry inside. She gripped her side to stem the pain as she hobbled to the cover of the smaller circle of pines.

She felt the pine-needles scattered on the ground for roots or stones before taking a seat, adjusting her skirt over her legs and pulling them to her chest, then fixing her cloak over her like a tent. It had grown so cold. Uncorking the bottle, she took a long draught, the spicy and tingly taste of Vieggo's draught from the night before giving her a warm and relaxed feeling inside, despite it not being warm.

Malcolm busied himself, and within a mere few moments, he had removed their packs, unsaddled the horse, removed his bit, and tethered him to a nearby tree after rubbing him down and cloaking him with a piece of oil-cloth that would help keep him dry and warm throughout the night. He placed the saddle behind Rosalie's back and motioned for her to lean against it, which she did gratefully, several muscles in her back fairly screaming with overuse.

Malcolm unwound another oilcloth that had been wrapped tightly and placed in one of their leather saddlebags, tying the corners to the trees and sloping it to one side, allowing the extra water to run off it instead of puddling on top. Shaking out the last item that seemed to fill one of the bags, he draped the blanket over the pile of needles and motioned her toward him, still holding the corners.

She stood and made her way to him, settling on top of the blanket. She tucked her cloak around her, pulling her hood farther over her head, and sunk down onto her injured side, hoping that the cushion of the fallen pine-needles would give her respite. Malcolm draped the other half of the blanket over her, tucking in the edges, and the weight alone made her feel the smallest bit warmer as she hunkered close, shivering once to rid herself of the last chill.

"Rest now, my lady. You'll have need of strength on the morrow, but for now, rest." His voice softly blending with the whimper of the trees and the softly falling rain. But he had no need to tell her, for her eyes were already shut.

MALCOLM, PRESENT DAY...

Malcolm sank to the forest floor beside Rosalie, her soft breathing telling him she was already asleep. He knew she had been desperate for it; everything within her had to be exhausted. He hoped she suffered no ill effects and was grateful she had gotten some sleep over the last few hours once he had finally told her to rest.

A smile tugged his lips as he pulled his knees up and rested his elbows upon them. Valiant indeed. Just like her mother. A lump rose in his throat, and he reached for the bottle, downing several swallows of Vieggo's draught. He placed the cork back on top, the warmth in his stomach warring with the ice in his veins. The pain of his memories haunted him and he started at a rustle in the trees. It was as if those memories were ghosts, wandering the forest like wraiths, their ghastly figures trying to hunt him and drag him down.

She had been his charge. His responsibility. All had looked as it should, but he had missed it. Even with his vigilance, his loyalty, and the valor of those who stood with him, he had not been able to keep her safe.

He pulled his cloak tighter around his shoulders, again on alert. The dark knights should not be able to find them here. They had traveled much farther than most would expect, taking the more dangerous shortcut over the mountain pass. Zuko's men would not traverse it. As evidenced by the tragedy this afternoon, it had its dangers—some of them deadly.

He glanced over Rosalie's shoulder and saw her nose just peeking out of her hood, her lashes fluttering. In sleep she looked even younger, her face flushed with the journey and the chill, but so like her mother's. Her coloring was her father's from the brown hair, dark brows, and long lashes, but her eyes and features were her mother's. He had not known the queen long, certainly not as long as he would have liked, but her portrait hanging in the castle hall, bedecked with honorarium for the day when the people of Elira hoped she would return, had kept her face and her memory fresh in all their minds.

He had not begrudged the people the day they remembered their queen each year, a woman born of them, with their own heart beating within her breast and their hopes taking flight with her spirit. But for him, the day was a haunted reminder of his greatest loss.

Each year, as the spies brought back the same answer to what was fast becoming an empty promise of fulfillment, their hope died little by little. Elgon had remained true to the hope he had promised to cling to, true to the woman who had been the love of his life, but the people were overcome by despair. Over time, the tradition had become more one of mourning than of hope.

Another anniversary had passed on Malcolm's journey to rescuing her daughter, and it had been the first time in over a decade where he had been free to mourn. Free to let the tears fall, to curse the ground, the enemy, and the plans that had been laid and the thievery of youth that had pervaded his country.

He shook his head. He glanced back at the horse that had brought them this far on their journey and thanked the Lord for the animal's strength and presence of mind. Curling up, his back to Rosalie, he shut his eyes. Sorrow could not steal his focus. Memories could not ravage his courage. At least not this close to the enemy's camp and with danger near enough to whisper on the wind.

Malcolm felt the stiffness in his neck and the cold on the tip of his nose when he woke from his light sleep; a common occurrence for him when he was on the trail. Sleeping in the woods while on the run required a keen ear and the ability to snap awake at the slightest movement or noise. All was as he had left it aside from the dim light that made its way onto the forest floor, filtered through the pine tree boughs and the mist that hid the rest of the forest from his view. A soft layer of dew rested in tiny droplets on top of the stained, green wool of his cloak. He adjusted the knife at his belt, and reflexively his hand went to his sword that had been resting on the ground beside him

Despite it being the curved scimitar of the Rusalks, old habits remained intact; he cared for the weapon as if it were his own Eliran straight-blade. If they could just reach Mother Hobbs' today, he would finally be able to trade in this weapon, foreign in his hand every time he pulled it from its sheath, and replace it with his own.

A cough met his ears, and he glanced at their steed. He had covered him well for the night, and the oilcloth remained where he had tied it. The animal shouldn't have caught cold last night, and indeed, he seemed fine as he dipped his head and nibbled at a few pieces of grass from where it grew around the ground at the trunk of one of the trees.

The rasping sound came again, and he whirled on Rosalie, still fast asleep, much in the same position he had left her, the air from her lungs entering the forest in visible clouds as it hit the morning chill. She shook with another cough, and he rested a hand on her shoulder. She reacted to his touch with a shiver and a soft moan, almost indiscernible. His heart dropped with dread.

His stomach clenched, and he pulled off his leather glove, touching his large, callused fingers to her forehead. Despite the chill, her skin was hot to the touch and her nose was as bright as a cherry. Her eyes flicked open as another cough shook her small form and her face constricted in pain.

"Rosalie, are you all right?"

Her eyes looked foggy, as if she weren't completely awake or fully able to focus on his voice as he held her shoulder and placed his other hand beneath her head.

She nodded—brave lass—but cringed again as she moved a hand to her side.

"Do your ribs ache?"

She nodded again, her next breath wheezing as she coughed on her inhale. "My lungs hurt." Her voice was soft but harsh over the scraping of her throat. Her chin quivered.

Valiant child. He reached for the bottle and held it to her lips, lifting her head to meet it and giving her a few swallows of Vieggo's draught. She coughed at the spices, but her eyes cleared briefly before they fluttered closed again on another moan.

"Just rest easy, lass. I'll saddle the horse, and we'll get you to Mother Hobbs. She'll know how to care for you. A hot fire, warm bed; we'll have you right as rain in no time." Malcolm removed his cloak and wrapped it tightly around her like a cocoon.

In a trice, he had the rest of their gear packed, the horse saddled, and was bundling the oilcloth he had covered Rosalie with. She had not moved except to wheeze or cough here and there, but her moans concerned him. He knew he was pushing her hard, but if they could just make it to Mother Hobbs, they would be safe enough for a time.

Hopefully long enough for her to heal, gain some strength, and tire out the dark knights in their search.

Hidden under their noses might just be their safest plan.

ELGON, FOURTEEN YEARS AGO...

The rest of the lords of Pavlin still needed to sign the treaty.

Elgon buckled Sigeric's saddle for the ride into Pavlin, the old memories of previous haunts returning. He was near Raintamount. How he so desperately wished he could spare the time to make a running visit to Marcus and his new wife. Their wedding had been one he had been sad to miss, but it was sudden. Scarcely had Elgon and Violet heard of their engagement than the letter arrived announcing their marriage.

He knew Violet had been disappointed, but her delight in her childhood friend's newfound happiness had far outweighed her sadness. It would not do to divert to visit them at this hour, but perhaps he could make a short visit on the return trip home.

"Kenton, will you see that the other lords have all that they need and ensure we can be on our way within the next few moments?'

Kenton scampered off. He had been bobbing about, attempting to be helpful—but mostly just underfoot. Elgon preferred to have his mornings to himself, even if that meant doing the un-kingly task of saddling his own horse or packing his things. Un-kingly might be what others thought of him, but in reality, he found it far more kingly to do his own tasks and care for himself by way of showing his people that he was not the pompous man he had once been. It was a small thing, and even though he knew he had been forgiven, there was something in him that balked against anything that reminded him of the prideful, selfish, and entitled lad he had been in his youth.

He prayed under his breath as he took the brush to Sigeric's coat one more time and allowed the bristles to smooth away the dirt and bring back a beautiful sheen to the animal's black coat. Sigeric tossed his mane and reached back with his muzzle to nibble at the end of Elgon's cloak.

Elgon smiled and pulled his cloak out from between Sigeric's teeth and gave him a playful pat on the head between the eyes. Scratching the special place under his chin where Elgon knew the animal relished receiving affection, he spoke under his breath. "You've seen me through, haven't you, old boy? And taken care of my wife, which was the greatest kindness you could ever do me."

Sigeric nodded his head, using the opportunity to give Elgon's chest an affectionate shove, then tossed his mane again. The beast sniffed the air before he turned his gaze north and looked off into the distance, almost as if he too could sense that they were near to their previous home and his old haunt of Raintamount Forest. Despite being loose in the woods for many a day, the war-horse had not forgotten his training or kingly bearing and he still looked the magnificent, royal beast that he was.

"Ready to go, majesty?" Azriel asked. His eyes on the ground as he shuffled his boot through the grass. The captain of the two battalions that rode with them strode toward Elgon, his hand on the hilt of his sword at his side and the look of one in a hurry. Azriel had not let the men lag or take many breaks on the march here. Elgon was grateful for his efficiency, but the man needed to work on his confidence in front of his ruler and superiors.

"Ready, Azriel." Elgon shoved one side of his cloak over his shoulder before gripping Sigeric's reins in one hand. Placing a foot in the stirrups, he sprang upward, swinging his leg easily over the animal's back.

"What of camp?"

"The squires shall come behind and pack the tents, your majesty. They will follow, though of course, you will be welcomed in one of the homes of the lords tonight." Azriel hadn't once looked Elgon in the eyes.

Elgon peered at him sharply, his hackles rising for some reason. Azriel shifted under the scrutiny and turned abruptly, striding off, presumably to give his orders. Elgon shook his head to clear the cobwebs that readily clung to the corners of his mind just as they did in the corners of the Castle of Niran back home. He looked around his encampment to ensure he wasn't forgetting anything that he should be carrying on his person.

Gathering the reins in one hand, he pulled Sigeric over to the rest of the cavalcade that awaited his signal to move forward. Azriel mounted behind him, and Elgon caught him moving in his peripheral. He wished that Malcolm could be here with him. The man had discernment in ways that he did not and having been on the inside of the rotten forces for all of the years that Enguerrand had led Elira, he seemed to see more clearly the alliances of the Kingsmen and where they stood.

Rusalka was unpredictable, and that was what made Elgon nervous. Perhaps that was all this feeling was.

With a nod to Kenton and Lord Milton who sat atop his horse just behind him, Elgon set out, leading the entourage over the border into Pavlin…even though Raintamount and Padsley called his heart far louder than their neighboring country did.

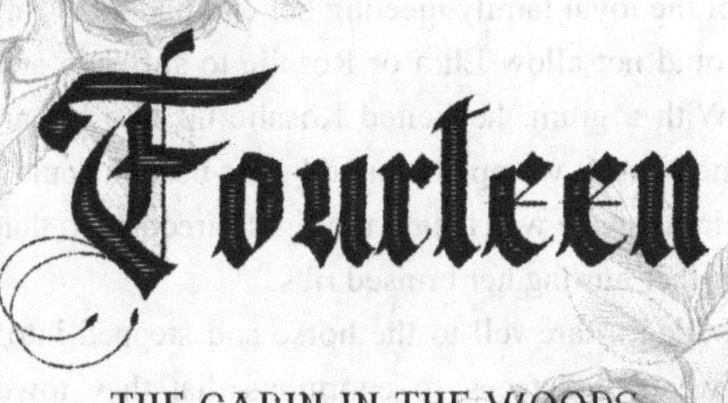

Fourteen

THE CABIN IN THE WOODS

MALCOLM, PRESENT DAY...

Malcolm threw the saddle bags over his shoulder after tying their trusty steed to a tree branch, everything in him anxious to arrive at their destination. A few hours of riding in this rain had left him wet and more concerned for Rosalie than before. The walk was far too narrow and steep for the mount to make it to Mother Hobbs' plateau chalet from here, but he would return to feed him, or perhaps send him back to Vieggo, hoping that the animal's homing capabilities would get him somewhere safe.

The last thing he wanted was for the princess to become ill on the road and… He stilled, momentarily paralyzed before continuing on with his rapid pace. The princess's life was at

141

stake, and his vision darkened at the thought of another member of the royal family meeting her end under his care.

He would not allow Elira or Rosalie to suffer in such a manner. With a grunt, he hefted Rosalie up into his arms, keeping the blanket wrapped around her as best he could and making sure that she was facing the right direction so that he was not further hurting her bruised ribs.

He nodded a farewell to the horse and stepped into the break between cliff faces so enormous that they towered above his head. The path was winding now, carved through the rock by the melting ice and snow that had eroded it over the years. He had to turn sideways to fit since he carried Rosalie and was burdened down with their packs. His sword banged and clanked as it dragged along the curve of the smoothly hewn slate.

Lord, help me get her to Elira. Don't let me have gotten this far only to have hope expire now. You promised that there would always be hope, and she might be the last remaining bit of it for Elira. The people have longed for years to see their queen reinstated, begged You, waited for You to move. Don't give up on us now. Heal her. Strengthen her for this journey, for this is only the beginning. Don't let my journey or the prayers of a nation be in vain.

He took a few more steps before an answering voice resounded in his spirit.

My word shall not return void, and I will accomplish that which I please. My word shall prosper wherever I send it.

Malcolm drew a breath, the rate of his heart calming at the reassurance of a promise that filled his heart. As he hoisted Rosalie higher, his feet nearly slipped on the steps carved into the stones that were now damp from last night's rain. He could feel the chill in the air, the pain in his own lungs at its sting, and he prayed harder than he ever had before. Words he didn't even know dripped from his mouth like the water trickling down the faces of the rocks as he squeezed through them. The words were ones that came from his heart, not from his mind, and they calmed his racing thoughts.

The rocks narrowed even more, and the pines towered overhead, the chill water coating the needles like ice yet unfrozen. He pulled Rosalie closer to his chest and grunted as he squeezed them both through a particularly narrow section of the path. Her eyelids fluttered but remained closed, even as she moaned in pain. The moisture clinging to her upper lip and beading on her forehead was definitely *not* from the rain.

"Just a little further, wee one." He whispered under his breath, daylight breaking above the open crevasse he walked through. The light was murky, clouded from the darkened day as the rain started again, the drizzle cutting through the crack in the rock above him and finding its chill way down the back of his neck.

Stepping through the last few feet of the crevasse, his boots touched pine-needle strewn, even ground. He had reached the chalet. A few more feet of woods and the door of Mother Hobbs' cabin met his gaze. It blended into the natural surrounding of the forest, nearly invisible unless one were standing close to it. Her home was cut into the mountain stone, the small clearing it sat in dotted with trees, giving off the impression of a chalet that seemed to have sprouted naturally from the forest surrounding it. Instead of cleanly hewn logs forming the home, they were still covered in bark; moss grew up its sides, and the branches were of different thicknesses, winding around the door as if woven like a basket.

He had barely stepped foot on her doorstep when the entrance flew open, and Mother Hobbs, face set like flint, with a dagger in her hand, met him on the threshold.

"Merciful heavens, lad! What took you so long?" Her posture eased, and she sheathed the dagger in the belt that wound around her waist overtop her apron strings and knitted shawl. A pocket dangled from the other side of the belt, as well as some shears and a flask encased in leather. She paused in her excitement. "What's wrong with the child?"

He stepped in, turning sideways to fit Rosalie through the door. "Exhaustion, infection, or a combination of the two. It's been a painful journey for the lass."

"Tsk." Mother Hobbs shut the door and scurried by him, her wool skirts swishing around her ankles as she ushered him to a bed that lay snug in the far corner of the room. The cabin was larger on the inside than it had appeared without, and the dark corners were alight with the golden glow from the fire and various lamps and candles scattered about the room. Everything gleamed like well-polished mahogany—old, worn, and meticulously cleaned. Everything had a purpose and a place, and the room spoke of rest and togetherness. "Lay the bairn here. I expected you nigh on three days ago."

Malcolm laid her down, removing the wet blankets and oilcloth that were wound around her. "Getting in took longer than expected, and she's traveled nary a step from the doorway of the castle her entire life."

"Shame, that. Everyone deserves a chance to feel the wind and sun on their face." Mother Hobbs grumbled a few curses toward the ruler of the land under her breath as she instinctively shoved him out of her way and started untying Rosalie's wet cloak from around her neck.

Malcolm shook the rain off his own cloak and removed it from around his shoulders. He hadn't realized how chilled he was himself, having grown used to living with whatever the elements gave him, but now he backed toward the fire, letting the flames chase the cold and wetness from his skin as he rubbed his hands together behind his back.

"I'll need more wood before you get dry and comfortable," their host threw over her shoulder. He tried to hide a smile and tossed his cloak back over his shoulders. Mother Hobbs wasn't one to waste time on pleasantries.

He stepped out long enough to gather an armful of wood and ducked back into the hut, dropping it within the woodbox beside the fire.

Mother Hobbs had changed Rosalie into a new chemise, probably her own as it was of hardy flannel and swam upon the girl's thin form. Rosalie's hair, some of it wet and stringy, was tossed over the pillow above her head, and the older woman was shaking woolen blankets over her.

"The lass is freezing. The weather didn't do you any favors."

"It did a few. They won't be able to find our tracks."

She nodded in agreement. "I suppose there is that. The horse?"

"I left him tied. I'll set him loose once I retrieve our things."

"Better to do it now. There's no telling who might be wandering the forest under cover of just such conditions that proved favorably for you."

Malcolm paused before reaching for the handle of the door. "Have visitors been more common of late?" His voice was soft, tense beneath the pressure and feeling that perhaps they weren't safe after all and he had relaxed far too soon. He remembered Mother Hobbs' reaction to his entrance and her ready defense of her home.

She looked up from her work, her gray eyes piercing and glimmering in the low light from the fire. "They, at the very least, now know of my presence and my general whereabouts, thanks to rumors that have been circulating in the villages."

He didn't take his eyes from her face.

She rolled her eyes and adjusted her shawl, gathering up Rosalie's wet clothes in her arms. "Vieggo sent a few girls through here. They stayed long enough, but they were sighted leaving the village and it was noticed that they never returned. Some support us in secret, you know that as well as I do, but when I left to see them along on their journey, I overheard the rumors. Children turned from me in the street, and whispers of 'witch' were passed on the breeze. People who fear another will readily give voice to that fear, and they do not often care to whom they share."

Malcolm gripped his sword. "They know of your home?"

She shook her head. "Not that I can tell. There are few who know the way or the proper path—nor that there are multiple of such. I'm ready to defend my home at any cost, but I hope to God they do not find it. 'Tis the safe haven of far too many to be risked. I have heard footsteps on my foraging trips into the woods, but as far as I know, I have remained hidden." She reached for a kettle of warm water heating over the fire. "But as the horse cannot enter my sanctum, he must be set loose before he is found and the entrance discovered."

Malcolm nodded. "I'll be back in a trice."

"Hurry back. The bairn doesn't know my face yet, and I would hate to have her startled in her current state if she woke and you were nowhere to be found."

Malcolm swept from the room and back into the cold rain like a thunderclap—there one second and gone the next. As he retraced his footsteps, he felt the chill all the more sharply for having spent some time in the shelter. He bowed his head against the rain, trying to avoid the frigid water from getting in his eyes. His hood was heavy with wet, and it took him far less time to reach the horse he had tethered to the tree than it took on the previous journey.

The horse whuffled and bobbed its head a few times at the sight of Malcolm, who removed the remaining saddle bags from his back and threw them over his shoulder. "All right, friend. Find your way home. You've served us well." He removed the bit, letting it dangle beneath the horse's chin and, with a sharp click of his tongue and a tossing motion of his arm, the animal backed away, snuffing into the wind and eyeing him keenly before turning and trotting into the evergreen mist.

The animal would be able to find his way home. Having been most likely raised on the moors and mountains, his footing was sure and his sense of direction was as keen as any human's when a warm stable, his master, and a hot meal were available to him. Malcolm sunk into the tree cover and held fast, listening intently to the sounds of the forest. He prayed from the bottom of his heart that this place was not being watched.

But as the wind whistled through the tops of the trees and the rain beat out a steady refrain, his heart rose into his throat. They may not be able to stay here long, if what Mother Hobbs had said was true. As she had mentioned, people acting in fear rarely kept information to themselves, especially when that fear was preyed upon and twisted against them. Their only hope was that none truly knew the way. That and their trust in a power who could make blind eyes see and seeing eyes blind.

ROSALIE, PRESENT DAY...

There was warmth on her face, and for the first time in a long while, she didn't feel the wind chafing her skin. But why was she hot? Had she tossed too close to the fire? Instead of feeling pleasant and warming her from the outside in, her whole body felt as though it were aflame.

She coughed, the congested wheezing of her own lungs frightening her not just with the sound, but with the pain as well. A stabbing ache like a blade slicing through flesh ran along her side, and she reached for it with a moan, half expecting to see blood on her fingers.

Her eyes were heavy, burning and filled with water when she opened them, blinking past the mist in an attempt to make sense of her surroundings. The forest sky no longer met her gaze, but the branches still remained. But they were dark, completely closed in, and rubbed to nearly a shine. Herbs hung from the boughs in bundles above her, and she caught a whiff of an earthy smell that permeated the air.

Was this the forest or something else? Low voices met her ears, and she tried to blink past the haze that pinned her to the bed, but there was hardly any strength left to fight it. It started to feel like the prison she had spent her life in, the inability to leave no matter how hard she tried or how good she was. The pressure grew on her chest, and she groaned, eliciting a coughing fit that wracked her frame until she was out of breath as she shoved against the blanket that rested on top of her.

"Shh, little one. You're safe." The voice was deep and hoarse, and she stilled. Malcolm was with her. They hadn't dragged her back. A large hand rested on her forehead, and it felt cool in a way that cut past the heat and the pain that was wrestling her into submission.

An earthenware cup was held to her lips, and it clanked gently against her teeth until she moved to swallow the warm, sweet and sour liquid that coated her throat and stilled the burning desire to cough. "Rest now; you need it."

The voice was a woman's, and on the same half-formed thought that wondered who it was, Rosalie drifted back into sleep.

ELGON, FOURTEEN YEARS AGO...

"May I take your reins, your majesty?" Kenton asked, the ever present energy in his movement evident by the way he bounced and rocked onto the balls of his feet and then back. Elgon dismounted, allowing the lad to take Sigeric's lead and arranged his cloak with a half-distracted toss over his shoulder.

The lords of Pavlin had all convened on the battlefield where some of their best had met their end at the edge of the Rusalkan scimitars. Pavlin had no wall as Elira's most eastern border did. It had no demarcation, but when the Rusalks had pushed on the front, merging out from their forest hideaway to ransack the local village. Its people did not take kindly to those whom they had trusted to remain on their side of the border breaching that trust so violently.

Several of the local serfs were killed in that attack, and a call to arms had quickly flown throughout the land. Pavlin had done themselves credit, and when called upon and provoked, they had risen to the occasion, ready to defend their homes.

But it had been too little in the face of the attempted invasion. They had succeeded in keeping the Rusalkans off their lands, but at the great cost of many of the husbands, fathers, and brothers of their people.

The air felt oppressive as he walked through the trampled fields toward the main house of Lord Elton that had been used as a battlement and was nearest the border. The weight of the sorrow, pain, and sacrifice was still as alive as the sun that shone brightly overhead. A sun too bright in a world that had been drained of life and the vitality of those that laid theirs on the line. It felt harsh instead of warm; the great yellow orb that brought so much brightness seemed to mock the very land it was created to fill with light.

The townsfolk had turned out to greet their new ruler, and he shrank inside, suddenly filled with the feeling of insignificance. Who was he to be honored in such a way? He had once been the worst of them, the harshest master and the lowliest servant. Yet they lined up in parade to welcome him as a savior he was far too ill-fit to be. He clenched his jaw as the moisture burned in his eyes, threatening to spill over.

Even the widows, black cloths tied around their hair and at their throats, had come out to welcome him. As if he were more important than mourning the loss of the ones they loved most in all this world.

Lord Elton stepped forward, his eyes red-rimmed and his entire face drooping as if he alone bore the weight of the loss. He bowed before Elgon, dropping to one knee. "Thank you, your majesty, for coming."

Without a thought, Elgon dropped to a knee in front of him and rested his hand on the lord's shoulder. Lord Elton looked up, his red eyes wide in surprise, and Elgon felt his own chin quiver. He gripped Lord Elton's hand in his, keeping the other on the man's shoulder, and drew him up to stand in front of him. "I'm so sorry for your loss, m'lord. I pray God's mercies and comfort for you and your people." Elgon's voice was husky with emotion he could not hide.

The lord's eyes misted, but he clenched his jaw and raised his head in a nod of gratitude. "Thank you, your majesty." He gestured with his arm to the people who served him and took care of his land. "Pavlin welcomes you, our king."

The two rows of people that lined the short drive to Lord Elton's home bowed, the women clutching their children's hands and pulling them down to the gravel beside them.

God, give me strength. He fought the urge to let the tears fall down his face; he needed to be strong for these people. Despite the fact that his own family was safe and sound within the castle walls of Niran, there was something in him that felt a kinship to these people. He could feel their pain, their fear, and their loss as keenly as if it was his own.

But strength poured through him, conviction filling his veins like steel. They weren't lined up to see a weeping king; they wanted to see the strong leader who would protect them and do his best to serve them. He knelt beside the first woman in line, a widow's kerchief around her graying black hair, and gripped her gently beneath the elbows. The young child clutched in her arms stared straight into his soul with the clearest blue eyes he had ever seen as he drew the woman back to her feet.

Though that strength not entirely his own still stood like a ballast within him, a tear edged its way from his eye and dripped down his cheek. The woman met his gaze, and her chin trembled as her own eyes filled. "I'm so sorry for your loss," Elgon said, his voice quiet and husky.

She bit her lip and all she could do was nod in thanks, overcome by an emotion so soul-ripping he felt it himself.

He would do what he could for these people. Preparations for protection, military assignments, and other arrangements could be saved for later. Their hearts were more important in this moment, and he would do all that he could to ease a burden he was grateful he did not have to carry.

As he moved down the line, a small hand slipped into his, and he looked down to see the child of the first woman at his side, her tiny thumb in her mouth and her large eyes gazing straight up into his. His heart stuttered in his chest, and the love nearly exploded in his heart. The closeness of his own impending fatherhood made the moment all that more poignant. He would go home to meet his own child in just a week or so. He would guide them by the hand, walk with them through life, and be the protector and provider that they needed. While this little one had lost the opportunity to be held by her father for the rest of her childhood. Her father had sacrificed everything to keep her safe and had succeeded.

He gripped her hand tightly in his much larger one, and she smiled around her thumb. Tears rushed to his eyes as she walked with him the rest of the way down the line. He had a new appreciation for the family and life he would return home to.

No child deserved to live without a father, and he would do his best to rectify the mistakes of previous generations. He would not abandon his child for the life and work of a king; they would be with him and he with them, every step of the way.

Fifteen

HAUNTED DREAMS

MALCOLM

A bright light pierced through the darkness, setting his head ablaze with pain. Shouting echoed in the distance and Malcolm rolled, trying to get to his feet, but only succeeded in managing to push himself to his hands and knees, his eyes still crammed shut against the pain that threatened to split his head wide open.

The echoes… They sounded different. They sounded wrong. A massive thud and crash slammed through his eardrums and flashed through every fiber of his being like lightning that sent his eyes flying wide open.

The pain threatened to drown him. But it was just a wave. Like the tide, it abated if he gave it a second.

His memory was gone. What had happened. Why was he here? These were not the halls of the upper castle, but the basement… No, not just the cellar, but the prison. A cell. He was in a cell…

Enguerrand's cell.

Where was that beast? Why was he here? Why was his head splitting open like someone had taken an ax to it? Where were the guards?

He blinked heavily and focused on the ground in front of him. The straw-covered cobbles were swimming in bloody, dark red stains—almost black. His blood. He shifted his weight and lifted a hand to his head. It came away dripping in sticky red, oozing between his fingers.

The door. He stumbled, pulling himself toward the cell door. Closed. Locked. Why?

The thundering from above him continued—footsteps, pounding. He used the metal grating on the door to pull himself to his feet. Shaking and trembling like a newborn lamb, his legs were knocking together as he leaned heavily against it.

There was no one in the hall.

"Help!" he shouted, but then sank to his knees with the agony that ran through his veins, trembling like fire.

"Guards!" He tried again, holding his head between both hands as if he could keep the firebrand from stabbing inside his head. Nausea overcame him, and he fell to his knees once more, vomiting into the bloodied straw beneath him.

Something was horribly wrong. He couldn't stay here. He needed to get out. He was responsible. Niran and the castle were his to guard and protect. He needed to make sure the queen and the castle were all right. Where was Enguerrand? Had the demon escaped from his cell and left him here to rot? Had Enguerrand attacked him? How had this occurred? And why was his memory as dark as the blood that coated the stones in front of him?

God, what happened?

Running feet, sudden turns, and then blinding pain. It flashed back. Someone had rushed him, slammed something into the back of his head. There was nothing else besides that scrap of a memory to keep him company. Loneliness filled his soul.

Engeurrand's absence made him fear the worst.

Screams met his ears, faint and echoing down the winding staircase at the end of the stone hall.

Lord, help us. Save us. Whatever enemy has entered these walls, protect us from what evil has conspired against us. Do not let our enemies flourish.

He had to get out of this wretched hole. He needed to find the queen. It was his life for hers. He had promised such. And a promise was as good as a covenant between him and his king. His friend. His brother.

He stood again, gritting his teeth and fighting through the agony, the darkness, and the nausea that threatened to level him yet again. He grappled at the latch of the cell, barely able to see it through the gray mist covering his eyes. Blood dripped down his face, and he tasted iron on the edge of his lip.

No luck. He was trapped here. Stuck.

"HELP!" he shouted again, holding himself upright this time and letting the pain roll through like a stormy sea tossing a wave upon the sand, waiting for that moment when it would recede. There, it subsided.

No response.

"Let. Me. OUT!" Jaw clenched, he stepped back, lowering his shoulder. He slammed his weight into the metal grate and hit the floor before he was even aware he was falling.

It was black as night when a final scream of agony reached his ears, echoing in the distance. Or was it his own?

"Malcolm!"

He jolted upright, the anxiety coursing through his veins strong enough to bring on another bout of nausea that he swallowed hard against. The darkness ebbed, and the soft, golden light of a fire met his eyes as he strained against the panic, willing his heart to cease from slamming into his ribs like a wave beating the side of a boat.

The voice that had hissed his name at his side was Mother Hobbs. He took in his surroundings and started when she rested her cold fingers over his and pried his fist loose from the hilt of his sword. He looked down, expecting to see blood as she spread his fingers wide, attempting to get him to relax.

"You're dreaming, lad. Don't let the terrors keep you, even now."

He stood suddenly and caught her elbow when his abrupt movement almost sent her tumbling over. Her eyes were wide, her gray, wiry hair in a long braid over her shoulder instead of twined around her head as it was during the day.

"I'll go check the perimeter." That dream had left his breathing ragged, his hair on edge, and his muscles taut. He needed to make sure they were safe. Protect them. He had made a promise, and he would die before he was unable to keep it.

She grabbed his arm as he moved away, stalling him. Her gray eyes were pleading, gleaming in the firelight. "Don't let the shame of the past follow you into your future. The horrors of what once was are not your companions, nor should they be allowed to burden you. Only the good Lord can see you through this storm, Malcolm. The lass needs ye."

He nodded, swallowing hard against the rock in his throat. "I'll secure the area."

Her shoulders wilted, but she nodded, her lips pressed tight.

He strode out into the stormy night, but not without first glancing at the little cot against the far wall and the sleeping form of his ward. She tossed, a soft moan on her lips that turned into an unconscious cough. Her face contorted in pain, and his heart thumped in unison with it. He fought against it, pulling himself away and flinging his cloak over his shoulder even as he shut the large wooden door fast behind him.

There was a phantom throbbing at the back of his head and base of his skull, and he reached up to press against the scars that still remained, buried beneath his hair. The horror that filled him still haunted him like an unbidden ghost trailing its way through the creaking shadows of his soul as he made his way to the edge of the woods.

The cold wind beat the rain into his face, and he let it sting, turning into it, allowing the cold water to wash away the last vestiges of the nightmare he could never quite escape. As clarity returned and the pain subsided, the ache inside his soul only grew in ferocity. The gates of his heart had been opened again. Seeing the perfect combination of Elgon and Violet's face in their wee lass had broken down something solid that had barred love from his life for far too long.

But as that feeling of love grew for the one who fought for her strength inside the camouflaged walls of Mother Hobb's domicile, he slammed the doors down, locking them as tight as they should have been that fateful day, fourteen years ago, when the life of another was taken from their kingdom…and his was forever marked.

ELGON, FOURTEEN YEARS AGO…

With a sudden start, Elgon jolted upright on his bedroll, his pulse pounding in his ears, the feeling of panic overwhelming him as every shadow in his tent seemingly threatened to attack him. He drew deep, shuddering breaths, one hand gripping the hilt of his sword, the other resting on his heaving chest.

He couldn't remember the details of the dream or if they had any merit, but he still felt the feelings of horror, panic, and dismay. He had learned not to dispel the dreams he was given, but this one, even though details were fleeting, left him begging that it not be true.

Wearied after a long day defining new policies and determining where the new outpost for the Kingsmen would be built, he had sunk into a deep sleep, fraught with nightmares he couldn't shake.

But something obviously had awoken him.

He heard a nearby gasp and paused, holding his breath to determine where it had come from. The soft glow from the torch hanging by its metal ring from the center tent pole did little to light the room aside from casting shadows. His bedroll was no better than those of the kingsmen, and few furnishings littered his tent, aside from a leather satchel with papers and documents that the lords of Pavlin were signing one by one and a change of shirt should he need it.

Another gasp and a gurgle sent him leaping from his bedroll, slinging the sword from where it rested on his belt even in sleep toward his back. Throwing the flap of his tent wide, he nearly fell over the form that rested at the opening, prone, face down in the dirt.

"Kenton!"

Falling to his knees, Elgon scooped one arm beneath the boy's shoulders, turning him over in the moonlight. Sticky warmth coated his hands, and horror stole his breath at the sight of the boy's midsection, completely covered in blood as it spilled from him and onto the ground.

Kenton's face contorted in agony, blood smeared across his forehead and down his neck. His hands were coated in it as they hovered over his midsection where deep cuts oozed more of the lifegiving red onto Elgon's knees, turning them a rich black. "H-he went." He choked on his own words and swallowed hard.

At the sound of the lad's voice, Elgon's horrified daze shattered like a broken mirror. "HELP!" he shouted, pulling

Kenton closer. He rested the boy's shoulders on his knees and reached over his head, pulling his shirt from off his own back and bundling it into a ball to press against Kenton's abdomen.

Kenton's eyes fluttered and rolled back in his head for a moment, a moan wrenched from his lips as Elgon pressed down hard to staunch the flow. The world seemed to stand still around them until Elgon finally heard distant shouts and hurried footsteps over the roaring that filled his ears. Kenton's hands shook, blood dripping from a few of his fingers as they rested on top of Elgon's, gripping the backs of his hands hard.

Forms materialized out of the darkness. More hands reached for the boy, the medic's voice a blur in the background of Elgon's consciousness.

A hand on his shoulder arrested Elgon's attention, and the thunder in his ears finally ceased. "Your majesty, lift your hands that I may attend the wound."

Elgon released the wadded up shirt and wrapped one hand around Kenton's shoulder, cradling it in the crook of his arm and pushing back the hair from his face with his other, blood smearing the tawny locks.

Kenton's eyes flew open again, wild and unfocused. "H-he left."

"Who left? Who did this to you?" Elgon whispered softly as the rest of the hands did their work.

Kenton cried out, trembling taking over every one of his limbs. "M-mont-montcalme." Kenton's voice wavered, his face as pale as the canvas of Elgon's tent.

Elgon felt his stomach clench. A shaft of anger and fear pierced his heart like a spear thrown with deadly accuracy.

Montcalme. His commander. The one he had pegged as acting strangely the other day.

He raised a hand, his voice authoritative despite the tremble that punctuated every word. "Quick! A headcount of the men! Do it immediately. There is a traitor in our midst!"

Action was taken, but Elgon focused on Kenton. It seemed as though the boy's life was leaving him moment by moment as the medic worked tirelessly over the boy, bandaging, wrapping them tight, and trying to stem the blood. His eyes fluttered closed again with another groan and did not reopen.

"Huxley. How is he?"

The medic brushed aside the hair that had fallen over his face with the back of his bloodied hand. Sweat beaded his upper lip, and his hands shook. This might have been the first battle wound the young man had ever seen. "I won't know for sure, your majesty. He'll need time, but I got the bleeding slowed at least. A surgeon may need to examine him. The knife wounds are deep, and I don't have the skill to operate. I need to get him to my tent to clean and sew up the wounds. That should stem the bleeding completely, at least externally. I'll need more light than I have here."

Elgon motioned to another kingsman, who stepped in, scooping his hands beneath Kenton's knees and lifting him as Elgon cradled the boy's head against his chest and wrapped his arms beneath his shoulders.

Walking slowly to keep from jostling the injured squire, they carried him to Huxley's tent as the sound of footsteps punctuated the evening stillness and bodies moved past them quickly, assembling for the headcount Elgon had requested.

They laid Kenton down on Huxley's bedroll, and Elgon turned to the kingsman who had helped him carry the boy. "Aid Huxley and get him light. I'll be right back."

The horror had washed from his veins, replaced by steel that snapped his spine ramrod straight. He tried to swallow against the fire that rose at the back of his throat, every muscle taught, squeezing tight.

Lord Milton strode over, a serious look on his face and his jaw clenched, the muscles standing out in eerie relief in the dim light of the moon and the torch that he carried.

"Walk with me," Elgon said quietly, his voice hard as he strode to his tent to retrieve his extra shirt.

"The men have been counted, sir."

"Don't stand on ceremony, Milton. What were the results?"

Elgon jerked to a halt outside his tent. The black of Kenton's blood stained the grass, and a bloody handprint marred the flap of his tent as it waved gently in the nighttime breeze.

His inhale turned hot, fire-laden as it caught in his chest. A trail of blood led up to the puddle at the portal of his tent and that handprint. While he had been dreaming just on the other side, Kenton lay bleeding out, giving everything he had to get to his king. He let his breath out in a gasp, drawing air back in, tears burning his vision as his jaw popped loudly in one ear from the clenching.

"Your majesty?" Milton raised a hand and touched Elgon's shoulder.

Elgon flinched away, the horrible, ghastly feeling that this had been his fault flooding over him like a wave that threatened to knock him off his feet and drown him. "This was my fault. I should have seen it."

Throwing the flap aside, he strode into his tent, pulling his shirt from his pack and over his head, cursing under his breath at the blood that covered his hands and had transferred to the crisp white linen. He tucked his clean shirt into his trousers, pulling his leather jerkin over his shoulders, tying it in the front. The knots got tangled around his harried fingers, and he huffed, the tension in his shoulders mounting.

"M'lord. Allow me." Milton stepped in, tying the leather strings with ease before Elgon could protest.

Elgon turned away lest Milton see the mist in his eyes. *Kenton.* His squire. His charge. Betrayed and left for dead on the ground outside of his king's tent.

The sudden hand on his shoulders held him fast like an anchor, and Elgon looked up through the haze into Milton's hard but sorrowful face.

"Your majesty, don't let the pain of this moment take from you the strength and purpose that you carry. Sorrow is not weakness, and suffering is not a lack of strength. Let it drive you to greater resolve instead of bury you beneath its depths."

Elgon drew a steadying breath, letting the weight of the man's grip on his shoulder relax a few of the muscles.

He nodded once so that Milton would know he had been heard. Elgon drew another breath, letting the rage settle to a place deep in the pit of his stomach. "What was the result of the count?"

"Montcalme is, indeed, missing." Milton drew a breath. "Along with nearly a third of the men."

Elgon's knees went weak. "A third?" His mind reeled, spinning with all of the signs that he had seen over the last few days—last few months. Wondering how he could have missed such an overwhelming amount of disloyalty to the crown from those who served under him.

Two battalions, and just over a hundred remained. He rubbed his throbbing temples.

Dread flew through every inch of him like a frozen river of ice. Niran. Engeurrand. If this had been an organized effort, who else amongst those that served the country of Elira had also taken arms and fled from his service?

"I'm placing the men in your command, Lord Milton. I'll inform the remaining battalion chiefs. I'll take a small detail back with me, but I must return to Niran." Elgon flung his cloak over his shoulders and strode from the tent, tying it around his neck as he went. Ignoring the stains on the grass outside, he gathered ground beneath his long and purposeful footsteps.

Milton followed closely in his wake.

"If that number were organized enough to desert their post, then I tremble to think what state the rest of the kingdom is in."

Violet held her distended abdomen in her arms, her hands tied together at the wrist. The covered wagon she rode in bounced over uneven ground, jostling its occupants. The horses' galloping hooves thundered in the night darkness, their exhausted snorts pulling at her heart strings.

She looked down at the blood that coated her hands, and vomit rose in the back of her throat. She willed it down, every muscle tense in protection of the life she carried within. The blood on her hands was that of her servants, her countrymen, her kin.

Her teeth clacked as she sucked in a breath through her nose and glanced across the wagon. Zehra's mouth was tied with a gag, her hands bound in front of her like Violet's. Tears cascaded down her cheeks and soaked the front of her dress, but there was no fear in her eyes. Instead they glistened and sparked like flint to stone, belying the fire that burned deep within.

Their eyes met, held, and Violet nodded. Fire met fire and kindled it higher.

Their lives were still in the hands of the King, and no one could steal them until He willed it. And even if that day came to pass, Violet would not let them steal her spirit. They may have taken her kin, her land, and her home, but they would not take her trust in the King who ruled more than mortal lands.

Sixteen

THE NEED FOR HEALING

MALCOLM, PRESENT DAY...

"You can't take her on like this. Not for a while. Ye know that, don't you, Malcolm?"

The weight that had built up in Malcolm's chest pressed a little harder. It was fear—fear that threatened to swell into panic like a storm overtaking the forest late at night.

He sat on the wooden carved stool at Mother Hobbs' rough hewn table, smoothed over with years of use and oil. The cup in his hands warmed his palms, steam rising lazily from the top of it. He wished he could have the same level of calmness Mother Hobbs seemed to possess in his soul.

Malcolm glanced over at Rosalie's prone form on the mattress against the far wall. Shadows of the herbs that hung from the ceiling danced over her pale face with the golden light from the fire. Her fever had worsened in the night instead of growing better, and there was little hope for anything more than a long recovery.

"You take her out in this before she's ready and you'll make her worse. Short of the Lord doing a miracle, she's far too weak and this world's a bit too rough for such a mite."

"But the world will always be a rough place, and strength is not built in a day. I don't know that anyone will ever be fully ready for this journey, Mother Hobbs. And not only that, but what are we to do if we are discovered? You already said yourself that the townsfolk have started to spread rumors about you that are not only untrue, but are also damaging. If the dark knights hear of it…" His sentence broke off as his throat tightened.

"They are smart men, far too skilled at what they do for their own good, but we have One on our side that doesn't just support His own heavenly host, but also those of the mortal realm that love and serve Him. He can do what the strongest force cannot, and I think ye know that. Despite having the very real fear that the ruler's own could come and bring their terror with them, there is more trust to be put in the One who does not fight with earthly weapons."

He nodded, though his heart had a hard time trusting in this moment. He might be the most trusted knight in the kingdom of Elira, but his faith in the Lord had been so obliterated that he had lost what little confidence he had in himself or the God he thought he knew was there long ago.

"Say it. I know ye're thinking it."

He shook his head, his jaw clenched as his knuckles went white around the steaming cup in his grasp.

Her voice was soft, like one who speaks to a small frightened child or a broken animal while still making them feel her equal. "You'll feel better for having let it out."

"He was in charge at the moment when my command was shattered. I too trusted Him once—still do, in my own way—but even in His keeping, the darkest of nights and harshest of storms may come."

Silence met his hard words that trembled with anger and sorrow lurking just beneath the surface.

Then her hand was on top of his. The soft, old skin punctuated by calluses that long years of toil in these woods had wrought. "The difference is, lad, He was still there in the storm. He was still there in the darkness. Just because His plans confuse and scare us, or the enemy diverts them for his own purposes at the hands of evil men…that doesn't mean He's gone and left us. Instead, He draws nearer, and His heart breaks when ours does."

He gulped. The moisture ever at the back of his eyes threatened to escape. He blinked it away. "I just worry that His hand won't stop it this time. It didn't once. Who is to say it won't happen again?"

"There is no saying, though I feel it deep in my spirit that He will not allow this lass to be taken. Why else would He raise such a strong warrior for such a time as this? For such a task as this? Do not doubt the capabilities and purposes the Lord has for ye, lad. He knew you'd need all you have gone through to bring this lass back to her father. Let Him fight His fight while you fight yours. Lord knows, she's fighting hers."

A moan punctuated the thoughtful stillness, and the wooden bed creaked as Rosalie tossed, a cough on her lips that rattled deep in her chest.

Mother Hobbs rose, her knees creaking with the movement, and brought a cup of tea to the bedside. Lifting the little girl's head, she held the cup to her lips. Rosalie moaned and rolled her head away.

"Aye, fight it all ye want, but the life-giving water is what ye need to get through this."

Malcolm stood and made his way to the side of the bed. "Maybe if she is more upright." He slid his hand beneath the girl's shoulders and lifted her up as Mother Hobbs again touched the cup to her chapped lips. A few swallows made it down her throat, but her eyes never did more than flutter.

"Lord, touch this child and bring healing quickly." Mother Hobbs rested her hand on the child's head for a moment. "Set her down, Malcolm. Let her rest again."

Malcolm lowered Rosalie gently down again upon the mattress, coupling his own internal prayers with Mother Hobbs'.

The child would need more than just to recover before they were to be sent out. She was little more than skin and bones, and there was much that would be required of her. The route would be a taxing one, but one that would keep them the safest. He had spent the last several years conferring with spies and journeying these mountains and forests. The crags and crevices, valleys and hilltops had been scoured and mapped. Their route would take them through havens of safety. The last fourteen years had not been for naught. While the king's heart had grown weary in waiting, the hope and prayers of the people gathered in store in the heavenlies, and spies and servants of the king had done their work—searching high and low throughout Rusalka for the lost princess, the only heir to the throne of Elira.

As the days went by, Malcolm and Mother Hobbs watched and waited. Rosalie's fever finally broke within a handful of days, and she slept easily. With nothing to wake her and her skin nearly as pale as death, Malcolm had thought her gone once or twice, but the sleep had instead rejuvenated her. She woke one morning, the golden glow of fire and the lamps chasing the shadows from her face, and though she was gaunt, her eyes were bright.

ROSALIE...

Her ribs still ached, but she felt as though she were finally over a hill. The worst of the fight and the climbing were over, and it was even ground from here. Mother Hobbs still had yet to let her out of bed unassisted, but she had little impetus to argue. The world still took a spin every now and then if she moved too fast, and the pain was much worse when standing.

Mother Hobbs brought a steaming wooden bowl of stew over to the stool she had moved to the bedside for the purpose and put it down, the wooden spoon that accompanied it clattering in its place. "There we are, dearie. The bowl will be too hot for you for a minute yet, so let's tend those bandages and see how your side is doing. The bones be mending, but we want to make sure they are knitting right."

Rosalie winced as she pulled herself off the pillows at her back and allowed Mother Hobbs to lift the shift she had lent her and unwind the linen bandages that had bound her abdomen. With the tightness gone, the pain increased, and Rosalie held herself stiffly upright in an attempt to keep it at bay.

Mother Hobbs' hand was cool as it touched her side, pressing gently on the bruise that had faded from a deep purple and blue splotch to something more green.

Rosalie winced, tilting her head and pulling away from the hand, gentle though it may be.

"Aye, I know 'tis painful, but not so much as it was a few days ago, eh?"

Rosalie nodded. "Much better. When can I start walking again?" The words tumbled out faster than she had meant them to, and she cleared her throat against the cough that threatened her throat. While much better, it still had yet to completely disappear, and Mother Hobbs said that the wet weather they were having wasn't helping in the slightest.

Mother Hobbs chuckled, her gray eyes shining behind the puffy silver hair that was braided back from her face but had partially fallen from its knots. "Ye sure are in a mighty hurry, aren't ye? Though ye can't be blamed. You and Malcolm both, ye feel it in yer bones. It's about time to be getting on. Ye'll have to wait a bit more, I'm afraid. Just because I'll let ye up and walk today, doesn't mean you are in any fit shape to be traveling. The storms outside have kept yer pursuers away and you'll do good to eat this here soup and more if you'll take it, and build your strength up afore you go. The walk is hard, lass, and I'll not send you out sooner than you need to. I don't want to hear ye succumbed to yer bed again because I was derelict in my care and let ye go too soon."

The old woman's hands were swift as she talked and had Rosalie's ribs rewrapped before she had finished. "Eat yer stew and I'll help you up for a spin around the room."

Rosalie took the bowl, hard pressed to keep the smile from her face. She had no idea of the journey Mother Hobbs spoke of, but this setback was nothing more than a nuisance and wouldn't keep her from her father a moment longer than she could possibly let it. Though she knew little of the decision was in her hands. The stew was heavenly though. Meaty, just the right temperature, and thick with rich flavor and a touch of pepper that warmed the back of her throat and made her tongue dance.

The door of the cabin burst open and Malcolm stumbled in, his arms loaded nearly beyond capacity with split firewood and kindling. The cold rain and chill wind poured in with him, and the sound of thunder in the distance grew louder with the open door.

"Sakes alive, Malcolm. The child's only just recovered! That wind is freezing!"

Malcolm used his shoulder and back to slam the door shut behind him as he nodded at Mother Hobbs. "This firewood will take away the chill, I think."

Mother Hobbs shook her head with a good-natured smile and huffed dramatically. "Men. Think they can fix everything with hard work and heavy labor."

The smallest smile tugged at the corner of Malcolm's mouth, and Rosalie thought it might have been the first time she'd seen it coupled with that sparkle in his eyes. "Can't it, though?" he asked with mock incredulity dripping from his tone.

"Law!" Mother Hobbs shot him a glare, her own smile threatening to escape as she gathered some of the wood from his arms. "Get on with you now. There's stew on the stove at yer disposal."

Sir Malcolm winked at Rosalie, and her heart fluttered with happiness as he dumped the rest of the wood in his arms in the stack by the fireplace, dusting the remaining dirt and bark from his hands before striding to the table, ruffling Rosalie's hair as he passed her.

They had grown comfortable in their days together, the rhythms and patterns of existence making Rosalie feel the safest she had ever felt. They were some of the first moments in her life where she had realized just how different an existence outside of the castle walls could be.

There was a certain glow to the days as they dragged on; the golden hue from the fireplace and the lanterns kept the storm outside at bay, and there was a tight-knit warmth that held her in its embrace, comforting her as she felt her body grow stronger and her injuries heal. The herbs and hearty meals that Mother Hobbs refused to stop giving her at every turn were working their God-given magic, filling her bones and strengthening her muscles, sending the pain retreating and giving her an energy she had never known could be hers.

It wasn't long before she was walking, traversing the small hut with its many cracks and crevices, cozy alcoves and shadows where the firelight refused to tread. It felt a little like what she imagined living inside of a tree would be like, and it filled her with a sense of wonder and comfort that had been sorely lacking in the stone confines of the tower.

Mother Hobbs had her pacing at regular intervals; at first, using the furniture for support, and then on her own. The first time she made it across the room under her own power, she had been nearly as winded as if she had climbed a mountain peak. But as the days gathered one on top of the other like threads woven into a cloth, she could sense the strength returning. The walks grew easier, her breathing more still.

The cough finally ceased, and Rosalie attributed that to Mother Hobbs' herbal concoction of tea that she sipped nearly nonstop the first week after her fever broke.

Malcolm wavered between peace and being on edge, his eyes darting at the smallest sound, and he stepped outside more than a few times a day to check the perimeter and determine that they were safe. Those moments made her nervous. The life she had left behind gathered close and tried to drag her memories back to the confines of the tower, her life being jerked about at the will of the Rusalk guards and the occasional visits from Zuko himself.

She slammed her mind shut on those memories, praying often that they would not resurface and that her life would never again be under such a strain.

But there were some days when Malcolm seemed at ease. The tension and straightness with which he carried his shoulders relaxed. The wrinkles at the corners of his eyes deepened, and he bandied words with Mother Hobbs, winking occasionally at Rosalie as if they shared some secret that entertained him and that Mother Hobbs would never guess.

It did something to her, that wink. The feeling of knowing and being known. Of being…loved. The man who had been a stranger slowly became someone of whom she could recognize the ever changing moods, read his face, and know the tone of his voice.

She wanted to know more. More of his story. More of her father, more of the kingdom, but there was little that she felt comfortable to ask. There was a hesitancy that stilled her questions; perhaps it was the guidance of her Heavenly King, staying her tongue and whispering, *Not yet*.

One night, footsteps sounded on the porch and the door flew open. Malcolm was on his feet and at the door, sword in hand before the intruder could take a step farther, but Mother Hobbs was in front of him even quicker than that.

She pressed a hand to his chest, shoving him back into the room and glaring first at him, then his sword with a pointed look that sent the blade back into its sheath at a trice.

Rosalie stood at the back of the room, her arms crossed in front of herself and holding her own shoulders, the fear that had sent her heart into her throat freezing her feet to the ground.

She didn't notice Malcolm's movements until he was beside her, his large hand resting on her shoulder in a weighty but gentle pressure, reminding her that she was safe without even having to utter a word. His fingers rubbed a small circle into her taught muscles, and she drew a breath. He would not let anything evil come to her.

There were two at the door—a couple. It was a large man, a beard grown so long and wayward that Rosalie couldn't see his mouth, his hat in his hand. His strong arm and shoulder supporting a young woman in a cloak, the hood thrown over her head. Mother Hobbs stepped to the woman's other side without a word, and they half carried the dripping figure into the room, laying her on one of the cots on the opposite side of the room from where Rosalie's rested.

The girl didn't even move after Mother Hobbs untied her cloak, removed it from her shoulders, and covered her prone form with a blanket.

Curiosity filled Rosalie, and she wondered so many questions about where the girl had come from, why she was here, and why none of them spoke a word but instead seemed to communicate only with their eyes, an invisible thread of knowing passing between them. Mother Hobbs nodded to the gentleman with the overwhelming beard, made a shooing gesture with her hand, and patted his shoulder.

He left without a word. The wind and rain rushed through the doorway as he departed.

"Off to bed with you, young one," Mother Hobbs whispered, gesturing Rosalie away from the back wall and toward her own cot.

"But what—" she objected.

"Tsk." Mother Hobbs cut her off, chiding her with a good-natured smile that was cloaked with a sadness and weight Rosalie couldn't understand. "Not an argument from you. it's late and ye need yer sleep."

As Rosalie closed her eyes, and as the soft sound of Mother Hobbs humming from across the room as she tended to the stranger filled her ears, she thought of the strange marking she had seen on the man's wrist as he rested the girl on the bed.

The dark sign of a dove, inked into his skin.

ELGON, FOURTEEN YEARS AGO…

"There is nothing else I can do, your majesty. I do not have the skill for such wounds. Would that I had hope he would survive, but the likes of these wounds are not ones many come back from. His chances are slim, and all we can do is hope that the bleeding inside is minimal and ceases soon."

Elgon stood over the bed of Kenton. Tears that had once threatened to spill over were now completely banished. He was too angry, too broken, too afraid to let the tears come. There would be a time for the spilling of tears later. Violet always reminded him that the Lord stored them in heaven and cherished them as He did His children, but there was a time and a place. Now was the time to act.

"I must take him to Marcus." It was scarcely more than a murmur that fell from his lips, and his mind spun with the realization of what he needed to do.

"Your majesty?" Huxley's brow pinched.

"Padsley. I must get the lad to Padsley. The medicinals there may know how to care for him. They are some of the most skilled I have ever known."

Huxley's eyes lit up with hope. He brushed the hair from his forehead with the back of his hand even as it still clutched a bloody towel. Relief lurked in the lines of his face. "That may be best, but…" Worry again creased his forehead. "While we are close, it is still a few hours ride at best, and he is in no condition to ride or be held atop a horse."

"We will fetch a wagon for him. We will make him as comfortable as possible, but we must leave with all dispatch and haste. See that he is made ready; we cannot wait."

Huxley nodded and threw the towel down, hurrying to Kenton's side and reaching for a blanket.

Elgon watched a moment more as the boy's pale, bloody, and bandaged form was covered with the woolen cloth. He clenched his jaw even tighter, his teeth hurting from the force. He would get Kenton safely to Marucs and Fendrel, but then he must ride for Niran. The dread that filled him and the anger that burned like a hot coal to bare skin inside of his chest was not to be ignored. If a third of his men had betrayed him, abandoned their brothers and their people without communication, there was something bigger afoot.

He strode from the tent to seek out Lord Milton and secure a small company of loyal Kingsmen to bring Kenton to Fendrel and then to go back to Niran.

He tried to draw a deep breath. He could rest in the fact that he had left Violet in the care of Malcolm. Even if he was right…she would be safe with his first knight.

No greater love hath any man than that he lay his life down for a friend.

Kenton had given the ultimate sacrifice today.

Kenton would not make that sacrifice in vain.

Seventeen

BETRAYAL AND DORMANT FEARS

ROSALIE, PRESENT DAY...

There was something about that little cabin in the woods that Rosalie had never tasted before, and the sweetness coated her tongue like a spoonful of honey after a dry and harrowing day.

Freedom. It called to her with the wind that whistled off the mountain pass, and it sang in her heart with every day that she grew stronger. It kept her warm at nights as she felt the joy of the Savior as she rested in a place where she was not afraid to lay her head.

Peace was found with the freedom, unlike anything she had never known. It had been one thing to carry internal peace within her heart, knowing that she was in the hands of her Heavenly King and could rely on Him in the greatest and smallest moments. Yet still spending her entire life on edge, waiting for the one thing that would send her captors into a fit of rage and bring pain and suffering down on her head.

But to be outside of that suffering, not worried that every time she laid down she could be awoken by abusive words or a foot to the side…

It was a new feeling to be allowed to fully bloom. To breathe.

She might have budded among thorns, a rosy glow in the upper castle room, but here she blossomed like a wild rose, the thorns and thistle making way for her petals, ever expanding out and taking up more space than she had ever been allowed before.

Begging to be put to use, she learned to cook with Mother Hobbs. Malcolm smiled on for a bit but spent much of his days outside, guarding, watching, or hunting near the premises. Nearer especially during the days the young woman was with them.

The stranger spent a few days in bed but was silent, with eyes that were haunted in a way Rosalie recognized. There was something about her that reminded her of those days locked in the tower—that desperate desire to get out. The inner ache that what you most feared would come upon you at any moment. She started at every creak in the floorboard and jumped when the door squeaked open on its hinges.

Slowly but surely, Rosalie watched as the pain and suffering waned in the young woman's eyes.

But there was still something there. Something locked and shuttered within. A beauty, a joy that Rosalie prayed every single day would come bursting out of the young woman's spirit like a dove set free to the air after a long captivity.

They fed her. Rosalie tried to talk to her, softly at first, as you would with a spooked animal. Using her time spent with the young woman to touch the worn and limp hands that rested aimlessly in her lap, Rosalie tended them. She wanted them to dance, to become alive with animation. To move about with excitement as she talked. She could see them as they should be, not as they were, and so she held them. Warmed them between her own palms, massaged the muscles, begging blood and life to fill them again.

The third day was when she got a name.

"I've always wondered what a name says about a person," Rosalie spoke softly, letting her thoughts run from her tongue with a freedom she rarely allowed herself unless she was alone. The woman reminded her of herself; there was a comfort there that she couldn't explain. "Names have so much power. To speak to a person much of what their parents hoped for them. To declare over them and whisper a meaning and a strength to their spirit. I often wonder if the Lord had a special delight in names. Surely, He let Adam name the animals, but He breathed over them the name of man and woman. And if what God did is something that He gave us permission to do, I think there is something important about naming another creature, especially those of our own flesh and blood. I wonder what your name is?"

"Chasta."

Rosalie's lips were open to continue speaking, but she shut them with a click in surprise. Three days of silence, finally broken. And with an answer to her question, no less. The world seemed to still, and Rosalie stared at the blank face of the young woman, holding her hand tight between her own.

She squeezed it lightly. "That is a beautiful name." Her voice was quiet, breathy with the weight of what had just occurred.

Some of the blankness left Chasta's face, and she turned her head slowly, taking Rosalie in for the first time. Some of the fog disappeared from those lovely dark eyes. Then they filled with moisture, and the tears trembled on her long lashes.

"Do you know what it means?" Rosalie asked, hesitant but desperately wanting to know.

"Pure," the girl whispered, then her head went down on the quilt that covered her lap, sobs shaking her shoulders.

Rosalie froze, her heart breaking and beating out of her chest at the same time. Tears filled her own eyes in empathy, and her body felt the weight of the emotions the girl in front of her bore.

Soft hands pressed into her shoulders, maneuvering her out of the chair and toward the door. "Go outside, dearie. Find Malcolm. I'll call you when dinner's ready."

Rosalie obeyed, grabbing her cloak from the hook next to the door and looking back as she did so. Mother Hobbs was holding Chasta much like a young child, her salt and pepper head bent over the shiny black one, her face twisted in grief, rocking back and forth as a mother would when soothing her child to sleep.

Malcolm was sitting on the front stoop, whittling a stick, feet spread wide and cloak thrown over his shoulder.

She stepped near him, settling down beside him, and shyly edged closer. There was comfort in his presence for her. The long days that had stretched into years since she had experienced a loving touch left her with an emptiness that longed to be filled. Hesitantly, she scooted still closer, reaching a hand to touch his shoulder.

His arm moved with a stroke of the knife, and she pulled back, clutching her hand to herself and feeling the heat fly into her face.

There was a long pause, and then a large arm came around her, wrapping her in the smell of leather, wool, and pine and cupping her arm in the crook of his. He pulled her in close, taking the knife from his other hand and placing it in her palm. Wrapping her other hand around the stick, he used his hands on top of hers to maneuver her through the motion of carving. The first few strokes were jerky, awkward, but she took a breath and settled into the rhythm, loosening her grip and letting him guide her.

"Where did Chasta come from?"

Malcolm paused, his silence and stillness lasting long enough that she looked up at him. The lines in his face were deeper, the pain hiding in his eyes closer to the surface as he stared into the woods. She saw him swallow, and his eyes met hers before he started carving again with her hands. She focused on the wood in order not to miss anything.

"Like you, she comes from a place where she was treated ill. Held against her will and made to do things that no human being should ever have to do outside of their own wishes or desires."

She swallowed as a bit of the darkness crept back into her memories. The feeling of being kept captive, that desire to run free and explore, just to harmlessly spend one day out in the sun away from the cloistered place where she was held against her will. That weighted feeling of captivity held her in a crushing blow, and she suddenly had to fight for a breath.

But the hand soothingly rubbing circles into her back pulled her out, and she gasped for air. The comfort swarmed and chased away the darkness of her grotto home.

"Rest easy. You'll not go back, even if I have to give myself to keep you free."

The words were spoken low, a deep rumble in his chest, and she felt the vibrations of it from the safety of the crook of his arm. Without the hesitancy of before, she nestled in closer. The comfort of a father's arms had long been denied her, and though this man was not her true father in blood, the sacrifice of his life, the comfort of his protection, and the purity of his promise to see her safe reassured her in ways that a thousand words could never do.

You could hear that you were loved a hundred times a day and never feel so, but when you know and sense that love beyond what you had ever felt before, there is a weight and meaning behind it that pours out the goodness upon the one who experiences it.

"We'll have to leave soon, you know that, Rosalie?"

She nodded, the sadness crashing back in. The burden of what she had always hoped for—a tiny cabin in the woods, dependent things to care for and nurture, a hearth to call home with the freedom to feel herself… It was all going to slip away again.

"You're almost strong enough. The journey will be a long one, but you have gathered a bit of strength, and your will is much stronger than even your physical ability. You have the heart of a princess even though you have been the slave of a king."

Rosalie fought the tears that rose to her eyes. Never in her wildest dreams had she expected to be royalty. Never in her desperate pleas and prayers of the heart that she had poured out from the rooftop tower of Zuko's castle had she ever once thought or expected that her place in this world would be one like his.

And despite knowing that she was born to it like a bird to flying and a goat to the mountain pass, there was a tiny piece of her that rejected that claim to a throne, to royalty, to the separateness that was her birthright. The only royalty she had known in her life was one of fear and trembling. Of lording it over those beneath you and of keeping your place of stature so far above those in your care that there was little they could do to ever feel safe or appreciated.

"Wh-what if I don't want to be princess?" Her voice was soft. Almost afraid of what he might say or do. His hand shifted upon hers, and she recoiled, feeling suddenly trapped and wishing that she was not stuck within the crook of his arm. She made a move to roll away and cover her head.

But Malcolm didn't pull back. Indeed, he completely ceased to move. He didn't raise a hand to strike her; his face didn't register anything but sadness and pain. Trembling, her breathing slowed at the look on his face. There was no anger there and her clenched hands released.

Were his eyes filling with tears? Her cheeks flamed. Malcolm had never done anything that would cause her to fear being in his presence, but his movement had sent some primal fear pumping through her veins in an uncontrollable wave of panic.

"My lady, I would never, should the world press in and my hand be forced, ever hurt you in any way. It would be my greatest shame and fear that I should even unintentionally make you fear me."

She drew a breath, and the feeling of tears rose to her own eyes, burning them as she tried to see through the haze. She had always had to fear a certain kind of man her entire life. Learned to hide, to pretend, to shun honesty, and if, by chance, she spoke her mind, she recoiled, pulling deeper within her shell and preparing for the moment when all hell would break loose upon her.

And here was a man, a knight, a servant to her father the king, and he was not only protecting her, but he was giving her the space to act and feel and be something she had never been allowed to be in the past.

"There is nothing wrong with not wanting to rule, your ladyship. Even your father can relate to that sentiment. There were several moments in his life, some of them recently, when he questioned his own calling. Questioned whether he should be ruler, in charge of a country with the needs and resources like those of Elira.

"But truthfully, every good ruler questions their right to a throne or to any sort of lordship at all. Humility and kindness are necessary traits for a king or queen, though I doubt you have seen much from your short experiences. A true leader is one who can place themselves in the shoes of those they rule and, instead of bending them to their will, tend them as a shepherd does, making the hard decisions and protecting what is put in front of them for the good of the people and to further the kingdom of God. *Not* to further their own ideals and goals."

Rosalie's breath slowed. The hand on her back never left. His was a soft presence that stilled her pulse and gave her peace in her questions.

They sat in silence for a moment, and Rosalie picked up the carved piece of wood that had fallen to the stone step beneath her feet in her panic. Turning it over in her hand, its rough bark and etched wood still in the beginning stages of being an article of any kind, she used the tip of her finger to trace the subtle shape of a bird's wing in flight.

"You may keep it if you wish. We can continue to work on it over the course of our journey. A little something to remember the path you have embarked upon." He took the item from her hand gently and used the knife to make another swatch through the wood. A bird's head took shape. He handed it back.

"I-it's a dove." There was a bit of wonder in her voice as she fingered the wing.

He nodded, standing and adjusting the sword that never left his side. "I'm going to check the perimeter. Stay within the coven of trees." He nodded to her and strode off into the mist.

Chasta left only the very next day. A woman came to escort her, the same tattoo of the dove etched into the skin of her neck above her collar. Chasta didn't say anything when she left, but she gave Rosalie's hand a squeeze before she headed out the door.

The weather brightened, and Rosalie took to the outdoors. Having spent the majority of her life within the same room, being outside in the bracing air, smelling the pine and the sharpness of the wind, hearing the birds and woodland creatures in noises of the forest gave her soul a level of delight she had never experienced before.

She loved tending Mother Hobbs' animals. The chickens were delightfully entertaining with their strutting, heads bobbing up and down whenever they walked or clucked. There was also a small nanny goat that kept them provided with lovely milk and even cheese that Mother Hobbs took the time to teach her how to make.

She laughed daily now, spilling the seeds she had been given onto the ground, amused at the chicken's display of territorialism as they chased each other away with the ends of their beaks and fought over the seeds that fell, never realizing that Rosalie had far more in the bucket and that they would be full if only they knew how much was in her control.

It made her pause. How many times did one greedily snap up the small bit of beauty and treasure that the Lord dropped at their feet, instead of taking it with gratitude, knowing that the Lord owned cattle on a thousand hills and was more than capable of giving all that is needed?

It reminded her of how the children of Israel had often not seen the provision of the Lord's hand, assuming that what they got might be all they see, desperately fighting over scraps instead of resting in the promise of God to feed and provide for them.

The sun was high, and it almost chased the chill of the mountain pass straight from the clearing. She raised her head, letting the warmth of the rays seal her eyes shut in the brightness of the light.

A crack from the forest shattered the tranquility and peacefulness of the moment, and her head snapped up. Malcolm came dashing from the tree line, his face flushed and horror in every line about his mouth and eyes. "They've come. Quick, we must hide." He grabbed her hand and yanked her toward the cabin. The bucket of seed fell from her hands with the force, scattering every ounce of provision onto the ground.

Feeling separate from her body, she watched the chickens descend upon the seed as if it would be their last meal on this earth as she dashed toward the cottage.

ELGON, FOURTEEN YEARS AGO...

The creaking of the saddle set Elgon's taught nerves on edge. Every movement and jerk would have been pure torture to Kenton, but he was mercifully unconscious, riding in the back of the wagon that they had been able to borrow from the local farmers in Pavlin.

They were nearly to Padsley. Prayer filled Elgon's heart. For his friend Marcus and for Fendrel, begging the Lord for a miracle that they would be able save Kenton and that he would be able to experience a long and prosperous life after the viciousness of the attack from Montcalme. The poor boy had been merely trying to raise the alarm, and he had paid a deadly price for it.

Sigeric tossed his head, rolling it, almost as if to check in on his master, sensing the king's uneasiness in the saddle. Elgon was so desperately anxious to get home, to ascertain if Violet was all right. To make sure that his inkling of fear was false and that this betrayal of his kingsmen was just a random act and not in fact a kingdom-wide experience that would put his wife and unborn child in danger.

As they approached the gates to Padsley, his hackles rose. There was an air of fear that buzzed in the atmosphere, and he tried to steady Sigeric as he pranced sideways on the King's Highway in reaction to Elgon's heightened tension.

One of the wooden gates was awry on its hinges, a few men working hard to repair it. When they saw the king's colors and the Eliran banner, they immediately bent to pick up the broken door as a group, lifting it with grunts and straining backs to allow them through.

"Keep going," Elgon commanded his men. They continued to lead the horses, pulling the wagon past him and the broken gate. Pulling Sigeric off to the side where he would be in earshot of the men, he leaned forward in the saddle. "What happened?"

They bowed, and Elgon tried not to be annoyed with the waste of time the deference was. "The kingsmen raided us last night, majesty." There was a hesitancy in the man's tone, but one of the others threw Elgon an angry look. These people had only just grown used to not being ruled with a tyrannical hand and a leader who would send his soldiers to plunder and tax the people in a selfish and outrageous manner. There was little they could trust in the authority of a king, and if his men, under his colors and wearing his armor, had raided Padsley on the way through, it was he who would be held responsible for their actions.

"I had nothing to do with the raid. I am so sorry. What of the fort?"

Another man nodded his head toward a second coming up the street, his kingsman uniform apparent and a stack of boards weighing on his shoulder. "Not all have fled, but many have, stealing what food and goods that they could easily carry. It happened during the night watch."

"Was anyone hurt?" Elgon gripped his reins tighter and prayed there were no casualties.

"No, majesty. No more than a few bumps and bruises."

Some of the pain and tightness in Elgon's muscles relaxed and gave him the space he needed to take a deep breath.

The kingsman had made it the rest of the way to them and as he joined the group. He bowed, a fist to the shoulder that sported the Eliran crest pressed into its pauldron. There was a pain on his face, frustration at probably the same thing that Elgon himself was feeling.

"How many have gone, soldier?" Elgon asked. He glanced past him to see the cart still in view on its way to Fendrel and Marcus, yet his mind was also overrun with thoughts and fears for Violet.

"About thirty of the garrison, m'lord."

Elgon sighed, the weight on his shoulders growing with every passing second as the energy inside of him wound up tighter, burning hotter and filling him with the desperate need to act, to move, to explode. "Your commanding officer?" The markings next to the Eliran emblem on the man's shoulder showed him to be a captain and therefore not the head of the garrison at the outpost.

"Gone with the rest, sir." The man lifted his head to meet Elgon's gaze, and there was a flash in his eyes. He straightened his shoulders and held firm in the gathering light of morning.

Elgon nodded. He could relate. "I'm leaving you in charge. A third of our men abandoned us in the middle of the night and one of my soldiers was injured. I am fearing that this was not an isolated incident. I must see that my friend is taken care of and then ride with all haste to Niran. Are you capable of that, soldier?"

The soldier dipped his head in a nod. "Aye, sir. I shall do my very best to be worthy of the station."

Elgon gave the kingsman a slight bow of thanks. "See that the townsfolk are cared for and protected at all costs. And those that are left must gather forces, prepare for the defensive, and be ready for word from the capital. If the treachery that has occurred is spread, as I suspect, the betrayal will go with us beyond this night."

The soldier bowed, raising his fist again to his shoulder pauldron and then in a salute to his forehead. "I shall strive to be worthy of such trust, sir."

Elgon nodded to him, then the townsfolk who had been standing by with folded arms and slack jaws, and nudged Sigeric into a trot, his hand holding his sword steady at his side.

This day would see no rest until he was assured of his wife's and child's safety. It was at this moment that he wished beyond anything he could ever wish that he was not the ruler of the country. Even kings could spurn their crown and leaders could desire to be the lonely soldier in the barracks, with little responsibility and nothing to lose save the life that was given them.

And there was something in him that hated himself for thinking such a selfish thing.

He caught up with the wagon in enough time to reach the Medicinal Lodge at the same time. Kenton's face was whiter than the undyed wool blanket that covered him, the handprints and smears of blood marring the fleece and bringing to mind the image of the spotless Savior, wounded, torn, and bloodied for the transgressions of His children. Elgon swallowed. He would not weep. There would be time enough for that at some later date.

The moments mounted like the sand the waves brought upon the seashore, pounding more earth on top of itself, again and again, tireless and persistent, but oh so slow, chipping away, one moment at a time. No one was moving fast enough, and he himself felt as though he were caught in quicksand that glued his boots to the ground, making every step heavy, hard, and slow.

The door opened and there was that face. Wide-eyed, tired, but ready for anything.

"Marcus." Elgon drew his brother into an embrace.

"Elgon? Of all the… What on earth are you doing here?"

Elgon drew back, motioning with his hand to his squire resting on the stretcher the men were sliding from the wagon.

"I've a patient for you. He's given much, and I hope to return the sacrifice he has made and spare his life."

Fendrel came up behind Marcus, his face drawn, slightly older looking, but those gray eyes were just as bright and knowing. He was sliding his arms into his jerkin and tying the front closed over his tunic; his long, nimble fingers made quick work of the knot even as his eyes surely took in every single detail of what lay before him.

He motioned them over the threshold without a word, and Elgon stooped to grip a side of the stretcher. Kenton barely moved or made a sound, and were it not for the fluttering eyelids, Elgon would have thought him already dead.

Marcus's hand was on his arm as they made their way up the step and through the doorway of the lodge. It had undergone some improvements since Elgon had seen it merely a year ago. A large room had been built off the back, and more beds separated by curtains hung from the rafters with metal rings. They took Kenton to one such bed, and with directions from Fendrel, they lifted the boy as carefully as they could and laid him gently upon the white sheets.

A young woman, brown hair tied into a braid far down her back and a shawl wrapped tightly over her shoulders, crossed in the front and tied in back, slipped past him with a basin and cloth in hand. She cast him a shy and wide-eyed look, her brown eyes reminding him of the doe he encountered in Raintamount Forest.

It must be Dilara, the young woman Marcus had written them about. Now his wife.

Few words were spoken, and what few were uttered were whispered in soft tones as Fendrel and Dilara worked in tandem, their bodies and hands flowing like water over stones in a gentle stream as they cleaned and ministered to Kenton, unwrapping the bloodied bandages and examining the wounds.

Elgon turned away from the sight, guilt, fear, anger, and sorrow washing over him in waves. Two steadying hands rested on his shoulders, and he looked up into cornflower blue eyes. They were as clear and strong as ever, a few lines around them pinching as Marcus examined his face.

"You've been through much this night, my brother." It was a statement, and Elgon's shoulders loosened as he took a shuddering breath. Despite the months between their last meeting, Marcus needed no words to know a little of what Elgon had experienced. It was his gift—to see what others could only guess.

"I must make haste to Niran." He turned and glanced back at Kenton who was already being prepared for surgery by Fendrel and Dilara's helping hand. "Take care of him, won't you?"

Marcus nodded, following his gaze and walking beside him as Elgon headed for the door, his limp reminding Elgon to slow so that his friend could keep pace with his longer strides. Marcus was using his light cane, but he seemed more able and stronger than when Elgon had seen him last.

Elgon smiled softly, pushing the worries from his mind for just a second. "Married life treating you well, old friend?"

Marcus paused and gave him a long look as if he were reading his mood before letting a small, sad smile slip out. "Aye. I know you can relate."

"The months will grow sweeter yet, though you know not how at this moment."

Marcus's smile broadened. "I'll have to take your word for it. What a beautiful mystery it is to love a woman and to be the object of her affection also."

"The Lord loves mysteries."

Marcus nodded as they moved once more for the door. "It's Violet, isn't it?"

Elgon halted in the doorway. "What do you mean?" His fingers returned to the hilt of his blade and gripped it fiercely.

"I woke with a nightmare. I know not what it means, but you are in a hurry to reach Niran. She is your greatest treasure that resides there."

Elgon fought back full blown panic that felt like it had snuck up and attacked him from behind, his head pounding with the sudden force of it. It stole his breath, his strength, and made his very thoughts collapse into chaos.

Until that hand rested on his arm again. "Don't forget who your God is. You are not king alone, my friend. Despite what sorrow you have faced this day or what you are about to encounter, know that His throne has not been left vacant. He was betrayed once too; he knows the feeling well. Ride with God, and know that His rule still stands, though others may have fought to steal yours from you again."

"How did you know?" If Marcus had been asleep when the division and mutiny had occurred at the garrison and Elgon had not said a word about the events…

"I don't, but the Lord does." There was pain and worry in Marcus's eyes, and Elgon could tell that his brother was fighting to remain calm. Emotions were etched into every line of his face. "I worry for you both, but even my worry must be surrendered to the King. I shall pray for you through your travels and after. Whatever state of affairs meets you, remember that your name and Violet's will not leave my heart in prayer for a second."

"Pray for the country too, Marcus. That it would recover whatever the extent of the loss it has endured this night."

"I will. But it's morning. Ride on the wings of the sun and remember who placed it in the sky."

Elgon clutched Marcus to his chest in an embrace that the medicinal and seer returned with as much grip as he could muster, the pressure and whispered words of prayer in Elgon's ear as settling and grounding as an anchor to a ship in a storm.

"Go with God, my friend. My king." Marcus pulled away, bobbed in a bow, and gave Elgon a subtle shove toward the door. "I will send word of the state of your young squire."

Elgon and his company of kingsmen were mounted and on their way without delay. As they cantered through the gates of Padsley, the sun mounted the horizon, its red-orange hue casting shadows across the ground to their left, their movement setting them to dancing in the tree line just off the King's Highway.

The blood red hue set Elgon's mind on the worst he might face when he returned home. Sweat beaded on his brow despite the sun's slow ascent. He prayed that there was little blood spilt in his capital city… or within his palace walls.

One broken body was enough for one night.

ROSALIE, PRESENT DAY...

Malcolm's large hand dragged Rosalie quickly toward the little hut built into the side of the mountain. If one wasn't looking for it, one could easily miss it, so overgrown by its habitat as it was.

She was breathless by the time they reached the door. He dragged her in, slamming it shut behind them.

"They're here. They're after her."

"Saints alive, Lord preserve us." Mother Hobbs shoved the kitchen table across the floor and threw the woven rug off the floorboards. Dust shook out in a cloud from the rug and Rosalie coughed, covering her face with her sleeve. She wanted to fly into action, but the weight bearing down on her made the war within her threaten to explode.

Removing a few cuts of the plank floors, Mother Hobbs gestured her in, gripping her by the arms and pulling her toward the dark hole in the ground.

Suddenly everything in her balked against her own will. She wanted to be brave, to step foot into hiding for her own safety and for the safety of those that protected her, but her body was outside of her rational mind and her fears wrapped her in their chain-like grip. Terror, like lightning, poured through her veins.

"I-I can't." She breathed her words past the lump in her throat that was threatening to gag her.

"You must; there's no time." Rosalie saw the fear that gathered in Mother Hobbs' gray eyes. It flashed there for a moment but then was gone the next as her mouth whispered unintelligible words and she threw her gaze heavenward.

Rosalie might as well have been frozen in a block of ice. Stone solid, stiff, and unyielding.

You have to go. You have to get in. Save yourself, clawed at her mind with deep scratches that still didn't penetrate the stillness.

Hands gripped her beneath the arms and brought her toward the hole. She wanted to scream, to fight them, to beat them off of her, but just like every time, she didn't fight. She couldn't. The fear of fighting was worse than the fear of the darkness closing in around her.

Until it did. She gasped for breath, and the shadows caved in on her, the boards placed over her head and the scrambling sounds above barely making it past the roaring in her ears. She couldn't breathe. Couldn't move. Every muscle was taught against the intangible fear that something, anything, would swallow her in this pit and she would die here, alone, forgotten, tortured with everything she dreamed of and everything she would never see again.

Horses' hooves shook the ground and the panic intensified. She gasped for breath.

Mother Hobbs' whispered words filtering through the floorboards met her ears. "Hush, little one. Keep still. Christ is with you in the darkness as He is in the light."

She must have placed the rug over the floorboards again for even the tiny slivers of light that shone into her hideaway disappeared…and with them, every vestige of control or calm.

Quote the light, Rosie. Don't let the darkness swallow you when you know the lamp to your feet by heart.

Words. Light in the darkness. She swallowed back a sob and the nausea and tried to keep her breathing steady. She couldn't be heard. Couldn't be seen. Couldn't be discovered.

Hide me. Hide me in your tent. Shelter me in your secret place. Don't let me go. Don't let me be found.

"For thou wilt light my candle: the Lord my God will enlighten my darkness. I will not leave you in the darkness. The light and the darkness is all the same to me. I can see you. I won't lose you. I won't abandon you to the shadows. I'm here with you in it. My light dawns even in darkness. Shadows cannot harm you in my presence and my presence is with you wherever you go."

She pulled her knees to her chest, wrapping them tight to hold off the feeling that wanted to explode within her. She stretched her heart nearer that of her Savior, squeezing her eyes shut against the darkness. Willing, praying for the light to return.

"My light dawns in the darkness. Those that I love, that I protect, that love me and my ways, they will always have my light to guide them. Darkness is not dark to me, no shadow overwhelms me. Night is as the light to Me. I shine like the day against the shadows. I am the light of noonday. My word is a lamp unto your feet and a light to your path."

Tears chased each other down her face, her nose filling, and she tried to refrain from sniffing. Not a sound, not a movement. Not the slightest scuffle could be heard from above.

She jolted as a heavy fist pounded on the door and the loud, commanding voice with a Rusalkan accent echoed in the stillness.

"Open the door by order of the king!"

She heard soft footsteps—Mother Hobbs shuffling across the floor. Dirt shook down and landed softly on her head and shoulders. She cringed away from it, the sensation taking her by surprise and ratcheting up the tightness in her muscles.

Whenever I am afraid, I will trust in you.

The door creaked open, and heavy footsteps, more than one pair, entered the room above her, the vibrations rattling in her head, intensifying the pounding that had started in her temples.

She heard more shuffling and someone stumbled into the table that rested over the opening above her. The rattle of the heavy wooden furniture made her start, and she held her breath, trying to remain as still as possible.

"Who else do you have in this cabin beside you? Who is that?"

"Oi, easy, soldier." Mother Hobbs' voice was weaker than Rosalie remembered, trembling and thin. "Spare a poor old woman. My aches be acting up something fierce these days."

"I said"—the strange, deep and angered voice growled through clenched teeth—"who is that? Answer me before I drag them from their bed."

"Och, ye're grip is rough, laddy." Rosalie tensed at Mother Hobbs' strained and trembling words. "'Tis my poor son. He took ill something fierce, and I've kept the neighbors away ever since. I'm afraid it'll be catching. Wouldn't be the least surprised if I came down with it myself. He's been burnin' with fever and he's been outta his head these last three days. I've been feeling mighty poorly myself of late. The fire hasn't seemed to keep away the aches and chills."

The table creaked again, and the footsteps moved away from Rosalie's spot under the table. Curses flooded the room and burned her ears. "If you've got me sick, woman…"

"Sakes alive, I didn't break *your* door down in the middle of dusk," Mother Hobbs retorted with that innocent, shaky voice.

He growled back, then shuffled further away. "Get up, man! Is there anyone else in the house?"

Rosalie heard the bed-clothes rustling, a moan, and incoherent chatter come from what must have been Malcolm. She drew a deep breath.

More curses spewed from the intruder's mouth, and even though Rosalie daren't move, she so desperately wanted to cover her ears.

"Search the hut, men. Leave no stone unturned," he barked.

"I ought to warn ye, soldier. The plague's been spreading in these parts like sparks to dry timber. We've stayed in me cottage this time to protect the neighbors and the townfolk, lest we be carrying it. Me son did come home sick from the time he spent with the Vagari, and ye know how they be known for carrying such filth from where they go, hither and yon over all creation."

Another expletive laced the air and a few stomps across the room, then pots clanging, furniture moving. Rosalie shuddered in the darkness. *Keep them away from the table. Don't let them near. Don't take me back.*

"I can give ye a rabbit's foot and some herbs if ye'd like to keep the plague away. It has worked for me thus far." Mother Hobbs shuffled across the floor, seemingly toward her herbs that Rosalie knew she kept strung from the back wall.

The air was thick, frigid suddenly, and Rosalie couldn't get a breath. She tried to stifle her gasp for air, but not enough met her burning lungs, and her throat seized. She felt as though she might be buried alive in this hole. All of their stomping and creaking of the floorboards felt like they would cave in on her at any moment.

"Let's go, men! Keep your witchcraft, woman. And if you see a young lass, ye're to report it to the knights stationed in the town below."

"A lass, ye say?"

"Oh, shut up and follow orders," he muttered as he stomped from the house, and the cottage door slammed shut in his wake.

Rosalie's head pounded, her eyes feeling swollen, dry, and hot. She clung to her skirts with her hands in fists in the fabric, her jaw popping from the tension. They weren't out of the woods yet.

The table grumbled as it was scooted across the floor and light filtered in. She couldn't move. She was still frozen, her head feeling hot, but every other limb was shaking and frigid. Suddenly the golden light cascaded down onto her, and her eyes flared against the sudden barrage of radiance.

Hands gripped her around the arms, startling her, and she lashed out, her mind half thinking the knights had returned and were dragging her from her hiding place.

"Oi, lass. Breathe deep, dearie. They be gone for now. They'll not trouble ye while Malcolm and I still have breath," Mother Hobbs whispered, but it was Malcolm who had pulled her from the dank and frigid hole in the floor, pulling her close even as she struck at him with a hand she could barely feel until she was held.

Tighter than she had ever been in her life, even by Zehra, and those memories were long lost to the deeper recesses that held those childhood years in the golden glow of companionship before the vast gray of loneliness.

Strong arms held her stiff form. The muscles in her neck kept her head at a distance until the arms didn't let go and she collapsed against the strong chest and into the warmth of an embrace that seemed to break something in her.

The panic fled. The fear departed. A sob slipped from her lips and a hand cradled the back of her head as she clenched the shoulders of his tunic in her hands.

"Let it out." The whisper was soft in her ear and deep of tone. "You don't have to hide anymore."

As the silent sobs shook her shoulders and her entire body trembled all over, she knew he didn't mean hiding from her captors. There would be plenty of that ahead. But pretending with him, hiding from him, worrying what he might think or do… She didn't have to hide her spirit.

In that moment as the fire crackled, the warmth returned to her body and to her spirit. Blood flowed into her sleeping limbs as tears flowed from her eyes, and she felt truly known. Held despite her fears. Not berated for them, or forced to hide them.

But loved in spite of them.

She wasn't alone against the world anymore. She let the sobs come, the tears, long hidden and dammed up, finally sprung free like a glacier lake, suddenly rid of the ice that had held it captive so long.

And with the ice cap melting, there was room for new growth. Spring was coming.

Eighteen

FAREWELLS

ELGON, FOURTEEN YEARS AGO...

Elgon's heart beat in time with the pounding of Sigeric's hooves as the moor sped by beneath the swift black feet. The canter had long since given way to a gallop again, and even Sigeric's lighting speed was not fast enough for Elgon. His heart was already in Niran, wandering the streets, trying desperately to guess what he would find there.

His men were behind him, doing their best to keep up with his pace. Instead of slowing when the gates of Niran rose from the fog of the moors to meet his gaze, he dug his heels in. The sea air was sharp in his nostrils, the salt in the mist coating his skin until he tasted it as he licked his lips. A storm was mounting on the horizon, black clouds roiling over the sea and mist like steam from a boiling cauldron gathering thick and blowing in off the water.

The gates were barely tended with two guards when he reached them, and already the dread that filled every fiber of his being sprung into action, making his vision blur and his body feel physically ill. As the doors swung open, Elgon noticed the proper guards were missing and the bedraggled kingsmen ran to him, their mouths open with shouts frozen on their tongues. He swept past them, urging Sigeric to greater speed as he wound his way through the smog-infested city streets. The sound of Sigeric's hooves on the cobblestones clattered and echoed off the stone walls that suddenly felt much too near, as if threatening to collapse and bury him alive.

God, please. Please. Please.

Every iteration breathed in time with the beat of his heart as it thundered in his chest.

The streets steepened, and Sigeric faithfully conquered them with the same speed even as he wound and turned sharply around every corner. The palace walls rose above him, and the sight of them, quiet and still, set his mind to racing.

Elgon pulled Sigeric to a stop in the stableyard harsher than he had meant to, and the horse tossed his head. Throwing his cloak over one shoulder and reaching a hand to the hilt of his sword, Elgon's fingers toyed with the golden crown on the end of it. His footsteps ate up the space in front of him even as his legs wobbled beneath the intensity of the ride and the adrenaline coursed through his veins. The feeling was so explosive, as he turned every corner, he worried he would react and hurt someone who came at him, even if they were on his side.

But who could he trust now? Who was to say that any of the kingsmen were on his side?

Malcolm… Surely he would still be standing.

Why were the halls so empty? He turned another corner before he met the entry to the throne room, and he moved to pass it to go directly to the family quarters. He would not rest until he had Violet in his arms.

But his feet froze to the cobblestones.

Blood. So much blood. Dark brown mixed with the red of the rug. The wooden archways of the doors hung battered, askew from their hinges. And bodies.

Bodies covered in red-stained sheets lined the hall. The throne room stood empty, arrows broken and scattered across the marble floors. The gray, thin light pouring in from the cathedral windows cast murky shadows across the floor.

He gasped for air, tears of horror gathering in his eyes as he stared. Nothing moved or breathed in that hall or that room.

He turned, stumbling over his own feet and the cracks in the floor as his walk turned to a full sprint down the hall toward the family quarters.

"Vi-" He choked on his own words, far too soft in the darkening stillness. The hallway lengthened under his feet, and the walls stretched in to crush him between them. "Violet!" He shouted into the darkness as he ran to the door of their room and flung it open, his hands fumbling with the ring and catch.

Nothing greeted his call. No warm, soft body came to his embrace. Not a breath stirred in the apartment or the sitting room of the next.

Violet. "God, help me," tore from his throat like a sob.

He turned and ran. The kitchens, the medicinal hall. Anywhere. There had to be someone in this castle. His servants were too many to hide for long…if they were still alive.

His footsteps faltered at the thought, but he pressed on.

Turning a corner, he fairly ran into a maid, and she dropped the dish she was carrying, its earthenware pieces shattering and skittering across the floor. He gripped her shoulders to keep them both from falling. Her face was tear-stained, eyes wide and her cap askew on her brown hair.

"Where is everyone?" He didn't let go of her shoulders, his hands like vices gripping her flesh.

She bobbed her head from side to side and moved her mouth, but no words came out.

He shook her. "Where?" He was almost shouting with his hoarse voice, the hand of terror squeezing it tight in its grip.

"Th-they're in the m-medicinal hall." She gasped and he released her, running before she had time to say another word. His wife, his child. Perhaps the baby had come early. How many were wounded? If there were that many dead, Violet had her bow and she would do what she could to protect their child, but perhaps the shock had sent her into labor. Would he have two to embrace instead of just one? God forbid she was hurt…

The doors to the medicinal hall were cracked open, and they squeaked and then slammed into the stone walls as he threw them wide. A few medicinals and their apprentices looked up in shock, their bodies moving into the defensive, then relaxing as they recognized him. He headed toward the main healer.

"Raphart." He breathed a sigh of relief as he trotted to the older man and lifted a hand to his shoulder. "Where is my wife? Has she given birth? Why is she not in our apartments?"

The man froze. He opened his mouth to speak, but nothing came out before he clapped it shut again, his eyes wide as they darted to a corner of the room and then back.

Elgon followed his gaze, but there was nothing there but a curtain. Perhaps they had given Violet some privacy. He turned to go, but Raphart gripped his arm in a vice like grip, a tremble making its way from his fingertips. "Majesty, m'lord. You must know..."

The dread in Raphart's voice threw Elgon, and he tossed his arm free of the healer and dashed to the corner, pulling back the curtain. His feet arrested from further movement, he stared in disbelief. Violet was not in the bed holding a babe, or cradling her swollen stomach... Instead, it was Malcolm.

His second in command. Blood in his hair, deep purple bruises and cuts covering his face and chest beneath bandages that were wrapped tight and stained with more of the blood.

He swallowed back the bile rising in his throat. He swayed on his feet until a steadying hand grabbed his arm once more.

He turned back to the healer. "Violet," he gasped.

"She's been taken, m'lord."

His knees buckled and he met the stones.

ROSALIE, PRESENT DAY...

Rosalie stuffed the pair of wool socks Mother Hobbs had knitted for her into the leather satchel that would be hers to carry and rolled her head, trying to loosen the stiffness in her neck from her foray into the darkness beneath the cottage.

Malcolm had forced her to get some sleep before they set out, and it took her some time to come down off the ledge of heightened emotions, fears, and worries over the very real possibility that the Rusalk knights might come back. But they needed to give the soldiers time to wander away from the cottage and conduct their search elsewhere before she and Malcolm ran off into the woods. The knights might be waiting for them, a trap set in the thickness of the brush to take them the moment they fled.

When sleep had come, it had been nightmarish, filled with the shadows of her castle prison and the very real and foreboding fears she had experienced in the darkness. She had woken with a start, sending the bedclothes flying as if they had been rope that held her bound.

Malcolm had rested a hand on her shoulder, the presence and weight of it bringing a comfort that chased the shadows away. So much of her life had been dictated by her loneliness, by isolation and the need that her captors had of making her feel helpless in her captivity. There was something about knowing she wasn't alone anymore.

And yet, even as she had a companion, a protector, a comfort, it was just as much a confusion to her. She had been taught to avoid contact, to keep others at a distance. To truly know someone was to know the depths of the evil inside, the pain that made them who they were and the darkness that crafted the inner workings of their heart. And from that, she hid. The curse of seeing who one was at their core had been hers from the earliest of days, but instead of it bringing her wisdom or strength, it had taken her into the depths. She had crawled out of those painful places on the steps and handholds of the Word and of the truth that had been drilled into her heart that could take even the darkest shadows and send them fleeing.

Being held, letting the walls down, allowing one person to see inside to the places and emptiness that was her own, came with its own fear. What evil would they see in her? What would she see in them?

"Rosalie, we must go."

The words startled her, and she clutched her bag to her chest, avoiding Malcolm's eyes as he towered over her. She drew in a steadying deep breath and tried to still the shaking of her hands all wrapped up in the leather strap of her satchel.

Mother Hobbs must be thanked, and in that, there was ample distraction. But tears sprang to her eyes. She had not known the woman long, but everything in her wished she could stay. That the woman who had cared for her and tended her could be with her always. The hunger had been stoked, that burning desire to be loved, nurtured, mothered. It had her clinging to this cottage, this home. These happy memories of recovery and coziness and freedom amidst the painful journey of hellos and farewells.

Her chin quivered, and she stopped in front of the old woman, who promptly pulled her into an embrace. Rosalie dropped the satchel to the floor and wrapped her arms around the woman's middle.

Mother Hobbs held tight and smoothed the hair that had escaped Rosalie's braid back from her face. "Dear child, don't let the evils of what you have gone through shape you. Don't let hopes dashed make you cease hoping. Don't let abuses make you shy away from being loved. Don't let farewells bring you pain, but only the remembrance that we will meet again one day in heaven."

Rosalie clung to her, tears spilling from her eyes. The comforting smell of rosemary, thyme, and clove clung to the woman who held her, and she hoped to remember it as long as she could. Perhaps when she was queen one day, she would be able to bring the people who had such a hand in her rescue to her new home that they might be together always.

Rosalie finally pulled back, her eye catching on a darkened spot behind the neckline of Mother Hobbs' chemise. There it was again—the dove, tiny, but etched in black on her collarbone. Rosalie couldn't help but stare at it until Mother Hobbs turned and took something off the table.

"This is for you. God forbid that ye should need it, but better supplied than not." It was a knife, its handle twined in leather and worn to fit comfortably in her small hand. She took it from Mother Hobbs and tested the weight, the leather warming as it molded to her hand. She pulled it out of the leather sheath and shuddered at the golden light glinting off the curved steel.

"There." Mother Hobbs rested her hands on top of Rosalie's and guided the knife back into its sheath and helped her string it onto her belt, refastening the buckle at her waist when she was done. "I pray ye don't have to use it. But Malcolm will teach ye how. He's a master at the craft, and you couldn't ask for a better teacher. He taught me a few revolutions once upon a time." The old woman winked up at Malcolm who stood by, his feet wide, arms folded in readiness.

She helped Rosalie on with her cloak and tied it under her chin. Before either of them could move, she grabbed both their hands in hers and poured forth a prayer with her eyes closed and face upraised. "Lord, take these wanderers home. There's been an entire country waiting for the hope and promise of their daughter's return. Don't fail them now. We trust that you go behind and before them, you make a way where there is no way. You can part seas, and still the sun and make seeing eyes blind, and we ask that you do this on their behalf. Keep them hidden, keep them safe, and take them home."

Rosalie scrubbed at the tears that wet her face with a fist and pulled her cloak tight around her shoulders, already feeling the chill before they stepped outside the door.

"God go with ye, my children. I know He does."

A sob jerked from Rosalie's throat as they trotted on foot away from the cottage. Turning, she caught sight of Mother Hobbs raising a hand in farewell from her open doorway, her shawl wrapped tight around her shoulders. As they reached the rocky outcropping that protected the clearing, Rosalie paused. Would that these ceaseless farewells would one day be a thing of the past and new friends would not be gone to her forever after first meeting.

The hand on her shoulder urged her onward, and she followed its prompting, ducking behind the rocks and into the crevice that held its own version of gloom. She felt as though she couldn't breathe and tripped over her own feet and the gravel beneath them as she rushed through the narrow tunnel, cut through the boulders, and nearly fell through the opening into the forest beyond.

Would she never get away from the darkness? She trembled at the shadows that filled the forest, and the very real fear of the night before made her breath come short. Whirling one way, then the next, she strained her eyes to see what was lurking in the mist and murkiness of the foggy pine forest.

A pair of birds flew chattering from a tree beside them, and she spun hard, gasping, her feet catching and throwing her to the ground.

Malcolm's kind brown eyes swooped into her vision, the hair that had escaped the tie at the base of his neck framing his face as he bent, an arm extended to help her up.

Her chest heaved with each breath, and she hesitated before taking his hand.

"The darkness scatters before the face of the dawn we carry. Don't let it frighten you. Darkness in and of itself has no power over us and never will. Not unless we let it." His words were low, soft, but clear as Izevel's bell as it peeled over the mountains.

She swallowed against the dryness in her throat and reached forward to take his arm. He hauled her to her feet.

"My light shines in the darkness and the darkness will not and cannot overcome it. Walk in the light, child. Walk in the protection I have set for you. Fear not, for I am with you."

MALCOLM, PRESENT DAY...

Malcolm kept his hand low so Rosalie could catch it should she need assistance navigating any rough patches as they moved quickly through dense underbrush. They would have a steep climb as soon as they broke the treeline, and he wanted to make sure that they were well away from any area where the dark knights would be hunting. He veered farther east than he would have wanted, but he could take no chances after the surprise visit to Mother Hobbs' cottage late last night.

The ground tilted upward, and he grasped Rosalie's hand, helping her over a few rocks. He didn't let go. She would need his help to make it up this hill, and he knew that she would never ask for it. He towed her along after him, his hand holding hers tightly and maneuvering her expertly over rough terrain.

God, forgive me my foolishness. He cursed himself silently. He had been lulled to comfort by the time spent in the little clearing. By the freedom they both had felt. He had watched Rosalie blossom day by day as her strength grew and her injury healed. Seen her joyful discovery of one new thing and then another. Took note of the light in her eyes as she began making her own choices, even in the smallest of ways, be it helping Mother Hobbs in the kitchen, moving about the home and outside at will, or tending the stock.

He couldn't help but smile at that.

How she loved those animals. She was a natural with them. His delight dissipated quickly into anger that boiled deep as he realized that tending an animal of any kind and showing it love was a luxury that had never been afforded her. If only they could have found her sooner. What strength would have been hers had she been allowed the things that had always been denied her.

What joy would have been hers if she and her mother had never been stolen in the first place. He gritted his teeth and tried to keep the scenes of the past from flooding his mind, but they settled like swallows roosting in towers anyway.

He sucked air in through his nostrils. All these years, all the spies, the attempts at discovering her whereabouts, at rescuing her, and he had almost let it all slip through their fingers. He was the wrong man for this job, and yet Elgon, his king, had trusted him with something that he swore he could trust no other man with.

Didn't he remember the failure? The pain? The sorrow that had been theirs for the last fourteen years? Had he forgotten that it was all at Malcolm's hands that it had come about? His one failure had wiped out a queen, stolen their child, lost their most dangerous prisoner, and routed an entire kingdom that had fallen into disorder and mutiny of the worst sort.

His weakness had been the lynch-pin that had allowed the betrayal of the century to occur. His countrymen, his fellow soldiers, his king, queen, and princess—all those he loved as his own family—had been destroyed, broken, killed…because of his oversight.

He should have seen it. Should have recognized its presence. Should have felt the betrayal like the stinking worm that it was, poisoning the men and the country, working its way from the inside out, rotting them all at the core.

It had been his job to see it. Why hadn't he?

The hand in his squeezed back and tugged, and he turned to catch Rosalie's eyes. They were knowing, soft. Her hair blew in the wind, escaping her braid, just as unruly as her mother's. He felt her gaze go much deeper than the surface, pouring into him with an astuteness that she had hidden until now.

She tilted her head sideways, her eyebrows furrowing. "It wasn't your fault."

Four simple words. And they nearly undid him.

His eyes stung, burning with tears he had never shed, remnants of pain that had never seen the light of day.

He turned sharply, pulling her farther up the hill. She grunted and he stopped, remorse filling him as she rubbed her shoulder with a wince.

"Sorry," he muttered. He had let his emotions get in the way of his job, let his fears and worries shape who he was sworn to be: her protector.

"You pull like you're trying to escape something else entirely." Those eyes drilled into him again.

He didn't have the heart to tell her. She ought to know. He owed her his honesty, but just now, her faith in him was the strongest thing keeping him going.

She didn't know her mother was dead at his hands… Her blood upon his head. Blood he would never be free from until he had seen her home and safe again in the father's arms she had been stolen from for all these years.

Her fingers crept into his again, and he looked down, surprised by the trust and love that poured from her as if she were giving him permission. "Pull away."

He swallowed back the lump at the back of his throat and faced forward again. He needed to be strong, to protect her. He had to hold it together. He couldn't let her get to him. He couldn't let the feeling of family and the relationship formed by a brotherhood cloud his judgment. Not again.

Attachment was out of the question. He tried to ignore the fire burning in his gut as they climbed. That feeling elicited by the touch of someone smaller, weaker, more innocent than oneself.

He had sworn never to be a father for this very reason. He had seen what it had done to Elgon, what a life without that love and devotion, once tasted and then removed, could be. How after having it, everything paled in comparison, everything lost its appeal and sorrow became a constant friend. In his line of work, all it took was one wrong move to see your Maker by the end of day. One battle gone awry, one horse losing its footing, one slip of the watch and you would be gone from this world forever…and he would never do that to a family.

To a wife. To children…to himself. He had sworn not to be the reason someone bore a lifelong sorrow. Never again.

They reached the cliff face that they needed to climb to get up the escarpment to the next clearing where they would meet the band of Vagari that would be their refuge. If they could make it to them without being found, they could rest in the comfort of more protection and the knowledge of faithfulness in their ranks.

"Wrap this around you." Malcolm held out an end of rope after slinging it off his shoulder.

Rosalie followed instructions, her eyes darting down the path behind them with concern, then back up at the cliff face. "We're going to climb that?"

He nodded, tying an end of the rope to the straps of his pack. "Aye. Leastways, I'll climb it with you on my back."

Her face went pale, and her flushed cheeks stood out against the whiteness.

His voice softened. The harshness had started to grate on even his own ears. "We'll be alright. You did just fine last time." He took the end of the rope she had wrapped around herself and tied it off tightly.

"I might have, but the animal didn't." She shuddered, her eyes going dark.

Malcolm winced. The image of the pony going over the cliff with her on its back and her terrified screams still haunted him in his dreams. Thank God he had pulled her to safety in time.

He bent to one knee in front of her as he tied the rope around his own waist. Placing his hand on her shoulder, he held her gaze. "And just like last time, I won't let you fall."

She stared into his eyes and bit her trembling lip. She nodded.

"You have to promise me that no matter what, you don't let go unless I tell you to. No matter how uncertain it feels, or how frightened you are. Do you understand?"

She swallowed and nodded again, her face going a shade green.

He nodded back. "All right. Climb up." He turned, taking her hands and guiding them over his head and locking them around his neck as she climbed on his back and clutched his sides with her legs.

Reaching for a handhold and a foothold at the same time, he scuffed a few loose rocks with his toes and used them to propel them upward.

This wasn't a new experience for him. He'd spent the better part of the last few years forraying through Rusalka, getting closer and closer to finding Rosalie, meeting with other spies and conferring with accomplices via way of the crags and cliffs with nothing but a few strips of cloth wrapped around the palms of his hands and nearly as much weight on his back as he carried now.

He grunted, reaching again for a hold, and he felt the hammering of Rosalie's heart through his back where she clung on like a burr, doing her best not to move unless she shifted as he transferred their weight from one hand or foot to the other.

Good lass, she was holding on for dear life. "Breathe." He ground out through gritted teeth, reminding her as well as himself.

A gasp met his ear, and he tried not to smile.

Just a few more feet, and they'd be at the top. A branch cracking from below threw him off balance and Rosalie gasped, but he dug his hands into their grip with a grunt.

If they were being followed, Rosalie was fair game for any arrow shot their way. He heaved with all that he had, stepping one last time before his hand broke the top of the ledge, digging into the rock to pull them up.

He rolled over the top edge of the cliff just as quickly as he was high enough, throwing Rosalie behind his own body like a shield and rolling again, pulling them both away from the edge.

She grunted and scrambled away on her hands and knees as far as the rope between them allowed. He reached for the slack one that hung from his belt, heaving it hand over hand till his pack popped over the side and bounded across the space toward him.

Breathing heavily, he tried to still the roaring of his heart in his ears. He didn't dare peer over the edge without listening first lest an arrow between the eyes be the only thing that met him.

Silence.

No noise aside from the wind occasionally whistling through the pines.

Crawling on his elbows, he pulled himself toward the ledge, lifting just enough to see over with one eye. The hackles rose on the back of his neck, but nothing met his gaze. Shaking his head at his own foolishness he turned, and his heart stuttered to a stop as he froze.

A man towered over Rosalie from where she lay on her back, eyes wide with terror, her hands raised in the air in surrender. He held a curved scimitar of the Rusalk to her throat, but his eyes were on Malcolm. She made a low noise in her throat, but he didn't flinch.

Malcolm swallowed.

The man shifted.

ROSALIE, PRESENT DAY...

Everything stood still in that moment, every hope and dream of her heart suddenly lying shattered on the ground around her like a broken mirror—all reflecting back at her the desires of her heart.

The man suddenly cursed and dropped the hand with the blade immediately. "Malcolm? Saints alive, man, ye scared the living daylights out of me."

He reached down as if to grab her elbow, but she thrust a closed fist at his face—missed—and kicked at his shins before scrambling away, but the rope between her and Malcolm kept her from going more than a few inches. A scream rose in the back of her throat, but it stuck there, choking her.

"Sh, sh, it's all right." Malcolm was on his knees now, his hands out in a pacifying gesture until she was still long enough for him to pull a knife and cut the rope that held them bound. She gasped for breath, her eyes darting between the two large figures, trying to swallow back the fear that tasted like acid on her tongue.

"That's it, breathe. He's a friend. I promise."

The man nodded, the brown cloak tossed about his shoulders fluttering in the breeze. A faded red pattern peeked out from the underside when the wind lifted a corner. "I'm so sorry, m'lady. 'Twas a terrible mistake on my part. We didn't know what to think, and we have women and children to protect." He stepped back to give her even more room, sheathing his weapon at his side and lifting his palms in a placating gesture.

Malcolm didn't move toward her, but she could tell he wanted to. He opened his hand, palm up in invitation for her to take it. "He will not hurt you. He's on our side. They are here to protect you."

She swallowed and glanced between them. The stranger stood far enough away, his weapon sheathed and a look of remorse on his face. Rosalie slipped trembling fingers into Malcolm's outstretched hand. He pulled her to her feet, but her knees buckled, and he caught her around the waist.

She sucked in another deep breath to steady her, and he helped her to a rock where she could sit.

"The man below—one of yours?" he asked as he uncorked the leather waterskin and handed it to her so she could quench her thirst.

"Aye, a scout, like myself. We've heard the Rusalk knights have been up in the woods but not this near yet, thank God. But the travelers have been more frequent of late, and we didn't want them getting suspicious."

Malcolm left his hand on Rosalie's shoulder and held out his other to the man who clasped his wrist in return.

"Garridan, at your service, sir, m'lady. I'll lead you back to the caravan. Rominik will be glad to know you made it through. We've been expecting you for some time."

"Unavoidable delay. We almost got taken at Vieggo's place."

"Horse—" The man choked off the word and swallowed it with a sheepish look at Rosalie, running his hand through his long black hair and rubbing the back of his neck. "Glad you made it through all right. What happened to them?"

Malcolm patted Rosalie's shoulder. "The lass saved my life."

She looked up, surprised, and caught a slight smile on his lips as he raised an eyebrow at her.

"Either way, Vieggo said he'd be taken care of until we were out of danger."

"Oi." Garridan shook his head. "Well, if the lass is ready, I'll take you to the caravan. You look like you could use a good meal, a cup of tea, and a comfortable bed where you don't have to continually look over your shoulder."

"How could you tell?" Malcolm smiled softly. She could see the tiredness in the wrinkles near the corners of his eyes. He had kept watch while she had slept before they left Mother Hobbs'.

Shadows lengthened across the landscape as they entered another copse of trees. After traveling uphill most of the day, her legs shook with the effort of walking. Forget the meal, she was ready for a warm bed.

She bumped into Malcolm's side as she tripped over a rock with her weary feet, and he reached out a steadying hand. Taking it in hers, she pulled strength from his grip. What would life be like without fear as her constant companion?

The sound of clanking, the low hum of voices, and the noise of general bustle met her ears. And was that the echo of a child's laugh? The low buzz of activity grew in volume as they neared. How many people awaited them?

Garridan led them through the trees, and she gasped as they broke into the clearing. Her eyes couldn't grow wide enough to take in all of the wonder that met her gaze.

Nearly thirty covered wagons—their canvas tops stretched with colors and patterns like a quilt made of scraps of weathered reds, blues, greens, and brown—circled the area. Horses, unhitched and grazing, were tied to stakes in the ground and to each other, their tails flicking every few moments, and their heads bobbing to keep the flies away as they ate their fill.

A group of children chased each other, circling in and around the wagons, scrambling beneath them and squealing when another boy or girl got too close. Their dark locks flowed behind them in bouncing braids and luscious curls. Women in colorful skirts and headscarves were hanging lengths of cloth and clothes from ropes strung hither and yon between wagons. Their voices were happy, cheerful, and a few of them sang a lilting song that made Rosalie's toes dance with excitement and her nerves tingle with the desire to dance. She had no energy, but the music was begging her to sway to its rhythm.

A small group of men were cutting and chopping wood in the distance and carrying it to the caravan in armfuls, the echo of the ax splitting logs resounding.

Garridan let fly a sharp whistle between his teeth, and Rosalie flinched with the suddenness of the sound.

The children stopped their play and ran up to him, their feet bare, their sun-kissed skin darker than the Rusalkans' and weathered like the shepherds who spent most of their time out of doors. Rosalie was as pale as a piece of parchment compared to them. They were dressed in colors even brighter than the wagon coverings; their skirts and tunics were woven in bright blues, deep reds, and majestic purples, with intricate floral and detailed patterns in contrasting hues. Rosalie noticed the images of small animals mixed with the flora and fauna of the prints.

"Oi, you lot. Where's Romanik?"

A girl that looked to be around Rosalie's age spoke. "He's with the wood cutters." She stepped forward, her inquisitive and deep brown eyes pinned on Rosalie.

Rosalie was just as curious in return, but her gaze faltered beneath the steady stares, and she dropped her eyes to her feet, shuffling her worn boots in the dirt.

"Is she the witch from the castle?" one boy asked, eyes wide, but with a sparkle and a smile pulling at the corner of his mouth. His short hair was fluffy and curling around his ears.

Garridan swatted at him, his hand playfully striking nothing but the air around the boy. "Pfft, you know better than to repeat such rubbish talk. I oughtn't to hear ye say it again or your mother will get an earful."

The boy's brown eyes widened further, and he dodged out of sight with a giggle.

"Izabella, fetch yer father, won't you? I'll get these weary travelers to your caravan."

The girl who had mentioned the whereabouts of her father gave Rosalie one last look, a shy smile, and then took off toward the woodsmen with a twirl of her red skirt layered over cream and blue petticoat ruffles, her bare feet pattering off in the grass and dust.

The children clustered around them as they walked the rest of the way through the field to the caravans and slipped inside the ring, ducking beneath a sheet of vivid blue fabric that was somewhere between the blue of the morning and the evening sky, with golden patterns of stars, flowers, leaves, and winding dots and swirls. Eyes wide, Rosalie tried to take in every detail, but followed when Malcolm's tug on her hand pulled her away. She had woven and spun crude wool nearly her entire life, but never had she seen such finely woven fabric, silky threads, or vivid patterns. Only the wealthiest could afford such clothes, and she had never seen them up close.

The smiles on the little ones' faces and their anxious desire to be close to her brought a small grin to her own lips. They were so innocent, so charming, so artful. There was little of fear or concern behind those brightly shining eyes or in those upturned faces with the ruby lips. A small tot took

Rosalie's other hand and she didn't pull away. Tears pricked her eyes. The feeling of welcoming, of coming home to a place one had never seen before, but felt safe in, rose within her unbidden. She had never had the opportunity to be around other children as she grew up, and while at first she was uncomfortable in their presence and she certainly didn't know how to behave, there was something redemptive and life-giving about the acceptance of a small child. There was no judgment or malice behind those eyes, no expectation from their touch. Nothing but pure, unadulterated curiosity and a desire for closeness that she herself had felt many a time over.

Her heart ached for something she had never thought of before. What would it have been like if her mother had never been taken to Rusalka? Would she have had a mother and a father? Would she have had brothers and sisters? Little children like this that would be hers by blood and hers to love? To care for and to influence and teach? To pass down the things she had been taught by her own mother?

She tripped over another rock, and this time two hands tugged her upward. The little boy still bobbed alongside her, and they stopped next to a wagon with a wooden slat, rounded top, and a round door in the back. Four stairs led to the doorway, which stood open, revealing a dim but brightly colored interior.

"Nim, you in there?" Garridan called from the threshold with an energetic knock.

A beautiful young woman, her dark hair tied back with a bright red kerchief with gold embroidery, fringe, and coins hanging from the edges, popped her head out of the wagon. She glanced at Garridan, then past him to where Rosalie and

Malcom stood, and her face lit up. "Malcolm! And…" Her voice caught when her eyes bounced back to Rosalie. She stepped down, her mouth open in wonder and her eyes large in her tan face. "Lord in heaven…" she breathed, glancing back at Malcolm. "You've got her. After all these years."

She stepped down from the wagon with a spry jump to skip the last few steps, her large necklace with pounded metal charms and coins dangling and her long earrings jingling with the movement as she floated to Rosalie, her red skirts and fluffy white sleeves fluttering and twirling gracefully with her movements. She took both of Rosalie's hands in hers and held them as she bent slightly to gaze deep into Rosalie's eyes. Hers were full of tears, and love reflected in the golden flecks that rimmed her iris.

All of the tense energy that had held her muscles tight in its grip seemed to melt away, and Rosalie's lip quivered, her own eyes filling with tears. She was safe. Here in this camp, with this woman, with these people. She couldn't explain why, but they were hers, and she theirs. A sense of belonging and acceptance flooded through her. There was nothing in these people that wanted anything from her, demanded anything of her. She was accepted, loved—treasured even.

"Oh, child." Nim's face crumpled with compassion, and she pulled the girl into her embrace, her chin resting on Rosalie's head. Rosalie twined her arms around her middle, tears of exhaustion and every pent up emotion flowing from her heart and releasing every bit of tightly wound pain and worry that kept her tied within their grip.

Nim held her, a soft rocking motion and the gentle swish of skirts and tinkle of metallic jewelry a punctuation to

Rosalie's tears. When she opened her eyes, still unwilling to leave the woman's embrace, she looked down and saw the same small child, his hand wrapped in her skirt and his own brown eyes brimming with the largest tears she had ever seen. His little pudgy chin quivered with compassion. Releasing Nim, she sank to her knees and held out her arms. He dove into them, hugging her middle for a moment before squirming to get a good look at her face.

She smiled through the tears spilling from her eyes, sniffing them back and wiping them away to show him that all was well.

Nim chuckled, wiping her own cheeks with the corner of her skirt. "That's my little brother, Bogden. He's a quiet un, but his love runs deeper than the mountain streams. Izabella!" she turned over her shoulder and called.

The girl ran up fast, dust flying beneath her feet and her skirts whirling and dancing with her movement, the shawl tied around her waist jingling with its own golden fringe of coins and chain. A man trotted a ways behind her, his form large and hulking and far less agile than the young girl's.

"Fetch a few buckets of hot water for Malcolm and the young lady. I'll tend Rosalie in my wagon. Take Bogden with you, or he'll be sure to be underfoot. You can see her later, I promise, kochanie. But first she needs to wash and rest." The girl trotted off to do her bidding, leading a reluctant Bogden by the hand as his brown eyes kept Rosalie in sight over his shoulder till they disappeared around a wagon.

"Romanik." Malcolm stepped toward the man who pulled to a stop near them, taking his forearm in his hand and shaking it, their opposite hands resting on either shoulder.

The man was large enough to dwarf Malcolm, his shoulders and chest as wide as a horse. His tunic was blue like Bogden's but with a different pattern, far more faded and worn beneath his leather belt and jerkin. Doves with branches were tooled into the thick leather on his wrist bracers and belt, and his boots were laced high to his knee. His face was bright with welcome, his smile large beneath his frizzy black beard, his curly hair tossed about on his head as if it had a mind of its own.

"And ye have the mlødy. Lord be praised." His eyes twinkled, and he bent to one knee in front of Rosalie, his hand outstretched. "Welcome, lass. My name is Romanik. I'm the keeper of the caravan and overjoyed to offer you my services and my protection on our journey west. Ye'll be treasured here with all that we can give till our time comes to part. Even with our lives, should it be necessary." She took his hand, and Garridan, Nim, and the few men who had come up behind Romanik all bowed to one knee or curtseyed, their fists to their chest.

She nodded, too choked up to say anything, resting her tiny hand in his massive mit and letting him lead it to his face where he kissed the back of it, his beard tickling her skin.

"My daughter, Nim, will see to you. She'll watch over ye and ye may ask her for anything that ye wish."

Izabella returned, a wooden bucket swinging from her fingers, her tongue between her lips in concentration as the water sloshed to the edges of the bucket and steamed in the brisk mountain air. Bogden was in tow, his fingers gripped in her skirt, and another boy around Izabella's age followed behind, his own bucket balanced in his hands.

Nim took the bucket from Izabella, winked, and grabbed Rosalie's hand. "In ye get. Ye'll feel much better once you've had a wash, a sleep, and a new set of clothes."

Rosalie followed Nim but glanced back at Malcolm who nodded reassuringly. His face had lost some of the weathered lines since arriving. He looked the most tired that she had ever seen him. Even he seemed to feel safe and relaxed here. She could trust these people if Malcolm did.

Nim led her up the stairs, and Romanik scooped Bogden into his arms, swinging him high to his shoulder as he ruffled Izabella's hair, her kerchief falling from her head. She too laughed, swatting at Romanik's hand and diving for her fluttering kerchief before it caught the breeze and took flight. They led Malcolm off.

Inside Nim's wagon was a beautiful display of colors. Fabric lay across a small table, and after she set the bucket down, Nim moved a jar of gold paint and several brushes to a windowsill filled with sewing implements and other tools.

Rosalie watched with interested eyes, but her legs trembled. She sat hard on the stool Nim held out for her.

"There, mlødy, ye're safe here." The foreign word was coated with gentleness on Nim's tongue, and Rosalie drew a deep breath in, the steam from the bucket beside her warming and coating her throat. "Rest easy. I'll heat you some tea while you wash." She poured a bit of the water from the bucket into a kettle which she set on the tiny black stove whose pipe was angled outside of the wagon's roof. Nim barely had to duck under the curved sides of the roof and could stand up straight in the middle of the wagon, her skirts swishing and bumping into the table, the chair, and an orange-cushioned and embroidered ottoman.

Rosalie started tugging at the laces of her boots, but her hands fumbled over themselves, her mind feeling far too foggy to make her fingers nimble.

"Here, kochanie." Nim moved her skirt out of the way and crossed her legs, settling into a seat on the floor in front of Rosalie, and started unlacing her boots. Rosalie tried to help but Nim shook her head with a smile and gently pushed her hands away. "I'd guess you've had enough work to get here today without having to do a mite extra. It's an honor to serve ye. We've been praying for ye for years, mlødy."

Rosalie swallowed back the lump in her throat, wrapping her arms around herself. It was warm in the little wagon with the heat from the stove, but the shivers long pent up from the cold, fright, and trudge in the foggy woods still felt as though they needed to be let loose. She bit her lip.

The idea of anyone praying for her as she rotted away, hidden in a tiny tower, believed to be a witch, shook her to her core.

All of those years alone and she could have known this?

Nim gently peeled the woolen socks from her feet and tsked before pouring some water from the steaming bucket into a metal basin and softly guiding Rosalie's feet into the warm liquid.

A sigh escaped her, and her back muscles relaxed as her aching feet rested in the warm water.

Nim smiled. "Oi, I bet that feels grand." She took a cloth, worn and faded, but still just as brightly colored and patterned as the rest of what the Vagari wore, and washed Rosalie's feet.

"You've nothing to worry about here. My father, Romanik, won't let anything happen to ye. Once we outfit you like one of us, no one will be the wiser. Izabella will have some skirts and petticoats that'll fit ye, and I'll loan ye one of my bodices. Izabella and Bogden are also my sister and brother. They sure have taken a shine to ye. I haven't seen Iz so eager to fetch water or run errands in quite some time, mlødy." She shook her head with an eye roll on this use of the word, and Rosalie squinted, confused.

"What does that mean?" Her voice was dry, scratchy with the cold and dust.

"Och." Nim jumped up and poured the boiling water from the kettle into a pot and reached for a sprig of herbs that hung from the rafters over the stove. Grinding it in her palm, she dropped it into the water and set the lid on top, then poured it into a carved wooden cup and handed it to Rosalie. "Mlødy means young one."

Rosalie held the steaming cup in her hands, letting the warmth soak into her skin, her muscles and bones, allowing the warm water soaking her feet to do the same. She felt a little of that pent up feeling of fear slowly ooze from her soul—the constantly clenched feeling in her stomach, the pain of the taut muscles. Her shoulders relaxed for the first time that day as she realized that all of the worry tangled in her mind could now dissipate. The concern of turning a corner and finding a dark knight, wondering who the Vagari were, allowing Malcolm to carry her on the climb, then encountering

Garridan, and the shock of thinking she was caught and going to be dragged back to that solitary, lonely life in the tower.

Nim hummed a soft tune as she moved about the caravan, collecting items over her arm and then helping Rosalie off with her cloak as she warmed by the fire. The tune was somehow both mournful but rollicking, a similar style to the one Rosalie had heard as they approached the camp.

Gathering herself and letting the shock wear off, she looked around the inside of the caravan, marveling at all of the details. The bed was against the back wall, covered in colorful tapestries and quilts pieced out of the most beautiful fabric Rosalie had ever seen. Her green wool dress looked positively drab in comparison to it. Gold tassels and coins hung from the edges of the curtains over the tiny, arched windows. Paintings and tapestry hung from the walls, some in varying levels of progress, with half of the fabric covered in a design and the other half simply a solid color, waiting for its design.

The table Nim had moved the tools from had a royal blue fabric overlaying it like a tablecloth, that strange shade between morning and nighttime and richer than any Rosalie had ever seen. Nim had been using metallic gold paint to cover the fabric in a motif that seemed to have flowers woven in. Rosale squinted closer and her eyes widened. There were doves too. Many of them. Some of them poised in mid-flight, others resting on the branches with the flowers and fruit hanging from them.

The sign of the dove. It was everywhere. Everywhere they had traveled, everywhere they stayed. The people they met, the people they could trust.

"May I—" Rosalie paused, her voice giving out at the audacity of her question. She dare not ask it, for fear that Nim would think she was strange or ignorant.

"What is it, kochanie?" Nim's words were so gentle, so soft, as melodic as her humming, and Rosalie squared her shoulders in preparation to ask her question in return.

"Why do the doves seem to be everywhere? Are they a sign?"

Nim smiled, a sorrowful one that Rosalie didn't quite understand. She followed Rosalie's gaze and looked at the fabric, her hands clutching the clothing she held tighter, drawing it to her chest with a look of pain and love.

She knelt in front of Rosalie, and Rosalie flinched, unable to hold back the involuntary action, even though the logic in her mind told her that there was nothing to fear from the closeness of this woman.

Nim's dark brown eyes were full of compassion, soft with moisture, and that sorrowful smile played on her lips. She reached behind her head and swept the dark brown spiraling and fluffy curls away from her neck and turned her head so that Rosalie could see the tattoos. Two doves in varying stages of flight. Their wings flapping, their feathers cast in detail, but subtle against Nim's brown skin.

"They are a sign, my kochanie. A sign of who we are and what we have taken as our mission on this earth. Has Malcolm not told you of the creed of the dove?"

Rosalie felt a chill run through her as she shook her head. Not an unpleasant one, but one that filled her with a sense of wonder and excitement.

Nim smiled then. "Oi, have we a story to tell you."

ELGON, FOURTEEN YEARS AGO...

He had never felt so helpless. Never through all the years, the times when he had been at his lowest. Weaker than he had ever been. When he had needed someone even to hold his head up to take in a drink of water. When his memories had been lost.

Nothing could have prepared him for this. The utter blackness and waste that he felt.

If he had been adrift on the ocean with nothing but a scrap of wood to call his own, he would have perhaps felt as though he had more control than he did now.

They were gone. Not just his wife, but the child she carried. She and her servant girl, whisked away to who knew where with more of his people.

He clenched his hands, his legs shaking and worn out from pacing. The movement had given him some direction, some reason to keep breathing, but now that he had exhausted his energy, he had to put his trust elsewhere.

It felt so horribly wrong, after betrayal upon betrayal, to put any sort of trust at all in another living, breathing human. To trust the medicinals to work on the wounded. To trust that they knew better than he did. To let the loyal kingsmen who remained assess the damage he could not find himself. To allow them to do what they could to comfort those grieving over lost loved ones.

Men had been killed, their families devastated. Their wives, children, mothers, fathers, sisters, brothers...left grieving, in pain, lost forever.

Those that weren't killed had been taken. Thirty had gone missing, his wife and her maidservant amongst that number. He was grateful it wasn't more, but the hatred for what he had lost could not be relieved by even that small comfort.

He flexed his fingers, his hands sore from the tight grip that he held on the crown that lay in his hands. It felt too heavy to rest on his head.

Except it wasn't just the weight of the crown alone, but all that it represented. The years of ownership held by his family. The weight of monarchs past who had borne it before, their presence hanging about the metal circlet like ghosts crowded around their past lives.

He glanced up and to his left, to Malcolm, still on his cot an arm's length away from where Elgon sat. More of his body was covered in bandages than not. His head wrapped in linen, the skin showing beneath it mottled with purple. At least it was lightening now, though only slightly. He still hadn't woken up. His dearest friend lay beside him, somewhere between the living and dead, and there was nothing Elgon could do.

Nothing.

And there the pain spiraled.

He couldn't even trust himself. Shouldn't have.

The pain grew in his chest until he felt as though it would crush him. Exhaustion or no, he stood and strode from the room, his steps purposeful, though his legs still shook beneath his own weight. He couldn't eat, could barely swallow the water his attendants forced upon him, his pain so great that it welled up in his throat like there was a dam built up to hold it back.

Their concerned faces haunted him as he moved past, ignoring their sorrowful, sorry expressions. Ignoring the pleas for him to return to the medicinal room.

The wooden castle door slammed behind him and he was out in the air, the smell of the sea stinging his nose as he gulped back lungfuls of the salty mist. Even that failed to calm him, so he kept walking, his strides growing longer, faster, harder, as he pounded his boots against the stones of the castle parapet, then the wall's walkway. To the place not long ago where he had held his wife, her voice whispering in his ear and informing him of the impending arrival of a tiny human who would be a part of them and theirs to love, care for, and protect.

And he had failed them both.

His chest exploded with pain. He looked down, almost expecting to see blood. A wound like Kenton's. His very life flowing from a gash cut so deep it seemed as though it was really there. A cry grated on his ears, and he suddenly realized that the shout was his own. His knees gave way, his arms hanging onto the brick wall, and his bleary eyes tried to focus on the movement of the waves against the cliffs beneath him.

The words he couldn't even articulate—the ones that had been so jumbled inside his mind—tumbled from his heart like rocks falling in a landslide from a cliff.

"Why?" His voice broke on that single word. "Why has this happened? What have I done wrong? What do I do? Why did you leave me like this?" He sank farther to the ground, turning and resting his back against the wall. Turning away from the ocean and the freedom of the wind and the waves that only seemed to mock him in this prison of regret and sorrow.

The gentle coo of a mourning dove sounded past the dull roaring in his ears. The blaring headache settled into the back of his head, and the call came again.

The tears that had been as dry as a season of drought finally misted his eyes. The pain, trapped in him like a prisoner rotting away, finally sprung free and streamed down his face in droplets.

He glanced up at the return of the cooing and saw the mourning dove, her gray feathers ruffling in the sea wind as her head cocked to one side, her beady eyes taking him in.

"I never left. I never will. I'm right here with you. As present in the pain as I was in the joys."

The tears fell harder—no longer just tears, but sorrow, scalding hot and broken, pouring from him.

Hold onto hope. Don't ever let go.

Violet's words came back to him, and his shoulders heaved, the pain too great, but the realization sinking deep into his soul.

Perhaps she had seen this coming. Those beautiful forest green eyes of hers, so keen to things outside of normal sight. Her spirit often sensed what was to come even before it happened.

He had made a promise. A heart surrendered to hope was not void of pain, but it knew where to place it. At the feet of a Savior who was once just as broken. And then even more so.

His throat clamped shut, words trapped behind his vocal chords. He wanted to say them, but everything in him fought it. Fought the trust that he had to place outside of himself.

But every bit of trust he had had in himself had gone to waste. Disappeared as if it were a vapor. All of his hopes, his dreams, his faith in those around him had shattered like a blade ill-made and easily broken in its first battle.

Real steel was forged at the greatest heat, tempered with the greatest force.

He slumped over his knees. His heart wanted to say what his mouth could not. *I trust you.*

The dam broke. The tension eased, and his throat opened as he gasped for air, sucking in the chill, the damp, the salt. Tasting it on his lips.

"I trust you. Take away my doubt."

Let us hold unswervingly to hope, for He who promised is faithful.

He could hear Violet's words echoing that of the Word. Her voice reading to him by candlelight as they prepared for bed.

The burden eased slightly, the pain finally releasing him from the dark black hole it sought to drown him in.

Where there was life, there was hope. And where there was hope, there was life.

She was alive. Somewhere. Someplace.

They would find her.

They must.

MALCOLM, PRESENT DAY...

Blood. The blackness. It had risen to haunt him. The throbbing pain had returned. The back of his head felt as though it were splitting open.

He splashed water on his face, the cold sensation chasing a few of the aches away. He reached for the bucket of warm water, setting it in front of him, then peeled his sweaty shirt from his back. Dipping a cloth in the bucket, he used it to wash, the warm water welcome on his skin and the feeling of being clean even more so.

He dunked his head in the bucket, reaching the soap to the back of his neck and sloshing more of the water over himself. Ringing his hair as dry as he could, he raked it back with his fingers, tying it off with the strip of leather, weaving the leather around and into a knot at the base of his neck. The split in his scalp where hair refused to grow over his scar was covered. Malcolm shook the extra water from his hands before using the cloth to dry himself off.

The teal shirt he reached for was more colorful than he was used to, and the gold embroidery of doves flying between olive branches at the collar and cuffs was a touch that brought a slight smile to his face. The image was one that he held dearly to his heart. He lifted a hand to his chest, near his collarbone, and touched the ink that he knew was there. A dove in flight. A mark he felt unworthy to wear, but somehow it also felt as though it gave him a path to the redemption that he hoped to achieve.

It gave him a place of belonging. Something beyond himself to live for, even more than just the mission he fought for with every beat of his heart and fiber of his being. The mission that he would give his life for, if necessary. The one that he had spent the last fourteen years striving to bring to fruition. And one which, should he accomplish his aim, would restore not just his own heart, but the heart of the king. The man he loved like a blood brother.

He pulled the shirt over his head, then his jerkin, binding the leather ties in the front and fastening his belt, pushing the sword he dare not be without farther to the side so that it didn't get in his way.

Sleep awaited him tonight, likely more peaceful than he would experience again during the entirety of the journey that would lead them home. Being the sole protector for the most precious legacy of Elira was not a job that allowed for much rest.

But tonight he was in the company of friends. A haven. He smiled slightly as he threw his cloak over his shoulder. A covey of kindred souls and secret warriors.

He stepped from the caravan Romanik had been so gracious to allow him to use as he washed up and strode toward the campfires. Dusk had already started to creep into the haven, and he caught sight of flying skirts before Rosalie was beside him, out of breath, and still tired, but with a bit more life behind those green eyes. There was peace there, too, and a lack of fear he was grateful to see. She felt safe here.

She slipped her hand into his, and a sudden thought had him blinking hard. She felt safe *with him*.

After all that he had failed in, all that he had broken and allowed to happen to her, her family. Should she trust him? The first knight who couldn't even protect the castle? He moved to pull his hand away reflexively, but she held it tighter, gripping it with both of hers and looking up at him with a bright smile.

He swallowed and glanced away. "Are you finding yourself comfortable here with the Vagari?"

She nodded. "Now that you're with me again."

He nearly stumbled.

And then the hair on the back of his neck stood on end and he whirled, using her grip on his hand to push her behind him and into cover. A branch broke in the woods near the edge of the circle of caravans, and he reached his free hand for the hilt of his sword, his eyes darting in every direction, squinting to see in the growing darkness.

A shadow moved and he pulled his blade, stepping back with one foot for a better fighting stance and wishing that they weren't so far away from the rest of the group that sat unaware near the roaring fires in the covey's center behind him and Rosalie.

The shadow moved again, unmistakably the shape of a man. Did he cry out for Garridan or Romanik and alert their stalker that they were near? Or did he dart toward the fire, exposing Rosalie or his back to the intruder?

A man stepped from the tree cover, his broad shoulders stiffening, a dark cloak and hood covering his face. Malcolm pulled his sword from its scabbard, silent, the metal glinting in the distant glow of the firelight.

The man raised both palms out, but the movement sent Malcolm into action. He shoved Rosalie behind the cover of the closest wagon and advanced toward the enemy before the hooded man could harm either one of them.

The dark knights had found them already.

Twenty

SPIES, ENEMIES, AND FRIENDS

ELGON, FOURTEEN YEARS AGO...

"You know we need a secondary plan if we are to safeguard the kingdom." The words felt like sawdust on Elgon's tongue, even if he knew he was right. Elgon watched the frustration on Malcolm's face as his friend sat in bed, his fingers picking at the covers and his brows drawn in a harsh frown. Malcolm was still recovering, but he was the only man that Elgon could trust with his deepest secrets and with whom he felt comfortable allowing himself to process and plan.

"I just—I just don't want you to give up." Malcolm's voice was strained and laced with pain that Elgon knew he fought with daily.

A pain he knew all too well.

251

Though it had been just over a month since the coup, Malcolm's healing had been slow, and he had yet to be up and about. A broken skull, internal bleeding, and several stab wounds and broken ribs didn't make for the easiest—or shortest—recovery.

Elgon swallowed and stood from the chair placed at his friend's bedside, resuming pacing for the third time during this conversation. "I'm not giving up. On the contrary, this is the farthest thing from giving up. I will never—" He swallowed hard, his voice husky when he resumed. "I will never give up on Violet or our child. You know that. But the truth is that should things take longer than we hope—should something happen to me—someone that I trust must be placed as second in command so that Elira will not fall. My father tried to do it on his own; he couldn't trust those closest to him. With a council, there will be room for wiser, more experienced voices to raise their opinion, for us to pray together, and for us to plan together for the future of Elira."

Malcolm nodded, then grew pale, his jaw clenching at what must have been a spasm of pain. He held his head steady and wrung the sheet in his hand. "I'm—I'm so sorry." The words were a whisper.

Elgon sat in the chair once again and placed a hand on his arm. "Please. Brother. You know there is nothing to forgive. You gave your all to stop this madness, but sometimes, one person building a wall is not enough to hold hell back on his own."

"But why did God allow this?" Malcolm still had yet to meet his eyes.

Elgon sighed and leaned back. "I wish I knew. But what I do know is that Violet would remind us that the Lord works all things for good for those that love Him. We may not get to see what that means, what that looks like, or how the good will come about, but we need to trust that it *will* be good, no matter the circumstances. And He can be trusted to bring it about for His glory. His glory does not always mean our comfort, desires, or hopes will come to pass as we expect them to. The existence of God and His plan and purpose does not preclude the existence of evil. The enemy will always have emissaries who will do his bidding, even when he knows it's a losing battle."

Malcolm nodded, Adam's apple bobbing. "Who will you ask to be on the council?"

"You, of course, as chief military advisor as soon as you are well enough. No rush on that in the slightest. We will ask for a vote of the townsfolk that a representative of the larger towns and provinces will have someone to speak for them that they trust. One each from Padsley and the farming province, Pranvera, and Valhaven, and a few from Niran. I will also ask Lord Milton to assemble a small delegation so that their people will also be represented in decisions that are made. I will still hold final say, but the council will vote on an order of succession."

"My lord, I do not—that is, I am honored, but I do not see myself as being fit for such an office. Surely there is another who is more experienced and without—"

Elgon sighed. He knew those feelings of doubt, of regret. He fought them himself. There was only so much he could say to his brother, but only the Lord could do the work of mending a broken heart and reversing the weight of regret that rested like a boulder atop Malcolm's shoulders. *Lord, do it quickly.*

"We will wait until you are well, but it is you that I want. I trust no one such as I do you, my brother."

Malcolm seemed to recoil from Elgon's words, as if they burned him.

Before Malcolm could come back with any response or argument, Elgon stood. "Rest, my friend, we will talk more when you are able. Let the Lord bring healing to your body and spirit."

Elgon could sense the turmoil in the heart of his friend despite the diminishing of the lines between his brows. *Lord, minister to him and speak to him, heal him in a way that my words cannot.*

Taking the lantern that rested on the bedside table, Elgon stepped from the room, leaving it in semi-darkness so that Malcolm could sleep, and softly shut the door.

Once outside, he sagged against the wall. Malcolm needed to see his king strong, to know that Elgon could handle the weight of the grief and pain that rested on his shoulders. To know that he still held Malcolm in high regard, despite whatever Malcolm thought about what had occurred. But being strong for Malcolm was as much a performance as it was truth. Setting aside the pain and fears for his wife and child that only grew as the days marched on was necessary in the presence of his first knight. Malcolm already shouldered enough guilt; he did not need to see his king carrying his own, or it would only make Malcolm's worse.

But pretending that the load he carried was lighter than it truly was took its own toll. His insides still quivered at the constant worry that nagged his inner core of what Violet could be going through now. The uncertainty of her existence. Was she alive? Was she well? Was she being mistreated? Surely their child had been born. Had it survived whatever journey had awaited them? Was his hope that they were being held as collateral against the kingdom of Elira a foolish one? Were his attempts to resolve peacefully whatever issue Zuko and Enguerrand had against him foolish ones?

Such questions ran through his mind unanswered during every waking second, and they haunted his sleep like monsters, devouring whatever peace lay within his slumber.

He allowed himself to sink to the stone floor, resting his head on his knees, drawing in a deep breath.

Lord, give me peace. Help me trust in you. Don't let me lose my hope.

Peace settled over his shoulders like a blanket. The kind he had felt before and knew was not of himself. Tears still burned in his eyes as he squeezed them shut, willing them to stay barred in place, but the pressure of holding them back built in his throat until he no longer could. That spot over his heart, where Violet had often rested the palm of her hand in a loving embrace, felt like it was on fire. Her touch had always brought such comfort, her presence and nearness a peace and a sense of home he had never felt before meeting her. The loss of that touch, that presence, burned like a wound exposed to open flame.

But then it soothed. Like her gentle touch, soft as dove's wings and gentle as a whisper in the darkness, the presence of the Lord filled the hall. As the tears flowed down his face and his shoulders shook with silent sobs, the weight of the world seemed to shrink back and hide in the dark corners, unable to face the Spirit of the God that lived and breathed within him.

"My hope is yours for the taking. My heart for you and your family—your kingdom, your legacy—is just as sure now as it was when you were together. My plan was not destroyed because of the circumstances. I can see farther than you ever could; and this is not the end. They who wait for the Lord shall renew their strength; they shall mount up with wings like eagles; they shall run and not be weary; they shall walk and not faint. I will be your strength. I will be your wings. I will be your courage to keep going in the face of pain and heartbreak."

The tears were now cleansing ones. No longer were they burning from the inside out, but they were a washing. A baptism of the Word cleansed his soul, and his heart filled with strength. Never had he felt the nearness of God so close as he did in that moment.

His pain and desperation became an empty vessel for the Spirit of the Lord to fill with a hope that could not be manufactured on its own.

"Your majesty?" A timid voice broke the spell of stillness and comfort that surrounded him, and Elgon shook the cobwebs from his mind, using the back of his hand to swipe at the tears that had drenched his face and his beard.

"What is it, Tobias?"

The small squire wrung his hands in front of him and struggled to meet Elgon's eye. "I-I was sent to f-fetch you, s-sir. There is a small d-delegation from Padlsey who are here to s-see you." His small stutter was only ever accentuated when talking to the king.

Elgon smiled softly. The mite had just become a squire since the attack and couldn't have been any older than eight. His brown hair was proper in the front but sticking out at all ends in the back from the three cowlicks that spun in opposing directions and would most likely never be tamed. He held out his hand to the lad who stared, wide-eyed, and stepped forward to grasp Elgon's finger and help pull him to his feet.

Elgon's legs throbbed from being curled up under himself for so long, and he leaned against the wall for support. "Thank you." He tousled the child's head and smiled even more when, as a result, the front stood on end as much as the back. "Let's go see what it is that they need, shall we?"

He strode through the halls, the little squire trotting at his heels to keep up. Malcolm had been moved to the family wing of apartments to rest once he was deemed out of danger by Raphart, the castle medicinal. Elgon wanted him as comfortable as possible as he recovered, and despite Malcolm's protests, he hoped that there would be some comfort and healing for him here where he could be tended to with easier access by the household servants.

He wondered who had been sent from Padsley. Though his letters and decrees to the villages had been sent out nearly a week ago, surely it was far too early for them to have chosen their provincial representative just yet. He hoped it wasn't ill news of Kenton. Though the lad's recovery had taken somewhat of a backseat in his mind, he had been anxiously awaiting news of how he was recovering.

He didn't bother going around the back of the throne room as he usually did. The back door ensured that he would come out on the dais and from behind the thrones, but he was in too much of a hurry to take the long way around.

The large wooden doors had been repaired quickly by the craftsman, but the missing carpet and darker hue of the stone floor was a grim reminder that sent a lump into his throat which he fruitlessly tried to swallow back. He would need an ocean of water to cleanse his mind from the scarring sight that was imprinted on his mind from when he had found the outer hall torn to shreds, littered with the bodies of faithful soldiers and stained with blood.

The small group that huddled near the front of the dais caught his eye, and his feet stumbled when one in a green cloak turned around and met his gaze.

Marcus.

All vestiges of kingly bearing left him immediately, and the tears so recently flooding his eyes sprang forward again. Two salty drops chased each other down his face as his shoulders crumpled. The compassion on his friend's face nearly brought him to his knees, but his feet flew until he met Marcus, who had taken two large swings of his crutch to meet him in the middle of the room.

The crutch fell to the ground as they embraced, Marcus's arms around him breaking him to sobs. A king holds an entire nation on his shoulders…but who holds the king?

His cries shook them both, and while he held Marcus steady, Marcus steadied his heart. All of the raw pain, loneliness, and aching brokenness was flayed raw and touched with the healing salve of companionship and compassion. Healing intermixed with the throbbing agony.

Elgon knew not how long they stood there before a large hand rested on his shoulder. He turned, taking a shuddering breath and let it pull his spine straight again before he felt his face break. Everard.

Those dark eyes, so like those of their enemies, but so full of compassion, love, and tenderness put him right at ease. Everard pulled him into an embrace of his own, Marcus's hand still on his shoulder.

Everard had never needed words to express his feelings and intent. When souls speak and faces tell stories, words feel shallow and unnecessary.

Elgon didn't know how many moments had passed when he finally stepped back, still staying within reach of both of the men with whom he felt a kinship like that of family.

"We did bring something we hope will at least cheer you up." Marcus smiled sadly and hesitantly, limping out of the way.

"Kenton!" Elgon pulled the young man into his arms for a gentle embrace before stepping away and holding his young squire at arm's length.

His usual bright and cheery grin still split his pale face, but it dropped quickly. "I'm sorry, your majesty." The lad had an arm around his middle and was thin and gaunt by comparison to the youth and vitality of merely a month prior.

Elgon blinked away the mental image of the lad bleeding out in front of him and drew in a shuddering breath to steady his nerves and clear the memory. "I'm so pleased to see you up and doing so well. I—" He shook his head. "It doesn't matter what I thought. My prayers for you have been answered." Hope whispered and flew a little deeper into his heart. The Lord had healed Kenton and brought him back from the very grave. Perhaps there was just as much hope for his wife and child.

"Tobias," he called to the young lad who stood at the doorway, hands respectfully folded in front of himself and his spine ramrod straight.

"Sir?" The lad jumped forward and trotted to his side, eyes like those of a puppy ready to do his bidding.

"Will you take Kenton to the room next to Malcolm's, help him get settled, and then inform Raphart that he is here and will need care until he's well?"

"I'm doing quite well, your majesty." Kenton tried to object and straighten his shoulders, but his wince and pale face—the freckles standing out like stones across a riverbed—spoke differently.

"Nonsense, you'll need quite a bit of strengthening and fattening up before you're ready for service or duty, lad. No argument. You'll be taken care of on my watch."

Kenton nodded, though Elgon tried to fight a smile at the disgruntled look on the face of his apprentice knight before Tobias led him away. He and Malcolm would make quite the pair. He shook his head as he noticed Kenton lean some of his weight onto Tobias's shoulder. *Quite well, indeed.*

Turning to Marcus, he took his friend's elbow and led him to the chairs along the side of the room, Everard following and standing by like some silent sentry while they both sat. "How is the lad doing?"

"Well enough. He tries to blame himself for what happened and insists that he should have tried to tell you sooner, but I keep telling him there was nothing he could do.

It might mean more coming from you, but the Lord will have to do that work."

"Aye, don't I just know how that is." Elgon sighed, shaking his head and folding his arms.

Marcus tilted his head with a quizzical look in his blue eyes.

"I'll tell you later. His wounds?"

"Healing, though it was touch and go for a while. He's not as strong as I would like, but he insisted on coming. He's probably exhausted and needs plenty of easy, hearty foods, rest, and some slow training to help bring back some of the muscle he's lost. He lost a lot of blood, and he'll need care to help with the weakness that is still persistent from his injury. It may last a long time, but I can speak with Raphart about a course of treatment Fendrell and I have been finding effective."

"Will he be able to resume his work or...?" Elgon was almost too afraid to ask the question.

"Oh surely! It may be some time before he's ready for duties again, and certainly, he'll grow frustrated at how long he will need to train in order to regain his strength, but he's so young and the Lord has been accelerating the healing process for him thus far. There were many I would not have expected to come back from so grave an injury."

"Well, that's a comfort that the Lord answers some prayers." Elgon tried to keep the bitterness from his tone.

"He answers them all, they might just not be what, how, or when we expect them." Marcus's soft voice spoke truth into his weary heart.

Elgon sighed, but nodded. "I know. Sometimes I need to be reminded of that."

Marcus leaned in. "How can we help?"

"Pray. It seems to be the best thing at the moment," he admitted. "I've been working on doing something that's been on my mind and spirit for some time, but didn't get around to when this all came up with Pavlin. The treaty was signed, and I would have done it sooner than later, but in absence of"—he choked—"the queen, we'll need a contingency if something were to happen to me. An order of succession. This whole thing seems to be some giant plot against Elira itself, or an attempt to free Enguerrand—which was unfortunately successful."

"Has there been any news? Do you know what has happened to Violet?" Marcus's voice trembled on her name.

Elgon shook his head. His heart was heavy, but then hope sprang back in that moment like a spring breeze over the fields of Padsley with the whisper of falling rain. "No, but she is not dead. She can't be. Enguerrand would have thrown that in my face if it were true. But instead our messages seem to have been completely ignored. I have this creeping feeling they are waiting until just the right moment to spring upon us, and that they are withholding showing their cards in order to set us on edge."

"Have you sent people looking for her?" Marcus asked, leaning on the edge of his seat and throwing a look past Elgon at Everard.

"A few, though our search may need to be widened. We still don't know how they got away so quickly and where they went. The spies we have sent into Rusalka have either been met with immediate resistance or have found nothing that denotes a caravan's passage. Their tracks seem to have simply disappeared without the slightest trace. I'll need to assemble more and send them farther afield, but short of marching across the border—which is as improbable as it is impossible at this time—I'm at a loss of what else to do."

"Send me." Everard's words were spoken softly, with that deep breathiness he had when he did finally allow words past his vocal chords.

Elgon turned and looked up his towering frame into the dark eyes. "What?"

"Send me. I will search for them like they are my own kin…" His eyes sparked and narrowed. "As they are."

Elgon drew a breath. Everard was the perfect spy. He was silent, quiet, loyal…and Rusalkan by descent. He would blend right into the landscape and make it farther than any of the native Elirans would on their own.

Before continuing, Everard glanced at Marcus, who gave him a nod. "I know their ways. I was one of them once. Not just one of them…but the worst of them." Sadness rimmed his eyes, and his jaw set with a click.

"What do you mean? The worst of them, how?" Elgon gaped at Everard. Violet had never told him even if she had known.

"I traded slaves in the Kaira mountains and deeper into the country before I was…redeemed."

Elgon stared. What he knew of this gentle man conflicted with the revelation that slipped from Everard's mouth with the strain and pain of hidden truths that were too shameful to speak of out loud.

He swallowed. Everard had been Violet's silent guardian from the day that her father was killed and had been a watchful eye over Padsley in ways that he himself could never really understand. The grace he had extended to Elgon when he had been struggling with his memory and fighting for the ability to return to his old life had stuck with him, and his presence had always brought him and Violet great comfort. Even on their wedding day, the hope he had spoken over them for their new life together would never leave his memory.

Elgon stood, holding out his hand to shake Everard's.

Everard paused, took his hand, and then pulled him into a hug. As Elgon was crushed against the man's chest, he heard the faintest whisper. "I'll give my life to bring her back."

MALCOLM, PRESENT DAY...

Malcolm strode forward, every nerve taught and every muscle at the ready, both hands gripping the handle of his sword.

The faint light of the evening and the shadows still cast the form in darkness till a small child ran from the cover of the forest and snuggled behind the man's cloak, clinging to his leg and peering around in fear at Malcolm.

Malcolm's steps hitched.

The man in the dark cloak stood his ground, his hands in the air in a pacifying gesture, his massive frame standing as solid as a rock. Neither advancing nor backing down.

"I come on the wings of the wind…" His words were deep and steady.

Malcolm drew a breath and dropped his sword at the passcode. "As a dove flying to the sun," he returned, his body still strung tight, so much so that the idea of sheathing his sword still didn't sit right with him.

The man dropped his hands and scooped up the young child, who nestled into his shoulder like a small animal curling up for a nap.

"Your business here?" Malcolm asked as they walked toward each other.

The man lifted a hand and swept back his hood, his bearded face coming into full view, and his long black hair tousled and escaping the braids of locks and leather that tied it back.

His beard was longer, but those shoulders and those eyes… "Everard? Is that you?"

A soft smile tilted his mouth as he wrapped his other arm around the child and returned her embrace, keeping his focus on Malcolm. "Aye." He puckered his lips and let out a bird whistle of three notes. Four more hooded figures stepped out from behind the bushes and the trees at the outskirts of the clearing and made their way toward Everard.

Malcolm felt himself tense again and then sheathed his sword when he realized that all of them were small, slight, and far too frail to possibly be anyone of danger. He rolled his neck, convincing his shoulders to relax. "Rosalie, it's all right. You can come back out. I have someone you will want to meet."

Her eyes rounded in concern and curiosity, Rosalie peeked out from around the wagon that had been her hiding place and then took timid steps toward him. Malcolm held out his hand to her, and she took it once close enough.

Everard's face changed, surprise filling his eyes as he handed the small child to a young woman who had sidled up to him, gaze never leaving Rosalie's face. He strode forward.

"Rosalie, meet Everard. The man who knew your mother when she was a child and cared for her. He was the one who discovered your whereabouts."

EVERARD, PRESENT DAY...

The moment had come. The child he had prayed over for fourteen years. The youngling that he had given those fourteen years to find. The one who had been his heart's cry and the purpose behind his work now stood before him.

This moment crashed into his chest, and he felt a twist in his gut, the pain in his heart so great. Why did rejoicing have the ability to feel like it was a crushing weight?

He saw Violet in her. The green, curious eyes, the wild hair. But more than that, her spirit drew him like a magnet. The subtle strength behind her gaze, the openness and pureness of a soul that has hope in the only One worth hoping in.

She quirked her head to one side, and it was all he could do not to scoop her into his arms and hold her tight. The full weight of all that this moment meant to him—to her father…to her people—hit him with the force of a stone wall falling from the sky.

His stoicism failed him, and a sob cracked his heart in two.

She was here. After all these years. All the prayers. All the hopes. At long last, the answer had come. Death had been cheated, evil had been thwarted, and here she stood. A rose blooming amongst the thorns of revenge and conspiracy.

She was the proof.

The proof of hope. Alive, well, and on her way to a life that awaited her with open arms… and a father who would see the fruit of long-awaited trust.

He saw understanding in her eyes as he reached out a hand, dropping to one knee in front of her, the tears spilling down his cheeks and soaking his beard. She bypassed his offered hand and wrapped her arms around his neck, burying her face in his shoulder.

He kept his hands gentle, the desire to crush her to him taking second place to his care for her. He cradled the back of her head in his massive hand and cupped her small frame to him like a shepherd holds his lamb.

She held him, and the broken, longing, painful place in his soul that had felt like a desert blown over suddenly had the cleansing flood wash over it, drowning it in grace and mercy.

This precious gift was theirs at last.

ROSALIE, PRESENT DAY...

Rosalie tilted her head from the place of safety tucked behind Malcolm's arm, her hand in his. There was something in this strange man as large as a mountain that felt like home. A kinship she had never known. Why did she feel as though she recognized him, as if she had known him her whole life and was coming back after a long journey away?

There was a familiar spirit in those shining dark eyes that were turning glossy. The rugged face had a softness and tenderness to it, while looking for all the world like he could crush someone if he had a mind to. A dangerous strength that was held back by a gentleness that could only be the Holy Spirit.

Those tears. They fell down his face as he knelt in front of her and held out a hand. It was massive, reminding her of a bear paw.

There was something otherworldly shining from that face, the dark skin like those who had tormented her all her life, but holding a flame that burned bright, warm, like a fire flickering in a frigid room. There was warmth, safety, comfort in this man.

There was Christ.

She took two steps and disregarded his hand entirely, instead stepping into his embrace and twining her arms around his neck. Tears started to her own eyes as his own arms wrapped around her, holding her tight, but not too tight.

She was safe.

Loved.

Held.

Never before had she felt such things. The broken, abandoned, hurting places inside her came together like two sides of a canyon long cut with the storms and wind being knit together again. Peace flooded her, and the hopes and dreams of her entire existence sparked to life, fanned into flame again as they grew. They weren't just far off things—these dreams of being loved, held, cherished. They were for now. They were real. And hopes and dreams really could come true.

Hope fulfilled is all the sweeter for its years of aching unfulfillment.

She didn't know how long she held onto this rock in the midst of the storm until she took a step back and their tearful eyes met. The broken joy in his eyes filled her with so much love that she felt as though her very heart would burst. He didn't have to say a word but she *felt* his words with a keenness she never thought possible.

And then he spoke. "You have your mother's eyes." His voice was deep but breathless. But she felt more than heard what he left unsaid, and her chest swelled with pride. She was her mother's daughter, and with that realization came a level of responsibility. She had been weighed and found not just enough, but everything that had been hoped and prayed for. She was seen. Was beheld and cherished for who she was. For what and Who she carried. The light inside of her met the light inside of this man, once a stranger, always a friend, and she stood tall.

The royal blood that flowed through her veins was everything that Christ had created it to be, and she had a destiny inside of her that no one could steal. Not a king, not a prison guard, not a life in captivity.

Her spirit soared.

"Everard! You're back!" Children's giggles broke the moment. Bogden, Izabella, and their cohorts ran into the group, tackling and climbing onto Everard's legs, grabbing his hands, and smiling up at him with an adoration and joy that made Rosalie's heart sing. She grinned widely and stepped back, unwilling to be alone. Involuntarily, she took

Malcolm's hand, and when he squeezed it in return, she looked up into his face.

Even his eyes were misty, and he opened his mouth as if to speak but nothing came out. As the children dragged Everard and the young woman and child that had been with him toward the massive fire in the center of camp, Malcolm swallowed and his voice was husky with emotion. "He was the one who searched for you. These fourteen years he's been traveling up and down Rusalka, over every mountain and forest, in every village, bringing the gospel to those that needed hope, rescuing others long held in captivity. The day he found of your whereabouts was the day he was rescuing a group of slaves from Zuko's castle with Vieggo's help. It took everything within him to leave you there that day. He would have taken on the very depths of hell to bring you back, but you were ill and there was no way to get you out. Vieggo had to talk him out of storming the castle and convince him to bide his time and return to Elira to form a plan."

Rosalie felt the tears sliding down her face. All this time. Every hour, every day, every year that she spent locked away in that tower. Every moment wondering if anyone even cared of her existence, and here there were people roaming the very corners of the land for her. To find her. To rescue her. To bring her home. A silent sob shook her, and Malcolm squeezed her hand again.

"The entire nation has prayed for your and your mother's return. He was the first to offer to come search for you both."

The aching emptiness of that realization felt like a blow to the gut. She was only half the return. The sorrow of losing a mother she had never had the honor and joy of knowing filled her with an aching sadness for what was lost. Not only was her father an unknown to her, but her mother had died when she was born.

Am I not a father to the fatherless? Am I not healing for brokenness, rescue for the lost, and hope for the weary? Take heart, your story is not yet fully written.

"Those people he had with him…?" she asked, settling her heart with a hand to the chest over the fluttering member.

"Rescued slaves, no doubt. The Vagari are a rescue caravan."

Rosalie froze. "A what?"

Malcolm smiled sadly and tugged on her hand, leading her toward the crackling fire, the music, and the voices of joyous and excited people. "They are smugglers. Except they don't smuggle for their own good or in stolen items, but in stolen people. Stolen from those that robbed them of their lives and livelihoods. They're all rescues, just like you. The Vagari shelter them on their journey across the mountains and to a new home in Elira. It's why we have come to meet them here. They offer us protection and safety amongst their numbers."

Her feet were moving but she hardly even noticed as her mind spun and whirred on the information that had just been given her, the stops along their way. The tavern and the dove on the door. Mother Hobbs and the dove tattoo they all had engraved into their skin. She glanced at her patchwork skirt, the vibrant reds, and blues, and purples a swirled backdrop for the gold painted leaves and doves that scattered across the fabric and were embroidered into the hem.

Even Malcolm and Everard's passcode…

"What was the meaning of what you said to each other when he first came into camp?"

Malcolm turned to her with a set jaw and straight lips. "You must never use that phrase except with the utmost respect in understanding that it is a passcode that keeps every one of us safe; every rescued and every rescuer. It must only be used to determine if a person or place is safe and a part of the creed of the dove. Do you understand?"

She nodded.

"Good. The first part, 'I come on the wings of the wind,' is a phrase that describes the person coming with the power and protection of the Holy Spirit. The response 'as a dove flying to the sun', describes the act of approaching the Son of God in the journey that we all make through life and into eternity. The Order of the Dove was created years ago when Everard first met the Vagari and understood their sign of the dove. It has since been used to establish the places and pathways of refuge for those who wish to escape and to find healing and redemption. All who have helped us and sheltered us thus far are members of the creed."

Awe filled Rosalie's heart as they stepped within the ring of the golden light of the flame.

Nim strode to meet them, her smile as bright and warm as the massive fire, and her skirts swaying with her every step. The joy on her face was heightened by the sorrow that hid beneath the surface.

Joy is not the absence of pain, but merely the delight and surety of truth even in the midst of it.

"Come." Nim's skin glowed and her eyes burned bright. "Let us take communion together." She took each of their hands and pulled them into the crowd of people around the fire. Men and women were seated in pairs and groups, near enough to each other to converse easily. Children sat cross-legged on the ground, playing and laughing amongst themselves.

Romanik stood and raised his hands, and the music stopped. The silence was filled only with the crackling of the fire as all of the chattering voices died down with whispers and shushes. "Let us break bread together and take the body and blood of Christ in remembrance and gratitude for his sacrifice."

Twenty-One

REST FOR THE WEARY

MALCOLM, PRESENT DAY...

He tried to shake off the anxious feeling that had settled on him since Everard had startled him, appearing as he did out of the edge of the woods, but that persistent worry that perhaps he had missed something tried to perch on his shoulders.

But as Romanik blessed the bread, broke it, and passed it around the crowd of families, children, parents, even the old folk, he felt a bit of the peace that Romanik prayed for settle on him. His shoulders released, and he drew a deep breath as he took the bread, broke off a piece, and handed it to Rosalie who sat cross-legged on the ground at his feet. She followed suit, her eyes wide, taking in everything around her. The weariness on her face was eclipsed by the curiosity and joy of the moment.

Malcolm thanked the Lord for His body silently, closing his eyes and letting the remembrance of the Lord's ultimate sacrifice and broken body touch his soul in a way nothing else could. That sacrifice had gone far, brought him into something new—this family, this way of life. He had saved him from eternal hell and gave him hope and peace through an earthly life.

They partook together, and after Romanik prayed in gratitude and blessed the wine, he took the cup that Nim handed to him, thanked the Lord for His blood, and pleaded its protection over them again this night and for the journey ahead. He drank of the wine, its sweetness mixed with the sour, and drew a deep breath.

The sour and the sweet. The juxtaposition of so much joy with the sorrow of the past flitting through his mind like a pair of butterflies that chased each other across the plains. One never quite separate from each other. Always together.

The Vagari rose to their feet after the last man, woman, and child had received the blood and body of Christ and raised their hands to the sky. Their smiles sliced through the shadowed skin of their face and gleamed in the fire.

"Let us praise the Lord for all that He has done, all that He is, and those that He has rescued and brought into our midst." Romanik spoke, his thundering voice loud enough to be heard throughout the group and over the crackling of the flames and the distracted children's whispers.

"Chwała Panu!" They shouted together, and Malcolm lent his voice to those of his friends.

He caught the questioning look Rosalie threw over her shoulder, and he nodded, leaning down to speak in her ear as the music started again with a shout from the people. "It means 'praise the Lord' in their language."

She grinned and tasted the words on her tongue, her pronunciation different from theirs, and he smiled at her wholehearted attempt.

He felt his own muscles relaxing as the music swayed and rolicked. The instruments were varied and handmade; fiddles, pipes, an animal skin turned into an instrument that one young man blew into with nimble fingers and more skill than ought to be allowed in one so young. Most of the women had tambourines, and a few even had some spoons going. The joy of their voices, their faces, and in the dancing and nimble movements of their feet—swishing, flowing, twirling and stamping into the dirt with vigor—reminded him of the verse 'the serpent you shall trample underfoot.' The Vagari certainly did that in every moment of their lives.

He closed his eyes and let the music wash over him, the praise and words of adoration to a King who resided beyond this earthly realm soaking into his very bones and revitalizing the wearied places. He felt movement near him and caught a glance of Izabella grabbing Rosalie's hand and pulling her to her feet, demonstrating with a bit too much speed and enthusiasm how Rosalie should twirl her multi-colored skirt, stamp her feet, and clap her hands over her head.

He shook his head with a chuckle building in his throat at her attempts but also at her puckered brow and pursed lips as she tried with all her might to follow Izabella's movements, which were as easy to imitate as a grasshopper's would've been.

Even little Bogden joined in, and his little feet stamped along as fast as his sisters, his clapping and finger-snapping showing up some of his older friends.

Malcolm clapped along with the rhythm and caught Nim's eyes as she turned in circles around her younger siblings, her skirts spinning in impossible shapes. She grinned at him and glanced pointedly at Rosalie, her smile growing wider as she raised her eyebrows and nodded with approval.

He gave her an answering nod, and she spun away, her tambourine joyfully clanging over her head as she disappeared around the fire.

The log beneath him shifted, and he glanced to his left at Everard, his bulky frame perched next to Malcolm on the makeshift seat. The look on his face was so hidden by the man's stoicism that only the few who knew him best would've been able to see it—and Malcolm saw joy resting in the lines about his eyes. Joy tempered by all that he had seen, all that he had sacrificed for this moment to become reality, and those eyes shone as they followed Rosalie's efforts to join in the worship of these people whom she had only just met.

Malcolm nodded toward the princess. "She does her mother credit, even from what little I knew of her."

Everard nodded and rested his palm on Malcolm's shoulder, his eyes saying more than words ever could. Pride, gratitude, praise, joy—all lay in their depths.

Malcolm nodded. "Now to get her home. I wonder what Elgon is doing with himself. He must be beside himself with impatience."

"He's waited fourteen years. The joy of his reward for his faith will be the sweetest thing he has ever known."

Malcolm swallowed the lump in his throat, trying to tamp down the guilt that rose to snuff out the happiness he felt. The darkness of his past mistakes made the back of his head throb, and the sorrowful tones of the music, interwoven masterfully with that of rejoicing, suddenly took on deeper meaning and pierced his heart like the keening wail of a mother.

"Don't carry past demons." Everard's eyes did not leave Rosalie.

"Past demons are not so easily rid of when the consequences of those actions follow you, stare you in the face each morning, and greet you with a smile."

"Don't let the past rob you of the joy of life. Stare down the lies and remove them. They will only fester and grow more bitter with time."

That arrow of truth seemed to lodge there and quiver painfully. Honesty from a friend was more painful than the lie of an enemy, but it would heal instead of scar. Malcolm nodded as he glanced again at Rosalie, her feet stomping and her skirts swaying in time to the music, a look of ecstasy on her face even as tears spilled down her cheeks.

His eyes burned at the sight. The girl before him was experiencing so much newfound joy—who was he to begrudge it on the merits of his own pain?

"Look at her. Her joy, peace, and freedom is much more powerful than that of a girl who has grown up in a palace her entire life in perfect safety. The Father knows what He's doing. Don't forget that even the most painful of pasts, the most broken of men, and the most woeful of tales can still be touched with redemption and goodness that we cannot even fathom."

They might have been the most words Malcolm had ever heard Everard speak, but they rang with a truth and an understanding that many could not know. Everard's past had been one of shock to Malcolm upon learning it, but the man knew of what he spoke. He, a slave trader turned man of God and rescuer of lost souls, would truly know more than anyone else ever could of the goodness and redemptive power of their Lord. Everard was not one to speak in niceties for the sake of it, and Malcolm fought past the walls that tried to keep his truth and his words from entering his soul and let them sink deep into his spirit like the cool water of refreshment.

"Don't live in darkness by choice, Malcolm. Too many dwell there against their will. Don't make your prison one of your own making." Everard's massive hand again landing on his shoulder brought a level of love and rest to Malcolm that he hadn't felt in a long time, and he closed his eyes, drawing in a deep breath.

The hand left a moment later, but he almost didn't notice. *I am the one who makes crooked paths straight. One who turns darkness to light with the touch of a finger and who speaks life into existence. You were not a mistake. My plans are good, and I will not leave you in your crooked ways. You will never be left alone. Trust and rest in me. I'll bring it to pass."*

ROSALIE, PRESENT DAY...

The music stirred something in her soul. It was like rivers poured through a desert, bringing life to dry places buried deep inside. As her body moved in time with the music as if of its own volition and with no planning or help from herself, the song filled her in a way that the songs in the Tavern hadn't. Music had captivated her, held her attention, whispered of better things, but now it felt like a direct line heavenward. As if the very words of her heart were being poured out in the richness and complexity of notes she had never heard before and expressed her very desires and cries to the Keeper of her soul. The One who knew her name. The One who chose her and set her free.

Sheer freedom pounded out from her feet and into the starry night sky. Her skirts swayed, the wind taking her hair and tossing it about, the kerchief flying from her hair and into her fingers. She mimicked Nim and Izabella as their faces shone with joy and the golden light of the fire, their kerchiefs twirling in her fingers and whipping over her head and around her as she spun.

Nim's tambourine chimed in time with the music, and her skirts threw smoke and sound across the evening as the golden bead work danced and sparked.

The light swirled before Rosalie's eyes, and her spirit danced within her. It was strange but marvelous to feel her body free of all encumberment and to experience the joy and delight in her Creator. The group was one, but she also felt as though she stood apart, alone, smiled upon by the One who had never left her soul to darkness. The One who had always been with her. Even on the harshest of days and in the darkest of pains.

And her soul cried out to Him in gratitude. Exhaustion slipped away and peace became her companion, her very heart cloistered and held in the hands of the One who made the stars.

ENGUERRAND, FOURTEEN YEARS AGO...

He was not always a dark and mysterious ruler, clamoring for anything he could use to get ahead. He had once been sought after; he had been the one the king trusted the most. King Indulf himself had only deigned to take advice from one man: his best friend and loyal confidant...Enguerrand.

Enguerrand paced the caverns of his dark and lonely castle on its own mountain cliff. Far smaller than he was used to, it held him imprisoned with only the memories of his past failures floating in the shadows like ghosts that had come to haunt him. They were in the voices that echoed in the halls, the terrors that woke him in the middle of the night, and in those ghastly shadows that flitted from one room to the next.

But instead of banishing them, he held them close and wore them like the black cloak that kept him warm from the cold air that seeped from the stone walls and floors like steam from a cauldron. His last plan had ended in chaos, and he had held on to just enough information that could be helpful. It was not his final request of Zuko—this castle, these servants, this named nobility—in the land he had once sworn to stand against to the one friend he had ever known.

But oaths died with flesh, and Indulf was too far buried in his mountain grave to ever haunt Enguerrand with the truth of what he had once committed to through the lies he had sworn in the throneroom of Elira. His mind swirled like the whirlpool it was. Lies blended into truth, and he could no longer remember if they had always been lies.

Perhaps, once upon a time, when all had been right in the world, when his friendship with the king was greater than anything else, they had been truths. But over time they had colored green with the envy and degradation that he had felt at losing his friend to a slow and incremental death. A death of distance instead of life.

Questioning glances.

Lost trust.

Whispered conversations behind closed doors or down shadowed hallways.

Actions made without or firmly against his advice.

And it was then that Enguerrand knew that not only would his trust suffer the effects of a slow death. But so would his friend.

For who was better fit to run a kingdom than the man who had been trained for it his whole life? Who had stood at the king's side when they had both been boys? Who had walked in the footsteps of their fathers together? Who had often been in the throne room hearing the advice and rule of his father and the king while his friend was out training for battle? He had listened, had watched. Had held close his desires to stand tall in the throne room, next to the dais, having the ear of the monarch. He had fought at Indulf's side time and again, in skirmishes or outright battles. They had won the victory together, their blades dripping with the same blood and their hearts beating as one.

But then the day had come when Prince Indulf became King Indulf, and it felt so terribly wrong to see the man who had been more passionate about wooing a wife and learning the art of the sword than about foreign politics and policy occupying a throne Enguerrand was far more suited for.

Indulf's young pup was easy to take care of. Dissuaded from duty by all that glittered in this world. Drink, gambling, women. Whatever he desired was provided by Enguerrand. If Indulf could be distracted as a boy, surely his son could follow in his footsteps…and perhaps wander far enough away from the father who was desperately trying to maintain the reins of a kingdom poisoned from within. If he could manage that, Elgon would never become a stumbling block to his plans.

Disgruntled feelings had steeped in the witches brew of bitterness till it had grown as potent as the poison he diluted into the king's cup with his own hand. And day by day, as the king grew weaker and weaker and his mind started to wander, Enguerrand slowly but surely, dealing under the table, amassed more strength than he had ever thought possible. An alliance with the foreign soil he now walked upon had given him the final nail in the coffin, and the day the king was buried was the same day he watched the man's son break even further and fall sway to the temptations at hand. Those distractions that would steal him from the throne that was rightfully his… And that Engueurrand would not give up without a fight.

But he had miscounted the loyalty of the kingsmen. The few who dared to stand up to him. And that girl… He spat, his heart hammering hard in his ears, drowning out the echo of his clipping footsteps as they paced the great hall. The peasant who had become a queen. And who had dared not only defy his orders and the kingsmen he had sent, but had stood up to him and ripped away the mask he wore and thrown it back in his face.

He could still see her green eyes, blazing like a forest on fire, and he lashed out, kicking the lampstand over, the glass shattering and satisfying something within him as the flame slowly flickered out.

She had paid for her insolence. At least she too had joined the mistrusting and weak Indulf in a grave that would never be found. Deep in the castle of enemy territory, her legacy lost to dust, and buried in no better than a prison. He had hoped her life would be a long and miserable one, but death would have to do.

And now Zuko held the one last link to a kingdom that had won in every conceivable way.

Chaos had descended upon Niran that day, the attack from Zuko's secret force swift and overwhelming. More had taken a stand against them than he had expected, and instead of a sweeping victory, they had been foisted from the castle, escaping into the forest with their lives and a considerably smaller force than they had originally intended. And for that small victory and foil of Engerurrand's plans, Elgon would pay…

But instead of allowing him to ready the troops and attack again, this time abolishing any and all hold that the royalty of Elira had over the people—a people far stronger and more resilient than he had given them credit for—Zuko had commanded Enguerrand stay put.

"You will not have my men on one more wild goose chase, Enguerrand." Zuko's voice had been calm while

Enguerrand, for all his restraint, had been breathing heavily after his impassioned plea to wipe Elira from the face of the earth. "That is the difference between you and me. You react out of passion and fury. I, on the other hand, play a game far more complicated and with more patience than you will ever be capable of understanding."

Enguerrand had fumed but clammed up, withholding one last piece of information as a bargaining chip. "If you are going to think that you can get rid of me that easily, you should think again. For though you sent many men into Niran that day—and you may ask them—but none that returned know the whereabouts of the tunnels. If your plan is to be accomplished and completed, the map that resides nowhere but in this head of mine will need to be yours." He knew the dangerous game he was playing, but he was no stranger to it. He had always looked it in the face and laughed.

Zuko's eyes had glinted, and the right one had twitched, though his expression had not changed. "I could have you tortured till you divulge such information."

Enguerrand kept his facial expression neutral despite Zuko's attempts to frighten him. "Torture would not yield you what you seek, my lord. And neither will soft words and bribery. You will give me what I require and you will use me when the time comes as regent of Elira…as promised to me some years ago now. You may not think twice of going back on your word or find yourself forgetful, but I will not."

Zuko's smile came a second later, spreading slowly across his face and revealing that enigmatic grin that made him handsome in a devilish way and setting the gold tooth three spaces over from the front to sparkling. He nodded. "As you wish. And what, pray, will you ask in return?"

Enguerrand smiled, casually flipping his cape over his shoulder and leaning an elbow against the pillar placed conveniently to his left. "Just a few sundries…" He ticked them off his fingers. "Land, title, servants, the usual. I should live in the manner to which I am accustomed."

Zuko's laugh echoed in the large hall that held alcoves of windows with black tinted borders. He slammed a hand down on the arm of his mahogany throne. "Is that all?" He asked, bellowing out another laugh.

Enguerrands smile did not slip. "I happen to know you have plenty of decrepit castles in your mountains, my lord. Something about a few lords and ladies who knew not who they were up against? Your people can not be expected to govern themselves, now can they?"

Zuko paused, his grin remaining on his face as he studied Enguerrand. He stood, flipped his fur lined cloak behind him to let it hang better on his tall frame, and strode off the dais toward Enguerrand. "And you think you would be better suited for the job, eh? You know why those castles have settled into disrepair and their owners were either forced to flee or lose their lives?" More swiftly than even Enguerrand was counting on, Zuko flicked a dagger out from his sleeve, gripping it point first at Enguerrand's throat.

Those dark eyes flashed and the grin grew wider, his tongue quiet and deadly with its whisper. "Because, my dear would-be-regent, I have a penchant for disposing of those that disagree with me. Do I make myself clear?"

Enguerrand calmly stretched his neck. He had done it once; he could do it again. "The mountain king has my allegiance. If my actions over the past few years have not proven that, I'm not sure if his majesty is blind or simply needs to be made to see loyalty that would sooner bite him on the a—"

The blade hitched the last word from his lips, and Zuko leaned in. "I. See. Everything." Their meeting stares refused to break a few breaths before the dagger was suddenly stowed and Zuko strode to the throne once more. "Give him Draikonsfort and see to it that the people know by my edict that he is now the legal Vassal of the fief of Draikonsfort, and as such he will hold authority over the region. Now." He flicked his cloak behind him once more as he sat again upon the throne. "I don't want to hear from you until either your peasants pay me tribute from their vassal, or I have called for you to share this—information"—he waved a hand benevolently with a mocking lilt to his voice—"that you have so kindly agreed to bestow upon me should the time arise. Now. Be gone."

Enguerrand nodded and spun, trying to maintain the grin on his face as he was led from the throne room by guards dressed in the traditional garb of Rusalk warriors. Once the heavy wooden doors squeaked shut behind him did he let out the breath that had been trapped in his lungs for the entire length of the encounter.

He had been nearer death than he cared to admit. But then elation filled him with new fire in his veins. And just like every other time, he had risen to the top. And perhaps, as a vassal, his luck was about to change.

ELGON, FOURTEEN YEARS AGO...

Elgon watched Malcolm guide the sword he held into a defensive position, blocking and throwing the kingsman he trained off-guard. The young soldier stepped back, and Malcolm pressed the advantage, his brows drawn into a harsh line across his forehead and absolutely no mercy written in the stoic and straight look on his face. Malcolm lunged forward in the space the young man created as he stepped back. Shoving with his sword against the frantic attempt at a raised blade from the inexperienced lad, he pressed harder and threw the boy back further. The trainee's legs collapsed under him, and he fell into the dirt on his rear.

Eyes wide and frantic, the lad spun out of the way of Malcolm's blade in an attempt to give himself room to stand. Malcolm stepped forward again, forcing him onto his back, and their blades clashed with a sound that set Elgon's teeth on edge. With a subtle and deft twist of the wrist, Malcolm's blade whirled in an arc and plucked the young soldier's from his grip, sending it flying with a flick to his right.

Malcolm rested the point of his sword against the lad's neck, and the boy raised both hands in surrender.

Malcolm's jaw was set fiercely and the glint in his eye made even Elgon uncomfortable as he held the advantage for a moment. Finally, he moved back, shoulders square, and sheathed his sword before standing with his arms folded. The boy sheepishly waited for a hand up, then blushed as he realized it wasn't coming and scuffled to his feet in the dust, head hung in shame and cheeks ablaze.

"You were vulnerable in your attack. Make sure that you do not give ground, and instead of leaning on your back foot, you must be on the offense. You left space for me to double my attack and throw you off balance. You'd best learn to be quicker with the blade and more stalwart with your footing if you ever want to see any advancement or survive any real warfare." Malcolm's training delivery was dry, and Elgon winced under the strong and unsympathetic teaching method of his first man.

"Get yourself cleaned up and off to the barracks. We will resume again tomorrow."

The sweating young man kept his eyes on the ground, swiped a hand at his forehead, and bent to pick up his sword a few paces away, sheathing it as a flush continued to rise up his neck before scurrying for the cover of the barracks—away from Malcolm's judging gaze.

"You could have been a bit easier on the lad. This is after all only one of his first few lessons." Elgon's tone was void of judgment, but he still kept it measured.

Malcolm turned and strode toward him, his gaze not once meeting Elgon's eyes. "If we expect to hold off another attack and prepare for whatever Rusalka has in our future, there is not the time for coddling and weakness in training. If I, in my weakened and still recovering state, was able to best him so completely, what hope does he have from a real enemy?"

"I just mean that not all training needs to be degrading. Sometimes the lads learn a bit better from an approachable teacher." Elgon tread gently but spoke with confidence. Malcolm needed to shake whatever this despondent air was if they were ever to succeed in recruiting and training an army worthy of Elira's defense.

In many ways, he felt as though they were starting over. So many of the kingsmen that had been handed down to him from Enguerrand's reign were infected. He hadn't known how many till the betrayal. And even in his attempts to clean and rid them of those that did not wish to serve under Indulf's rule had clearly not gone as planned. Now, with many of those men defected, it at least showed them where they stood. More strict scrutiny was upon those who had stayed, in hopes to weed out any moles or spies that might still exist. But new soldiers were needed. Especially after an alliance with Pavlin was made and there was more land to protect and fewer soldiers to protect it.

Malcolm, upon his recovery, which was still slow in some respects, had been set to training the newest wave of recruits in an effort to build up his own strength in the process. Elgon had made him in charge of plotting the course of training that was needed, and he would soon be in charge of recruitment, taking out a garrison of soldiers to approach those in the rest of Elira and Pavlin to ask for volunteers and men to join not just the Kingsmen, but the army in reserve.

The country was sorely in need of people who would protect their towns and farms, who would willingly answer the call to defend or attack, , should the normal army not be sufficient or the attacks from their enemies be so specific that they would need to be at the ready for mobilizations to protect what was rightfully theirs.

That meant training grounds would need to be set up in all the major villages; farmers, workmen, and marketers would take turns being trained in the art of battle and close combat. He would not let his country be left defenseless again. No man should have to endure what he did. No man should have his home violated and his wife or children taken forcibly from him. He would ensure that every man was equipped with a weapon, and every man aware of how to use it to defend himself and his home.

He blinked and swallowed against the ache. Never again would he put Elira so at risk and leave her open to such an attack from within.

"Are you all right, m'lord?" Malcolm swung his sword's sheath at his side, the leather creaking and the movement stretching out the fastening from sheath to belt.

Elgon did his best to smile. "As well as can be. How goeth the plans for our forays into the unknown?" he asked softly.

The men who milled about the training grounds must not know of their spying into foreign lands. The initiative was secret, though many probably assumed what was going on. Everard had gathered a small cohort of volunteers, those most trusted, and those that had interest in covert missions, and trained them in the ways of the Rusalkan.

The men who were chosen were of larger build, darker in skin and hair to mimic and fit in with those across the border, and of some skill in not just hand-to-hand combat, but also in knowledge of weapons, mountaineering, farming, herding, and more. There were many trades that those who entered into Rusalka may be required to take on to keep their plans to learn more about their enemy intact.

Rensen from Pranvera, the inn-keeper who had sheltered the injured during the skirmish last winter, had been instrumental in getting word over the border and contacting a group of traveling performers who still operated on the other side of the wall. He had been Rusalkan once himself, and he and his wife still had some family who would not only set up and take in any of Elria's spies, but had promised to act as a way-house and place of safety for those who came and went on their secret reconnaissance.

"The initiative is going well. Everard's training might even be more rigorous than mine, which might account as to why I am as sore as I am." Malcolm clasped his hands behind him and stretched out his back, turning his neck one way, then the other.

"Even a master needs to be trained, eh?" Elgon let a small smile slip into his voice.

"Aye, though for the life of me, I'm surprised I felt as strong as I did." Malcolm absentmindedly reached a hand to the back of his head with a wince. The hair had yet to grow back over the scar, the seam of flesh and the divots from the stitches still plainly visible when his hair was not tied back into a tail with leather as it was now for training.

As if conscious of the movement and embarrassed by it, Malcolm shifted and turned the movement into a sweeping gesture, getting rid of the locks of hair that had fallen from the confines of the leather and into his face.

A whinny at his shoulder sent Elgon's nerves scattering, and he jumped, the feeling of looking for something that was not there ever present these days. He almost thought he'd see Violet's flirtatious grin from above Sigeric's withers and her hands tangled in his mane. The warhorse had always been particularly gentle with his wife. Especially when she visited him after finding out she bore a child. Sigeric would sniff at her waistline and step to protect her with his shoulders. Funny that, how animals knew things their masters were scarcely aware of.

"Everard has the men in tight shape. They'll be ready to head out as we had planned in three days."

Elgon gripped Sigeric's reins and put a foot into the stirrup, pulling himself up and over after a quick hop on his standing leg. Sigeric stepped sideways, anxious for the ride home through the moors. The training grounds and garrison were on the east side of the city, slightly removed from the walls in order to prohibit them from disturbing the townsfolk, and so that they had enough undisturbed space for their training exercises. Children often came to watch. At least, they did before the last attack. Now, many mothers and fathers were too afraid to let their little ones out of their sight, let alone without the city walls.

He glanced out toward the open space that would be the sea if they were closer. All he saw was waving grass and heather before the earth dropped off into the cliffs that sank into the ocean. "Do you think I am doing the right thing, Malcolm? Many would wonder why I do not storm the very gates of Rusalka to bring back my wife and child."

"Many do not know the intentions of your heart and the pain, but wisdom with which you make such decisions, your majesty. A king does not listen to many, but to the One who guides his heart and soul in His ways. The men are fragile, the kingdom unsure… Mounting an all out war against a country that has so readily earned a victory over us would be questionable at best, a folly at worst. Many were lost…"

Malcolm's voice broke, and he cleared his throat. "How many more would be lost if we did not first ensure the integrity of our force and the skill with which they set out against a foe that has so recently overpowered them?"

Elgon nodded. He gazed over the ocean a moment more till Sigeric's prancing, snuff, and toss of the head proved that he would be off. Perhaps a gallop was in order. He turned back to his friend, who despite his own misgivings still spoke wisdom and comfort. "Thank you, my brother." The words were heartfelt, and Elgon turned his horse's head and kicked him into a trot, then a canter, drawing a deep breath before he gave Sigeric his head and let him gallop toward the sea, pretending he hadn't seen the broken and sorrow-filled face of his friend at the word *brother*.

Twenty-Two

STALKING SHADOWS

MALCOLM, PRESENT DAY...

Malcolm threw a splash of water on his face, letting the frigid temperature sting and drag him a bit further from the death-like sleep he had endured the night before. Something about the words from Everard, the long day, and the worship of the evening prior had driven him into the deepest dreamless sleep he had experienced in as long as he could remember. Fitful, awake, watchful, or dreaming was his constant state; he almost didn't know what to think of a good night's sleep.

The sun was just peeking over the cliff tops that were framed by the forest and towered over the caravan's clearing. Orange and yellow light filtering with blue into the world around him. He splashed another handful of water over his face and used his wet hands to comb back any flyaways before drying them on a towel that hung next to the barrel. Something sounded in the forest—a crack. Perhaps a branch falling to the forest floor, but he whirled anyway, his nerves on high alert. He strained his eyes to see into the murky darkness and thought he saw shadows flitting amongst the trees.

He stared for a bit longer, wondering if his mind was playing tricks on him or if there were indeed shadows that shimmered in and out amongst the tree trunks and beneath the flickering leaves.

He was being ridiculous. Romanik's men would surely catch any lurkers in the forest. They kept a watch every hour of the day and night. This caravan and clearing housed their most precious possessions—the souls of their women and children. No risk was taken, and no watch left unattended. Rusalka was not a place for trust and easy living. But these people had thrived here. Or as close to it as they could under the circumstances.

"Good morning, Malcolm." The voice was bright and musical.

"Nim." Malcolm turned, handing her the towel as she stepped forward. Dark smudges under her eyes from the fading liner the Vagari women used were the only things that marred the bronzed skin of her face. Her white teeth flashed in a comfortable smile.

He turned to leave but she stopped him.

"Wait a moment, won't you? I've someone for you to meet."

Malcolm paused and waited while she splashed water on her own face and patted it dry before tying her curls back with a purple and blue kerchief. Some of the locks that had beads and charms tied to them in braids fell from the glorious mess and chimed softly as they swayed with her movement. She fell into step with him and swung her arms by her side as he strode next to her, his own arms folded over his chest.

"One of the slaves who made it in with Everard last night served at the castle."

"Izevel?" Malcolm breathed, incredulously. What if they should recognize Rosalie? Would it put them at more risk?

"Oi, pokój my friend." Her word for peace reminded him to take a deep breath. "They were *serviced*." Nim grimaced, anger flashing across her face and turning her skin a ruddy color. "To the garrison, so I doubt she knows anything about the hidden child that was secreted away in a tower. But she does know that something was amiss in Izevel. She has come from there more recently than you, and Zuko seems unhappy."

"He can take his unhappiness and cry an ocean for all I care," Malcolm spat, the words bitter on his tongue.

"Zuko is not in the habit of crying; unfortunately he is in the habit of killing." Her words were spoken in a monotone, but a chill ran down his spine. Not because he was surprised by them, but because they were true, and Nim was one of the few who knew how true.

"I'm sorry, Nim." His words came out of a tight throat. He had known her husband. Had met him on more than one occasion during his own forays into Rusalka for reconnaissance.

She nodded, her lips pressed together, and her easy stride tightened as she brought her arms up and cradled her elbows in her hands with a shrug. "At least I know where he is, and I'd rather him be there than anywhere else on earth."

Malcolm nodded and he clenched his jaw. One more thing to add to his list of reasons to avoid marriage and children. The ache of loss was already so deep when they *didn't* mean everything and the world besides to you.

"Here we are. Rano, Everard." She smiled up at the large man who stood guard outside the caravan that housed his rescues, his arms folded and a restful but aware look on his face.

He nodded with a slight smile, first to Nim, then Malcolm, neither speaking nor moving in any response to her greeting.

"Is the young woman we spoke of awake yet?" she asked him, rubbing her hands over her upper arms as if she were cold.

He nodded and rapped on the door of the caravan three times. A young woman opened the door, glanced at them all before blushing and dropping her gaze to the ground. Stepping out of the caravan, she held her skirts out of the way as she descended the stairs and wrapped her arms around herself, keeping her gaze on the dirt beneath her feet without saying a word.

"Tomsia." Nim stepped to her side, her voice soft, like she would use when comforting a frightened child. She placed her hand on the young woman's shoulder, and the girl did not shy away from her touch. "This is the man I told you about. Will you tell him what you told me of Izevel and what you witnessed there before you were rescued?"

Her face grew pale, and Malcolm regretted the need to drag up such memories from her of a place that most assuredly was filled with pain and suffering. She drew a shuddering breath and still couldn't seem to meet any of their eyes. She pulled her shawl closer over her shoulders and shivered slightly in the morning air. "They were upset. Many of them were grumbling about what had occurred, and there seemed to be a lot of casting blame amongst them. I overheard a few of them angrily discussing the need to 'find the king's prize,' and there was something said about 'they think they've won by stealing her, but we'll get her back and do more damage than would have been done before.'" She swallowed against what must have been a lump in her throat as her voice cut out at the last.

Malcolm felt the tightness winding about his shoulders. Something prickled at the back of his mind, pressing on the fight or flight feelings that coiled inside him like the tension of an arrow being pulled back against the bowstring just before it let loose. They needed to get this caravan moving. The sooner they could put some distance between themselves and any of Zuko's dark knights, the better. Zuko was not a merciful king.

"They also said something about 'better laid plans for the future of Rusalka than any the king has afforded us yet.'"

Malcolm swallowed the anxious feeling that gripped his throat with its icy claws and took a step back. The plans that Zuko had for the future of Rusalka that would need Rosalie so intimately was something he couldn't even begin to comprehend. Something dark, shadowy, and too disgusting to think about niggled at the back of his mind. Too shadowed to be named, but there nonetheless.

"Thank you, for telling us this. I—I am grateful." Malcolm's voice was shaky, and he caught the questioning tilt of Everard's brows.

Malcolm turned and strode from the back of the refugee wagon and set out to find Rosalie. He knew she had been sleeping in either Nim's caravan or with Romanik and Immanuella. Bogden had been loath to let go of Rosalie last night. The child fairly adored her.

His steps were long and fast as he made his way across the clearing. Turning around Romanik's caravan, a bevy of mourning doves sprung up in his face, their wings fluttering loudly with their soft, warning whistles echoing back in the early morning of the clearing. The hair on the back of his neck stood up straight.

Up the steps, he pounded on Romanik's door, realizing that he might be waking them up as he did so and softening his fist on the last knock. Movement from inside met his ears, along with soft whispers, and then creaking footsteps upon the wooden floor. The ornately carved, rounded door swung open on its hinges, the brick-a-brack and filigree in the wood carving catching his attention. The very same bevy of doves he had startled seemed to be caught in relief across the doorway and turning around the corner of the caravan.

"What is it, Malcolm?" Romanick strode out, still pulling a red and gold jacket over his linen shirt and trousers. The bright colors of it contrasted against the plain and somewhat disheveled shirt untied around his throat. "Is everything all right?"

Malcolm nodded, but still glanced around, half expecting a dark knight to leap out of the forest at a moment's notice.

He had let someone down before; he wouldn't do so again. "Where's Rosalie?"

"She's sleeping peacefully in Izabella's bunk. Shall I wake her?"

"No! I mean—" He spoke hastily and then ran his thumb along the hilt of his sword, feeling the metal crown that adorned the straight blade. "That's all right. Let her sleep. When do you have plans to move, Romanik?"

Romanik squinted, and he was far more alert than Malcolm would have thought with it being so early in the morning and having just been roused from his bed.

Malcolm gazed into the forest, Romanik's observation grating. He might be paranoid, but being hesitant and unconcerned was not what had gotten him this far in the first place.

"We'll be leaving as soon as camp is broken. Do you have concerns that we should get started on that right away?"

Malcolm shifted again and swung his arms behind him. There was something that was eating at his insides. He almost wanted to take Rosalie and run this instant, but that would be a foolish mistake. Riding with the Vagari was a surer way to get closer to their destination. The people of Rusalka left the Vagari alone for many reasons, some of which were true, and others were simple prejudice or misunderstanding. He ran his hands over the top of his head, shoving back the few locks of hair that had fallen in front of his face. While those assumptions may be untrue, it at least kept them safe.

"As long as you think we can depart today. I'm worried, Romanik. Something doesn't feel right. I was just talking with one of Everard's refugees, and there is grave concern for what the dark knights and Zuko's warriors might choose to do. The king is very displeased, and there is something in me that is terrified he might catch us off guard."

Romanik strode forward, and his hand hit the top of Malcolm's shoulder like a brick with its weight and size. "We'll get moving as soon as we can. But you're safer here than you might think. The Rusalkans don't like to tangle with the Vagari if they can help it."

Malcolm nodded and swallowed against the lump in his throat. "I wish I could trust in that, Rom. But this is a hornets' nest that has been left to its own devices for far too long. I'm worried that this might have been the poke that forces them out of hiding and into attack. We didn't exactly let sleeping dogs lie, and they won't either. Ghost stories in the wind won't keep them away this time, my friend. Not if they find out that we are here."

Romanik nodded and buttoned his jacket, tying shut the top of his shirt and pulling a matching scarf from his pocket that he tied around his throat, tucking the ends rakishly into the front of his jacket. "I'll wake the men and get things moving. Making sure you and the girl are safe is our utmost priority. Let me wake Immanuella first." He returned to the caravan and shut the door behind him, leaving Malcolm on the doorstep.

Malcolm felt some of the tension dissipate, but the anxiety that still curled in his stomach and coiled like a snake ready to strike merely seemed to sleep, not disappear entirely.

He turned to see where else he could help and caught Nim's eye. She was standing off to the side. Far enough away not to have interrupted but close enough to have heard the conversation.

She pulled her shawl closer around her shoulders and gave him a nod. "God goes with us, Malcolm. He hasn't brought you this far to let you fail now." Her chin was set; the muscles jumped in her cheek, but it was her eyes that caught his attention. The murky depths of pain with a tinge of fear that a woman with her past would struggle to live without. She knew exactly what the dark knights were capable of.

ROSALIE, PRESENT DAY...

Rosalie was jolted awake by Izabella kicking her in the shin. It was still dark in the bunk, but she drew in a breath and squinted, trying to see where her new friend was headed off to. "Izabella?" she whispered into the darkness.

"Oh! You're awake! Rano! I was trying to get out without waking you, but I'm sorry that I did. You looked all cozy and sleepy in your little den." Izabella ducked into her bunk, her head bent to avoid hitting it on the wooden slats above her, and she was pulling on socks in the opposite corner from Rosalie. She smiled. The girl looked so at home and natural, curled up in her tiny bunk.

"What time is it?" Rosalie yawned and stretched, her muscles aching from their use in dancing the night before.

"It's mid-morning. The camp's been up and roaming around for about an hour. Papa said he wanted us to sleep as long as we could because we hope to make it far today. But Mama needs my help getting the dishes packed and the caravan in moving order. I tried not to wake you."

"That's alright." Rosalie rubbed her eyes. She had slept all night, and so soundly too. She reached for the foot of her bed, but Izabella beat her to it, handing her the small bundle of clothing she had trundled away the previous night before pulling her own bodice on over her head and lacing it in front. Rosalie followed suit, sorting through the ruffles of material to pull her Vagari skirt over her head and fasten it around her waist, making sure her chemise was tucked in and out of the way. She reached under her pillow and pulled out her wool socks, slipping them onto her bare feet and pushing her hair back and out of her face.

Izabella reached past her and pulled aside the curtain that separated the cubby hole from the rest of the caravan, and light from the open door streamed in, making Rosalie blink against its brightness. The sound of birds chirping outside, voices, and axes, pounding, and general milling noises met her ears, and she smiled. These people were hard workers, and that was something she could relate to.

"Rano, little ones!" Immanuella took her daughter by the hand and helped her down from the cubby that rested about waist length from the floor. Kissing the top of her daughter's head of messy curls, she then reached for Rosalie. She felt the woman's kiss as her feet hit the ground, and her smile blossomed again before she had a chance to think about it. There was so much delightfully cozy love in this home that her heart fairly sang with it. Bogden slammed into her legs, his own mop of black curls bouncing with his movement as he grinned his toothy smile up at her.

She hugged him back and watched as Immanuella shoved a wide-toothed wooden comb into her daughter's hand and pointed at the wayward curls before scurrying back to the little stove in the corner where two pots bubbled in chorus together. She gave them each a vigorous stir while the music of preparation continued outside.

"What does 'rano' mean?" Rosalie whispered, dragging Bogden across the floor with her since he refused to release her from his clinging grip.

Izabella smiled, then yelped as she dragged the comb through her hair. "It means, morning! Like a-a—" She grimaced at the comb, now stuck in her curls, and stamped her foot impatiently.

"It's a greeting, mlødy. Izabella, what have I told you about the comb?" Immanuella smiled and shook her head with an eye roll while she rescued the comb with a swift motion and ran it through the ends of her daughter's curls.

Izabella rolled her own eyes in remarkable resemblance to her mother. "To start at the ends. But, Mama, it takes so long! Why can't I have it cut short like the boys? All they have to do is tie theirs back."

Immanuella was already mid-shaft and transitioning to combing the tangles from the scalp by then. "It doesn't take very long if you do it right, and trust me, you'll appreciate your long hair soon enough. Here." She swept it into three strands and braided it swiftly, then pulled the scarf from around her neck, wrapping Izabella's head and braid in the purple and blue silk and tying it around it. "There, hardly any time at all. Your turn, dear."

Rosalie allowed herself to be pulled nearer to Immanuella and suddenly felt the comb being swept through her own long curls, gently at first, working out knots, and going from ends to the top. When Immanuella had finished with the comb, she swept back the pieces near Rosalie's face, twisting them back and then tying them off into a braid that traveled down her back and swung against her hip after Immanuella tied it off with a string. "Here, młødy." She stood and reached over the two bed cubbies that her children slept in and pulled a golden yellow and red scarf from the shelf above them, wrapping it over Rosalie's head and tying it around her braid just like Izabella. "Don't you look lovely."

With a smile, Imanuella patted Rosalie on the shoulder after laying the braid softly over it and to the front before she turned back to the stove. "Your father might need your help with the rigging outside, girls. I'll have śniadanie ready in a few moments."

Rosalie followed Izabella as she careened from the caravan and out into the glittering sunshine and crisp mountain air. The girl had a gracefulness about her that was only punctuated by her energetic nature as she dashed here and there with all the focus of a squirrel searching for its winter stash of nuts.

Rosalie gasped as Izabella leapt off the caravan without the use of stairs and onto her father's back as he was bent untying the tent bindings from the ground.

"Oi!" he shouted and reached around, grabbing his daughter's giggling and squirming form and hopping from one foot to the next as if he had a swarm of bees after him. "I've been attacked!" He groaned and wailed dramatically.

Rosalie almost tumbled to her backside when Bogden barrelled past her and clambered down the steps to prance around at his father's feet, giggling with his arms outstretched to be welcomed into the group. Romanik let his son grab his knees and pretended that they buckled under the weight before toppling into the wet grass and letting the children crawl on top of him while he bellowed like his life was at stake.

She didn't feel like she belonged. Awkwardly, Rosalie stood at the top of the stairs, her heart beating hard in her ears and a smile on her face. But it was a hesitant smile. She wanted to join in, to partake of the closeness they shared, but she was at a distance, an outsider.

"You look lovely. I almost didn't recognize you with that beautiful scarf."

Rosalie turned. Nim stood at her shoulder, her shawl tied over one of her own and under the other, her sleeves rolled up as if coming from working and her arms folded across her chest. The fringe of the shawl blew in the breeze, and Rosalie noticed that the scarves on their heads matched in color if not in pattern.

Rosalie lifted a hand and touched the silk, soft and cool to her fingertips, a bit like water from the mountain streams. "It's so pretty. Did one of you make it?"

"My mother is known for her linen silk. Weaves the flax down smaller and tighter than anyone I know. Her scarves are the softest and brightest in color." She toyed with her own. "I'm still learning to master the skill with hardly as much grace as she has. It's a hard one to learn."

"You all make such beautiful things. I can spin and have nearly my whole life, but nothing as fine and dainty as you have."

Nim glanced at her and her eyes twinkled, a small smile tugging at the corner of her mouth. "You're a spinner? Do you also weave? You sure are full of surprises."

Rosalie nodded and glanced over her shoulder at the play of Romanik and his children as he roared at them and chased Izabella toward the center of camp with Bogden under one arm like a wayward log. She bit her lip. Her chest ached with it; the reality that this would never be her childhood, that it hadn't been.

A hand on her shoulder drew her attention. "It's okay to mourn, kochanie."

"I'm being brought home. Shouldn't I be rejoicing?"

Their footsteps were nearly silent in the dew-soaked grass of the morning as they made their way across the clearing. The birds singing in the trees grew louder as they walked and the sounds of camp being broken faded behind them.

Nim drew a breath and Rosalie looked up to catch her staring off into the woods. "One can rejoice and mourn at the same time, mlødy. Pain and joy dwell together more often than they do apart. Mourning something you never had can be just as real and painful as mourning something that was stolen from you." Her voice choked on the last word, and her dark eyes welled.

Rosalie reached up and took the young woman's hand and squeezed it in her own.

Nim smiled down at her, and a tear fell at the drop of her head. She pulled Rosalie into an embrace, her chin resting on the top of Rosalie's head. Rosalie wrapped her arms around Nim's waist and held tight as a silent sob shook her new friend. They held each other as the sunlight topped the cascade of mountains and flooded the clearing with golden light so bright, Rosalie had to shut her eyes. Rosalie didn't have to know the details to know that Nim's sorrow ran as deep as the underground well of her own.

Nim let go and took Rosalie's face in her hands, using her thumbs to wipe away her tears, her gaze soft, sorrowful, but awe-filled. "Let me show you something." Taking Rosalie's hand again, Nim led her to a caravan out of the way, already packed and waiting for its departure. The horses were hitched, their massive golden bodies and long flowing manes just as showy and beautiful as the Vagari's colorful clothing.

Rosalie stepped up behind Nim as the woman opened the door for her, heaving the ornate wood on its hinges and letting Rosalie move past her into the dark space. Nim struck a match and lit the lantern above the table, cracking a window and letting some of the outside light in.

Books. Rows, stacks, and piles of them. A little table in the center with a map spread upon it and pages of handwritten notes in some semblance of order. A tiny sliver of light from the slatted window mixed with the golden haze of the lantern and filled the room with welcoming shadows—dancing movements from the tassel of the curtain that hung just above the slatted window. The deep, jewel-toned hues of the Vagari decorated the edges of the shelves; doves and patterns of crosses, birds in flight, filigree, and scrolls decorated every piece of wood within the cart. Cushions of deep purples and reds rested on the floor and were strewn against the wall in what looked like a makeshift couch.

"Biblioteka," Nim said softly, her voice filled with a mixture of awe, delight, peace, and joy.

Rosalie drew a breath. She touched the scattered pages with delight, her fingers trailing across the ink, words strewn across it. She looked up as Nim stepped toward the shelf and reached for the largest book amongst them, pulling the painted leather spine from its place with reverent hands and resting it on the table in front of Rosalie.

"Malcolm told me you had no Bible where you lived."

"Only the words that live inside my head."

"'But the Comforter, which is the Holy Ghost, whom the Father will send in my name, he shall teach you all things, and bring all things to your remembrance, whatsoever I have said unto you.'" Nim's smile grew wider. "He gave you a teacher and then brought them to mind for you, mlødy."

Rosalie reached for the book and flipped through its pages, a hunger in her to read more of the words that she never knew existed filling her heart and soul like a fire ablaze. The chapters Zehra had taught her and she had committed to memory had stood her in good stead for years, being the only tie to the Living Word that she had. But there was something that always hungered for more.

"This is our greatest treasure, and we copy off as much as we can in secret for others as we journey. It's the reason we don't stay in one place for too long. Too many need these words, need the life that they bring. That's why we came to Rusalka in the first place." Nim's eyes were filled with reverence and love as her hands stroked the pages filled with words.

Rosalie glanced up. "Where did it come from? When did you come here?"

Nim smiled, her gaze distant as she stared at the pages. "We've been here for decades now, longer than I've been alive. The story goes that travelers brought the story of life to our country over the mountains. They risked everything to journey from the land where Jesus was born to spread the gospel and His words with everyone they met. Many spurned their story, but when they came to my home country, my people heard their story and believed their words. They were saved and filled with the Holy Spirit, and now, in their honor and in answer to the call of our Savior, we too have become travelers, Vagari, those without a home, but with the truth of life."

Rosalie blinked. "The doves?"

Nim grinned and absentmindedly reached for the place on her neck where the tattoo rested. "It first represented the place where the Holy Spirit dwells. Like the spirit descending from heaven like a dove and indwelling Jezus Chrystus, we bear the mark of His spirit, the mark of His children. It's become known for those that are peacekeepers. We do not adhere to the politics of this world, but a higher one, and so the safe-havens of Rusalka were born. It's how you journey with the protection of those that have seen the darkness and been saved from its hold on them and now walk with the light of Christ inside of them."

"Malcolm said that where there are doves, there is safety."

Nim nodded and flipped through the pages. "As much safety as prayer and people can provide on this earth. We came over the mountains many many years ago with our wagons and our families to dwell in a place that needed to hear of Christ's sacrifice, and as we did, we realized that the need was greater than we had thought. For people here do not just need rescue from the darkness of the devil and the slavery of the mind, but from the slavery of their bodies as well. Many who serve Zuko distrust us, and stories of witches, spirits, and seances with ghosts in the deepest part of the forest keep us safe." She grinned, finding the page she had been searching for and turning the book around so Rosalie could read. "But there is only one Spirit here, and He is more powerful than they will ever give Him credit for. They mock and label what they do not understand and what they do not wish to understand."

Rosalie suddenly reached for Nim's hand, a thought having sprung up in her mind. "Why do you live in your own wagon and not with your parents?"

Nim froze, her demeanor standing still as if shocked into silence. The smile was gone from her face, and she took her hand from Rosalie's, rubbing hers together as if they had suddenly grown cold. "It was not just my own caravan once." Her voice was tight, and the muscles in her jaw clenched. "Many of the Rusalkan warriors and Zuko's men do not wish to understand the power of what we carry. Instead they fear the threat to their way of life that we are. But my husband would not let one be left behind, and so he sacrificed himself that another might be free."

Rosalie's heart clenched. Had not the same men snuffed out the life of her own mother before she had a chance to know her? Her mother's death was not just about what Zuko does to his enemies, but about what he feared would take over his country from within. "I'm so sorry," she whispered.

Nim nodded and drew in a sharp breath, clearing the emotion from her face and shuffling the loose papers on the table together into a neat stack that she placed inside a carved wooden box. "I am too, but I won't let his legacy die if I can help it." A "hiyup" from outside startled them as the wagon creaked and started forward. "It seems we are on the move." She reached for the door as if to go out.

"May I help?" The heart to read and write the Lord's words like Nim did filled her with a passion and fire she wouldn't easily be distracted from.

Nim stared at her for a moment, then let a small smile seep back into her features. She flipped the latch so that the door would not fly open as they rode. "Of course. What better way to wile away the travel? Let's write the words of life."

ELGON, TWELVE YEARS AGO...

Elgon rested his chin in his hand, his mind distant. He stared at the intricate wood grain of the table and traced the golden pattern of rings with his other hand. The conversation stirred around him like a hornet's nest, buzzing like it was about to explode. Or perhaps the conversation had already exploded.

"I don't care how weak and disorganized our army is. It's been two years! We should have gone in and demanded Zuko return to us what is ours! At this point, he is just mocking us to our face. We don't even know that our hostages are alive!" Lord Rowan shouted. He was Niran's councilman and a distant cousin of Elgon's father's.

Elgon winced at the insinuation. Rowan's intentions were pure, his heart angered for his familial sense of duty, but his words echoed harshly in the silence of the otherwise empty room.

"And?" Lord Loucas, the representative from Wood River, bounced his closed fist on the arm of his chair. "We just march all the way across Rusalka, over two mountain passes and into Izevel and demand he show us proof of life and return to us what he stole? While his men pick off our army one step at a time? The land is too vast! As much as I dislike this cat and mouse game, what can we do aside from declare all out war and risk losing the lives of countless more in an attempt to, what? Demand Zuko stop ignoring our messengers?" As keeper of a city so near the border of Elira and Rusalka, Lord Loucas's words were not without insight. His border had been weakened under Enguerrand's rule, and while they had experienced nothing close to what Pranvera had the year before Violet was taken, he had still lived in a level of fear that few could grasp.

"Our armies are stronger now and our country better fit to protect itself, but what would knocking at Rusalka's door do that sending messengers and spies have not? Surely the quiet and stealth-like approach may be better than demanding a war be waged between two countries." Fendrel had been elected by the people of Padsley to speak on their behalf, and his wise words and quiet manner seemed to calm the other councilmen, as if his tone tossed a peaceful herbal tincture into the atmosphere.

Rensen, elected to represent Pranvera, nodded vigorously from his seat beside Fendrel. Neither man had dressed in anything fancier than their best for this meeting and Elgon fought a small smile. These two men had more wisdom than the rest of his fancily-clad council members. As a merchant, Lord Rowan knew little more than his sea trade and the inside of the city of Niran.

"What many of you forget is that the loss of life is always more numerous on the side that cannot defend themselves," Fendrel went on. "While we do not cower in fear from Rusalkan warriors, it is rarely just the soldiers that risk life and limb, but the inhabitants that suffer most. I know time has gone on, but perhaps if we rest in a season of waiting while the spies and messengers do their work, the return of our queen will be more assured than if we had stormed the gates and ransacked home and vale in an attempt to get her back. Can we not trust that the Lord is working even while we cannot see it? I for one do not feel any peace about sending a war-party into Rusalka to stir up trouble. Are we not better than the Rusalkan warriors who follow the orders of a king who shows no mercy and no allegiance to anyone but himself? Are we not better than the traitors who gave up their own land and people for something that glitters?" Fendrel's words were not forceful, but the passion in his voice was met with another nod from Rensen.

Elgon glanced at Malcolm, who sat stiff as a tree trunk and with a face as austere and immovable as the mountain passes. Elgon knew that he always took in more than he let on. He drew a deep breath and turned to his friend. "Do you have anything to say from a military perspective, Malcolm?"

Malcolm shifted in his seat. "I'm sure that my king knows how desperately I would like to get the queen back." His tone was unemotional, but Elgon knew his friend well enough to know that it wasn't for lack of emotion. "But I too would advise against running roughshod into Rusalka with a military plan tantamount to a battering ram in an attempt to rescue anyone. I would hazard that such action would do more to anger our opponent and potentially even drive him to do more than just hold hostages. Hostages rarely remain so when pressure to retrieve them is perceived."

Elgon felt the lump in his throat grow. As much as the conversations of the past few years had constantly centered around this one object, the thought of his heart's desire and passion languishing away somewhere within the confines of the Izevel mountains or castle made his stomach turn.

"But that's just it—my pardon, your majesty." Lord Loucas of Wood River spoke. "It's been years. How do we even know that anyone who was taken is still alive? What if we sent a larger envoy and more than just a messenger? Something so large and official that Zuko would not be able to ignore it. Surely he would prefer not to lose face, and the entire continent would hear of such an act if we were to do so."

"And who would volunteer, Loucas? You?" Rowan's voice had a mocking edge to it that made Elgon want to cringe. "You know what Rusalka does to intruders and what has happened to some of the messengers we have sent."

Loucas paled. "I-I would if my king asked it of me." His voice was shaky, but firm in its response.

"As honorable as that is," Lord Milton spoke for the first time during the entirety of the meeting. "Such an envoy, though large, might net a larger disgrace should Zuko take it into his head that the world ought to know just what he thinks of Elira. As painful as waiting has been, I do not wish to rush myself or my men into a war for which we cannot ensure an outcome. The fact remains that we have little information to go on. While there are allies being made in Rusalka, surely, they are far too few and too little is known to do anything of grave import without risking the lives of an envoy, an army, or civilians. And be it many or not, a few lives put at risk is thought enough to give me pause."

"If no one is going to do anything, perhaps we should just give up altogether." Rowan huffed in frustration and adjusted his cape and himself on his chair.

Elgon's slow tap of his forefinger against his thigh halted. The ringing quiet that met his ears echoed louder than the shouting of moments before. He never thought silence had a taste before, but there it was, palpable and salty with a bitterness that made him want to scrape it off his tongue. He avoided catching anyone's gaze and drew in a deep breath.

"I-I'm sorry, Elgon." There was true remorse in Rowan's voice, but the man couldn't possibly know of what he spoke or how painful it was.

Elgon stood, the legs of his chair scraping the stone with an ugly cry that resounded harshly in the vast stone room. The bitterness burned on his tongue like a flame in the mouth of a dragon, begging to be let out and overwhelm all in its path. "I know that you couldn't possibly understand my position, Rowan. It seems that a man of little sense would wait with hope and baited breath so long for something he doesn't even know is promised. But the silence speaks of hope to me. I cannot help but think that if Zuko had done"—he cleared his throat—"had done anything to my wife and child that he would have flaunted it for all the world to see. Instead, he sits in silence, locked away in his domain, waiting for us to move. I'm sorry if it goes beyond your hope that the Lord may not perform some miracle and return the queen and heir to the kingdom of Elira, but I can do nothing *but* hope. Now, I'll let Malcolm discuss the plans for the new recruits that we plan to send to Rusalka next week. If you'll excuse me, I will get some air. Malcolm, send Tobias for me if you have need of me or if anyone feels the need to object to our carefully laid plans." He nodded stiffly to the group, tucked his trembling hands behind his back, and strode through the door, letting Tobias scramble to open and shut it after him.

Once through, he drew a deep breath, heaving in and out, the weight on his chest seeming to lighten the farther he traveled away from the council room. He knew that there would be strong opinions and even sharper words today. Something about the lack of perceived action on his part was rankling to a few of the men, but there was little in him that had any desire to provoke an attack from Rusalka.

He fumbled with the door's latch to the upper walk up on the wall, his hands shaking. He finally got it open and shoved the wooden doors with a shoulder, nearly tumbling from the castle and gulping in the sea air. His feet took him swiftly over the wall's walkway, and he drew in calming breaths. His body no longer seemed to tremble, and he rested his hands on the curtain wall and stared out over the sea. He closed his eyes, letting the chilled sea wind blow the hair from his face and the cobwebs from his mind.

He knew that what Rowan said shouldn't rattle him, but as the months passed painfully beyond his grasp with no word from Rusalka and the return of only half the messengers they had sent, each more wounded or degraded than the last, his own hope grew shaky and thin. He fought the wave of nausea that came at the thought of the wounds the last one had received. Not again. The spies were far more successful, and Zuko had made it clear that he not only refused to respect a royal messenger, but that he cared not to hear from Elgon at all.

He'd inform Malcolm later and then wait to notify the council at their next meeting, but no more messengers would be sent.

Zuko knew what he was doing. The slow, painful death of hope was like a poison in its own right. If hope deferred makes the heart sick, then hope unfounded kills it completely. Every day that went by with no word, no sign…a tiny piece of him died, and he didn't think those pieces would ever be revived.

Rowan knew not of what he spoke. Of all of them, Rowan's life had given him little reason to be patient, to hope against hope, but if it were his wife and child who were being held behind enemy lines, his hope would be alive as long as it took to bring them back.

A cloud blew over the sun and blocked the light, the shadow making him shiver and reach for the cloak that was thrown over his shoulder. He would hope against hope, even if every tiny bit of it he had left seemed to be shrinking by the day.

MALCOLM, PRESENT DAY…

He couldn't find Rosalie. He had ridden all up and down the caravan and couldn't find her anywhere. She hadn't been with Izabella or Bogden as they rode on their ponies with the youngsters. She hadn't been near Romanik and the other men who led the caravan. And even Immanuella hadn't seen her from her spot on the front seat, driving their family caravan.

His mind was racing. There was something wrong. Why did he have this intense feeling of dread as if the worst was about to—or had—happened? He needed to tell Romanik and ask for help. Where was Nim?

He prodded his horse into a canter to ride past the varied and colorful wagons, their creaking and jostling on the rocky mountain road filling his ears along with the hoofbeats of the Vagar Mocny, the monstrous and blocky breed of horses with flowing manes and tales that were bred expressly for pulling the Vagari wagons.

The women drove the wagons, many of the men on guard from their own mounts, riding up and down the length of the train to ensure the safety of each wagon and that no one fell behind. They also guarded against attack and rode in the woods beside the road, making certain that they weren't being followed and that they tracked the whereabouts of anyone who would wish them harm.

One of the men astride a beast similar in coloring to Malcolm's trotted from the woods at his left and circled a wagon ahead of Malcolm, talking with the woman who drove it for a moment before he kicked his steed toward the front.

Malcolm prodded his own horse into a gallop and overtook the Vagari. "Garridan!" He hailed him with an arm above his head.

Garridan shifted in his saddle to look over his shoulder and pulled his horse up but kept the steed moving. Malcolm nearly froze at the look on his face. Something wasn't right. Garridan beckoned with an arm wave that Malcolm should catch up before prodding his horse toward the front of the caravan once more.

Malcolm leaned forward, the mane of his horse whipping him in the face as he rode faster to keep up with the Vagari scout. He must have something to tell Romanik—and whatever it was, it couldn't be anything good.

MALCOLM, PRESENT DAY...

With a howl that made the hair on the back of his neck stand on edge, the wind burst over the mountain pass into the valley they wound through. It was surrounded on either side by forest that seemed to reach its shadowed hands toward him. Malcolm rode after Garridan, though he fought hard with himself not to turn around and continue his search for Rosalie. The insatiable desire to find her, know that she was safe, have her in his sight and care, unnerved him beyond anything he had ever experienced.

Something was wrong.

Breathlessly, he pulled up his steed beside Garridan, who was already talking and gesticulating wildly to Romanik. "What is it?"

Romanik threw his head over his shoulder, his piercing black eyes vibrant in his fierce face, his jaw beneath his black beard set and hard as he inspected the edge of the forest, squinting into the shadows.

"A scout," Garridan said, low. "A dark knight. Our group found him in the woods, and he headed for cover before we could capture him. He answered not our call to halt. Something is amiss. We lost him in the woods, but we heard voices and horses." Garridan's face, similar to Romanik's with the same high cheekbones, dark hair and beard, square jaw and aquiline nose, but much younger, had a look of concern that Malcolm did not often see in the Vagari men.

Garridan must have felt it too. That unnamed, uneasy feeling that was creeping up behind Malcolm and digging its icy fingers into his spine.

"You're sure it's a dark knight? How could you tell at such a distance?" Romanik held his horse at bay as it pranced sideways, sensing the uneasiness of the group.

"As sure as I can be, Romanik. You know their ways. The weapons they carry. The silence and cold stares. Despite not knowing for certain, my heart tells me so. There is a chill I feel to my soul. Something must be done. We must gather the bevy." Garridan's words were not soft, his intent clear, and though his facts were lacking, his emphasis on their needed action put Malcolm even more on edge.

"Have they come for us?"

A beat of silence met his question, and Garridan's answer was written on his face, though, out of deference he waited for his leader to answer, adjusting his reins and his legs as his horse hopped sideways, no doubt sensing the unrest and worry of his master.

Romanick kept his gaze focused on the woods. "Circle or flee. If we stand and fight, it gives you a chance to retreat." His words were low, only for their ears as the woman driving the wagon behind them seemed to have a look of concern and awareness on her face as her hands clenched the reins of her team. Another beat of silence and Romanik lifted his fingers to his lips and issued a piercing whistle. He nodded to Malcolm and reached out a hand, which Malcolm took gratefully. "Get her out of here. Protect her with your life. I'll hold them off as long as I can. Head farther north to avoid them through Wraith Forest. Few will follow you there, and those who do won't make it far."

Malcolm nodded, glancing past Romanik to the northern woods and the shadows that awaited them there. They were named Wraith Forest for a reason, but he wouldn't dwell on that now. He shifted his reins to leave, but Romanik had not loosened his grip. Malcolm turned back, his heart telling him to gallop after Rosalie as fast as possible. Already the wagons were circling in silence, the Vagari familiar and practiced with the exercise and aware of how to limit the amount of noise and chaos such an order from Romanik caused. Garridan galloped down the line, ensuring that everyone had heard the signal and repeating it himself as he approached the end of the wagon train.

"Malcolm. See her safe. God will protect you."

Malcolm gave a strong nod, his teeth aching as they clenched together.

"God will not fail you. Now go. On the wings of the wind." Romanik raised three fingers to rest over his heart in a salute.

"To the sun," Malcolm returned, jerked the reins to the right, and galloped down the line of caravan wagons. Rosalie had to be either in Nim's or with her in the library cart.

While he hoped against hope that Garridan was wrong about the dark knights, the secret warriors initiated into the rites of Zuko, he could sense their presence too. The darkness they carried and the fear they instilled as a result of their brutal and inhumane attacks could be felt by anyone discerning, even from a distance.

Nim's wagon was first, the purple and gold flag hanging from the back of the wagon waving in the breeze. Malcolm shivered in the chill wind. He felt as though he had eyes on him. He glanced over his shoulder again. Nothing met his gaze, but he felt them watching, lurking, waiting.

Without dismounting, he banged on the side of the caravan, the ornate patterns painted and fading from sun and rain catching his gaze and reminding him of the hidden messages of the gospel that his and Rosalie's life was not within his hands alone. He was grateful that he had remained packed at all times and that the saddle bags on their horse held all they would need for the journey ahead. He had hoped something like this would never happen, but had prepared for it in case it did.

The wagons had circled into a tight ring, preparing a blockade as they would for setting camp, but arranging themselves closer to each other than usual in a defense against any outside attack. Be they human or animal, the Vagari were used to and trained to ward off attack and protect those that they loved.

The sudden silence after the constant clopping of hooves unnerved him. And where was Rosalie?

"Nim!" he hissed, but no response met his ear. *Please let them be in the library cart.* He prodded his horse into a trot, now winding in a circle around moving wagons.

Nothing seemed to breathe, to move. The sounds of the wagons creaking almost faded into silence, and the horses even tempered their unease. The giant, gentle beasts were well trained and loved by their owners, and they could calm and silence them with a word or a touch. Not even a bird chirped to break the stillness in the dense foliage of the woods.

There. The library cart. He watched as Nim stepped out of the door, her eyes piercing and her hand gripping the side of the door frame as she angled her upper body out of the opening while protecting something behind.

With a crack, the woods erupted with a bevy of birds, their frantic calls filling the air with a cacophony of panic as they took off, swooping in a group over the Vagari, and then righting themselves as they took off into the sky. Every muscle tightened in preparation for what was to come. For he knew they were not startled by a mere wanderer.

The battle shout echoed over the clearing. Rusalk warriors, the dark knights, their camouflage cloaks whipping over their shoulders as they drew their curved scimitars from their belts, poured onto the road.

An explosion of movement, activity, and shouts took over the caravan, and the men drew their swords, women disappearing into the wagons, pulling children after them and locking hatches. Malcolm drew his sword and turned his horse, facing the attackers and ducking as an arrow shot past him. Nim's sharp whistle cut through the melee, and he backed his horse to the wagon.

"Quickly! Get her out of here!" Nim shouted above the din, guiding a hooded and cloaked Rosalie from behind her in the wagon and lifting her to a seat in front of Malcolm. He held his sword to the side, his eyes trained on the action as the Vagari men surged forward to engage the Rusalks, their swords clanging against each other, metal on metal causing his teeth to clench.

No sooner was Rosalie settled on the horse before Nim gripped the bow that had been leaning against the wall and whipped an arrow from the quiver over her shoulder, nocked it, drew, and shot. The arrow flew into the arm of a swordsman a second before he plunged his sword into one of the Vagari men. "Go!" she shouted, already pulling another arrow and setting it on the string. "Behind the wagons!"

Malcolm's rein hand pulled back, holding Rosalie beneath the grip of his forearm as he spun the horse and prodded him with a jab of the heels to the flank. The horse hopped before starting into a trot but drew up sharply at the Russalk warrior that faced them. The man's hood was drawn down over his eyes, the forest-colored and variegated cloak thrown over his shoulder to reveal black leather armor and the scimitar gripped in his hand. The horse whinnied in fright, hopping on his back feet in a half rear to get beyond the reach of the blade.

The man reached up and caught a fistful of both Rosalie's and Malcolm's cloaks on the opposite side from where

Malcolm held his sword. Malcolm tried to swing it over Rosalie while keeping his grip as the man sought to pull them off the horse's back. His muscles strained in opposite directions, trying to keep them from falling, while also attempting to defend them. Rosalie tried to duck out of his way, but before that could happen, the flat of a longsword came down on the man's arm, and he released their cloaks, crumpling to the ground as he let loose a cry of pain.

Everard stood over the Rusalk, his longsword in hand and his eyes flashing fire. "Run!" he shouted, as he brought the sword around to meet the Rusalk's scimitar as it rose in a counterattack. Malcolm saw enough to catch the Rusalk's sharp face and flint-like gaze as he rolled swiftly to his feet and out of reach, parrying against Everard's advance.

With a kick to his horse's flank, they were in the woods, the beast's pounding hooves driving them farther from the melee behind.

But two riders, their cloaks matching the trees flashing in Malcolm's peripheral, had spotted them fleeing and were giving chase. Malcolm leaned forward, pulling Rosalie into his chest and urging their mount to greater speed with his heels. Weaving through the trees, he tucked his sword arm in so that the blade did not endanger himself or the horse and would be free from knocking against a tree. He needed his weapon at the ready. This was far from over.

ELGON, TEN YEARS AGO...

Elgon's muscles tensed as the court gathered on the eve of Violet's day of birth. A banquet was held in honor of the traveling dignitaries, and they came to pay their condolences and honor the memory of his wife, the queen of Elira.

He had been advised to offer the banquet and host an event that would remind the people of her legacy and bring them together to pray and break bread and intercede together for her return. But this year, it felt like a sham, a funeral, a celebration of a life lived and…lost.

No. He had not lost. He would not believe it. Hope had not died within him, despite those that would do all that they could to snuff it out "for his good." As he mingled, he tried to see past their words and to their hearts. He let his mind wander and float to some other place and time while they talked and waxed eloquent on what they would wish for him.

This year, there was less of the "I have been praying for the queen and her return" and more of the "I have been praying for your majesty."

Of what prayer did he need? Why did they waste breath praying for someone who was home, safe, waiting? Why did they not pray for resolution? For return, for recovery of all? Why did their eyes flicker with those elements of sorrow woven together with pity? He recoiled at the touch of one of the lord's wives as she patted his hand with her elderly, wizened one and lifted sorrowful eyes to his face. "I pray often for you, majesty, that the Lord would comfort your heart."

He stumbled a single step backward and could not even bring himself to mutter any thanks when he received a sharp look from Malcolm, who hurried to smooth things over as Elgon retreated.

While the room was filled with bouncing golden light from a thousand candles and many fires that chased the damp and chill from the brick, those fires could not chase the chill from his heart. Shadows gathered in the corners, held at bay, but mocking him with their presence as if they could jump upon him at any moment. That familiar ache gathered in his chest. The dresses and courtly clothes of the diplomats, council, and their families swirled in his vision, and he would have fallen to his knees were it not for an elbow suddenly materializing with fortitude beneath his hand.

"May I take you to the dais, majesty?" Malcolm. His saving grace.

Elgon nodded, drawing a deep breath of the warm and heavy air that was laden with the scents of many people, steam from the tables filled with food, and the acrid smell of wine that had been provided to his guests. Nothing in him wanted the stuff since his injury and memory loss years ago. The feeling of not having control over his own mind and memories still haunted him; the idea of drinking anything that dulled or stole the senses made him shiver with distaste.

He took a few steps up to the dais, thanking Malcolm with a nod. There were more diplomats to meet. These had come from over the Syrene sea, their trade partners from countries far away. They were dressed differently. More vibrant colors, the ladies wearing golden yellows that spoke of Bear's Ear and Rudbeckia, another in a rich red, like a rose about to shed its petals. Golden filigree and embroidery trailed the fabric over the men and women's clothing and their heads were held high. They reeked of wealth they desired to show off, and he tempered the frown he knew was twisting his face.

"Majesty, our condolences and regrets." The lead lord bowed at his waist. At his side, his wife gripped his hand and dipped into a curtsey that had her golden skirts pooling upon the rich wood of the throne room's floor. Elgon bowed in thanks but could bring no words to his lips. The man helped his wife up the steps to approach Elgon. He held out his hand to her and she took it, bowing over it and bringing her eyes back up to meet his own. Something beyond sadness rested in their depths. Admiration? Appraisal?

"Perhaps your majesty ought to add a ceremony to such an event. In honor of your wife's name and her memory. Perhaps a monument where violets would be planted?"

Elgon felt the weight on his chest build again, and he tried to stifle a gasp for breath. The room seemed to buzz with a noise and energy that swirled around him.

"We, my husband and I, on behalf of our country of Eris, wish to gift such a monument in her memory and to further her legacy."

Roaring sounded in Elgon's ears, and the gathering of pain and sorrow welled within him to a depth he could not even express. All semblance of control was gone, and while he wished he could bring himself to nod and bow out subtly, the effort it dragged from him only made it worse.

"Don't give up hope...promise me..."

The whispers floated on the breath of her voice inside his heart, and his vision blurred. He took a trembling step backward and shook his head to clear his sight while he moved to his right. He must escape. Escape these walls that moved inward as if to crush him. Escape the eyes staring and burning holes in his chest. Escape the voices, the noise, the roaring of a thousand opinions all at once.

Something clattered and fell to the floor with a crash, broken glass crunched under his boots, and the wooden door met his palms with force as he fumbled with the lock and staggered through.

The pressure in his chest built as his boots ate up the ground. Air. If only he could get air. He unclipped the decorative pin of the Eliran crest that held his ceremonial burgundy and gold embroidered cloak around his neck. His hands shook, and he jabbed the pin into his thumb before it was clear and the cloak floated to the floor behind him. The pin hitting the stone floor clattered in the stillness of the walkway.

He threw the door to the upper walkway open, and the sea air embraced him, heavier than he had hoped, and he nearly fell to his knees right then and there.

Hope. Why did he still have hope? When everyone else demanded he give up? Acknowledge her absence. Act as if it were for good, forever.

He wasn't supposed to live without her. They were supposed to be together, forever. Tears stung his eyes and streamed down his face, chilling his skin in the night air. The flickering fires in the torches scattered incrementally along the balustrades did nothing to light the fog and darkness that was untouched by the moon or stars.

"Majesty?" Malcolm's voice—quiet, cautious.

"I promised!" He screamed the words, whirling and collapsing back against the curtain wall with his elbows. They echoed off the stones and the courtyards below. Courtyards that should be full of joy, of light, of laughter, of the pattering of little feet.

"I know everyone thinks I should let go." Tears streamed down his face as he stared into Malcolm's. "I've heard every argument, fought through every doubt I have. But I cannot let go of hope. Not ever. Not even for a second. They could be out there somewhere. Waiting. And I promised her…" He drew a shuddering breath, his shoulders heaving with the effort. "I promised I'd never let go of that hope. The minute I do, I'll sink into nothing, and I can never betray her, never betray my King. Not like that. Don't ask it of me, Malcolm."

Malcolm's face twisted into pain that Elgon knew he tried to mask. Pain he would not give in to in the presence of his king, at least not entirely.

No words were uttered, and in the hesitant silence between them, Malcolm stepped forward with purpose and wrapped his arms around his friend. Elgon stiffened momentarily before returning the embrace with a ferocity that mirrored the gutting ache in his chest. A raw cry climbed his throat.

No tones of comfort were needed. Only those that were uttered without sound. From the deep recesses of the heart and spirit where no eye could see, but where one could feel.

Malcolm finally spoke. His voice cracked. "Hope is yours, and no one can ever take that away. Hold onto it for all you're worth. You won't betray them. You never could. It's not within your nature because your nature is His. Hope doesn't go away because we can't see the fulfillment of it with our eyes. Hope grows deeper the longer between proof, because it's in the places where most give up that the faithful find their strength. Where they dig in deeper. Where they stand firm upon promises spoken in spirit and they say, 'I will not yield.' I know you won't. I know you can't. I'll never ask it of you, and those that do are fools."

ROSALIE, PRESENT DAY...

Rosalie clung to the saddle, doing her best to move with the beast as their mount wove in and out amongst the trees, serpentine fashion. Malcolm's breathing was heavy and quick in her ear, and the muscles in the arm binding her to his chest were tense. She prayed under her breath, some of it coherent, some of it only coherent to the Lord.

They turned sharply around a tree, the force of it pressing Malcolm's arm into her middle so fiercely she lost her breath. The sickening thud of an arrow in flesh coincided with the sharp cry of their horse as it fell, plummeting forward and throwing them as he did so. Fear gripped her as she flailed for control before hitting the ground on top of Malcolm. They rolled twice, his arm still around her as if it were glued to her.

Gripping dead leaves and twigs in her bare hands, Rosalie fought for a breath that finally came and smashed into her lungs with a force that made her limbs go weak. She frantically looked around her. Malcolm had released her and was scrambling across the forest floor to a group of heather, where he pulled his sword from where he had flung it in an attempt to keep either of them from getting cut or injured in the fall.

"Quickly," he rasped, stumbling toward her and throwing a look past her into the woods where the distant sounds of the conflict—screams, shouts, and metal upon metal—rang through the trees.

"But…" Tears started to her eyes at the massive animal as it tried to roll to his feet with an arrow protruding from his left flank. The animal huffed in pain, and she was relieved to see him reach his feet, his back leg suspended in the air to keep from putting any weight on it and his head bobbing with the pain of it.

"There's no time." He grabbed her shoulder, his head constantly on a swivel to catch a glimpse of the horses that had been following them. Their hooves thundered nearer, and Malcolm propelled them with quick feet and pushing hands over the terrain and toward outcroppings of rocks.

"We—won't—be able to—outrun them." She gasped between breaths.

"Don't talk. Focus on running," he snapped, pulling her farther toward the rocks. Then he swore under his breath as one of the dark knights galloped upon them and pulled to a stop, the rider flinging off his animal's back with a snarl, sword drawn.

Rosalie screamed when Malcom shoved her down a small incline, and she rolled to the bottom of the hill, leaves getting caught in her tangled cloak and the sky spinning overhead broken only by the harsh and crooked lines of the tree branches.

Metal on metal rang at the top of the hillock, punctuated with grunts and shuffling feet as Malcolm's sword met the Rusalk's again and again in combat. Rosalie untangled herself from her cloak and stood to her feet, staying low and praying with all her might that the evil man above would not win and drag her back to her prison.

Protect Malcolm. Be his rear guard. She gripped her blouse over heart in her fist, willing the thumping member to stop beating hard in her chest.

Malcolm disarmed the knight with a subtle twist of his blade and stepped within the reach of the man's fighting arm. The curved Rusalk sword slid down the hill toward her, and she stumbled out of the way, watching as Malcolm twisted the man's arm over his shoulder and flipped him onto his back. He glanced down at Rosalie, their eyes catching, and she saw the raw and uncontained anger burning like a blaze within him before she turned away.

A gasping sound met her ears and then the sound of crunching leaves as Malcolm slid down the hill, tossing the Rusalk's now ownerless blade and gripping her hand, pulling her with him as they again started running. The forest was pitched, and they were forced to run uphill, though they wound their way around and over uneven places in the ground. She tried not to think of what Malcolm had done to the Rusalk and focus on one step, then another, her feet pounding out the ground as her side knotted with the effort, and her breath came hard and fast.

The trees grew darker, closer together, the branches stretched to the heavens twirling like the Vagari dancers, the contortion of limbs and leaves matching the contortion of her insides. The sounds of battle and chaos faded behind them, and the stillness of the forest met their gasping breaths and frequent steps with a closeness that felt suffocating.

The only thing that held her steady was the arm on her shoulder, the reminder that she was not alone in this fight. The knowing that there was at least one person who would fight to the death to keep her from returning to the hell she had left. But fear gripped her anyway. Hope seemed a distant bird on wing, flying off into the gray sky and leaving her heart shuddering in her breast. So much hope, so much faith in what was to come. That peaceful lull of comfort letting her know that she would reach home soon, only to be snatched away in one blinding moment of pain and hate. The ones she had grown to love standing guard behind her, her heart still with them as her mind registered the fact that she may never see them again.

Her footsteps pounded out a refrain of regret and brokenness.

Nim.

Everard.

Izabella.

Romanick.

The Vagari.

Vieggo.

Mother Hobbs.

All lost to the days behind her and standing in protection of her heart and her calling, her very person—someone they had never met, would never see again, and would never get to experience the outcome of her safety... And yet they protected her anyway.

Of what worth was she? Why was she the one who received the gift of rescue? Why was her life brought to a place of restoration? Why would such as these fight with their last breath to see her set free? What of the slaves? The maids, the squires, the men, women, and children, young and old, left behind in prison, in bondage, possibly to never taste the freedom she had tasted. Never to experience the joy she had felt. Never to return to a home that gave everything to see her return.

What of them? Who saved them? Who prayed for their return? Who sought for a way year after year after year to set them free? What made her so special?

Malcolm's pull jerked her from her scattered thoughts and almost pulled her arm from her socket as they fought through underbrush and wound around trees. The burning in her lungs and the stitch in her side had grown to feel like the gut punches she had sometimes received at the hands of her captors.

Then, she heard them. Footsteps. Gentle ones. A harsh whisper from someone who most likely wished not to be heard. Hard to hear over her own heavy breathing and their attempt to wade through the heather and underbrush that grew as thick here as the trees overhead.

A sound behind them to the right, then another branch snapped to the left. They were still being followed. Closely. There was no way that she could move any faster than she already was, but Malcolm must have heard and sensed them too because he pulled her sharply on, shoving her up the hill ahead of him. The desperation in his touch and his movements made the fear ebb instead of accelerate. She drew a deep breath, setting her teeth, and scrambled up the hill as best she could, pulling her skirt out of the way and tucking it into her belt with a swiftness and lack of trembling that surprised even her.

An arrow flew past their heads and landed in a nearby tree trunk with a thud that only served to make her angry rather than afraid. Something took hold within her, and she fought up that hill with everything that was in her. She gritted her teeth and felt them grinding against each other as she sucked in air through her nose, fighting with all that she was worth to make it out of the reach of the evil men below. She would not be their slave again. Never again.

Just as they crested the hill and were about to descend down the other side, another thud rang nearby, and this time the bile crept into her throat. She reached out to her side as she sensed movement, her hand catching onto Malcolm's cloak as he jerked forward, plummeting down the face of the hill, pulling her with him.

They rolled, dirt and dried leaves getting into her eyes, her mouth. She spat and tried to catch her breath, but instead, she was met with a rock to the gut, then the shoulder, and she pulled her head down and tried to cover it with her arms even as she spun, dizziness taking her.

The spinning and rolling stopped, and instead her brain continued the spin as if she were still in a free-fall. Fighting for a breath again. She blinked hard against the stars and twirling blackness and pulled herself to her hands and knees before she had a chance to understand the pain that started to creep in around the edges.

A hand grabbed the back of her cloak, and she jumped, whipping her head around to see Malcolm, his face twisted in a grimace and a broken arrow protruding from his shoulder.

Twenty-Four

STANDING ALONE

MALCOLM, PRESENT DAY...

Fire tore through his shoulder. Searing, blinding fire. And Rosalie's expression in his bleary gaze—one of horror.

They had little time. He tucked her against his chest to protect her from more flying arrows, keeping their heads low as he scuttled them to the heather. Diving beneath the branches of the ground cover, he dragged her with him. A soft moan escaped him as the arrow shaft caught on the branches, and he gritted his teeth. He pulled his feet in and his cloak over them both, hoping the brown-stained-green would shield them from their hunters and match the environment of the heather they hid in. They were tucked into a depression in the ground beneath sharp and thorn-like twigs that clung to their clothes and hair.

343

He felt Rosalie's trepid breath against his chest, his arm over her and holding her close. Pain seized his shoulder, and he fought the urge to gasp, swallowing it down as a wave of nausea hit him and the vision of her father flashed into his mind. *Don't let me fail here. Let him see his daughter. Make seeing eyes blind, Father. Hide us from those that seek to harm us.*

She trembled, and he felt her breathing halt as a set of footsteps drew near. They were quiet, as if used to slinking through the forest. A branch cracked. Not as experienced as he would've thought. *Blind eyes. Please.*

The wind whipped above them, and the creaking and groaning of the trees that towered over them struck his ear. Sounding almost human and louder than usual. *Wraith Forest.* It was living up to its name. Whispers from the dark knights as they conferred with one another were unintelligible but loud enough to be heard. They were close.

He clenched and shuddered against the pain that seized him, traveling down from his shoulder as he tried to shift, and then a small hand was at his chest in an attempt to comfort. He drew a short breath. If only he could snap the arrow.

The dark knight's footsteps grew closer. And suddenly Rosalie was moving. Panic clawed at him, but he forced himself not to hiss at her to remain at his side. Her movements were as silent as possible as she crouched on her knees and reached over his shoulder. He tried to move to grab her wrist, but a seizure of pain took the breath from his lungs and forced darkness into the corners of his vision as he clamped his jaw and his eyes shut in reaction to it.

She rested one hand on his shoulder, her head still low, covered by the heather, and she pulled the unstrung bow from its place tied to his pack. Her movements were slow, measured, and he glanced up at her face. Dilated in the dark, her eyes were like flint, her lips pressed firmly, and the muscles in her jaw were tight.

She edged backward on her knees to create enough space between them and bent the bow, bracing it against her feet and pulling the string taught to wrap and tie over the top. She would not be able to create enough tension in this cramped environment to properly string it, but by the grimace on her face as her muscles strained to bend it and tie it off, Malcolm knew it would still shoot an arrow far enough.

Once finished, she let the breath leave her lungs, and he tried to reach for her hand once again, but his shoulder screamed.

She rested her hand on his shoulder and gazed directly into his eyes. No words, but there was an anger and a peace in her eyes that stopped him. Something whispered to him that she was acting on the internal guidance of the Spirit and to stop her now would be worse than to let her try.

She gave him a slight dip of her chin then broke his gaze, reaching over him for an arrow and fitting it to the string.

The wind howled now, amplified and strong. The sound resembled a human scream, and Malcolm heard the uncomfortable whispers of the men who sought them. Wraith Forest was not named without cause. Evil spirits were said to live in the trees, the wind carrying their cries over the mountains and through the hollows. Many grew lost and disoriented in the woods, and some were never heard from again. It was said that those who went in were not likely to return. And many did not.

Rosalie pulled the string back, her face lined in concentration. He watched her muscles straining with the weight of the tension needed to launch the arrow, and he saw sweat form on her brow. The girl who had never shot an arrow in her life was about to let one fly.

The arrow released with a soft *thwang* that was smothered by the sound of the crying trees. Malcolm shivered, the pain exacerbated by the movement as every hair on his arms and the back of his neck stood on end.

Rosalie's eyes grew wide and her mouth opened, and she quickly sank down next to him, clutching the bow in her hands.

The arrow had launched into the forest.

"What was that?" one man asked over the wailing of the trees, his voice a harsh whisper that was not in keeping with their objective of being silent.

"Shut up. They've gone this way." The voices grew more distant before actual whispers and growls filled the treetops. A low ominous snarl echoed into the gray and dark air of the woods, the creaking of trees and the snapping of branches against each other suddenly ringing through the hollow.

Cursing met his ears and the sound of muffled footsteps and a loud "hush."

"You know what will happen if we return empty handed." These words were sharp, heavily laden with the Rusalk accent, and rasped from a throat that seemed to be broken.

"At least we'll be alive."

"How long do you think that will last?"

More swearing. "They have to have gone this way. Come on. No one in their right mind would stay in this hollow. Not with these ghosts."

"We have to keep at it. The man was wounded. Surely they couldn't have gone far."

"They should flee this evil place."

The creaking and whispering from the trees struck up again, and more curses sounded farther away this time. The conversation was lost to him, but the chilling feeling of not being alone in the forest persisted, and he drew in a sharp breath when the low growl, harsh and deep, reverberated through the hollow. Rosalie jumped beside him. Galloping hooves shook the ground from a distance till they faded from hearing.

His throat was dry. He blinked hard to fight off the darkness that blurred the edges of his vision and caught Rosalie's frightened, wide-eyed expression. The fog of their breath mingled in the tiny alcove, and she shivered. It was then that he realized he was shivering too. Whose voices flitted in the trees, and why did he hear them? These woods were supposed to be uninhabited, and he wasn't one to believe in ghost stories.

The arrow embedded in the back of his shoulder throbbed, then tore into muscle as he moved. He couldn't contain the groan that climbed his throat, and Rosalie scrambled to her knees, gripping his hand where it clutched his upper arm against the pain.

There was only one thing to do. He panted, then sucked in a few deep breaths through his gritted teeth. Horror froze her gaze as he stared straight into those dark green eyes, shadowed in the gloaming of their alcove.

With a heave, he reached over his shoulder with his good hand, grabbed the shaft of the arrow, and twisted his wrist hard. He snapped the shaft at the point where it entered his skin in one clean break.

A bright flash of stars filled his vision right before the darkness.

ELGON, TEN YEARS AGO...

"Majesty, he's returned." Tobias was breathless as he ran up to Elgon on his daily walk on the balustrade, the ocean calming his nerves and reminding him of the memories he shared with his wife in this place. It had been four years, and his muscles ached more now, his back was a bit stiffer, but his memories and hope had not grown any less strong in the wake of the disappearance of his wife and child.

But his heart leapt at this bit of news, and Tobias's intense breathing and those eyes burning bright set the energy and adrenaline coursing through Elgon's own veins. He picked up his pace and followed the lad who had turned on his heel and was already trotting back whence he came with an energy and determination that Elgon could only hope for.

Was their child running about wherever she existed? Was she even a girl? Had Marcus's predictions come true? Elgon thought of his child as a little girl. Did she have room to grow? To run? To learn? Or was she holed up in some cell somewhere under the watchful eye of those that served Zuko?

But…no. He would not let his mind wander to a grimmer fate. It did no one any good, least of all him or his missing family.

A seagull screamed overhead, and he winced in surprise before striding long to keep up with Tobias and his trotting steps. The boy was constantly on the move. He took his job seriously and was loyal to a fault. Though only twelve, he had been trusted with more secrets than many twice his age. He and Kenton would get along.

Tobias swung the heavy wooden door open for Elgon to pass through, and he nodded his thanks to the boy. Small acts of courtesy must not be lost even in the day to day mundaneness of a young squire's life.

Elgon smiled slightly. Kenton was coming up the ranks and moving along in his own right toward knighthood. He would be needing a squire himself one of these days. And now Elgon knew just the person to assign to him. Lord Loucas's young son was nothing to be trifled with, whatever faults or doubts his father had. Lord Loucas wasn't exactly a flawed man, just one who allowed his pragmatic perspective to color his hope at times, but it allowed him to see potential problems before anyone else. Something that Elgon was in need of on a council that sought to direct the inner workings of a country that was only growing and gaining new ground and awareness from surrounding and oversea countries.

A good balance of dreamers and doers coupled with pragmatic and realistic minds was a good fit…even if they didn't see eye to eye all the time. Elgon huffed. His own bitterness at Loucas was driven by Loucas' constant no-nonsense approach to the underlying tensions with Zuko. Loucas hated things that were subversive, hidden, or underhanded. And he also saw little sense in hoping for the impossible.

But then, wasn't their God one of the impossible?

Tobias rushed ahead and threw open the great wooden arched doors of the throne hall. Elgon smiled; the rush of excitement, relief, and hope filled him and made his skin tingle. Impossible indeed.

"Everard!" He embraced his friend without care to remain dignified. Everard looked even more the part of the Rusalk. His heritage came in handy with the dark beard now growing long on his face; the dark gray camouflage leather clothing and the rusted cloak flung over his shoulder were a mirror image to the men over the border. Even the curved scimitar at his hip could be mistaken for one of the Rusalks'.

There was a smile somewhere behind that facial hair, even if all Elgon could see of it right now was the upturn of the large man's eyes.

Elgon was far from short, but Everard towered over nearly everyone that he met with the broad shoulders, square jaw, and tree-trunk limbs of a mountain-born Rusalk.

"What news have you?" Elgon glanced beyond his friend in hopes of catching sight of something, anything, though he dare not put detail to those dreams.

"M'lord." Malcolm strode in from behind the throne, his hand resting easily on the hilt of his sword that swung at his side and the closest thing to a smile on his face that Elgon had seen in years.

"Good, you're here. Should we take this into the conference room?" Elgon glanced over Malcolm's shoulder at the court members who hovered between the colonnade and the windows, awaiting open court.

Malcolm nodded, all seriousness again, and led the way across the courtroom, through another wooden door, down a hall, and into another room. Tobias had again run ahead and held the door for them, and after they entered, he hovered on the threshold as if wondering if his presence was wanted.

"Fetch some water, bread, and oil for our guests and then you may stay and guard the door." Elgon nodded to Tobias who scurried from the room, shutting the door and latching it behind himself.

Anticipation thrummed in Elgon's veins like fire licking at oil. "What news have you?" he repeated.

Everard shook his head. "Nothing on the royal family, but there are other things at play that have taken form over the last few months that I must notify you of."

Elgon felt the drop of disappointment but immediately steeled himself for the rest of the meeting. Finding his family would be too easy. He had to remind himself that if Zuko could play the long game, then he could too. He was not giving up. There were many things to prepare for the return of the queen and their child one day, and for now, that was where their focus would lie.

"I have three more spies trained for entry into Rusalka. Cover stories and all. They'll be ready to depart with you at first light tomorrow." Malcolm folded his arms and stood rather than sat at the round table where the council met each week. Everard waited for Elgon to sit before he pulled out one of the large, ornate wooden chairs and sank into it. Elgon could see the weariness in his friend—the dark circles under the eyes, the slightly more relaxed set of the shoulders, and the elbows leaning heavily on the table.

Everard nodded at Malcolm.

Elgon tapped his fingers on the table. Either a practice duel in the garden or a gallop through the moors would be needed to settle his nerves after this. Before he could allow the disappointment to get to him. "We'll meet with you after you've rested to discuss their stories and where they would best fit into the Rusalkan byway."

Everard nodded again, his dark eyes seeking Elgon's face.

Elgon swallowed. There was something about Everard's gaze that cut straight through the bone and marrow of a person and examined the heart. Everard seemed to know and sense his innermost feelings, the pain he struggled with, and the sorrow he was holding at bay till this meeting was over.

Tobias reentered a few minutes later, a platter laden with a pitcher and earthenware cups, a steaming loaf of bread and a dish of seasoned oil and herbs in his arms.

The boy set it down between Elgon and Everard, poured each of them a glass of water, and swiftly returned to the door. Reading a hand signal from Elgon, he closed it and stood on the inside, privy to their conversations. He would answer and shoo away anyone who knocked for entry till the conspirators were dispersed.

"You speak of progress. What else has occurred in Rusalka?" Elgon asked, resting his elbows on the table and folding his hands to keep from fidgeting while Everard tore off a piece of bread and dipped it in the oil.

Everard swallowed his bite, then took a drink of water before reaching into his pocket and pulling out a small item and tossing it onto the table in front of Elgon.

Elgon reached for the item. He turned the carved token of a bird in flight over in his hand. "A dove?"

Everard nodded. "A fitting call sign for a secret fellowship designed to offer passage to a lost royal family."

Elgon turned it over in his fingers once more. He blinked hard against the sheen that covered his eyes. The bird had come to mean more to him than simply another feather-adorned creature that filled the skies. The remembrance of the purpose behind the dove and its first association with the Holy Spirit as Christ experienced the power of the Godhead on the day of his baptism filled his mind. It was the bird who cooed on his walks along the balustrade. The same bird who had signaled comfort and peace on more than one occasion.

"Fitting indeed." His voice sounded raspy, even to himself, but he didn't care. "How does it work?"

Everard rolled up his sleeve and extended his arm across the table.

A dove in black ink was marked on the back of his hand and his wrist. Small, about the size of a coin, but clear for all who would know to look.

"There are many hungry for the gospel in a land like Rusalka. Hungry and ready for a hope and faith in something beyond themselves. But also dissatisfied with the acts of their own ruler and ready to partner with a country that they see as holding the key to their salvation."

Elgon felt heat, white and hot, course through him. He shoved his chair back and stood. "We are no savior." His voice trembled. He just wanted his family back. Was that too much to ask for? "I'm grateful that these people are willing, but I cannot drag my people into a war with a king who has tried to crush us on more than one occasion. Freedom is not something I can offer them in their own land."

Everard's gaze was steady, watching him with an upward gaze from his sitting position.

Elgon turned and started pacing.

"Your majesty…" Malcolm's voice.

"No! I cannot take on more than a simple rescue. It could put Violet and our—" He cut himself short, his fingers curling into a tight fist. "It could put them both at risk, and I'll not do that. We've discussed this in council. I can set no one free. You know that. Enguerrand had stolen my throne, and I had a right to it. What right do I have to a country that borders mine? It would be suicide! The council would never agree."

"Elgon." Everard's deep voice rumbled through the room and echoed off the walls.

"No. I appreciate their desire to help, as I said. But nothing can be done. Not now. Not until Violet is returned home. Safe. Unharmed. I will not risk either of them for…for…" The words "other people" froze on his tongue, but still seemed to reverberate throughout the room. Elgon shook his head, ignoring the guilt that pricked him. "No, they cannot expect anything from us. You must make that perfectly clear. I—"

"Obed." Everard's voice was louder, more emphatic but still somehow not a shout, though it pinned Elgon to the floor like it had been one. No one had used that name on him since he had last seen his wife.

Trembling, he stared at the man, his jaw clenched and his hands in fists at his sides.

Everard glanced down at the table and back up again as he drew a deep breath. "No one is expecting anything. I know you fear for your people. Your family. But is not the suffering of another just as important as your own? The people ask for nothing. Nothing but hope that their lives may one day experience more freedom than they do now. You know Elira has felt that hunger pain before. You knew it yourself while you lived among us." He had slowly risen as he spoke, his gaze never leaving Elgon's.

Elgon's chest was heaving and he folded his arms in an attempt to hold himself together. He had been doing well, but now he felt as though he would fly apart into a million pieces that would never be put back together again. His next words were a mere whisper as he opened his palm and stared down at the token of a dove that had bitten into his flesh when he had clenched his hands. "But what if all I can offer them is hope?"

"There is no shame in hope. Hope is the greatest gift one can ever receive. Because hope clung to will one day reap a reward far greater than anything you can accomplish. The people do not expect a savior who marches over the mountains and wages a bloody war that sets them free. That debt has already been paid. Blood has already been spilt. Freedom can exist for those that still live in bondage. I know of this hope. That is the hope that these people desire and earnestly seek. The freedom of the gospel is not bound to a man who can break chains, but to a God who can speak and it is so.

"God would make known what is the riches of the glory of this mystery among the lost; which is Christ in you, the hope of glory." Everard quoted what had already been echoing in Elgon's spirit. And then his hand was on his shoulder. "You carry a hope inside you that no man can take away. Not even if they try. They just ask for the same hope."

Elgon nodded. "So they just want to help us in exchange for hearing the gospel?"

Everard smiled. "In a sense. But they do it because they believe not in you, but in the God whom you serve. They believe that their time will come, just as surely as ours did."

Elgon drew in a steadying breath and handed the dove back to Everard. "Then so be it. We will offer what help we can from within with our spies, and…" He swallowed. There was one thing he had already done once and would do again. Every time. "And whoever makes it to the border will receive sanctuary. No matter how they get there." He raised his steely gaze to Everard's own. "Zuko's time will come. And though his time is not today, the Lord will not let the enemy rule over His people forever."

First, he would see to the safety of his wife and child. Anyone who sought shelter would have it till then. But after they were rescued, all bets were off and Zuko would have his reckoning.

ROSALIE, PRESENT DAY...

Rosalie pressed the scrap she had torn from her skirt to the wound on Malcolm's shoulder and winced as she tried to peer past the torn fabric of tunic and jerkin. Nothing but blood.

The arrow was embedded deep. She couldn't see the metal head. Malcolm moaned in his sleep, and she felt the worry of hurting him even worse rise in her throat.

They needed to get moving. The ungodly voices and sounds that echoed through the hollow had her shivering. She knew better than to believe in ghosts, but was there something or someone else in this forest that would cause them harm? Thankfully, her arrow diversion had led the dark knights farther away from their position, and the voices had coerced them to flee the hollow and head farther away. That had been close to an hour ago, and Rosalie had seen or heard nothing from them since. But the day was well past noon, and if they were not found, surely the knights would return. They had seen her. Or at least, she thought they had, and what reason had they to give up a search for Zuko's prized possession?

One had said as much. Death awaited all who did not follow through with his orders. As much as she loathed the evil men who were trained to hunt those like her down, she hoped they would meet Jesus before meeting hell first.

She pulled her knees up to her chest and hugged them, resting her chin on top of them and trying to ignore the bite from the bruises and scrapes from the rocks that had cut through her clothes on her tumble down the hill. She rolled her scratched arm so she could look at her elbow. Blood covered the torn fabric around a hand-sized patch of scuffed skin, and she tore off another strip from her skirt, dusting off the wound with a groan to remove the debris before tying off the makeshift bandage with her teeth.

Another howl cut through the valley, and she jumped. "That's it. We need to move." She shook Malcolm's good arm gently. She hoped it was enough to wake him up without adding too much to his pain.

Nothing.

Scooting closer, she used her hand to brush the stray strands of hair out of his pale face. His eyes flickered beneath the lids as if he were trying to wake up.

She gripped his cloak and shook again.

Groaning, his face contorted into a grimace before he opened his eyes and blinked them a few times until they focused on her face. Then they flew wide open, grabbing her shoulder and pulling her down beside him, attempting to look back over his shoulder.

The movement fell shy of the mark, and he groaned.

"Shhh… We're safe. For now. They took the bait, and these terrifying noises drove them even farther away. Don't move too quickly, but I think we need to get going. We should get farther away from the direction they took before dark falls. We won't be able to see past our hand in this forest after nightfall, even if there is a moon." She reached up and parted the heather to catch a glimpse of what little of the gray and overcast sky she could see through the dense branches above.

"Once we're free of this brush, I'll wrap your wound. Here, let me help." She lunged forward as he tried to push himself up with his arms but growled under his breath and clutched his wounded arm to his chest.

He took her offered arm, and they both stood through the top of the heather. Rosalie ignored the sharp twigs and branches clawing at her face and hair and simply tried to hold the heather open to allow Malcolm to stand unimpeded by anything that would catch on his arm or cloak.

He stumbled but quickly righted himself as they stepped out of the little depression in the ground that had been their hideaway. Rosalie guided him to clearer ground.

He cast a searching gaze into the trees at every angle, and she kept still and silent, knowing that he was listening and looking for any sign of danger. He nodded absentmindedly and tried to take a step, but stumbled again. She caught his good arm and then looped it over her shoulder. "Come, sit down for a minute. I need to remove your cloak and wrap that wound. There's no way I can take the arrow out. Should we go back to the Vagari wagons? I know Nim could help with—"

"No." He gritted his teeth as he angled himself down to a sitting position on a smooth rock. "No, we can't go back. They'll be expecting that. They'll stalk the wagons for however long it takes to convince them we won't be coming back. We have to continue on. Deeper into the woods."

Another howl ripped through the hollow. "What is that?" Rosalie gasped, her heart stuttering.

He smiled slightly. "Unnerving as it is, it's nothing to fear. The hollows and trees of this forest are shaped in such a way that they create and echo sound. Everything you hear is made by the wind whistling down the mountain pass and into the valleys and hollows on this side of the mountain. Some with active imaginations say they see wraiths in the forest, ghosts of those who got lost and never came out, but it's mere gossip. Though we must be careful." He hissed as she carefully peeled his cloak away from his wound. "Many have been lost and disoriented in the forest on this side of the mountain. The hills and hollows run on for what seems like forever, and the constant changing of the altitude, the noise, and the denseness of the trees make it easy to get lost. There is no path, so we must make sure that we are still moving upward to ensure we are heading north. There are those that dwell in the highlands of the mountain, on the passes and over them. They might help us if we can reach them." Malcolm's words cut off on a moan as the fibers of the cloak that the arrow had caught and carried into his shoulder snagged as she began removing them.

"I'm sorry." She tried to sever the threads that retreated into the wounded flesh. His muscles seized beneath her hands. The wooden shaft, though broken off, left a jagged end still protruding from the gash and even after looking closely, she couldn't see the metal tip. Shaking her head, she placed the piece of fabric she had already torn off in a folded up square over the opening, then tore a longer strip which she wound over the shoulder and under his opposite arm. She also fashioned a sling from her headscarf and blinked away tears at his look of pain as she helped him lift his arm into it.

She pawed through his pack till she found a skin of water and handed it to him, uncorking it so he didn't have to use one hand or his wounded one. While he drank and dragged in deep breaths, she tied the straps of the pack tighter and slung it to her own shoulders. Tottering under the weight, she swallowed and strung the bow over the other shoulder, the string running across her chest. Better to leave it at the ready should she need it again later. Though, she had no grand hopes that her aim was any good on its own.

"Here. Unstrap the dagger from inside my boot. You should carry it, just in case."

Her eyes widened. He had strapped the one Mother Hobbs had given her to his ankle for safe keeping, but now he was entrusting her with it.

Kneeling at his feet, she pulled the cuff of his boot down far enough to reveal the small leather harness that wrapped around his calf and held the small hand dagger in its sheath. When she had unbuckled it from his ankle and transferred it to her waist, she took the edges of her skirt and re-tied them into her belt in a more orderly fashion to ensure that they wouldn't trip up her steps, especially while traversing uphill.

She took his good arm and wrapped it over her shoulders, bracing her legs to take enough of his weight to help him to his feet and shushing his mild protests. "Sun sets in the west, which I should keep on my left and make sure I'm always heading uphill, no matter how many valleys we have to climb through."

He smiled down at her. "Strong of mind, just like your mother. Something needed doing and she did it. No questions asked. No arguments offered. You'd make her proud."

Her heart swelled in her chest with pride, and her eyes burned at the thought of her mother, but she blinked back any more wayward tears. Gripping his hand over her shoulder, she supported him as she led him up and out of the hollow north. They needed to make it as far as they could before night fell on the mountain.

It was slower going than Rosalie would have liked. As the day drew on, Malcolm stumbled more and more frequently. The weight of her burdens and his support dragged at her body, and her muscles screamed in fatigue. She would have left her cloak in the middle of the forest as sweat dripped down her face, but Malcolm insisted she keep it. "Nights are cold, and sweat turns into chill," he said.

She glanced up at him in between lumbering steps and drew a breath, trying to still the ache of worry in her stomach. Sweat dripped off his own face and dampened the collar of his shirt. She thought his skin had a gray pallor to it, but perhaps that was because what little light from the day they had possessed was now dwindling at an alarming rate.

The terrain was more intense than she had expected. Rocky outcroppings, deep piles of dead leaves, constant clambering up and down steep hills, and fighting upward the entire way.

Just as she was helping Malcolm clamber over a rock that was taller than she, his grip slipped and he fell to the forest floor on his wounded side, his shoulder hitting the ground first and wresting a moan from his throat that made her stomach clench. Every muscle in her screamed as they tightened in empathetic pain at the sight and she dropped to her knees beside him, the rocks digging into them as she gripped his good shoulder and felt him convulsing. He hadn't even been able to catch himself because his arm was tied up in the sling.

"Are you all right?" Rosalie whispered. The paleness of his face stood out in the dimming light of the forest. The creaking of the branches overhead as they swayed to the wind filled her with dread.

Only a moan met her ears? and her heart sank. "We can't go on any farther. Not tonight." He didn't reply, and she touched a hand to his forehead. She couldn't tell if he was warm and sweating from the exertion of their hike or from any other feverish reason. She hoped it was just the former. But first, she would need to tend that shoulder.

"Here." She spoke softly, her voice drifting off into the night and the breeze as she helped him roll over. His eyes were squeezed shut, his teeth gritted together, and she reached for the injured arm to support it as she rolled him. The ground was too pitched. She needed to get him to a more comfortable spot. Lying sideways on an incline was going to be far from comfortable for a night, and they needed to be protected from the wind, mountain cold, and any stalkers in the woods that might attempt to come this far.

His breath was coming in rasps now, and his eyes were still shut, as if he were attempting to will the pain away.

"Don't move." Rosalie let the pack drop beside him and pulled his cloak over him better to keep him warm. Sweat dripped down his face, and she lifted a hand to wipe the drops away from his forehead before they fell into his eyes. Turning, she scurried back down the hill into the hollow they had just climbed. No sun meant no clear directions, and the shadows wavered in the early evening light, hardly enough to see by, but enough to get the general outline of trees. Even so, her eyes strained into the darkness, the feeling of unsurety in the grayness making her heart beat harder and faster in her chest. There, behind that rock, tucked into the bottom and back of the hollow would be a perfect place to hide themselves. She could cover them with fallen leaves, and they would be hard to spot from anywhere, especially in the dark. She just needed to get Malcolm that far.

Clambering back up the incline, she gripped his foot, on her knees beside him. "We need to move. I found someplace for us to rest tonight. Do you think you can make it?"

He grimaced but opened his eyes with a set to his chin and reached a hand toward her for her support.

She swung the pack onto her shoulders again, grunting under the effort and ignoring the muscles that grumbled at the added weight. *It's a short walk. You can make it. Then you can rest.* Gripping his good left arm once again, she wrapped it around her shoulders, and this time they both groaned as they boosted Malcolm to his feet. The height difference didn't help either of them as they tried to walk their way down the incline, their feet slipping all over the brown leaves piled and scattered on the ground haphazardly by the wind. At the bottom of the glen, he tripped and tumbled to his knees, his breath coming heavy and his head hanging as he swayed with the effort.

Near tears, Rosalie fought them down with a gulping sob, pulling and pushing him to his feet once more. "Almost there. I promise."

He fell to his knees again at the corner of the rock that would be their shelter, and instead of standing, he reached forward with his good hand and crawled into the tiny hollow. He settled with his back against the wall of dirt and tree roots at the back of the alcove and rested his head, wincing as his shoulder touched the rock he was tucked against. He drew in a shuddering breath and swallowed hard.

Rosalie handed him the water skin, nearly empty now, and then set about arranging his cloak to cover him. She raked the leaves with her hands till they covered his legs up to his waist to camouflage him even farther. Kneeling beside him, she started unbuckling the sheath of his sword. He needed to be comfortable—for tonight at least.

He grabbed her wrist and caught her gaze. "I-I need to—" His voice was weak and shaky, as if speaking was more effort than he had the strength for. She tried not to let the fear overtake her. She had never seen him this way. "Don't worry. I'll leave it right beside you, but Lord willing, we won't need it tonight." Sliding it off his belt, she rested it beside him, and he relaxed, letting his head fall back, his eyes closing even though he seemed to be trying to keep them open.

There had been a stream just in the glen over. She needed to replenish their store before it was too dark to see. Giving him one last look to make sure he was settled, she turned and darted into the open, clambering up the hill, nearly on her hands and knees to top the steep incline. Sliding down the other side, she avoided the hulking rocks on either side and found the tiny, nearly silent stream of water that flowed from some larger source at the top of the mountain. Her breath came in heaving gasps, and her muscles were shaking now that she could gather herself for just a moment. Dirt and scratches covered her hands and forearms, and she surmised that her face showed much of the same. The water was frigid, but it felt good on her warm and pulsing wounds. Her hands shook as she filled them with water and splashed her face. Whatever cuts existed there stung, and she sucked in a sharp breath before splashing her face again, scrubbing the dirt from her hands and filling the water skin. She drank as much as she could before filling it again and replacing the cork.

Drawing a deep breath, she let it out in a heavy sigh, her eyelids drooping now. "Lord, keep us safe tonight. Let us have found a secret place," she whispered before slinging the water over her shoulder and gathering herself to clamber back up the hill and down to their spot in the corner of the glen.

Malcolm was either fast asleep or unconscious when she arrived, and she rolled up the one blanket they had in the pack and gently tucked it behind his head. He didn't move, and something urged her to check his wound. She should at least clean it, shouldn't she?

She pulled him forward gently by the back of the neck, unwinding the bandage. The scrap of cloth she had placed on it hours before was soaked with blood. Her stomach clenched, and she tried to peel it away from his skin. *It wasn't bleeding this much before.* Perhaps his fall had aggravated the arrow still embedded into his shoulder muscle below the bone. She sucked in breath between her teeth as the wound oozed, and she rested him back down to tear another strip from her petticoat.

He groaned, and she caught his eye as he woke; the pinched grimace seemed etched into the lines of his face like a statue carved from stone. He opened his mouth as if to speak, and she shook her head as she smoothed the fabric in her hands. "Save your strength. I'll just rewrap it and then you can sleep."

"I need to—watch—" He blinked hard before catching her gaze again.

"I think we'll be safe here tonight. You need sleep. Isn't that the best thing for healing?" She tried to smile, but felt as though it was forced more than genuine. She would contemplate her worries later. Just now there was something to be done, and her mind and body seemed to be doing all that was necessary without her even telling it what to do. Something inside of her whispered a checklist of items to perform. Water. Wound care. Rest. Watch. Move on in the morning.

She placed the new bundle on top of the wound and cringed when he started at the touch, caught his breath, and stifled a groan. Wrapping it again, she helped him settle his head back against the folded blanket, making sure his shoulder was situated with as little pain as possible.

"I'm sorry," she whispered, but his eyes were already closed. His breathing steadied and elongated. Her leg muscles cramped from crouching in the stillness beside him.

Alone. The aching wilderness, creaking and howling branches, and the vast night sounds and darkness of the forest suddenly seemed to expand around her and she felt utterly alone. It was then she let the tears come.

But so did the whisper. Deep inside. *I'll never leave you nor forsake you. I never left. I never will.*

She curled up beside Malcolm, shivering now in the cold air of the night as darkness closed in. Tucking her cloak around her, she wrapped her arms around herself and settled, drawing in a shuddering breath.

Protected from the wind that whistled through the trees above, she felt her eyes slide shut, and suddenly the whispers in the treetops no longer held menace, but instead sounded like song. A guard of angels, singing in the night.

Rosalie startled awake at a bird's sharp cry. She flew upright. Fighting the spinning feeling in her head that was exasperated by the echoing, racing thud of her heart in her ears, she rubbed at the sleep in her eyes. It was still dim in their alcove, but the gentle light of the morning sun sent fractals through the forest floor, sharp shadows slanted so far over that it almost made the world twist and turn as she tried to focus. Her nose was numb from the cold air. She shivered and drew her cloak closer over her shoulders, pulling her hood up over her head, the leaves rustling with her movements. Nothing seemed to live in the forest except the singing and chirping of the morning birds. A mourning dove cooed nearby, and she drew comfort from the sound.

Malcolm.

With a start, she whirled. His face was gray and shadowed from where he was tucked behind the rock, but he didn't move, and his eyes stayed shut. Trembling, she untangled a hand from her cloak and held it over his nose and mouth.

A soft puff of air met her hand, visible like a thin cloud in the morning air. She drew a breath of relief as her stomach cramped with hunger; she'd been too exhausted the night before to be concerned over food.

They had stayed safe all night. Nothing moved in the forest that wasn't wildlife. Rosalie was somehow still exhausted this morning even with what little sleep she had received. The sudden understanding of all that Malcolm had gone through to keep close watch over her the entire journey till now filled her mind. Fumbling about between deep sleep and wakefulness was more exhausting than being awake. Her heart was even more grateful to him for all of the ways he had guided, protected, and watched over her in the last weeks.

But they would need to get moving. Malcolm had said there were people who might help them on the other side of Wraith Forest, above them in the pass. The sounds that had kept her awake had grown a bit more familiar and less terrifying with time. She couldn't shake the feeling of there being guards and angels in the treetops, their whispers and calls filling the air and reminding her of their presence.

But there was also a darkness to the sounds this morning. Something didn't feel right. Wishing that she didn't have to wake Malcolm up and could let him sleep and recover, she knew that they needed to press on. Kneeling beside him, she shook his leg instead of his shoulder.

Nothing.

Her heart sank with that sickening feeling of falling from a height. Something was indeed wrong. She knew his injury was most likely causing his unconsciousness, but she had hoped he could muster up the strength to make it over the mountain.

She held her chilled hands up in front of her; they trembled and she wrung them together. *Lord, help.*

The forest seemed to press in on her, and she felt terribly alone. The voices in the trees were empty, echoing in the hollows and glens and off the hillsides.

"Malcolm?" Hesitant, she called him again, then once more, growing louder each time. Nothing. He didn't even stir.

But he was breathing. She had made sure of that. Wincing at the thought of paining him, she shook him harder this time, calling him louder and cringing when her voice echoed through the wood. Hopefully no one who wished them ill was near enough to hear.

Still nothing.

She shook him again, and this time jumped when he groaned and his face twisted into a grimace, but his eyes never opened.

Tears gathered in her eyes, and she dashed them away with her hand, trying to see, to think. Her breath came in shallow gasps, and she hugged her arms to herself. Thoughts crowded her mind, flooding with words and ideas from every direction, contradicting each other, and she raised a trembling hand to her mouth to cover any sound of a sob that waited to escape.

Should I go for help? Stay and wait for him to wake up? What if he never wakes up? What if he dies here on this side of the mountain? What if no one ever finds us and we rot here like all the others before us? Didn't Malcolm say some never escape from this forest?

She clapped her hands over her ears as the wind whistled through the branches and leaves over her. *Think. If I can only just think.*

Glancing around frantically, blinking away the fog from the tears that still burned in her eyes, she tried to remember what Malcolm had said. He had told her to go up, but every hill pitched and wavered. What if she diverted from the path? What if she got even more hopelessly lost in these woods and couldn't find her way back to Malcolm? Which way was the right way? What if she accidentally wandered back the way they had come and was caught? Brought back to Izevel?

Tears coursed down her cheeks, and she shook harder. The thoughts of every moment of her life and the pain and terror of being dragged back to her prison in the mountains suddenly seemed like a fate worse than death. Her fingers and nose had numbed, and terror coursed through her like ice.

Glancing up at a howl from the hollow trees, she caught her breath on a sob. Perhaps if she could climb high enough, she could get a feeling for which direction to go and how to stay the course. Malcolm needed help, and the sooner she could get it, the better. Sucking in a deep breath of air, she stood, turning about to find the tree with the branches closest together to assist her in her climb. They twirled around her, the dizziness catching her before she had even attempted to start the climb.

There. The tree at the top of the hill they rested under. The roots mingled with others that formed the little alcove in which they had found shelter all night. Its branches seemed close enough together to allow her to climb them with her limited experience, but reaching the bottom ones and pulling herself up would be the hardest part of all.

She glanced again at Malcolm and unfastened her cloak from around her neck. It would only get in the way. Leaving it in a pile on the ground, she scrambled up the hill, the leaves slipping and sliding beneath her feet until she stood at the base of the tree. Her heart trembled within her as she looked up the trunk of the tree and drew in a sharp breath, shaking out her hands at her sides.

One must do what must be done. The longer she sat thinking about it, the worse things would get. Her hands were still numb, but hopefully they would warm up as she climbed. She just needed to reach that bottom branch.

It took her a few tries to reach her first hold, jumping and lunging for the low hanging bough. The first time she grasped it, her fingers lost their grip. She fell to her knees with a grunt, then stood with concentration, a growl almost escaping her lips as she shook her hands again and coiled to spring.

Drawing a deep breath, she heaved herself upward, and this time, both hands caught. Holding her breath, she swung as she turned and used her feet to climb up the tree. Her muscles quivered, but she heaved upward, her feet bracing the trunk till she was able to get her elbow over the branch and clutch it to her chest. First the one arm, then the other. Every single muscle in her body screamed, trembling under the strain, and her sight blurred. The bark of the branch bit into her skin through her woolen dress as she hauled herself farther.

Don't. Give. Up.

She angled one leg over the branch and pushed herself up with her shaking arms till she was sitting on top of the large lower branch, and it was then that she drew a deep breath. She gasped it in, her lungs burning with the length of her hold, and her body aching and revolting at the effort to hoist itself up.

She held on for dear life, the branch gripped hard between her hands and her legs before she drew in one last breath, coaching herself against the feat that swallowed every other thought.

That was the longest reach. At least now, she could stand and the next branch was only at chest level. She tried to avoid looking down, but the leaves that blew with the wind danced on the forest floor, and she felt herself tipping.

"No," she ground out, squeezing her eyes shut and digging her nails into the bark beneath her grasp. "Keep on."

Reaching above her head before she could think about it, she grabbed the next branch and hauled herself to her knees, then her feet, wobbling, trying to find her balance, before she stepped closer to the trunk and reached for another branch, just farther up than the next one.

Climbing grew easier as she went, focusing on where to put her next hand, then her next foot. She sucked in a breath between each reach; she had a ways to go till she reached the tree cover. Her stomach cramped for want of food, and her muscles then followed suit. She gasped as her calf seized. Holding two-fisted to the branches and bracing the good foot, she lifted the cramping calf and tried to move her foot.

Rosalie felt the pangs of forgottenness fill her stomach. The little whispers that perhaps, she was not good enough. Not enough. She had come all this way and was supposed to be a royal princess, but how could she be worthy of such a life? She couldn't even climb a tree, wasn't strong enough to make it on her own without turning to tears and wallowing in pain.

You could never be enough.

She staggered beneath the weight of the words that plagued her. The ones that snuck in between the constant running of thoughts of what to do, what *she* should do, and how. She felt her muscles giving way beneath her, but she sucked in a huge breath. Pulling at all of the strength within her as she reached from something beyond herself to give her the courage she needed for this next moment.

Perhaps it had all been a fluke. Perhaps her rescue was not meant to be. Perhaps she too would succumb to the darkness of the land of Rusalka, Wraith Forest swallowing her whole as it had done so many others. Her bones lying rotting somewhere beneath the dead leaves that covered them. Perhaps she would be found, dragged back to a life of imprisonment, loneliness and guilt till King Zuko finally found her fit for the horrible purpose for which he had held her so long.

The crushing confusion crowded in, and the tiny thread of light that connected her to the source of strength and courage grew dimmer and dimmer.

But it never snapped.

I will never leave you or forsake you.

The words were different. They weren't the chiding, biting, dark ones that sucked the life from her soul. Hope seemed like a fickle thing until she realized that what anchored it was the strongest force in the world. The most unwavering of truth and the most unshakeable of presences. No tie so strong could ever be severed, and no heart could be destroyed that trusted in the King above all kings.

Mustering the strength within but not of her, she reached above her head and pulled herself up one branch higher. It swayed beneath her weight, thinner now than they were at the bottom.

Malcolm would not die. Not if she had anything to say about it. He had risked his life to bring her to the safety of what should have always been her home, and she would not let him lose it.

She couldn't. Not after all that they had been through. She may not know the full reason as to why she was the chosen one. Why she would be able to go free when so many lived in bondage, why her chains were severed and others remained so tightly locked.

Seeing over the ocean of trees and through the fog, she recognized the slope Malcolm had spoke of, noting the way the land gradually tilted upward as if rushing toward the sky, she strained her eyes in the pallid rays of overcast light and caught sight of smoke filtering through the tops of the branches, stroking the gray sky with a dark and wispy finger. Relief flooded her heart like a tidal wave. Marking the direction in relation to the tree, she took one last, long look. The thread of smog gave her the hope she needed to set not just herself free, but her protector as well.

The child had become the protector, and the protector, the protected.

She bit her lip and glanced down at the dizzying maze of branches that would need to be her way to the forest floor. Sucking in a breath, she straightened her shoulders, gritting her teeth. She would do anything to repay Malcolm's sacrifice.

Even if it meant giving up the bliss of freedom she had only recently tasted.

Twenty-Five

BROKEN HOPE

ELGON, EIGHT YEARS AGO...

Elgon finished tying off the laces of his ceremonial velvet jerkin and reached for his matching emerald and gold embroidered cloak all while feeling like he wanted to collapse onto his bed, pull the curtains surrounding it closed, and bar the door. But nothing would assuage his determination and desire to join with his people and pray for the return of their beloved queen.

He tied the cloak around his neck, fastening it with the golden pin of the Eliran emblem and throwing one side over his right shoulder, displaying the pauldron marked with that of a military officer. Stepping to the wooden and glass boxes

377

that rested on a shelf in their room and held the royal crowns side by side, he glanced at his wife's dainty circlet lit with pearls and emeralds, a lump growing in his throat.

Today wasn't just for him; it was for his people. A country on its knees in prayer, year after year, the name and rule of his wife—a queen for too short a time—living in the minds and hearts of the nation like legend. He opened the box and took out his heavier gold crown studded with emeralds. The heads of roaring lions decorated the crosses that rose from it, and he fit it atop his head. A few wisps of hair escaped their confines and brushed against his forehead. Resting his hand on the other crown, the unused one, he clenched his jaw.

"If only you were here to see how treasured you are, my love," he whispered, hoping that against some divide, perhaps somewhere, she would be assured of his faithful and undying love to the woman of his youth.

But six years. Some called him foolish. Some, insane. He had grown used to those that thought his moves—or lack thereof—insanity, but when God told him to do something, when he knew it, felt it deep inside his spirit, the very thought of going against that order filled him with a sickening ache in his gut that he could not be rid of. Waiting for a wife and child that had been gone this long. Refusing to step foot into Rusalka in battle. Refusing still to give up on hoping, on waiting… Many knew the outward signs, the decisions he did or did not make, but few knew the true import of what was occuring behind the scenes.

War was not something to be trifled with. It may yet come to that one day, but that time must not be hastened. In secret, his people, his spies, drew closer to the truth. Every day more inroads were made within a country that was supposedly "closed off" to the people of Elira. Every second that he waited, prayed, breathed with hope and earnest prayer for what was to come was another second that a heart might be coming to his aid, someone may be meeting another piece of the puzzle, another pawn in the match who would tip the balance in their favor, prepare a way of rescue, or bring more information to light.

Setting his shoulders and drawing his head back, he took a deep breath, the sigh emanating from deep within him as he rolled his neck to eliminate the knots that seemed to be his constant companion these days.

No man was meant to live life alone. Not like this. Not having tasted the goodness of a wife who was his strength, his light, his hope, and then losing her to the great unknown. He tried not to let himself dream about the moment she would return.

His steps ate up the stone floors as he made his way down to the throne room where he would meet the delegates sent from each village and town far down the King's Highway and from the furthest reaches of Pavlin, Kaira, and even from those that sought his support from over the sea.

Would he fall to his knees at the sight of her? Unable to move or breathe? Would he rush to her, gather her and their child into his arms, swing them around, and laugh with a delight rarely known this side of heaven? Or would he hold them and weep, his heart fully undone by the power of a promise fulfilled, a hope assured and then answered?

He shook his head to clear the images and the cobwebs. Today was not his day to mourn and dream. It was the people's. His time would come after they had all gone home and dispersed, their lanterns swinging in the night as they found their home, their family, their hearts within their place of rest.

As he approached the back door to the throne room, he threw his prayers heavenward. *Father, help me to be all that I need to be for my people. Keep my focus on You throughout this day and let me speak hope and be a representative of Your Spirit. Give me grace, and keep the words and doubts of others far from my presence and my mind today.*

Drawing in a deep breath, he straightened his shoulders, adjusted his belt from which hung his sword. He was in full court dress today. Nothing but the best for a day that was set aside to honor his wife and child.

Touching the ring on the door, he moved to push it open but halted when a panting figure dashed around the corner. "Majesty! Wait!"

Young Tobias, on leave this day from his squireship with Kenton, his blond hair tied at his neck with tendrils escaping and flopping in his red face, came to a skidding stop within a few feet of Elgon. The boy's own ceremonial dress and leather jerkin with the stamp of Elira upon it were rumpled on his lanky frame. "Sir, there are special guests Malcolm put in the meeting chamber rather than in the throne room. He said to fetch you and that you would want to see them first." He sucked in a breath and attempted to remain stately, failing miserably.

Perhaps Fendrel had made it in from Padsley as delegate and Malcolm knew he would want to meet his old friend alone rather than in public before the entire court and the visitors that had arrived already.

"Lead on, lad. I'll see them first." He nodded and followed Tobias, who alternated between trotting and walking in an attempt to stay ahead of the king down the hall. Opening a side door, he tried to remain serious, but there was a look of curiosity on his face as he glanced between Elgon and whoever was in the room.

And Elgon halted mid-stride the moment he stepped through the doorway. "M-marcus?" he stammered. Too stunned to speak more than his name, Elgon took in the sight of his friend, years since they'd last seen each other, and the life and vitality and strength behind the cuts of the normally frail face were hard to miss. A journey like the one that had brought them from Padsley would have normally worn Marcus out, and yet, here he stood, the crutch gone and in its place a cane. And was that a bit of muscle he saw on the man's thin frame along with the blond beard that clung to his cheeks and chin?

The medicinal grinned and nodded before Elgon finally came to his senses, using his brother's proffered hand to pull him into an embrace. Marcus slapped him on the back and returned the hug with a chuckle that rumbled from deep in his chest.

Joy—the first he'd felt in a long time—welled to the surface from a place deep within him like water flooding after a drought, running over the cracked and barren earth, resting on the surface instead of truly sinking in. Incredulous, he caught sight of Dilara. The young wife of Marcus whom he had only seen once, and his eyes widened at the small cluster of little ones that gathered around her skirts, clinging to her and looking wide-eyed at the king and the man who must be their…father.

"Ho, Marcus, all these yours?" Elgon still couldn't fully embrace the joy, but it was overwhelmed by a greater level of surprise and shock. He counted three small heads as Marcus stepped back with a smile and nodded, glancing over his little tribe with pride in his eyes and a tilt to the chin.

"Aye, they are. They've come to meet their king."

Dilara's face looked unsure, but there was a strength behind the hesitancy that he read in the humble tilt of her head and the straight set of the shoulders as her hands gripped those of the two smallest ones.

"Welcome, all." His emotions of joy and sorrow were rarely isolated and instead mixed together in a beautiful cacophony of pathos. He smiled over them all even as his eyes brimmed. The beauty of each and every face filled his chest with delight and pride for Marcus, even as he ached for his own loss. "Come, children, meet your uncle Obed."

His friend's blue eyes were also full of tears as he grinned. Elgon knew that Marcus sensed what he was feeling, felt the man's compassion as he stepped closer and Elgon bent to one knee to meet the wee little ones that might as well have been his blood nieces and nephews.

Marcus followed Elgon's lead and beckoned to the oldest. "Come, Tavish, this is your uncle."

Tavish, his brown locks, curly like his mother's and spilling over his forehead and around his ears messily, cocked his head to the side, and his eyebrows were drawn together in a V at the center of his forehead. "I thought you said he was going to be the king." His hands were stubbornly at his sides as he glanced between Marcus and Elgon in confusion.

Elgon lifted the crown from his head and handed it to Tobias, who rushed forward to take it. Smiling at the young child, Elgon held out his hand, his other tucking his sword further behind his cloak so as not to intimidate the children. "I'll tell you a secret: I'm only king some of the time. But to you, I'll always be Uncle Obed."

Tavish stared for a moment longer, glanced at Marcus one more time, and must have sensed his father's approval because the look of confusion was wiped away instantly with a curious and excited expression as he reached out a hand to shake Elgon's.

The king shook the lad's tiny hand in his, and his heart squeezed. Tavish and his own child would be near the same age. Though his should be just a bit older.

Elgon stood and stepped to Dilara. He took her confusion out of the question, taking her hand, pressing it quickly to his lips, and then holding it tenderly between his callused palms. He hoped they would come to know each other over the years. Violet had been taken before any relationship or friendship could occur, but the strength in her eyes reminded him of his wife, and he knew that someday they would be fast friends. Perhaps even like sisters.

She smiled, her shoulders dropping, and when he let go of her hand, she brought forward the other two smaller tykes that clung to her skirts. "Tristan, Tamaska, meet your uncle. This is"—she hesitated a moment, glanced at Marcus, and then smiled warmly—"your uncle, Obed."

Elgon knelt again, bending his tall frame to be on their level. The young boy, his eyes and hair a perfect twin to Marcus's but with even more vibrancy and wayward locks, grinned up at him and grabbed Elgon's hand in his as if claiming it for his own. He tugged and pointed at the tiny one who couldn't be any older than two, solemn brown eyes massive in her round face with curls riotously falling around her cheeks and neck.

"That's my 'ittle sis'er." His voice was babyish, but emphatic and confident, as if it were his job to introduce her to Elgon.

Elgon smiled and took the tiny hand with dimpled knuckles in between his fingers and shook it gently. "A pleasure, my lady." Still kneeling, he bowed solemnly while both of the boys watched in wide-eyed awe at his movements, no doubt surprised at the deference he showed their little sister. She seemed to react as if it were to be expected, blinking those dark long lashes at him and then bringing her two fingers into her mouth in a thoughtful way.

"Here, love." Dilara scooped Tamaska up in her arms and held her on her hip in a smooth and easy motion that the tyke seemed perfectly familiar with as she kept her eyes on Elgon's face, studying him with more scrutiny than he had experienced in many a day.

He turned a smile to his friend, his brother. "They're beautiful, Marcus. Every single one."

Marcus clapped his hand on the king's shoulder. "No more beautiful than yours, I'll bet."

Elgon nodded without a word. Marcus had faith like he did. Of course he did. Marcus wouldn't be one to easily let go of his best and dearest friend any more than her husband would be. But there was still a relief and a breath of fresh air that filled his lungs. If Marcus believed that she were still alive, that their child would one day be recovered, then perhaps he didn't have to feel so alone.

Hope met with hope was stronger in the compounding of it. When the heart of another walked in the same faith as his own, it made the burden a little lighter.

"Will your family come in and join us at court? I would be so honored to host you. Where are you staying?"

Marcus acquiesced. "Of course. Fendrel is off rustling us up somewhere to stay, so don't feel like you need to go to any trouble for us. Today will surely be enough for you to manage on its own without our little ones getting in the way or into trouble."

Elgon shook his head almost a bit too emphatically. "No! Please. I'd—" His voice broke and he turned for a moment to catch his breath and swallow under the pretense of adjusting his cloak before turning back. "I'd be grateful for the company. These stone walls feel a bit cold and empty most days."

Marcus cast his eyes to his wife. She looked to him and then to Elgon. He met her gaze and felt the close scrutiny of those piercing eyes, compassion like fire scorching away any pretense he might have still held onto. He knew she saw him. Saw the pain, the sorrow, and the utter loneliness as if his soul were laid bare before her. He still didn't know her whole story, but whatever it was had truly uniquely gifted her with the ability to be Marcus's match and equal in reading another and sensing their inner pain.

"We would be honored to stay, your maj—" She paused at the good-natured frown he sent her at *your majesty*. "O-obed." She nodded in deference to his wishes with a small smile pulling at the corner of her lip as she stepped to her husband's side and claimed the place beside his heart. Her hand wound around his bicep with a perfectly gentle understanding and possession that somehow felt like a kick to Elgon's stomach, but healed something inside him at the same time. To see his best friend with the woman of his dreams, the heart of such a one, and the fruit and blessings of that mutual trust and love in their children was all he would've wished for him.

He swallowed. *Lord, keep me together today. Help me to spread the hope You have given me to others instead of the pain and despair that goes with it.*

"I will strengthen thee; yea, I will help thee; yea, I will uphold thee with the right hand of my righteousness."

A tiny hand slipped into his right one, and he glanced down in surprise. Tavish was holding onto his large hand, only able to grasp a few fingers rather than Elgon's entire palm, and there was something of the same compassion Elgon sensed from the boy's mother in his gaze—along with a large grin.

Elgon smiled at the boy and roughed up his hair with his free hand. "Would you like to see the throne room, young Tavish?"

The little boy nodded vigorously and hopped in his excitement. "Father told me all about it! He said it's beautiful and reminds him of the forest when the light is flowing through it in the sunny mornings, not when it's cloudy though, because the sun can't be out when it's storming. But he said the floor is made of trees from our forest! Is that true? Can I see the trees or is it just pieces of wood like a table and chairs?"

Elgon couldn't hold back a bewildered chuckle at the amount of words and speed with which they fell from the tiny lad's mouth.

Dilara chuckled and raised her eyes heavenward in mock exasperation. "Tavish, my love. You must remember to only ask one question at a time, or else how can anyone answer them?" She shrugged an apology to Elgon.

Tavish swallowed all of the words that must have been hovering on the edge of his tongue with a wide-eyed expression of consternation. "But, Mama, I'll forget them all if I don't ask them before they go away!"

Elgon clamped his lips around a laugh. That urge hadn't come to him in many a day and it felt…right, somehow. Today was, after all, to be a day of rejoicing in a life as well as praying for its return. Mourning would be for another day.

"You know, I sometimes have that problem myself. You may be on to something, Tavish." Elgon winked at Dilara who huffed at the same time that a grin split her face. Marcus never seemed to cease grinning and watching them both like one does a sparring match.

Taking his crown from Tobias, Elgon settled it on top of his head once more and beckoned the squire to lead the way. Tobias nodded and scuttled out into the hallway, his limbs all lanky and knobby at the joints as he trotted down the hall in an attempt at a dignified strut that came off as more of a bouncing walk.

The time in court was the hardest part of the day. Elgon offered for Tavish and Tristan to sit on the step leading to the dais off to his right, their little legs swinging and their tongues wagging to each other in a whispered critique of the ceremony, circumstances, and attendants.

Those that came were treated to a meal in the dining hall without much pretense. Simply the massive table laden with good food and conversation as some stood and others took seats at the smaller tables that surrounded the head one. Elgon mingled as was his duty, but he kept finding strength and just a touch of joy every time he glanced at Marcus's little family at their own table. The children on their knees on the chairs in order to reach their plates and little Tamaska in her mother's arms as Marcus tried to keep them in order and focused on getting the food in their mouths rather than the floor, table top, or tossed through the air at each other.

And finally the evening was coming to a close; the last ceremony would take place as dusk settled over the Sirene Sea. The part that always made his throat clamp shut and his insides quiver after a long day of talking and reminiscing and hearing the condolences and prayers of others. He knew their reassurances were heartfelt. He understood their desire to help, and they did at times. But he also sensed the lack of faith in some of their faces, the placating looks and glances as if to say that he was a fool for believing as he did. That their hearts knew that they were just here to show homage and honor to one who was once their queen.

He withdrew as the kingsmen and servants gathered the guests and led them to a table outside where bundles of violets were littered, the air steeped in the smell of the fresh wood and slightly floral note of the flowers. They would gather their bundles and make their way down the winding steps and roadway to the ocean, their golden lanterns bobbing in the waning light in a golden trail upon the cliffside.

He pulled his archer's gloves on, tightening the bracer on his left forearm. At least he was able to lead this part alone. He stepped from the castle walls and out upon the balustrade, pressing a violet to his nose and inhaling deeply. The flower didn't just remind him of his wife, the smell did too. Carted in from Raintamount Forest, their petals and leaves held onto the wet and earthy essence that reminded him of his time spent in those woods. The woman who held his soul in her grip and had spurred him on to the things of the kingdom here on earth and in heaven. Her memory seemed to grow dimmer each day, but things like this brought them right back. His heart leapt at the memory of her telling him the news of their impending child. Right here, near this spot. Just a few columns farther down she had stood, her skirt whipping in the wind as his cloak did now, that look of love and joy on her face, glowing against the golden rays of the sunlight.

He sucked in a breath as the wind, warm and yet chilling, blasted him in the face with a spray of salt. The sea was riotous today. He tucked the flower into the pin at his throat and nodded to Kenton, who stood with his usually bright and eager face solemn and still as he bowed his head in acknowledgement of the greeting.

Kenton knew Elgon often wished to be alone during the ceremony, silent in the memories and the breeze as it threw the smell of the sea and the violets in his face. He glanced over the edge of the wall and down the cliff face. Most of the guests had already reached the small stretch of beach to the left of the docks and wharves, and their line of lanterns could be seen trailing thin in their golden glow as the last few made their way to where they were supposed to gather.

Prayers were offered on the beach. He knew that some like Fendrel, Lord Milton, Rowan, or Rensen would probably lead them, their hearts standing in unity with him for the return of their monarch and heir to the throne. Silent prayers would also be offered, and he could see a few small figures lit by the glow of their lanterns make their way to the pyre, depositing their bouquets of violets in representation of their prayers upon the wooden raft resting on the edge of the beach.

The darkness was pressing in now, and only a thin line of gold split the horizon and signaled where the sea ended and the sky began. He could barely see the darker gray shape of the raft as it was heaved into the ocean, the surf and waves tossing about the kingsmen who completed the task, their cloaks flapping in the wind as the white foam roiled around them.

He sucked in a breath, his hands trembling as his heart filled with his own prayers. The begging of hope to be fulfilled, of sickness to be rid of as he waited in the deferment of that hope.

Six years. He clenched his jaw to keep it from quivering. His child was nearly six now. He didn't even know when he or she had been born. Was it a son? A daughter as he imagined her? "Lord…" Words too painful for utterance whispered past his lips as his spirit poured out a petition he had too much feeling to express in real words.

I'll bring a return. Instead of your shame there shall be a double portion; instead of dishonor they shall rejoice in their lot; therefore in their land they shall possess a double portion; they shall have everlasting joy.

Sucking in another breath, he set his shoulders, the emotion still crashing deep within him like the waves that thundered on the beach below.

He turned and took the bow and arrow Kenton held for him, nocking the arrow and lifting the tip towar Kenton. Taking the torch from its loop on the wall, Kenton held it beneath the arrow's wrapped point till it caught flame with a hiss.

Aiming at the faint, bobbing pyre on the dark waves below, Elgon counted the waves three times before he pulled back on the arrow and released it.

The soft *thwang* of the bow sent the fire streaking toward the beach and over the heads of the bystanders. Striking the pyre, it exploded into flames after a few seconds, the color flooding the sky and lighting the beach in the blackness of the night. The flames reached for the sky like a sacrifice of old, only this one was fueled by the prayers and faith of the people. The pyre bobbed about on the waves, taken by the receding tide and floating out to the horizon, now the thinnest slit of hazy light, barely yellow against the black of the ocean and the sky.

He dropped to his knees, the bow falling on the floor at his side, and rested his elbows on the wall as he stared at the pyre. The symbolism of it filled his aching heart as the notes of a hymn floated up the cliff walls to his ears. His shoulders heaved in sobs.

"Let our words take flight,
Our impassioned plea for help.
Hear our hearts as they cry
Our souls broken as they melt.
You delivered your children,
From enemies long ago.
You heard their cry and answered,
With food and water that flowed.
Return what has been lost,
Return our hope again.
For as the sea never fails to rise and fall,
So your love and promise remains.
Your love remains,
Your promise is sure.
Even though the darkness falls
Your heart toward us is pure."

The soft, mournful words floated over the stillness of the night air and struck his heart like an arrow that had found its mark.

"Never let our hope die out,
For surely as the sun will rise,
Our faith must waver not,
Through flood or drought.
Your love remains,
Your promise is sure.
Even though the darkness falls
Your heart toward us is pure."

Elgon stood, his heart pouring out, then still as he felt the wind run over his face with gentle hands that cooled the heat and whispered hope and relief to a heart aching, burdened with pain and a bitterness that was reminiscent of hope deferred.

He hadn't noticed that Kenton had left him alone till footsteps pounded on the stone and a lantern swung in the distance till its golden glow reached him. His muscles were stiff, his knees sore, and there was pain that stabbed through his feet when he tried to stand.

"Your majesty! It's Everard—" Kenton's voice was breathless, his eyes wide and his chest heaving. "He has people with him."

Elgon stumbled forward, his jog turning into a run as feeling returned to his numbed limbs. His mind spun. What should he expect?

ROSALIE, PRESENT DAY...

Breathless, Rosalie clung to the root she was using to hoist herself up the steep hillock in her way. With a grunt, she pulled with arms that ached from overuse and scrambled with her feet for purchase in the smooth dirt that was covered in leaves and offered no traction. Reaching for the brink, she looped an elbow over and clawed with her fingers for anything to grip as she heaved her foot to the root and pushed with all her strength.

Rolling over the top of the hill, she squeezed her eyes shut as her chest rose and fell in rapid succession. Every hill seemed to grow steeper, and she didn't think it was just her reaching the end of her strength. More rocks were packed into the dirt, and often between the breaks in the trees she would catch a glimpse of the mountain top. Its precipice reared ever closer to her right, its gray face intimidating and frigid, stalwart and unyielding to the wind that whipped through the hollows and tore at the tattered edges of her ripped skirt.

Groaning as she pulled herself to a sitting position, her stomach muscles knotting and aching with the strain, she blinked slowly and reached for the hem of her skirt. Using her teeth to get another rip started, she pulled at the linen, wishing that she didn't have to tear into such beautiful fabric, fully aware of all that one soul had done to harvest, spin, weave, and so much more. But finding her way back to Malcolm as one inexperienced and quite possibly lost in these woods would require some sacrifice. These markers would guide her back. The green with the soft golden paint of the Vagari pressed into the fabric was now muddied and grown dim with dirt, and she ran her thumb and forefinger over an imprint in the fabric, the shape of a flourish that looked much like a dove.

Sighing, she hauled herself to her feet and tottered to the tree whose root she'd used to haul herself over the hill. Knotting the strip around a lower branch that was still above her head, she felt tears rush to her eyes at the realization that the daylight was almost gone and she still hadn't reached her objective.

She shivered at the thought that she had no idea who she was meeting—didn't know if they were friend or foe—and had no clue as to how they would receive a bedraggled girl child stumbling into their clearing and begging for mercy and help.

Glancing down over the hills and valleys below, she wavered on her feet and took a step back to regain her balance as she strained her eyes for the other ties fluttering in the wind. She was still headed in as straight a line as possible. The torn ribbons of fabric flapping in the breeze in a line down the mountain had met her gaze as she crested each hill.

Surely it couldn't be that much farther. Doubt crept in like the dark shadows that stretched out over the forest floor at night. But what if she hadn't been headed in the right direction this whole time? Should she climb another tree and search for the smoke? Would she even have enough light or energy to do so? What if she fell when her muscles gave out?

Crying out in frustration, she buried her head in her hands and scrubbed at her face to clear some of the fog and wake herself up enough to continue.

A branch cracked in the woods, and her head whipped up. She darted a glance in every direction. Was it just another trick of the woods? Another sound of an animal? Or was it a foe? Her breath came in shallow gasps as she backed up against the tree and strained her eyes into the dim forest.

God, please, protect me.

With one hand over her thundering heart and the other reaching for the dagger tied at her belt, she pulled the knife from its sheath, holding it at her side. She didn't breathe, didn't move, until her lungs screamed for air. Perhaps she had imagined the sound.

Her hands trembled, but she sheathed the knife again, too scared to carry it as she climbed lest she cut herself with the blade she had discovered was far too sharp for her comfort.

"Please, don't let it be much farther." Her whisper blended with the others that tore through the forest at another gust of wind. Her limbs were shaking, and she fell to her knees, rolling to her side as she slid down the other side of the hill she had just scaled. With a cry of pain, her hip caught on a rock hidden beneath the fallen leaves, and she gritted her teeth at what was bound to become a bruise. At the bottom, the rocks twisted beneath her feet, and her ankles bobbled trying to carry her over them. There was another creek. Crouching near it, she dipped her hands in and brought the water to her lips. Her hands stung like needles from the chill of the glacier water, and they quickly grew numb as she carried mouthfuls of water from the stream to her lips.

She shook her wrists harder in hopes to warm them up before attempting the crest of the next hill. It was even steeper than the last and was made of more rock ledges than dirt, with some roots crawling over and through them. She might as well be climbing a tree. It was nearly a rock face, straight to the top.

Lord, give me strength. Summoning what little was left, she searched with her eyes first for the easiest path she could climb, with the most places to grip with her hands and feet. At least it pitched forward a little and wasn't entirely vertical. Identifying her starting point, she reached for the rock that jutted out above her head and gripped it. Her knuckles strained, and she reached above that for another hand hold as her feet found the root of a tree.

"Just. One. More." She gritted out through her teeth with every handhold. Her breath came in shallow gasps. She sucked in a deeper lungful of air when black started to crowd the edges of her vision. "Keep breathing," she chided herself as she reached above her head once more. And again. And again, until she neared the top.

Throwing a shaking arm over the top of the ridge, she used the entirety of her arm to pull, her muscles at her neck cramping with the effort. Shoving with her feet, her right foot missed its mark and skidded off the rock, swinging out into thin air, jerking at the arm that tried to anchor her to the top of the hill. A squeal snuck past her lips, and the sound echoed down the cavern and through the hollow to who knows where else.

Before her arm could slide any farther, she threw her other hand up and clawed at the rock, her hands and fingers stinging till she caught purchase and pulled, her feet swinging and scraping the wall for a step. Her left foot finally found one, and she heaved with her arms, rolling over the crest and crying with relief.

Closing her eyes, she pulled her right arm to her, trying to breathe through the pain that shot from her neck down into her shoulder and all the way to her wrist. Nothing was broken. It couldn't be. But those muscles were screaming beyond anything she had ever felt before.

Pulling herself to her knees, she gingerly circled her arm around, trying to get the muscles to release. They were pulling her head sideways with the cramp, and she sucked in as large a breath as she could, closing her eyes and trying to focus on relaxing the muscle rather than panicking at the pain. It finally released after more than a dozen slow, even breaths, and she dropped to her hands, swaying on all fours as she shivered in the air, turning cold as the sun, hidden by clouds, threatened to disappear entirely.

She needed to tie the next ribbon and continue on. Malcolm needed her. She had to be close. She was sure of it. Ripping off another piece, she stood on shaky legs and turned to find a tree, but her breath tore from her lungs in a gasp.

Standing in the shadows was a man, his face covered with a stretch of cloth, looming over her at nearly twice her height and with his hand resting on the weapon that was sheathed at his side. A hood was over his head, but she could make out the bright spots where his eyes held her in a stare.

Without a thought, she reached for the knife at her belt and pulled it out, the dagger glinting, and the man started to pull his blade from his sheath. It was at least five times the length of her dagger. What on earth was she going to do with her pitiful weapon against this man?

A wave of heat flooded her body, followed by ice, and she wheeled and started to run, her arms pumping at her sides. Was she close to the house that was supposed to be her haven, or would she end up a pile of bones on the forest floor? Would she be dragged back to the castle that had been her prison?

Footsteps pounded behind her, and galloping reached her ear before a horse reared up on her right, exploding out of the forest, its front hooves leaving the ground as a scream ripped its way from her throat. She spun, but her foot caught and the earth rushed up at her, the brown leaves attacking her face as something sharp pierced her hand. Then a crack, and blackness flooded her vision.

MALCOLM, PRESENT DAY...

Pain laced Malcolm's tongue with a bitter flavor, and he groaned. Throbbing, hollowed out, hot pain coursed from his shoulder down his back and arm, his hand numb and limp at his side. He tried to open his eyes, but everything felt cold, then hot, like being plunged into the fire after diving into a glacier stream.

The sounds of whispers and groans, cries and moans met his ears, and he sucked in a breath between his teeth, fighting against the darkness that tried to hold him down, pinned to the ground.

Gray light finally met his vision, and he blinked. Some of the shadows turned to shapes, then to tree branches and a boulder looming at his right. He tried to move his legs and succeeded in shifting his weight, only to knock his shoulder into the rock. Moaning through breaths, he welcomed the darkness again as it swept in with his closing eyes. Squeezing them hard, he started to see stars and bit his tongue till the feeling of pain there took away enough of what throbbed in his shoulder so he could open his eyes.

He was alone.

Shaking, he pushed off with his good hand and heaved with his muscles to a sitting position. His head spun, and sharp pain stabbed through his shoulder. He gripped the bad arm to hold it still as he tried to look around the rock. Perhaps Rosalie had just gone for water?

"Rosalie?" His voice was raspy, hardly loud enough to be heard by himself, let alone someone else in these woods.

"Rosalie?" His voice came a little louder this time, and he swallowed against the dry heat of his throat. The water bottle. Its leather blended with the leaves, and he reached for it with his left hand, trying to keep his right arm immobile as he gripped the cork, pulled it out, and tried to switch his grip to the bottle without spilling.

The icy water took some of the bitter taste with it as it washed down his throat, and he sighed in relief after several hard swallows. Thank God for small blessings.

His gaze landed on the leather waterskin in his grasp. If it was here, she couldn't have gone for water. But her cloak was laid over his legs along with his own. Was she seeking food? "Rosalie!" He called louder this time, hoping his voice would be carried to wherever she might be, but not far enough that someone else would hear it. He had no understanding of how far they had come yesterday. Most of it had been far too blurry and anything after that slip and fall and the blinding pain was nearly gone from his memory.

Panic seized him. Where was she? She should know better than to wander too far away to be heard. What if a dark knight made it this far into the woods? What if she had already been taken?

Nausea rose in his blistering throat—but no, they wouldn't have left him alive if they'd found her. Unless she had led them away from here?

His mind filled with dark images and visions of what could have happened to her. "Lord, keep her safe. Please let this all be something simple."

The trees howled, and he tried to crane his neck to see outside of the hollow of rock and root and dirt wall where she had safely tucked him. He had to be completely hidden from view. A spark of pride gripped him. She was learning. She was smart. Too smart to have wandered too far to hear him call. He strained and shifted his hips to lean farther out and realized that the sun was past midday. Was it afternoon already? How long had he been asleep? Had he left Rosalie to watch all night while he blacked out completely?

Guilt and shame shot through him. He was supposed to be rescuing her. He was supposed to protect her, guard her with his life, and here she had guarded him. "Rosalie!" he called again, his voice breaking. He needed to find her.

Reaching over with his left arm, he found a craggy hold in the granite and pulled, growling and moaning through his teeth at the fire that flashed through his wound and ripped across the muscles in his back and down his side. Panting, he managed to place a foot beneath him. Shaking, he made it to standing, but stars flashed in his line of sight, and even when they cleared, the edges of the glen were too dark. Nothing met his gaze.

Nothing.

He needed to make it to the hilltop. Maybe she was on the other side or down the slope.

His feet seemed to be working against him as he tried to haul himself around the rock and begin the climb. Every step sent searing pain across his entire body, but he shoved away the blackness that tried to claim him and pressed on. One foot in front of the other. One step at a time. He needed to reach the crest of the hollow. Reaching for a root that stuck out of the ground with his left hand, he stepped up and pulled. The bending and pulling of his muscles caught on the arrowhead still in his shoulder, and he nearly screamed, biting off the sound that almost felt more animal than human as he choked on it instead.

He caught sight of a fluttering piece of fabric tied to the tree whose root he was using to haul himself upward and he squinted, pushing past the blurriness and the flashing lights to make it out.

It was a piece of Rosalie's skirt.

Horror filled him at the thought that she had tried to make it the rest of the way to the highlanders on her own. She could never make it to the plateau without help. And to make it past the brothers' traps and maze of entry—that was impossible.

He had to get to her. Frantic, he pulled at the dirt around him, the leaves falling and sliding beneath him. He gripped another rock, but it pulled from its place in the dirt and without his right arm to catch himself, he slid to the bottom of the hillock with a shout, agony ripping through his very bones.

Twenty-Six

THE HIGHLANDS

ROSALIE, PRESENT DAY...

Gray swam in her vision. Rosalie rolled to her side—blinking hard, but it didn't clear the haze over her eyes. She was half blind. She would have pulled herself to her feet were it not for the hands that gripped her shoulders and arms, tugging her back to the ground. She sucked in a deep breath. Something blotted at her eyes and a bit of the cloudiness went away.

"Oi, ye've given 'er a cut that'll leave a scar, brother!"

"Do shut up, as if I did it on purpose." The voices growled at each other, and she flung her arms, scrambling backward to get away from their sources.

She scrubbed at her eyes with her forearm, realizing her hands were stinging. She must have fallen. A sharp pain near her right eye made her gasp and still her movements, holding her arms out to protect her injured face. She blinked again and saw blood all over her hands and the tattered sleeves of her dress.

Then she saw the blurred forms of the men who crouched in the leaves before her. She squinted at them till something dripped again over her eye, and she had to close both to keep it out.

"Och, ye're bleeding, lass. Lemme take a look at it for ye." She held up her hands to keep them away and dabbed at her left eyebrow with her forearm again, more gingerly this time. There was something in the man's accent that felt familiar, though she couldn't quite place it. She wanted to scream at them. To tell them to leave her alone. Beg them not to take her back. But perhaps if she kept silent, she could spare Malcolm. Perhaps if they couldn't find him, one of the Vagari would before he… She shook her head. He couldn't die.

"Now see ye've gone and scared her off, Gavan."

"Me? What on arth are ye blamin' me fer?

"Yer the one as made a move on her."

"Och, ye daft fool. Twas simply trying to help."

"Shut up, you two lug heads." There was a third voice and some stomping boots that made their way closer to Rosalie.

She cowered. She couldn't fully see him, but she could sense the man's nearness, and the dread of the moment filled her. This was her last taste of freedom. She would never see the world the same way again. Against her bidding, tears stung her eyes and made whatever wound was across her head throb more fiercely.

"There, child. I'm not going to harm ye. None of us will. How did ye reach these parts?" The voice was gentle, and even though everything that made sense screamed danger, something released inside her spirit. Perhaps it was the exhaustion, perhaps it was the utter despair. But there was nowhere for her run or hide. And the softness in the deep bass of that voice made her want to understand the man who owned it.

She tried to dab at her vision again.

"Lemme help ye with that. It might hurt a bit, but I've got to bind that wound. Here, ye'll be able to see once we stop that bleeding." Gentle but callused fingers tipped her chin up, and she flinched but remained still as someone wiped at the stickiness on her face and eyes. "Cam, you and Alex ride ahead, get the gate, and let Jennie and Ma know we're comin', and refrain from yer theatrics."

Rosalie could finally see, though not clearly. She almost jumped back at the sight of the man in front of her. His massive hands were wrapping a cloth around her head and face, but his crouched figure beneath the green and brown cape that matched his forest surroundings couldn't bely the massive frame hulking beneath it. His shoulders seemed to be as wide as she was tall and his hands larger than her face. They were covered in blood. Her blood.

She swallowed the bitter taste in her mouth at the site and winced as his fingers probed a tender portion of her forehead.

"I'm sorry we scared ye. It's not our way to chase wee bairns about in the forest, but those 'at set off our traps aren't usually little uns. If we get visitors this far up in the mountain 'at make it past the forest, ye know they aren't usually of the friendly sort. Sight unseen, we took ye for someone I'm sure none of us would want to see." His face was kind beneath the massive red beard that covered his mouth and jaw, though she could still see the squareness of it behind the whiskers. Bushy eyebrows to match hovered above green eyes that were sharp and focused.

"W-what happened?" She reached her fingers up to feel the bandage. He leaned back on his heels and handed her the cloth to wipe the blood off her hands.

"Ye tripped and hit yer head. Right sorry I am, but ye'll not have any worry to make us more so. Our mother'll do that enough for all of us." He caught her eye and made a deliberate movement to his hand, pushing his sleeve as if to get it out of his way, but she saw the ink there, a bird in flight.

With no more reserves in her to hide or stay the movement, her shoulders relaxed and she sighed a sob, every muscle relaxing into exhaustion as tears filled her eyes and fell down her cheeks. She was safe. These were her people.

His voice was even softer, husky at the sight of her tears. "Aye, ye recognize it then?"

She nodded, her hands shaking as she used the handkerchief to wipe the blood away.

"I come on the wings of the wind…" His voice was a whisper, but the words triggered a memory.

"As a dove to the sun." Her voice was husky, and she hardly had the strength to lift her head up. These were the people Malcolm had told her they would try to find.

"Och, let's get ye home then. Are ye alone? All this way?" There was gentle surprise in his voice, and a raise of the eyebrows that made her wonder if he was impressed.

Rosalie stared into his eyes when he turned them back on her. She didn't know how she would know, but she hoped there was something in them that would tell her she could trust him with her secret—with their safety. She knew the doves were a sign, but her entire life had molded her to be prone to the opposite of trusting others.

But there was kindness in his gaze. Gentleness. Something that reminded her of an oak tree that softly whispers in the wind, but remains steady in a storm, sheltering those beneath its branches while the world rages around it.

She held out her hand; it shook with the weight of her journey, and her body trembled from exertion. "Will you help me?"

His shoulders straightened with something she couldn't quite understand, and his gaze turned sharp, scrutiny over her face and features. He took her hand in his firm grasp. "With my life." There was a hoarse sincerity in his tone that flooded her heart with complete and utter trust in him.

She swallowed hard. "The man who brought me here. He's injured and I left him hidden. I've been climbing all day, and I left a trail so I could find him again."

"Aye, a smart one, ye are. Let's fetch 'im, shall we?" He helped her to her feet, but she wavered, and he changed his grip to hold her beneath the elbow while his other arm wrapped around her waist. She barely felt the weight of her own body as he led her to his horse through the rattling leaves on the ground.

Another man sat mounted behind her protector's steed, his head on a swivel and eyes alert. He wasn't quite as large as his companion, but had the same red hair—though darker—

set shoulders, and auburn beard. His face was thinner and his eyes dark instead of green. He had a bit more of the look of a Rusalk about him, but there was still that steady safety in his sharp gaze as he took in the sight of her.

"Gavan, call Ian. Send him on to tell the others we have another visitor to retrieve and to keep the braziers glowing. Then follow behind us."

The man gave a sharp nod, brought his fingers to his lips, and sent a keening whistle that sounded eerily like the trees but at a different pitch than the forest. Galloping hooves thundered, and another horseman rode into sight. His green cape billowed behind him till he pulled to a stop, his eyes resting on Rosalie in curiosity. There was an openness about his countenance and a brightness behind the look on his face that made her want to get to know him instantly. He had a more excited energy than the others, and he held himself in the saddle like a younger, clean-shaven version of the giant who lifted her to a seat on the front of his saddle before climbing up after her.

She swayed till he had his arm about her waist. The height made her dizzy.

The young one trotted off into the woods after exchanging words with his companion, and her protector pulled their horse around. "Now, wee one. My name is Duncan, and this here is my brother Gavan. The other three lug heads you caught sight of are my brothers. Now, how do we go about following this trail of yours?"

"Mine's Rose." Her full name didn't come to her lips, and perhaps keeping a bit of her identity hidden was a good idea. Malcolm would have said so.

After explaining which direction she had come from that day, the brothers exchanged glances and kicked their horses into a trot. The ride was rough, though not as rough as it could have been. The ground she had covered today required more than a bit of up and down, but the brothers seemed to know how to guide their horses over the terrain, in and around the ebbs and flows of the hills, and around the rocks in such a way to make the ride as easy and swift as possible. The constant up and down, jockeying back and forth would have been worse were it not for the massive arm that held her waist and tethered her to the saddle, moving her in counterbalance to the horse's sure-footed and quick movements over the rocky terrain.

It was growing dark, and she strained to catch sight of each fluttering strip of cloth she had tied to the trees, pointing them out to the men as they went. But nausea crept up on her, and she sagged forward after a particularly circuitous route around a rock and the muscles in Duncan's arm tensed. "Och, lass. Perhaps I shouldna ha' taken ye this far. Mother and Jennie'll have my hide fer it."

"I wouldn't be left. Malcolm needs me."

He stiffened at the name. "Malcolm, ey?"

She squeezed her eyes shut and willed her stomach to calm. There was nothing for her to wretch anyway. Her stomach cramped in protest, and she gripped the pommel of the saddle till her knuckles turned white.

"Well, I hope fer your sake that we're almost there."

She nodded, her body trembling beneath the effort to stay upright. The ground dropped away beneath them into the dark, and she recognized the tree she had used to climb for a view—

was that this morning? It felt like a lifetime ago. She tried to push Duncan's arm away and slide to the ground, but he held her tighter. "Wait a moment, lass. I'll not have ye falling and getting hurt worse. Where'd you leave 'im?"

"In the bottom of the hollow, behind the large rock and under the tree."

Duncan clicked his tongue at his mount and brought the horse to the right, following his brother around the sharp drop and to a more shallow incline that allowed them to enter the hollow on hoof rather than foot.

Gavan was off his horse first and trotting forward when they reached the bottom. "Duncan." His voice was sharp with a hint of warning in it.

Duncan pulled up his mount and hopped off. "Stay here, lass." He gave her a pat on the knee and would have turned, but she had already thrown her leg over and was sliding off. He caught her so she didn't land hard on her feet and set her down with a grumble under his breath.

"Malcolm?" she called, stumbling into a run, nearly falling to her knees had Duncan not caught her arm. He helped her kneel beside a prone Malcolm. He was farther from the rock where she had left him this morning and face down in the leaves. His shoulder and the bandage she had wrapped there were stained with dark, red blood. Gavan took the uninjured shoulder and rolled him.

Rosalie let the tears loose as she gently brushed the dirt, gravel, and leaves away that had pressed into the side of Malcolm's face. "Macolm?" she whispered brokenly, her voice rasping. She had forgotten how thirsty she was. "Please wake up. I got help. I promised and I'm back." His skin was burning beneath her hand, and he twitched, but otherwise didn't react to the movement or voices.

"Give us space now, Rose. We'll get 'im up and get 'im home. The sooner the better. Mother and Jennie know medicine. They'll tend to 'im better than we could. I promise ye. He'll be all right if we've anything to say about it."

She sat back on her heels, swaying with exhaustion as the two massive men lifted Malcolm's tall and limp frame as if he were kindling, carrying him over their shoulders till they reached Gavan's mount.

She was too spent to move. Not one bit of strength ran through her veins. She thought about getting up, about walking to the horses, attempting to climb back onto Duncan's mount, but it was only her thoughts that took her there.

It was darker than she remembered. Night was falling. Her eyes drifted shut, but her body still stayed upright. Her head bobbed on her chest as the throbbing took hold behind her eyes and along the cut above her brow. Hands lifted her, and she felt the movement but relaxed against the chest she leaned against. If she could just rest for a minute…

MALCOLM, PRESENT DAY…

The sights and smells of blood came to his mind. The puddle of it beneath him. The roaring pain in his head as if he were in a cavern, the shouts of many echoing off the walls. He saw the prison doors and his hands gripping the metal grate, his knuckles white.

He was there again. The shouts and screams of the servants and soldiers alike roared in his ears. He saw the kingsman fall in front of him and raised his sword.

The blade came down on the back of his head, and the blackness rushed up to meet him, stars enfolding him in their depths. Pain ricocheted around him, his entire body an inferno as he descended into blackness, then fire, then blackness again.

Stones, cold against his face. Sharp on the palms of his hands. The taste of blood in his mouth—the bitter, metallic tang. He tried to spit it out. Tried to move. But he was tethered to those rocks. His body pressed into them harder and harder till he was sure they left an imprint on his face. All this time he was burning hot, scorching.

Water. If only he could fill his mouth with it. Taste it, feel it. Touch the coolness of it.

Something soft stroked his face, drenched him into ice. Cold now, he shook, the desire for the fire filling him just as assuredly as he had desired to escape it.

His brother's face. The pain that lingered there. The disappointment. Then anger. The anger he had never seen but knew beyond a shadow of a doubt should have been his. Years of it, aching, twisting, roiling from that face he loved.

And the guilt. Because he knew it was all his fault. The loss, the sorrow. It poured out of that look like scalding fire that burned him to his very bones. But the voice was like ice. The pain lacing it sent daggers to his heart.

"You could have saved them. How could you let this happen? How could you let them take my pride and joy? You, my brother, the man I trusted with more than my life, and you betrayed me. Just as the men who left that day betrayed me, you left me in my hour of direst need. You let them get past you. You let them take her. Beat her. Kill her with their poison and their plots."

Please... He gasped. The ice flowing through his veins made him shake beyond his own control. He would melt. Disappear right here. The fire in those eyes was righteous. Was right. Was all that he deserved. But still he didn't think he could possibly bear it.

"And now you lost the last link. The one who holds the promise of all those years of waiting. The years of sorrow. The reward for my suffering, and you left her. Abandoned her in the woods to herself. Where do you think she has gone? Would Rusalka let her out of their sight forever? And now my family is gone. Every last one of them. Every last hope of a legacy. Gone with the wind."

And it's all your doing...

He writhed under the inferno. The pain. The suffering. The guilt and shame that ate at the very core of who he was.

But it was right. It was true. He had failed. He had given up. Perhaps this hell was his penance.

ELGON, EIGHT YEARS AGO...

With his heart in his throat, Elgon followed Kenton down to the receiving area near the kitchens where he had once snuck into his own castle disguised as a kingsman. The memory pressed in on him now as he remembered what his purpose had been that day. To find the fabled woman he wished to marry and set her free. To remain undetected from those that sought him harm in his own castle and kingdom.

He slowed up just before reaching the large room where the kingsmen gathered, prepared for the day, kept their armor, and went about other menial tasks. He would direct the head housekeeper to have it cleared of kingsmen and allow the rescued to use it to clean up, get changed into new clothes, and find some comfort before they were fed a meal. His mind ran through the list of tasks that needed doing, hoping it would distract him from the hope exploding in his chest that perhaps, just by chance, his wife and child were amongst those that had come.

Kenton held the door for the king, and Elgon stepped through, his feet frozen at the sight of the ragtag crew before him. His eyes sought something familiar in every single face that met his gaze.

Everard stood, his cloak and pants caked in mud, dirt even clinging to his long black hair and fading it to a brown that matched the streaks on his face. Was that blood scabbed over a cut on his forehead? He held a small child in his arms who was also covered in dirt, her eyes huge in the emaciated and stretched skin of her face. Elgon swallowed back the bitter taste in his mouth and set his shoulders, tamping the disappointment that reared up at not finding what he'd sought back into the deep recesses of his heart where it would no doubt swallow him later.

Now was not the time.

"Welcome, all. Please, do not fear. You are safe here." The looks of worry and hesitancy on their faces remained despite his reassurance, and they all stepped back as if controlled by one mind.

He took in their haggard faces. There was no meat on their bones. Their clothes hung off of them like scarecrows. There were more women than men, most of them young, but there were a few boys and young girls amongst the group, as well as older men who looked too thin and exhausted to put up any kind of a fight. Silver locks laced the black of their bedraggled hair, and he swallowed again. The pain of what he saw was something beyond the depths of his own grief. He felt their pain. Understood their fear.

His voice was lower, huskier when he again tried to speak. "Please. I want you to know I'm sorry for all you have been through. But it is over now. You will not bear such harsh treatment in this kingdom, if I can help it. This place is yours. There are baths in the room beyond, and I'll have the servants fetch clothes. They will be yours to keep. There will also be food provided for you. I'll inform the cooks to start on that immediately. We will find a place for you to stay tonight. Rest easy. I know it's hard to do such a thing when your life has been as it has. But I promise you have nothing to fear here. Not from me, not from my men, and not from my servants."

He nodded and glanced at Everard, who gave him a thankful look while also subtly signaling with his head that he wished to speak to Elgon outside. He handed the child he held to one of the women close to him, and Elgon took Kenton's arm, leading him from the room till they were behind closed doors in the hallway.

"Inform the maids that they are to find clothes for every one of them. Send to the treasury. I want each of them to be given three gold pieces each to help them on their journey. Have Raphart called as well. They should be looked over for any injuries or illnesses. They may all sleep in the infirmary till new homes and occupations are found for them if they wish it. I'll speak to the cook myself. Oh, and tell the kingsmen they will need to remain away from the premises until the refugees are through with using it. The armory is as far as they may go. You may enlist Tobias with your needs."

Kenton nodded and spun on his heel, headed for the infirmary and whistling for Tobias, who was always within earshot if he could help it. Elgon caught sight of the lad at the end of the hall where he fell into step with Kenton and trotted after him as they turned the corner.

"Fourteen." Everard's voice behind him made Elgon turn. The hope in his heart sprung to life but he shoved it back with the hand of cynicism that tried to balance the emotions inside of him.

"Are they all from Rusalka?"

Everard nodded. "Slaves mostly. Some were even pulled from bordellos. Many of the women and children never experienced any kind of childhood. They'll need a place where they will feel safe and where they can start to understand what it means to be young and carefree."

Elgon nodded. "A-any news of…" His voice trailed off, and he glanced at his hands where he smoothed an imaginary wrinkle from his jerkin.

Everard didn't say anything, so Elgon looked up into his face and saw compassion there. Everard shook his head.

Elgon felt the choking feeling of tears rise up the back of his throat and grip his voice in clenching fingers as the burning started in his eyes.

Everard's hand on his shoulder made him feel like a child again, but he lifted his head and nodded to let his friend know that all was well. "No, I'm all right. I know…it may be a while yet." He straightened his shoulders.

He looked past Everard at the huddle of people through the door his friend had left open. They seemed at a loss, scared—hands gripping each other tightly, pain rippling beneath the surface of a carefully portrayed indifference. Bruises visible, and some scars no doubt hidden beneath the surface.

Compassion rose up in him. Sorrow for those who had experienced the illest form of humanity on this earth.

These ones here were deserving of just as much love as his Violet and their child. And they were loved. Not just by someone here on earth who had done it too poorly, but by the King who owned the cattle on a thousand hills.

Elgon reached a hand to the stone wall to hold his weight, suddenly too heavy for his own strength. In that moment, the power of love and compassion from his Heavenly Father crashed through him like an avalanche, and his mind exploded with the understanding and realization that this was more than just a few peasants rescued from an ill life.

Had Violet never been taken, these slaves would never be standing here, in his armory, afraid but free. Free forever from the life of abuse, pain, and sorrow they had endured. He prayed for his wife. Every moment of every day. The pain of her missing, the emptiness at his side. All of it plagued him like a thorn in his spirit he was not sure he would ever be rid of.

But as desperate as the pain was, as long as the sorrowful days and nights were, as much as he *hated* every single second of this living, gut-wrenching, horrendous tale of woe…he saw something of a glimmer of the hope that came from it.

Because even in despair, hope was alive and well. It flourished in the dark shadows of a broken world where a God existed beyond the natural order of space and time and held the power to flip the entire universe on its head. To do the impossible. To work evil for good. To turn mourning into dancing, sorrow into delight, and take the very depths of one's despair and use it to set others free.

And for that brief moment, the revelation of all that was wrong in his world tilted just enough to be put to right. He saw the freedom, the lives of these refugees stretched before him. Women like Dilara who would now experience a new world of hope, healing, and love that they had never known. He saw their paths even before they could. He saw the way that God was going to take the lives that had been broken and stolen from them and turn them into a thing of beauty and goodness that would bring healing not just to themselves, but to many.

Men who had lost their manhood; their authority would be given a new turn at experiencing the power of heaven.

Children who would know what it would mean to be loved unconditionally. To experience the power of a family where they had had none. To grow up as children of a King who could take the broken and put them back together again. Take the lame and make them walk, make the blind to see, and love the unloved in ways that no one else would think possible.

Hope surged in him. Not because his story was reaching its end. Not because he saw the fruit of his prayers. Not because he held his missing family in his arms. But because he had been granted a vision of what a God of love can do for those too broken and downtrodden for any other. He served a God who wasn't just able to take the pain and suffering of his people and turn it to their good…but one who *delighted* in doing so.

His time would come. This he knew beyond a shadow of a doubt. But for now, his place was here. Pouring forth the goodness of God onto a small band of people who needed to experience that love.

Elgon rose to his full height, throwing his cloak over his shoulder and out of his way. He wiped the tears that had spilled down his face unbidden and tangled in his beard with hasty hands. His voice rolled with strength and new passion, awoken from the depths as new faith and conviction sprung within him like the well of living water, never to run dry.

"Come, Everard. We have work to do. This is just the beginning."

Twenty-Seven

LIFE ANEW

ROSALIE, PRESENT DAY...

Voices, thick with a familiar accent, beckoned to her like a soft cooing of mourning doves, begging her to open her eyes, to see the brightness of the sunrise. She turned her head and felt the slight throb above her brow again. Blinking away the darkness, she pushed herself upright. The world tilted and shifted to gray as she lifted her hand to her head, willing it to stay still.

She swallowed. Her throat was so dry, her mouth parched beyond reason.

"Och, she's up, wee bairn. Here, lass. Drink this, love." The voice echoed distantly, as if from another room, but a cup was lifted to her lips, and she drank greedily.

When had she encountered the last stream, drunk from its ebb and flow?

The mountains. It all came rushing back with the force of an ax splintering wood, and she blinked into the light that shone in her eyes. Her vision cleared, the fuzziness banished to the corners and then gone completely as she sucked in a breath and her heart stalled in her chest.

There were so many of them. The memory of Duncan the giant and his band of brothers crashed back into her memory, and now she had the opportunity to see them all up close. This had to be them. Varying shades of red and black hair on heads that towered taller than anyone ought to filled her vision. Little faces peeked at her around legs and over the tops of chairs as the children all stood or sat around a table bigger than any she had ever seen before.

Her eyes widened as she took it all in.

"Och, ye're safe here, lass. My name is Mam'Nessa. Though this lot o' sons o' mine and their bairns are intimidating enough to take the salt out of anyone, gentler giants ye'll never find."

Rosalie searched their faces, arranged like a sea of stoicism till she found Duncan. She remembered that face. His broad shoulders bumped into those of the woman beside him, and there was a child in his lap, another one clinging to his arm, her small head barely peeking over the top of the table from her seat on the bench beside him. He nodded to Rosalie with a reassuring smile—or at least appeared to be from what little she could see behind his beard.

The food on the table caught her attention next. She placed a hand to her empty middle just as it cramped in hunger.

"Child, ye'll need food straight away. Now, everyone keep yer mouths from jabbering like a bunch of jaybirds. Lassie'll probably have a headache the size of a mountain cat with the way ye sent her flying into that rock." The older woman who had handed her the glass of water glared at the men around the table and helped Rosalie to her feet. "Here, lass, let's get ye something to eat. Don't worry, they won't bite, even if they are lug-headed sometimes."

Leading Rosalie to the table, she helped her to a seat. While the woman dished her up a plate, Rosalie lifted her hand and fingered the bandages neatly wrapped around the wound on her forehead.

"Sorry we are about that. Ye'll have a scar to show for that bump. Ye ended up with a bit of a cut over that left brow o' yourn. I told the lads those traps of theirs will end up doin' more trouble than good this far in the mountains."

Duncan closed his eyes and shook his head. "Oi, mither o' mine, as if them traps haven't kept the lot of us safe from those without that don't exactly see eye to eye."

The old woman set the plate down in front of Rosalie and handed her a linen napkin and a wooden fork with a sigh. "Don't I know it, but something must be done if those who seek refuge are to continue coming up the mountain pass to our bit o' land on their way to freedom. We can't as injure them afore they even get here."

Rosalie froze with the piece of bread in her fingers on the way to her mouth. They sounded a bit like…Mother Hobbs, though hers was far softer. But it was the same inflection.

"What is it, wee bairn?" The older woman rested a hand on her shoulder. "Isn't the food any good? Have ye all been lying to me about the taste o' me food again?"

The men shook their heads and leaned back as if scared to be roped into a row.

Rosalie glanced between the woman and the dish of food. "No, ma'am, it's not that. You…that is—you sound a bit familiar is all."

The woman grinned, her voice gentle and reminiscent, her eyes softening. "Ye've met me sister then, have ye?"

Sister? Glancing at the woman in front of her, Rosalie didn't doubt it, what with the black hair streaked by silver tied in a braid and wrapped into a bun at the base of her head. Her brown kirtle and apron were caught up and tucked into the belt at her ample waist, and her rounded figure and face was one of comfort. She gave off the air of having tended to many a young one with gentle hands and eyes filled with love. But there was a snap behind those eyes that rivaled Mother Hobbs, and the wrinkles at the corners of her dark eyes were those of joy and laughter.

"Your sister?"

"Aye. My older sister. Fiona Hobbs. She's in the wooden cabin that's all grown into the woods? Ye look as if ye've seen it. She married and left us long ago, but she still sends messages with those she directs on from her corner o' the woods."

Rosalie was starving, but she had forgotten about the food for the moment, surprised and a bit shocked by the revelation of these women's relations.

"Now, eat up. I'll introduce ye to the rest o' these crazy cattle so ye know they're friend nae foe, despite their looks." She winked at the line of massive men on the other side of the table and clutched the shoulders of the young child who had slipped to her side.

"Come now, dear, lay up on the boys." The oldest giant present grunted as he laid his crumpled napkin by his emptied plate. "Ye know they did nothing to berate 'em so fiercely."

Nessa grinned at him and stole a kiss as she walked by to take his plate to the dishboard against the far wall.

Rosalie chewed slowly, not wishing to feel worse for having scarfed down her food too quickly. The bread was warm with a sharp tang, and the crust had a bite and crunch to it that made her mouth water. The cheese was sharp but creamy on her tongue, and she thought for just a moment that she could eat what was on her plate for the rest of her life. She nearly choked when the small child who was holding onto the older woman's apron reached a small hand into the pocket without even looking.

"Oi, ye little minx! Trying to get a bite o' the sweetuns Mam'Nessa made fer ye! Ye know me better than to try to sneak a bite when ye've nae finished yer dinner. Ye'll have to ask yer mither if ye want to jump the gate and eat the sweet afore yer dinner." The little girl pouted but scampered back to a seat on the other side of the table.

The woman sitting beside Duncan, her dark hair wrapped away from her face in a kerchief and falling down over her shoulder in a long braid, bit back a smile and wrapped her arm around the young one, directing her to eat the food in front of her on the plate. "Ye heard Mam'Nessa. Eat yer food."

The woman everyone seemed to call Mam'Nessa came back with a steaming pot and ladled a creamy, tan-colored liquid into a wooden cup with a handle in front of Rosalie. "There ye are, dearie. Give that a try. That'll settle yer stomach and fill ye up all at once."

Rosalie cradled the cup in her hands and blew on it before taking a sip. It was the same spicy blend that she'd tasted during her short time with the Vagari, but this was creamier and sweeter than the strong brews they had served with barely a dash of cream. It warmed her stomach, taking away the pinched, empty feeling.

"Now, I'll introduce ye to my man so that he'll do the honors of showing ye the family." Mam'Nessa grinned at the old giant sitting at the end of the table. He shared a look of love and humor with her that made Rosalie suddenly feel comfortable and not so alone. These people loved and loved deeply. Despite the good-natured teasing, they were kind, and if they were anything like Duncan, she knew she could trust them. "That old one there at the end o' the table is Mac. He's the head o' the home and father to these lads." She winked at him and threw him a kiss, which he caught out of mid air and pressed it to his heart with an overly dramatic swoon.

Rosalie giggled along with the deep chuckles rumbling around the table.

Mac's eyes turned serious as he caught her gaze, and though they sparkled beneath the disordered array of white and red hair on his head, there was a comfort and a softness to them that he extended to her in the silence. A camaraderie and a compassion. "I hope ye know ye're welcome here lass. Welcome and safe. These lads o' ourn may look terrifyingly ugly"—a grin pulled at the corner of his mouth as his sons let out a collective groan—"but they've hearts of gold that serve the Lord and honor his people in all things." He pressed his hand to his chest. "It's our sincerest hope that ye'll feel welcome here even when others deny ye a place at their table. While ye're here, ye're treated like one o' our own, even if that means to the death."

His eyes never strayed from Rosalie as if to ensure that she knew the veracity of his words. She glanced around the rest of the table and saw the same look of welcome and care from Mac's sons and two daughters-in-law.

"Thank you," she whispered. It was all she could think to say, but those two words barely made it past the dam of tears that filled her eyes and clogged her throat. The feeling of loneliness that had plagued her through the mountain climb and dangerous flee for help yesterday fled screaming from the room like a ghost that couldn't bear the light. These weren't just strangers offering friendship, they were family offering kinship.

"Alrighty then, that there at the far end of the table is me oldest lad, Duncan. Next to him is his wife, Carlissa, and their young'uns are bouncing around the room, but I'm sure they'll tell ye their names if they can stand still long enough. They're Levi, Song, Jaelinne, Jubilee, and Jude."

A few of the children waved when their names were announced, but Mac was right; many of them were energetically climbing over the other men around the table or shoveling bread and cheese and meat into their mouths. Carlissa smiled at Rosalie when she was introduced, and her dark eyes were soft and welcoming. Rosalie thought she and Duncan seemed a pair who fit together. Despite the fact that Duncan looked like a redheaded oak tree and Carlissa looked more like a dark-haired willow.

Mac pointed to the rest of the men around the table. "My second son Knox, and his wife Rowan, and their little one, Liam." Knox was almost the spit and image of his older brother, just with no beard gracing his face. Rowan was blonde and seemed timid from her place beside her husband, but she threw Rosalie a shy smile. When she turned to wipe the food from her toddler's face as he sat in his father's lap, Rosalie caught sight of a red scar that cut from the side of her forehead, down her cheek and neck till it trailed off beneath her hair. A dove was tattooed over a part of the scar next to her ear, but Rosalie swallowed hard at the sight, wondering what would have caused such a gash and how she would have received it on her face.

"The other lads as yet haven't met their match, but their time'll come. Cameron, Alexander, Gavan, and Ian. Ye might 'ave seen a few o' them yesterday when ye met 'em in the woods." Each of the men nodded at her when their names were mentioned, and while some had Nessa's dark black hair, and some sported varying shades of scarlet thatches, they all had the family resemblance of the square face, large jaw, massive shoulders, and hands the size of shovels. They all reminded her of Everard in build, though these men were even larger. Malcolm had told her how Everard was from Rusalka, and while many of the men who served on the military force for Zuko were large men, they tended to be more wiry and had little in the way of resemblance to these giants.

The door behind her opened, and she turned on instinct, her heart beating hard in her chest.

A young woman in russet, with a linen apron tied over her dress, her red curls messily tied up in a scarf with locks escaping in every direction, entered the room. A large basin rested in her hands and clothes hung over her arm.

Rosalie flinched when a hand came to her shoulder, but it didn't move and instead made small circles of comfort on her back. "And this"—Mam'Nessa had a softer tone in her voice, one of comfort to soothe rather than to tease—"is our daughter, Jennie. Born in the midst of these crazy men. She's been tending to yer Malcolm."

Jennie nodded to Rosalie, her blue eyes large in her round face. Somehow she looked like these men, but not of them. Her features were softer, more like her mother's, but her hair was flaming red and tossed about with curls just like the wildest of her brothers. Freckles dotted her cheeks, and her nose scrunched when she smiled. Setting the basin down in an out of the way spot and taking the empty seat beside Rosalie, she held out her hand. "It's nice to meet ye."

The smile in her eyes beckoned Rosalie near, filled her with welcome, comfort, and a sense that this woman, instead of being rougher for the presence of so many men, had instead been made soft. The compassion in her tone and in her expression was tender, while her shoulders were set in a solid line that intimated that she pulled her own weight and had her own say. Like her mother, she was dwarfed by her brothers, but she had the same set jaw as they did, and there was a dancing light in those blue eyes.

Rosalie took her hand, calloused yet gentle, and Jennie grinned at her. "Welcome to this clan o' crazy that we call home."

Rosalie couldn't help giving a tired smile back. Jennie turned and gathered some food on her plate while elbowing the youngest of the Highland clan with a smirk. "Ye daft limmers take up sae much space it's hard to even turn around in 'ere," she groused good-naturedly and winked at one of her nieces across the table, who grinned back.

"Rose, is it? I expect you'll want to know how Malcolm is doing."

Rosalie nodded hard. There was little else she wanted to know more than that.

Ladling herself a cup full of the warm mixture Rosalie had drunk and then adding some more to Rosalie's, Jennie took a long swallow and started piling bread and cheese on her plate, while one of her brother's served her a spoonful of meat stew from the still steaming pot in the middle of the table. "He's doing as well as can be expected, though the fever is the hardest part now. We got the arrow out o' his shoulder, and after that he did much better, but the wound had already festered, and we daren't sew it up yet with it infected the way it is. If it gets any worse, we may have to burn it out, but I'm hoping mother'n mine's herbal mixtures can take it down afore we have to resort to that measure.

"He hasn't wakened yet, but I'm sure he'll be glad to know ye're near if ye want to sit with 'im when ye're finished."

Rosalie made a move to stand—food could wait—but Mam'Nessa touched her shoulder again. "He'd want ye to finish eating, luv. Ye had a rough day yesterday and need yer food and rest, same as anyone. I'll go sit with him till ye're done. Ian, ye and yer brother'll need to stock the wood in the kitchen when ye get finished with yer meal. We've a need to lay in more afore the night."

"Aye, Mam." Ian nodded vigorously and winked at Rosalie before he excused himself from the table. Nessa disappeared into the room Jennie had come from, and Rosalie tried to put another bite of cheese in her mouth, but she was distracted by the commotion across the room. Two of Duncan's children clung to Ian's legs, sitting on his feet and giggling while he tried to walk like nothing was amiss.

"Och, Mam must 'ave weighted down the stew today. I'm awful heavier than I was a mite ago."

More giggles overwhelmed the last of his words, and Rosalie couldn't help but smile as Ian stomped across the floor with two children for boot straps, grunting and groaning beneath the weight. He even pretended to bump his head on the low hanging rafters that were just a hair above the top of his head, and the children giggled harder.

"Uncle Ian, we're on your feet!" the young girl shouted.

"Ye don't say! And this whole time I thought Mam had put iron lead in that soup o' her'n." He smacked his forehead as if flabbergasted, then bent double, tickling the tykes who fell off his feet and ran screaming across the room to climb under the table.

"Oi, hide, ye cowards. I'll be back fer ye later. Make no mistake about that." Ian growled at the children who squealed and clambered further beneath the table, laughing all the while.

"Give it a rest, Ian, er I'll have to choose sides before I capsize," Duncan grumbled, but the twinkle in his eye relayed his enjoyment of their game.

"And that's my cue to leave. Cannnae be beating my older brother and showing up the power of the family, can I?"

Duncan scoffed, and Ian waggled his eyebrows before closing the door behind him.

Carlissa stood and kissed her husband on the cheek. "All right, little'uns, since you seem to have finished yer food and moved onto other things, let's get washed up and help Mam'Nessa with the dishes to surprise her when she comes out."

Scampering feet thumped across the floor, and four little ones followed her like a clattering mob into the connected room off the back of the house where Carlissa started scraping the dishes she had brought with her.

Rosalie watched it all as she kept eating till her plate was empty. There was something in this house she had never experienced before. The same love, joy, and delight that the Vagari life had shown her was somehow captured into this one large lodge these people called home. The simple conversations, elbows and hands resting on shoulders. The good-natured teasing and the ready laughter as well as the subtle motions of service and deference that was done in silence didn't escape her sight. The way they served one another, even if it were Gavan reaching something for Jennie that was beyond her grasp, Duncan holding his wife's hand as she stepped over the bench to help her balance. The children crawling all over their uncles' laps as if they belonged there and would never be turned away.

Her heart swelled, and that feeling of loss and longing she'd experienced with the Vagari rolled into one as if the thing she had never known existed had been missing her entire life, and she prayed it would be hers one day. But even in that, the realization that siblings would never be hers choked her throat, and she had to work hard to swallow the last bite of bread.

Malcolm was still asleep when she finally went in to visit him. Indeed, he didn't wake for another four days. Jennie, her mother, and Rosalie—when she wasn't forced to lie down and rest—took care of him around the clock during those four days. Cleaning, feeding him what little broth they could get down his throat. Tending to his wound and washing his face and arms with a cold cloth to keep his fever down.

Rosalie's throat and heart clenched at the way he faded before her eyes. His once strong frame shook with chills and burned with fever. The gray pallor of pain on his face made her want to weep, and the words from his lips gave her a little clue into the broken places of his heart that he had tried to hide from her.

Even as her heart broke at his scattered mutterings of the night her mother was taken, she couldn't bear the anguish and the words of shame he uttered when the fever wracked his form.

After a few days, it was too much, and she ran out of the house, finding herself in the Highlanders' clearing and letting the cold mountain air bite at her face in a way that stung the tears that dropped from her eyes like raindrops in a storm. Her chest heaved, the scattered memories Malcolm's mumblings dredged from the depths of her mind—her own pain and suffering inside castle walls—plagued her, but the sorrow from knowing the man who had risked everything to set her free thought of himself as nothing better than worthy of death or to be cast aside split her soul in two.

A soft hand rested on her shoulder, and she turned, startled, folding her arms around herself. Instead of Jennie or Mam'Nessa like she had expected, it was Mac. His blue eyes, the only ones that matched Jennie's, were like melted ice after the winter, and their softness made her relax. Her shoulders shook beneath his touch, and he followed her gaze out to the mountain peak that towered over the clearing.

"Fever brings back the ghosts of a man's past to haunt him. The ghosts he thinks are dead and buried. One runs from shame, hides the guilt where he thinks no one'll see it, and will do anything to expunge a debt he perceives he owes. Even though the truth is, that debt's been paid. Sometimes a body'll still fight to the death to carry that burden because he can't see he's been called worthy of the price the Prince o' Peace paid to set 'im free. So even though his chains have been unlocked, he'll still carry 'em around till he realizes that he's worthy enough for 'em to be unlocked."

Rosalie's lip quivered, and she wiped at her tears as the man pulled her into his side. "All one who loves 'im can do is pray that in the Lord's good time and way, He reminds 'im that he's worthy. That the debt's paid. Ye can shake a man and shout at 'im the truth, but he'll not listen till the Spirit's finished the work in 'im and made blind eyes to see the reason sacrifice was made isn't because he's worthy, but because he's *called* worthy by his Lord and Master." He gave her shoulder a squeeze that rested some of the ache in Rosalie's heart, the old man's fatherly words and touch filling her heart with the reminders of truth and rest. "Just keep on praying for 'im, dearling. He'll see the light one o' these days."

Rosalie took his words to heart and prayed over Malcolm as he tossed and turned, dead to the world, but awake to the terrors within.

She also found a certain comfort in the rest of the Highland clan. The men treated her like a little sister and convinced her often to step out of the house for a walk to check the traps, a ride through the forest, or a game with the "little'uns." Ian even showed her how to shoot the bow and arrow, and she practiced, straining her arm muscles and going to sleep with them sore every night. The bow string was hard to pull, but after four days of shooting at logs in the wood pile with Ian, her arrows were beginning to hit the log he had painted with rings instead of flying off into the woods behind it.

"You'll hit the bullseye one o' these days, young Rose! No mistake about that!" he exclaimed as he jogged over to fetch the arrow.

"I can barely hit the log." She shook her head but smiled at his words nonetheless. Praise had been nonexistent in her life, and yet it awakened something inside of her that filled her with pride in her hard work.

"Och, nonsense." He grunted, jerking the arrow from its place in the wood. "That'un went deep! The faster and deeper the arrow, the more powerful when the aim is finally true. Ye're learning more than where to shoot it, m'lady. How hard and how far matters too." He handed her the arrow and motioned her back to the shooting position.

She enjoyed the rides the most. The painful recollection of the forest that had claimed every last ounce of energy from her seemed to melt away beneath the hoof beats and the masterful guidance of the men on their horses as they maneuvered the reins and led their mounts through the maze of howling trees, animal calls, valleys, and hilltops. It was as if the forest was painted on their memory in ink so black they could navigate it with their eyes closed.

They would set her on the horse blanket in front of their leather saddles, the pommel between them, and a soft quilt folded for her to sit on so that the horse's spine didn't jar her tailbone. She felt the power of their movements and the horse's beneath them as they tethered her against them with one arm and grasped the reins with the other.

The speed and agility, the up and down of the hills, and the energy of the moment—feeling constantly on edge to ensure that she moved with the horse beneath her rather than straining against it—filled her with a special kind of exhilaration that made her suck the fresh mountain air into her lungs and breathe deep of the forest smells. They took her with them on their trapping expeditions, pulling animals for food from the traps and checking them for enemies. Their traps were two-fold it seemed, and she was grateful they didn't find any human prisoners on any of their trips.

The power of the towering mountain and the way their land was nestled into the shadow of it made her feel safe instead of worried. The ominous look of it could have made her sense the danger, but instead, they felt away from it all and in a place where she would be safe because few would dare to tread this land.

Each night they gathered around the bed where Malcolm slept through his fever, completely unaware that in the dark watches, candles flickered and kept the shadows at bay while hands were joined and voices merged into pleas on his behalf. Pain, the destroyer, circled the room like a wolf hunting its prey, but he was kept without by the cries and declarations of a people who knew that their standing with God was one that necessitated an authority they were given through the blood of a Christ who had set them free.

Their voices mingled and tears burned her eyes, her hands swallowed in Duncan's and Jennie's on either side of her, the golden light dim in the room, the moans from the bed nearly silent as deep voices floated in and on top of others, no turns taken, as some in her own tongue and others in ones she did not recognize, mingled together in a symphony of something that should have been chaos, but somehow fit together like well timed music. The hums of one person's murmur, and the flow of another's voice, the lilting prayer of scripture, filled her heart to overflowing. Tears cascaded down her cheeks, and she didn't lift a finger to dry them. They wet the front of her dress, but she couldn't bring herself to break the connection that felt like a current of lightning flowing through one hand and into the next as they joined in unity of purpose and heart around this bed.

The music then united into an actual hymn of praise and hope, the deep tenors, tender even when not in the best tune, combining with the few female voices, floating like angels of light above the depths of their men's voices.

"Softly He calls us
Whispering nigh
His gentle heart
Calling us high.
We respond out of love,
Hearts overflow,
As we praise Him forever,
His faithfulness known.
For dark though the storm,
His light pierces pain,
Love like a mountain,
Stands firm in the rain.
Nothing shakes it,
Can send it away,
It dwells in the darkness,
As sure in the night as the day.
Praise Him for all that He is,
Praise Him for what He has made,
Praise Him for setting us free,
Praise Him for all that He paid."

The fever finally broke that night. Rosalie was awoken by a soft hand on her shoulder, her head cradled on her folded arms across the quilt that covered Malcolm. He was still. Blinking away the sleep that covered her eyes like flog, she squinted up into Jennie's face.

"Come lie down, dearling. The fever has broken. He'll be all right now, but ye both need yer rest."

Rosalie turned to Malcolm, the pale shade of his face still concerning, but the quietness of his features and the look of peace that covered them made the tears well up in her eyes and chase each other down her face. She laid her hand over his where it rested on his chest and felt the skin—no longer hot to the touch.

Drawing a breath, the tension in her shoulders evaporated into the night air, and the shawl that Jennie tucked around her felt like a comforting embrace of peace in the darkness of a quiet night and the aftermath of a hard fought battle. Neither of them said a word as Jennie drew her from the room, one arm around Rosalie and a flickering candle in the other hand.

Rosalie's mind was elsewhere as she was led without thought or resistance to a bed, settled in it, and had her boots slipped from her feet, a pillow fluffed under her head, and a quilt pulled up under her chin. The deep sleep of relief stole any other awareness from her as the flickering golden glow retreated.

MALCOLM, PRESENT DAY...

The light met him first. So bright that his eyes revolted against it. He tried to blink, but even his eyelids felt tired.

How long had it been? With a start, every muscle in his body constricted at the thought of his charge, his child, his girl.

Rosalie.

He felt pain rush through his body despite the absence of the pulsing fire that seemed to burn him from the inside out.

But still his eyes would not focus on what was around him, and he sucked in a breath between his teeth.

"Shh, easy." The voice was soft and gentle, the hand on his shoulder the same, though cool in touch.

His throat was raw, but he drew in another breath and fought the weight of the blanket that held him captive.

"Rosalie." The word was hardly more than a raspy whisper.

"Hush, she is fine. Breathe deep a moment. Don't fight the pain and the weakness; they will pass but they are to protect your healing body."

The words were wise but the exact opposite of what he wanted to hear as he sucked in another breath, letting it fill his chest and his muscles expand to make room for it. The heaviness that weighed down his head like a brick to the face slowly lifted, and he drew in another breath, the air a remedy to his pain and his fear.

A cup touched his lips with the firm but gentle command to drink, and he sucked in the liquid. It was frigid and went down hard around the rocks in his throat, but the more he swallowed, the more thirsty he became, and he was almost angry when it was pulled away again.

"Shh, not too much or you'll make yourself sick. Just keep breathing."

The urge filled him to leap from his prone position and search every last nook and cranny till he found Rosalie and had her beside him, her hand in his, her nearness putting him at ease, and he shoved with his good elbow, intimately aware that his right shoulder wasn't just weak but was one wrong move away from blinding, searing pain. It's dead weight as he tried to lift himself up with the other arm pulled at muscles torn and raw.

The arrow. The forest. The emptiness of the woods without Rosalie. She had been missing. What had this voice said? She was all right?

"Rosalie." It was less of a rasp this time and more of a desperate plea for relief.

"I'll fetch her but please lay back. You've pushed yourself further than you ought already. Trust me. She is fine. Safe. Decidedly worried about you, but better than most would expect." The words brought him comfort even as his blurry vision tried to take in the fuzzy form in front of him, and he allowed her to push him back against the mattress as a groan escaped his lips. The worry over being broken and in need of a rest filled him with dread.

They had to keep moving.

The dark knights were far too close. They had come too far into the forest. They had come too near to them. Surely they knew he was in possession of the lost princess. Surely they knew that he was the one who had stolen her from under their very noses. His life would be forfeit if they were ever caught, and who knew what new horrors Rosalie would return to if that were the case.

He needed to see her. If any more seconds passed, he would hurl himself from this bed and crawl across the floor to the door if he had to.

The hinges squeaked upon someone's entry, and suddenly there was a small, cold hand against his face, rubbing against his beard, and were those tears in her voice?

Her voice…

"I'm so glad you are all right."

Every one of his muscles relaxed in an instant, his mind sure and sound in the knowledge that the young one left in his charge was safe. His chest ached with the realization...

He loved her like his own.

And the fear that coursed through him like a lightning bolt shattered any possible arguments that would come to his lips. The fear in him broke free, and it grew greater instead of went away, but the fear and terror of losing this wee one was dwarfed by the overwhelming love that burned red and hot like an iron pulled from the fire—molten, moldable, pliable, though it would cool to be tough as steel.

That love would do anything to keep her safe. Climb any mountain. Ford any stream. Fight any battle. She would be safe no matter what. No matter how, no matter where, and his life would be forfeit. Not just because of an oath given, a promise extended in faith.

But because his love for her knew no bounds and could not be contained. Was this what a father felt for his child?

His hand floated over her hair and pulled her to his chest. Her tears wet the front of his shirt, and he clutched her harder.

How heartbreakingly helpless he was, floating about on the edge of a hook to which she held the pole.

He blinked again, some of the haze leaving him, and he saw the redness of her cheeks and the health and light in those green eyes. Shining like the forest lit on the sunniest of days.

"Rosalie."

"I'm here. I'm so glad you are all right. I prayed and prayed." Her words were punctuated by a sob, and she kept one hand on his shoulder as if loathe to break their connection and used the other to mop at the tears that wet her face.

He quickly glanced her over. She was well. There was a red and swollen scratch through her right eyebrow, the skin split and the mark marring her face, but otherwise she seemed fine.

He could hardly believe it.

"I thought I lost you."

She shook her head, her eyes filling again. "No, I went for help." Her words fell to a whisper, and the fear and sadness floated over her face once more. "I couldn't lose *you*."

His throat closed up around the emotions, and he let his hand cup her face. "I'm so glad you were brave and took action. And you found your way."

Her head bobbed in a short nod. "And I thought I would lose you! I'm so glad that we haven't." Her voice broke on the last word, and he squeezed her fingers.

His gaze roved the room. She must have found the Highlanders, and Mac and Nessa would have seen to her. She had made it this far.

His eyes gravitated toward the window, and his lungs contracted when he saw her standing there, her red hair a silhouette against the bright morning light casting shards of bright golden light through the panes.

Her red curls were tossed about like a halo and caught the light, and her hands were folded in front of her as she watched them, giving them the space they needed to greet each other.

"Jennie." Her name came easily to his tongue. Of course it had been many months since they had seen each other, but his heart swelled with an overwhelming sense of hope at the sight of her.

There was a brightness Jennie carried, much like the light from the morning mountain air that backlit her. She shone from a place within, roots that ran deep with the hope and joy of a life spent with Christ.

"It's good to see ye, Malcolm. And grateful I am that ye're not just here but on the mend. Ye gave us quite the scare." Her voice was soft, her highland lilt less demonstrative than her parents', but there nonetheless.

Her blue eyes shone with the brightness of sapphires, and she stepped closer, still holding enough distance to remain out of their way, but she hesitated, almost as if she wished to come even closer, and her hands twitched till she tangled them in her skirt, wiping the palms in the russet linen. He noticed the movement and wondered at it.

"How long have I been lying here? How did I get here?"

She smiled, and Rosalie squeezed his hand as he looked between them. "You've been here for five days, but as far as how you got here, I'll let Rosie tell the tale. She's quite the wonder, this wee one o' yourn." The smile rose to Jennie's eyes, but there was a sadness there that battled with it as she patted Rosalie on the shoulder and turned to leave the room. "I'll prepare ye some broth. Ye'll need to get your strength back. I'll be back in a few moments."

When she had left, Rosalie hugged his hand in both of hers, and her shoulders shook.

"What is it—Rosie?" The name felt right on his tongue. Jennie had used it and he mimicked her, giving this girl a nickname for the first time and the tenderness of it made his heart swell. How had one so small captured his heart so completely? He had sworn never to feel this way about another—ever. Seeing the way it wrecked his best and dearest brother to lose one so close to his heart had stolen any desire or joy in the thought of a wife or children of his own. He had steeled himself against it—but he now knew he wouldn't just die for her because she was the daughter of his brother. He would give his last breath to see her succeed, to grow up, to become the woman he knew would make her father and her mother proud. And he would be proud with them.

A curse slipped into his mind as he tried to separate the feelings of paternal love and care in his mind to that of a distant uncle or what he was and should be—merely a servant tasked with her protection.

"I thought I was going to lose you. I was so scared, but…I knew that I had to get help. You…you wouldn't wake up."

He stroked her hair. He hadn't just worried her, he had left her alone in the forest, terrified, broken, with nowhere to go, and the pain of that was almost worse than the wound that marred his shoulder.

Again, he squeezed her hand in his and blinked away the tears that threatened in his own eyes. How was he so blasted vulnerable to the tears that fell down her cheeks? He was supposed to be the strong and distant one. Not a blubbering fool who felt the very pain of the one he had been tasked to protect. "I'm so sorry, Rosie. Truly. Not just for this…" His words trailed off, and he cleared his throat.

The thought of all that she had endured in life came crashing back. The understanding of what she had been and what her purpose would be if Zuko had his way. He sucked in a breath between his teeth as the remembrance of the guilt he tried to bury deep inside came crashing back like an avalanche from off the top of the mountain, cascading into his very soul. "I'm so sorry that any of this came upon you. I—" He wrested the admission from the depths of his being, unwilling for her to remain unaware any longer. "It's because of me that you've been held captive all this time. It's all—" He clenched his jaw as scalding tears flowed from the corners of his eyes and ran toward his ears. This broken flower in front of him was his doing. His and no one else's. "It's all my fault."

"No." The firmness and lack of emotion in her voice caught him off guard. The scar on the back of his head throbbed in time with his shoulder, and he stared into her eyes, her voice most certainly stronger than he had ever heard it before.

"It's not your fault." Tears still trembled on her lower lashes, but there was no daintiness about the flower that stood before him now. There was sharpness on her tongue, not that of a blade to wound, but one charged with the cutting away of damaged flesh with the precision of a medicinal trained to the art. Her eyes were a forest afire, blazing with a passion that seemed to come from something deeper than herself. "Nothing I have been through is your fault. Not one bit of it. Evil lives in the hearts of men who submit to it, and you have never submitted to such evil. You never could. Not because you are strong in and of yourself, though the King made you such. But because He has cleansed you and set you free, even if you can't see that yourself. Through His sacrifice, He made your heart pure and holy and void of any blame or sin that you think you committed."

Even as a remonstrance and argument rose in his mouth to refute her words, it was silenced like a flood pouring upon a campfire.

"Don't you think perhaps you were saved that day so that you could one day set me free? Your life is not still stirring within you because you were a coward and failed. But because His plan for you was greater. Don't you see? What you thought was a plan for evil was the purpose of a greater story that now sets me on a path for freedom and for…" She choked and swallowed, two tears like raindrops glistening in the sunlight falling from those lashes. "For home."

Her words struck his chest, and he couldn't deny them.

Her chest heaved with the passion that still sparked from her eyes, and his hand ached from the strength of her grip. He couldn't steal his gaze away from those eyes. There was something otherworldly in them. Something akin to the same look that would come over her mother's face when words of life fell from her lips like drops of water into the heart of a dying man. But there was also the passion of her father in the set brows and the hard line of her jaw. Somehow she simultaneously mirrored them both but was someone altogether different.

Jennie reentered and paused at the doorway. Rosalie released his hand and wiped her tears, stepping away so that Jennie could take her place, a wooden bowl of broth steaming in her hands and a carved spoon sticking out of her pocket.

She glanced between them, but Rosalie seemed suddenly shy, the fire in her eyes dying down to gentle coals, and she couldn't meet his gaze. He felt as though some spell had been broken, and he regretted it. Wished that he could have that moment back, that hope, a different story that was written in a way he had never considered before.

She turned away then, facing the window, and must have caught sight of something without. "Excuse me. I'll go help Ian with the firewood." Her voice was almost disappointed as she stepped toward the door.

"Don't worry, child. Ian can manage for—" Jennie paused when she caught sight of Rosalie's face, and her voice softened, glancing once again between Rosalie and Malcolm with her ever discerning eyes. "I'm sure he would be grateful for the help."

When they were alone, Malcolm shifted uncomfortably. The words Rosalie had spoken had struck a deep chord he could not fully comprehend. Something about Jennie tending him suddenly made him feel out of place. He knew he needed the help and the care, but there was something unspoken between them. Something that had followed him into the depths of Rusalka and given him hope even though he knew that it would never come to pass.

It was a desire that he had buried almost as deep as his guilt. He understood that being a husband and father was not what God had written in the stars for him. Yet here he sat, in the care of the only woman on earth he would give anything to stand beside, and she tended him. No doubt with the same Christ-like love and empathy as she would and had for any other. But their closeness made his unerring decision harder, not as strong.

He tried to swallow the broth she spooned into his mouth, but her blue eyes held questions, and he choked on it instead.

"Here." She set the bowl down and moved another pillow behind his head, wincing when he clamped his lips together to keep from groaning at the pain the movement caused to his injured shoulder. "Sorry."

He didn't know what to say in response and lifted his good hand to take the spoon from her.

"She's right, you know."

The crashing realization that she had heard all that Rosalie had said to him made his face heat, and he almost wished to be back again, buried in the unconscious world where thoughts couldn't bother him like pesky flies that seemed destined to distract him from his purpose.

She held the bowl and let him spoon the broth himself, not making a comment or changing facial expressions as his shaky hand spilled more than he managed to get to his mouth. "Ye weren't yourself for nigh on five days, Malcolm." The lilt with which she said his name in her accent sounded like the last few letters held a secret. "Ye said a lot of things ye would'nt've if ye'd been awake. She heard more than ye know, and it nigh on broke her tender heart. Ye'd do well to listen to what the Laird said through her lips. She knows more than ye think she does, and just because she's a bairn doesn't mean the King can't speak through her just the same's anyone else."

The broth, though delicious, lost all appeal, and he set the spoon down with a gentle tap against the bowl's rim. She wiped his chin with the napkin she pulled from another pocket and set the dish aside. "Ye're appetite'll be tossed for a while. Going that long without solid food and burning such a high fever'll take it out of ye. Ye'll have to be patient with yerself, which we all know isn't exactly yer strong suit." There was a lightness and a smile back in her voice, and he threw his gaze her way, confused by the sudden change in tone. She grinned back, and he couldn't help but let a small smile through at her joke, deprecating though it may be.

"Good. I thought ye'd forgotten how to smile, Sir Malcolm. 'Twoulda been a pity. Rest. Ye need it."

"I feel like I've been sleeping for days."

"And days more will be needed yet if ye're to make it the rest of the way to Elira." Her eyes sparked with excitement, and her words turned breathless. "I'd just like to see the day she sets foot on her own ground for the first time." The sheen covering her eyes made the blue of her irises deeper. "The joy on her father's face'll seem a touch like heaven, I think."

"Funny, he said almost the exact same thing, once." His eyes couldn't stay open another second, no matter how strong his will. "Actually, he said a lot of things that sound much like his daughter's words…"

ELGON, SEVEN YEARS AGO…

"I know you are aware that many in the counsel think my belief that the spies will one day find what they have been looking for is a hopeless one." Elgon paced across the private room and then back again, his boots making agitated clicks when he turned. He had his hands tucked behind his back to keep himself from wringing them. The anger in his words were only for private company. The utter disgust that roiled in his chest made him feel like the tiniest boat tossed about upon an angry Sirene Sea.

"I am aware, and I think they are as well, that it makes no difference what they think. The word hopeless is not one that fits within your way of thinking. Nor mine." Malcolm always stood by him—he could be relied upon for that.

"The counsel is split down the middle. Fendrel will always stand with us, as will Rensen. My cousin and the lords from Valhaven and Wood River stand firmly against continuing the search. Raphart will straddle the line, as he often does."

"Which might as well make his voice of no import in the discussion. You must not forget, majesty, that though you have those that doubt and disagree, you are still king. Their power only extends so far as to advise you and help rule only should you die before they do."

"Yes, but their 'advice' grows not just tedious but angersome," Elgon growled. The council had just left and their attempts to "temper expectations" and "prepare for what would most likely occur in the long run" made his blood run hot and his skin crawl.

"Those without eyes cannot see."

Elgon sucked in a strong breath. "And yet they see enough evidence to the contrary of my plans and hopes. I know that. I understand that. They see the spies come back every time with empty hands and naught else but a more detailed map of our enemy's land. The slaves set free and rescued by Everard and his band of merry men are little more than a bonus to them and less like valuable human lives wrested from a life of sorrow and tragedy." Elgon stilled his movements and whirled upon Macolm. "What will it take for them to see that this is something that I must do? Something that I must stand for?"

He watched Malcolm's face, waiting for some bit of encouragement, for him to affirm that if only he just waited, perhaps the answer would come. Perhaps the desire and reassurance he hoped for would appear. But instead he watched the truth flicker behind Malcolm's brown eyes and saw the resolve in the set of his friend's jaw and the sharp line of his eyebrows, glowering at the men who were no longer within this room. "They may never see it."

The words were like a painful weight stomping on already broken fingers. So much so that Elgon cringed and almost recoiled. "But—" He turned and strode to the window, needing the light as a comfort.

Malcolm's voice held strong. "There's something about resolve. About a purpose beyond ourselves that means that the hope within us is utterly misunderstood by others. The truth is, they won't ever see eye to eye with you, and that is going to be a good thing in some areas. But it's also going to be painful in others. They don't owe you their hope, and blind eyes cannot see what is right in front of them…unless it's shown to them. And for whatever reason, what has been shown to you has not been to them."

Elgon's shoulders sagged. Malcolm's words rang true, as much as Elgon wished the opposite.

He shook his head. "How can they not know that hope is all I have to cling to? How can they not see that the thought of my wife and child coming home to be within my arms again isn't just a wish, but something that is pressed so deeply in my heart it can never be wrested free? All I can think about is the taste of heaven I'll experience when I hold them again, that feeling that perhaps, just for a moment, all can be right in the world once more."

Elgon heard Malcolm stand, and he turned to watch his friend cross his arms over his chest with resolve. Something lurked in the depths of his friend's eyes. Something that disquieted him. Elgon saw the muscle in Malcolm's jaw twitch and felt the understanding course through him like a broken dam. Elgon tilted his head. "It's not wrong for you to hope."

Malcolm avoided his gaze even though he gave the impression of facing him. His muscles tensed even more.

"Malcolm."

"It's not that I don't have hope. You should know that by now."

"Yet you do not let yourself—"

"Let myself what?" Malcolm's voice simmered with a long suppressed rage that took Elgon off guard. "Let myself revel in a hope that isn't mine? Let myself believe that even if your family is restored to you that I somehow am not still the scum of the earth for letting it happen in the first place?"

Elgon took a step back without even thinking about it, the pain so raw and real it might as well have been a blade to the chest.

Malcolm stepped back as well, his feet fumbling and the normal look of strength and steel melted away in the fire of embarrassment. "I'm sorry, m'lord. I should not have spoken to you thus."

"Words that wound come from wounds." Elgon's voice was soft as he watched Malcolm turn and stare at the tapestry on the wall, the muscles in his neck twitching as his hands gripped his arms tightly.

Fire burned in Elgon's chest for Malcolm. For the one who would give all to set Elgon's wife and child free on his own, but who was driven with a purpose beyond even that love and duty. Driven by something darker and more sinister that haunted his steps and his thoughts with painful reminders of an ugly untruth.

"Malcolm." He sighed with regret and pain for his brother. "If only your eyes were not also so blind. I pray that one day you see the truth."

Malcolm flinched. "M'lord?"

"I pray for the day when the pain of this imagined failure falls away from you and you can let go of the chains that hold you in a despair of your own making. There's no one I would trust more even now. Even after what happened. Despite the way you see things, I thank God every single day that you were spared worse. I know the story you hold is not finished yet, and the story that has been told thus far isn't half as ugly as you think it."

Malcolm didn't face him. Elgon sighed. He knew of the burdens his brother carried because they weighed on him like fetters of his own. A brother, when plunged into darkness or prison, doesn't dwell there alone. Those that carry love for him in their hearts haunt the darkness with him, begging and praying for the moment when they will be released.

Just as assuredly as they rejoice when they finally are.

"You'll see one day, my friend. They'll return, all will be set right, and the truth that you are more valuable to me and to the King will come back to you. Then you'll understand why the guilt you carry was a useless fetter every moment that it was worn. You've been set free already and you just don't know it yet."

Malcolm straightened but still did not look back at Elgon. "Excuse me, m'lord. I have duties to tend to."

"Of course." Elgon's words were more of a sigh, and he barely blinked before Malcolm had flung open the door and disappeared from sight. He shook the tension from his own shoulders, the heaviness of despair that he could sense in the atmosphere around Malcolm whenever he was near.

He thought of the time he had spent with Marcus and Dilara when they had last visited the castle. Smiling, he remembered their little ones. The aching hole in his heart longed for some light, some laughter, some echo of goodness that felt too far away in the cold castle walls of Niran. Perhaps a visit to Padsley would be in order; there was not much else to do but wait.

Twenty-Eight

WATERFALLS AND FINDINGS

ROSALIE, PRESENT DAY...

At times, Malcolm seemed to be recovering quickly, and at others, his recovery seemed to drag on, and the constant swaying was wearing on Rosalie's frayed emotions. The itch to get her feet moving again filled her. How she could long to stay in one place forever, tie herself to a people that felt like family in a lonely world, yet yearn for what was to come with a passionate thirst that could not be quenched was beyond her grasp.

The answer to how joy and sorrow mixed so pertinently together and created some sort of beautiful tapestry of life that left scars as well as beauty was more than she could ever figure on her own.

Slowly she had slipped into a life with the Highland family, feeling the bond of comfort and camaraderie tie her closer and make her feel more at home as each day passed. Each of the small children considered themselves her special pet, nevermind the fact that there couldn't possibly be a favorite when there were six of them. They dragged her hither and yon when their fathers and uncles weren't carrying her off on adventures. "To prepare her" the men said with that insatiable twinkle in their eyes as they threw her on a horse and galloped off into the woods to teach her something new about living life in the remote mountains.

But there was something that always rang like a warning in her mind anytime she was away from Malcolm for too long. Panic started the longer the hours stretched, and the idea of being caught without him near, or the thought of him being ambushed while she was away, was something that haunted her dreams. The day she had climbed through the forest to reach the highlands was something that troubled her in her sleep. She would wake, shaking from the images of being dragged back to Zuko's castle, or the dark knights chasing Maclolm down, running him into the dirt and their horses' black hooves pounding him to death as an arrow lodged in his shoulder.

She worried over what had happened to the Vagari encampment. Were they all right? Nim, Romanik, Izabella, all of them. Had they won in the fight against the dark knights? Had anyone been taken captive? What if she was the reason some of them had been hurt? The fear and guilt haunted her like a ghost over her shoulder.

But just as the highland siblings drew her from the house and taught her new things, distracting her with adventures and exploration, Malcolm just as readily demanded with a twinkle in his eye and a smile behind his beard that she needed to give him at least a few moments' peace or he'd never heal with her eyes staring a hole into him.

The highland life was idyllic, creating an untouched feeling within the mountains. As if free air blew through their home and over their plateau. The mountaintop that towered over them stood like a guard that kept the world at bay and protected them from the intruders and interference of the Rusalkan military. Many were too afraid to come this far into Wraith Forest, and the highland family practiced their faith and their way of life with a modicum of peace that seemed almost too sweet to be true amidst the rest of Rusalka.

But even as she practiced shooting her arrows till her fingers ached from holding the bow string, chased the children about the yard or hid from them during one of their favorite games, worked with Mam'Nessa, Carlissa, Rowan, or Jennie in the kitchen, tended to the house, or even trotted through the woods with one or more of the brothers searching for the hidden traps, restlessness grew in her spirit. She tried to shove down the feeling that something was stalking them in the woods. The men told her it was impossible and that they would have advanced warning, but the feeling of shadows flitting behind trees and watching from hidden places filled her with an impending sense of dread that made her pray for Malcolm to have a speedier recovery.

It had been nearly two whole weeks and Malcolm was finally up and about, stretching the muscles of his arm and being told to take it easy more often than he listened. Rosalie watched him and sensed within him the same uneasy feeling that she carried. He felt the need for movement as well. They were lingering too long. She could see it in the way he worked his bad arm till the sweat poured from his face and soaked his shirt, fighting the pain and ignoring the soreness that sent him to sleep before his head hit the pillow.

The sun was bright one day when Duncan took her with him and a few of his brothers on a hunting trip that utilized the entire day. She was hesitant to go, but they said they had something they wanted to show her before they were forced to say goodbye. They traversed down the mountain ridge from their home, taking hours of trails till they came upon a mountain lake, gorgeous in its glacier splendor. She gasped at the sight and then held her breath when they descended into the basin.

Crystal clear blue and green water with every stone and fallen tree trunk resting on the bottom in perfect detail met her gaze, and her heart leapt at the beauty. The men grinned at each other, and when they had dismounted, Duncan gently shoved her shoulder toward the water.

"We'll check the traps, wee one. Go and see the wonder of it while we prepare the noonday meal."

She didn't need to be told twice and stumbled down the rocky shore till she reached the water, kneeling beside it and feeling the iciness when she reached out a finger to touch the surface of the glass. It was almost as if it couldn't be real, even more beautiful and clear than any mirror she had ever seen. The icy water enveloped her hand, the sharpness like needles touching her skin. She scooped a rock from the bottom and nearly didn't feel it in her frigid fingers.

The rock was smooth and had a green and blue hue to it as

she turned it in the sunlight, letting the air and the warmth from the sun dry the surface. It faded to a dull gray when dry, and she dipped it back in the water till its brightness returned, and she smiled. Hidden beauty.

It reminded her of the secret inner beauty of the joy of Christ that she felt in the very depths of her soul. The way that the people of this country were forced to hide it, to dull their colors on the outside when, without the water of the word, they were surrounded by the air that sought to destroy them. But, in the comfort of their homes, their communities, those that followed the symbol of the dove could shine and sparkle with a beauty that was unseen to those from whom it was hidden.

This place was a feast for her eyes, and she would never forget it.

The men had already checked the fishing traps, and she ate the meal they had prepared for her, smiling at their teasing, comfortable in their presence, but utterly swept away and distracted by the breathtaking sights around her. She didn't want to tear her eyes from it all.

"Ye keep staring, and yer eyes will freeze open." Ian laughed, pushing her playfully in the shoulder.

She grinned but didn't look away from the sparkling mountain lake. "If my eyes had to freeze open, I'd rather it be with this view in sight." When she finally glanced back at the group, Alexander was smiling softly.

"Ye know the Lord's been at work when there's places 'at look like this, fer sure," he said.

"I hate to ask it of ye." Duncan rested a hand on her shoulder. "But we ought to head back. The hunting is good the way we'll take, and ye might even shoot yer first dinner." Smiling, he packed the remaining loaf of bread into his saddle bag.

Rosalie grinned back, her heart sinking at the same time, realizing that she would probably never see this place again. "That would take a miracle, Duncan."

"Good news is we serve a God who's full of 'em." He chuckled, hefting himself to his feet and reaching out a hand to haul her to hers.

"I'll have you know, I've been teaching her quite well, and she's good enough not to need a miracle, by my judgment." Ian placed his hands on his hips, standing next to Rosalie.

"Is that so?" Alex asked. Though the tallest, he was usually the quietest of the bunch. But when he did speak, his humor was the driest and the most cutting of them all. "Maybe we should pray for a miracle to have yer judgment fixed." He winked behind his hand at Rosalie to assure her that he was picking on his brother and not on her skills. She tried to hide a chuckle, gathering the blanket they had been sitting on and shaking it out to fold while the men tied their supplies back to their saddles.

"How dare you question my training skills." Ian put a hand to his chest and growled with a sparkle in his eye, but his lips twitching despite their dramatic frown. "Just because she's the first person anyone's let me train. I had all of your experience to glean from, so if I'm a poor tutor, it's more your fault than mine." He humphed with a strong nod as if that were the end of the conversation.

"Her success'd be more on Rosalie's shootin' arm and her perseverance at practice more than it'd be on your tutelage, brother." Duncan's shoulders shook in silent laughter.

"That's the last I talk to you boys. This is ridiculous. Rosie, help a fella out."

"I guess I'll just have to do my best." She couldn't help but giggle at their antics and allowed Ian to whisk her atop his horse. He placed his foot in the stirrup and swung himself up after her. "I guess we'll just have to show 'em, eh?"

Though Rosalie tried more than once, she didn't hit anything, but they encouraged her that her time would come and her desire and continued practice would go a long way to getting her first bullseye. Their good natured jibes were interrupted when something in the woods made Alex jump and whip his mount around, his hand raised in the air in a universal sign of hush.

Rosalie's heart leapt into her throat, and the thought that perhaps her greatest fear of being separated from Malcolm came upon her.

"I hear the bells ringin,'" Alexander whispered, and Duncan moved his horse to stand beside him, both of them staring off into the woods and straining their ears for any sound.

"Ian, take Rosalie home," Duncan hissed beneath his breath. "Don't let her out of ye're sight and keep ye're weapon drawn. Take the battened path."

Ian directed his horse's head away from Duncan and Alexander and led her down a hollow and higher up the mountain. Rosalie knew this wasn't the way they had come, but while her heart was beating heavily in her chest like it wanted to escape, she trusted Ian even as she prayed. Words fell from her lips of which she knew not their meaning.

Riding up a valley toward the part where the two ridges met, he pulled up his mount and slid from its back, grabbing the reins and leading the horse to the rock wall that shot straight up in front of them. With a hand that knew exactly where it was headed, he reached under a root and peeled away a false cliff face that opened like a door.

Rosalie tensed but let him lift her from off the saddle with his hands around her waist, and he guided her hand to his sleeve. "Grip here and don't let go. We don't have a light."

She gulped, staring into the recesses of the dirt grotto that disappeared from her view into inky blackness. "You won't n-need it?" She stuttered, her skin crawling.

"No. Know these tunnels like the back o' me hand. Don't let go, no matter what."

He didn't have to tell her twice. He'd have to pry her cold, dead fingers from his sleeve to make her let go.

Gripping the reins in his hand, he led them all in, including the horse, and then pressed the reins into her hand, his body a shadowed outline against the light of the open door. "Hold this a moment. I have to sneak past Tupper and shut the door. I'll be right back."

Rosalie was too terrified to reply and gripped Tupper's reins in her stiff fingers. *God, help.* Her knees knocked together, and her teeth would have been chattering if it were not for the way her jaw was locked in place.

Then the door shut, and the roar in her ears drowned out her awareness as she strained to hear or see anything in the pitch blackness of the tunnel.

She wanted to call Ian's name, to ask him where he was, but nothing came out save for her fluttering breath. The images and panic of her childhood descended on her like the roof was caving in.

Long days and nights cramped in a cell when she'd "misbehaved." Terror in every corner, abuse waiting for the wrong move or the wrong word to fall from her lips. The memories of the pain that kept her company in that darkness, with the only light coming every few hours to ensure she was still there, brought all the fear and anguish rushing back.

Alone.

Broken.

Nothing to hold onto but the tiniest light within. She grabbed for it now, desperate. The presence of a Being that transcended past the darkness and dwelt here with her in it. She focused on that light, the tiniest flicker in the back of a cave that was her soul, and she held it. Willing it to grow, willing it to live.

A cold hand fell on her shoulder, and she squealed, the touch sending her to her knees in a panic as the world of the castle and her guards came rushing back. The words whispered in the darkness were so far away, she had to beg her heart to quiet to hear them.

"Shh, it's just me. It's Ian. Are ye all right? Rosalie?"

Gasping for air, she caught onto the voice, heard the kindness and concern there, and shook the mental cobwebs of fear and terror from her mind. But they clung to her still, dragging her kicking and screaming back into the darkness.

"I-Ian." The words rasped from a throat that was clutched in a panic, trying to hold back her words and any peace they gave her.

"I'm here. You're all right. I promise."

The words that reminded her of life, of truth, of light flowed through her head in broken snatches, but her muscles were too frozen to move. The need to speak them out loud pounded in her spirit like a growing urgency to do something she couldn't seem to do. Her throat closed, and no words came out even though she willed them to. Her breath trembled on its entrance and exit from her lungs.

Determination built like a fire in her chest, and she fought the iron grip the fear had over her.

"Jesus," she whispered, her lungs being squeezed by an invisible hand that felt more real than those that existed in this world. But it eased at that one word, and a snarl seemed to surround her, the terror edging ever closer.

The reins in her hand tugged, and the sound of Tupper shaking his head met her ears. The movement gave her something else to focus on and pulled her farther out of the grip she couldn't seem to shake.

"Jesus." The grip eased again and this time she pushed it away with her mind. "I will not fear."

The growl was deeper, but farther away now, and she pressed against it, sending it farther from her with every breath and every word. "Though the earth be removed and the mountains be cast into the sea." Her voice grew stronger. "Though the waters roar and be troubled, though the mountains shake with their swelling."

A hand touched her shoulder again, and she let it linger there, drawing strength from the nearness. "There is a river whose streams make glad the city of God. The holy place of the tabernacles of the Most High." She remembered the lake, the towering mountain that stood solidly in the path of anything that sought to steal her away from the presence of her King. "God is in the midst of her and she shall not be moved. God shall help her, and just at the break of day."

Ian's hand moved to grip hers and pull her to her feet, his deep voice joining hers. "The heathens raged, the kingdoms were moved, he uttered his voice and the earth melted."

"The Lord of hosts is with us. The God of Jacob is our refuge," she continued.

He is with me.

Light filled the caverns of her soul. Not just something to see by, but a light that sent the shadows crying for mercy, flinging themselves into whatever corner they could find. But they no longer mocked her. No longer held her in that grip. She did not belong to the terror. She belonged to the truth.

The truth that the King walked among them.

"Let's go." Ian tugged at her hand, but she didn't open her eyes. Gripping Ian's fingers, she handed him back Tupper's reins and grasped his shirt sleeve with her other hand for good measure.

She kept speaking as he led her feet onward, through a darkness she could not see. "God is our refuge and strength, a very present help in trouble."

A SPY, THREE YEARS AGO...

The uproarious sound of laughter met his ears, and he slunk farther into the shadows, divesting himself of the bright ribbons that had clung to his clothes and pulling the collar of his black linen shirt higher around his neck. His way in had looked like nothing was amiss, merely a group of troubadours and magicians entering the castle for the night's performance. The colorful, Vagari-made additions to his costume had been little more than a cover for him to blend in with the other performers. But the echo of singing met his ears as he leaned farther away from the light and slipped behind another pillar of the throne room, the voices of those who had brought him in with them joining the song and the act.

Glancing around, he noted that the guards were focused on the attraction. A knife-juggling giant of a man was the center of attention, his dark hair tied back with leather, his costume light and allowing him to move as twelve knives spun in an arc far over his head. They moved too swiftly to be distinguished from one another, each blade catching the light as they formed a perfect circle in front of him and around his head.

Vieggo was an expert at keeping many distracted for as long as was needed.

And all he needed was a few minutes.

His footsteps, soft from the extra padding added to his boots, were light and indiscernible as he turned the corner and slipped from the room through a private door that was unguarded and known to few but those like the servant he had bribed for the information. Zuko's options for entrance and exit from the throne room were more varied than it would appear, and he seemed to like the idea of a quick and hidden escape being built right into the room he himself had designed.

Grateful to be out of the room that had cavernous ceilings flying so far overhead that the light didn't reach it, he drew a breath and felt his way through the dimly lit hall and around the corner, where a lone torch burned in a ring on the wall. He needed to ensure that his destination existed and the rumors were true, remain undetected, and make it back to the throne room, all in time to join the next song and throw his partner around like she was a plaything on his arm. Only the best of the best made it into the castle to perform.

If his intelligence was true, he would find the object of his search just up this winding staircase, the private door leading to an even more private staircase that abutted the back of the tower, known only to the king and some of his most trusted servants.

One of whom now lay tied, gagged, and unconscious in the back of the performer's wagon. He couldn't be left behind to tell the tale of his indiscretion. The future of an entire country was relying on the secrecy that this night afforded them all.

Gripping the torch, he pulled it from the ring and slunk up the stairs as fast as he dared. They wound round and round, carrying him up and up within its stone-walled and coiling hall. Out of breath near the top, he hid the torch behind him as he approached the last few stairs, the sound of voices on the other side of the door sending the noise of his heartbeat roaring in his ears. He crept to the door and laid his ear against it. The wooden planks afforded him hardly any extra amplification of the sound on the other side, but just enough to make out words.

"Get her back into her room. Her time in the cell's been long enough, and Master said she wouldn't survive the night. Too cold outside, though I don't know why we don't let the child rot, sick as she is anyway. It's not as though she's any good to anyone."

"No good but that of a special pet. You fetch her yourself. I want to get a look at the women performers that came in with the troubadours."

A curse burned his ears through the wood, and he laid the torch on the second stair, using both his hands to feel around the door for the knob and the peephole that the servant had sworn existed.

The voices faded. They must have gone into another room. His fingertip caught the catch of the spy hole and he gripped it in his cold and shaking fingers. This was his only chance. If he was caught, he would be dead before morning.

Don't let me fail. He prayed in silence, breathing out slowly as he slid the metal slat sideways to open the spy hole. It gave way with a scratch, but only partly. He brought his eye up to it and noticed that it was like looking through some sort of gray haze. There must be a disguise on the other side of the opening to allow Zuko to view what went on without being detected. The servant had made it quite clear under duress that he was one of the few left alive who knew of the stairwell, the guards being oblivious to it.

He almost leapt back but schooled his twitching muscles to calmness when a figure dragged a child through a doorway and toward the larger wooden door at the end of the hall and the top of the staircase. The hall only held the three doors. The invisible one, the metal one that led to a darkened room with no light, and the larger wooden door at the top of the stairs with the golden flickering light of what must be a fire on the hearth.

The child's long, curly hair nearly brushed the floor when she tripped over her own bare feet and stumbled against the hand that gripped her arm like a vice, dragging her despite her loss of footing, and her knees banged against the bricks. The pale face turned, the hair whipping over her shoulder and out of her way, exhaustion written into every line and drawn corner of her expression—but those eyes.

They were green and vibrant as the mountain forest; even burning with fever, they shone bright in her hollow face that held terror in every twitch and movement.

His eyes widened as he watched them drag her to the end of the hall and deposit her in a hurled heap on the threshold of the lit room near the stairs.

The guard cursed her, shoved her with his boot, and slammed the door shut.

And he could fully wrap his mind around what his spirit leapt at already knowing.

The princess was alive.

Everything in him screamed to tear this door from its latch, leap into the hall, and rip the man in two who dared handle the heir of Elira in such a manner. But he prayed beneath his breath, the words unknown even to himself as he used his trembling hand to shut the spy hole. He sank against the cold stone wall, the light of the torch flickering as it rested on the stones and didn't have enough oxygen to keep it fully lit. He swallowed against the lump in his throat and put his hand over his chest, willing his heart to return to its normal rhythm and still the vengeance and anger that surged through his very blood like molten iron just off the fire. He needed to get down these stairs and join his act immediately or someone would notice that things were amiss.

Proving the rumors of a young child locked in the tower

since birth to be true was only half his mission.

Everard needed to know the truth, and then Sir Malcolm, captain of the guard, the man who had trained him within an inch of his life…and then the king.

The king must be told. Hope had been fulfilled at last. Sucking in one last breath, he snatched the torch from its spot and took the stairs two at a time. At the bottom, he gathered himself as he placed the torch back in its ring and pulled the colored scarf that went around his neck from his pocket. Stepping cautiously to the door, he listened for anyone on the other side and slipped out, shutting it softly behind him.

No one had seen him. No one was near.

His feet padded softly against the stone as the echo of Vieggo's singing grew louder and he crept from pillar to pillar, remaining outside of the light. He caught the eye of his partner, who stepped to his side as if conferring over their act, and helped him tie his scarf. Her black hair, curled and clinking with chains and charms woven into braids and tied with colored ribbons and golden string, swept over her shoulder as she looped the scarf over his neck and tied the knot.

Her eyes met his and he dipped his chin in a single nod, his teeth clenched tightly. She trembled for a moment, and he steadied her with a hand to her shoulder, lifting the strap of her bodice that had fallen from her bare shoulder and looping it back on top. His finger brushed her skin and she shivered. The ruffles on her gown swayed with her movement as Vieggo's voice died off in an echo of applause from the court and she gripped his hand in hers, pulling it to her side, the softness of the material of her skirt caressing his skin.

The power of hope surged in him as the music danced to life, and he twirled her into the center of the courtroom, the stones whirling beneath them as he grasped her waist in his hands and lifted her above his head, twirling her from one hand to the other as her skirt billowed over him like a multicolored sail of golden flowers and flying birds.

He dipped her beneath his arm, his muscles surging at the practiced movement it took to maneuver her weight in the graceful, flying dance that made the lords and ladies in attendance gasp with admiration and awe.

Her hair brushed against his face as he swung her upright, her hand in his, trusting, light, needing nothing more than subtle guidance as he spun her away from him, the hem of her skirt spinning out into a perfect circle and flowing against his leg till he pulled her back in toward him.

Their ribs met, and he coiled his hand around her waist, her dark eyes meeting his for a moment, the excitement and fear mingled together that he saw there a reflection of his own heart.

Just one last performance and they would be on their way. The performers, the bound, gagged, and blindfolded servant, a group of rescues, shaking and grateful…and one piece of precious information that would fly over the route of freedom with all speed and change the course of the secret battle hidden across the mountains and valleys of Rusalka.

MALCOLM, PRESENT DAY…

Malcolm nearly dropped the bundle of firewood he was carrying for Jennie when galloping hooves in the distance met his ear. Catching his breath, he felt his pulse pick up, turning his head and straining his eyes into the shadowed forest to see if he could determine what was going on.

Alexander dashed into the clearing, pulling his horse up as he did so, the steed's front hooves leaving the ground at the sudden jerk of his rider's hand on the reins. The Highlander threw himself from the saddle, his hand on the hilt of his sword, and jogged toward them, his mount shuffling sideways nervously with his reins dragging on the ground.

"Have Ian and Rosalie made it back yet?" His voice was anxious, his red head turning around as if looking for them.

Malcolm's muscles tensed, and he felt the hair on the back of his neck stand on end. "No. Weren't they with you?" His hands twitched at his side as he clenched and unclenched them, adrenaline coursing through his veins.

Alexander paled. "We heard a group approaching and sent them on ahead. They need to be here, and you need to get ready. We're sneaking you all out the back. Now." His words were staccato short, the steadiness of his gaze broken only by his frightened, searching glances past Malcolm toward the barn in the back.

Returning his eyes to Malcolm's, they exchanged a non-verbal question and answer. Something was wrong. Malcolm and Rosalie were being stalked, and they needed to get on the move again. Their time of peace and safety was at an end, and Malcolm felt it deep in his soul with a foreboding that caught him by the back of the neck and shook him with a tremor that chilled his soul.

A hand slipped into his and instantly the terror abated, sent packing with a peace that was meaningless. He turned.

Jennie's blue eyes stared into him, past his outer appearance and directly into his heart. A prayer in tongues was whispering on her lips, and she squeezed his hand in her own. His shoulders tensed, the still healing wound nowhere near whole, but well enough that he could get by. Something in him ripped away at the thought of leaving Jennie behind. They had found something these weeks that hadn't been there in his brief visits before. Something he could not fully make out, but something he didn't want to leave all the same.

He squeezed back. As much as his heart begged him to take her with them, Rosalie was his first priority, and getting her home would be accomplished, even if it was the last thing he did.

She seemed to read it all in his eyes, and without breaking his gaze, she lifted his hand to her lips and left a kiss upon it, soft, but burning like a live coal that heated him through. It felt like a promise, a mark as permanent as the doves that inked their skin, something to hold onto, no matter the wait or the storm.

He nodded to her and she spun, picking up her skirts and dashing to the house to gather their things. He refocused on Alexander. "What's going on?"

"Come on, I know where they're supposed to arrive." He led Malcolm across the yard in massive strides, eating up the ground toward the barn. "There are refugees coming up the mountain. Duncan and I headed them off, and he's bringing them here. But they were followed. Too close for comfort, and we need to use the passage to get you all out."

Malcolm swallowed back the tightness in the his throat and the queasy feeling in his stomach. The passage was rarely used, and the secrecy of it would cover them. But, being with another group of refugees could either be a blessing or a curse. Either Malcolm and Rosalie would be more easily hidden, or their presence would be that much easier to detect. More bodies were bound to slow them down, and it was easier for two to slip away where more could not follow.

But leaving the refugees here meant letting them meet a certain doom. The dark knights had never ventured this far north, but there was a first time for everything, and their actions spoke of desperation.

Alexander threw open the barn door and entered the third stall, shoving the horse that rested in his stable out of the way and kicking the hay and manure across the wooden floor. Bending to one knee, he inserted his finger into a knothole and heaved, his shoulder muscles rippling as he peeled a hidden door off the ground and stared into the dark abyss below.

Nothing.

The hair on the back of Malcolm's neck stood up. No light or lantern greeted them.

"God in heaven…" Alexander breathed, murmuring in prayer and kneeling to peer further into the darkness.

Suddenly a mourning dove coo echoed through the tunnel, and Alexander's shoulders dropped with relief. He sent a bird call back and smiled with relief up at Malcolm. "They're safe."

None of Malcolm's muscles relaxed in the slightest. Safe was relative, and while they were for the moment, nothing about this predicament and uncontrolled reaction felt safe.

Soft footfalls and horses' hooves met their ears, and Ian's face was the first one they saw. The youth blinked and squinted, shielding his eyes as they adjusted back to the light. He led Rosalie up the ramp with his other hand, and Malcolm reached down, pulling her up and to him, crushing her against his chest. She trembled beneath his touch, and he pulled her away from him to look into her face. She was squinting and shying away from the light as her eyes tried to adjust, but she seemed fine. Just paler than usual and with a frightened tremor in her every movement.

"We have to hurry. There is a group of refugees, and they are being followed," he explained to her, drawing her hand into his as Alex helped Ian lead the horse up the ramp and into the stall, slamming the door shut and covering it once again with the straw.

She gripped his hand back and, still blinking hard, allowed him to lead her to the house. Alexander trotted ahead, making a whistling screech that sounded like an owl but was sharp enough to get the attention of everyone in the clearing— alerting them.

The highland children rushed from a place behind the main house and entered it, just before Alexander reached it. When Malcolm stumbled through the door, the wee ones were climbing into the loft, their mothers scooting after them.

Mac gripped Malcolm's shoulder and pressed his pack into his hand. Mam'Nessa helped Rosalie with the straps of her own, and Jennie was bundling food on the table, tying it deftly with string and putting it in Rosalie's pack, knotting the flap shut all while they ushered them to the back door where the well house was stationed.

"The boys'll be followin' ye, but ye best get moving afore they come. Follow the tunnel down and make a left and ye'll find yerself at the dock. Get the boat ready. We'll get the refugees down as soon as they come and afore anyone else shows up." Mac led them into the small shed and around the stone-stacked well. The area that was cut into the rock behind it was used for keeping food cool, and Malcolm could sense the drop in temperature as soon as they entered the room. Mac leaned forward, scooting a few sundry food items over with his foot, and gripped a piece of stone that he pulled from the wall, revealing a rope latch. Pulling it, the stone gave way beneath his hand to reveal a wooden door covered with false stone to mimic the wall around it.

A dark tunnel met his gaze, and Malcolm sucked in his breath. It was even colder in there, and he could feel moisture in the air.

There were already the sounds of many others piling into the room behind them, and he felt himself pressed forward. Mac gripped his hand as he passed. "God go with ye and keep ye safe. He'll see ye through."

Still gripping Rosalie's hand in his, Malcolm ducked and stepped into the cavernous tunnel and dragged her after him. She stumbled and he helped her on, the path turning into narrow steps carved into stone. He went before her, still keeping her hand in his as they descended. The air grew colder and more damp as they went, and the steps were covered in water, the sound of dripping echoing in the tunnel.

Her foot slipped on a stair, and he barely caught her elbow before she careened past him. He hissed at the sharp pain of partially mended muscles in his shoulder from where her weight had pulled at the wound.

Her breath came in gasps, and he could tell that she was

shaking, adrenaline driving her onward. A roaring and rushing noise he nearly mistook for his heart pounding in his ears grew louder as if they were nearing something that sounded of thunder.

While he'd been to the highlands more than once, he had yet to know all of their secret byways, cut and carved into the mountains as a means of escape for some, protection for others, and a way out and down the mountain, tucked away from the prying eyes of Rusalk spies or warriors. There were a secret few who knew in an effort to keep many safe in a time and place where one word out of turn could be the difference that either saved a life or lost one.

A soft light ahead met his searching gaze and the muffled footsteps behind them, accompanied by frightened whispers, propelled him onward. The steps grew slicker and the roaring louder, drowning out all other sound until it seemed as if the very walls shook beneath it. The light grew brighter, and he squinted against it when they emerged from the tunnel, frigid spray striking him in the face and sending him back a step in surprise, stumbling into Rosalie, who tripped and fell to her knees on the pebbles at their feet.

He helped her up as another rescue emerged from the tunnel, and he cast his gaze around the grotto. A—waterfall? The water plunged in front of their eyes, roaring like thunder as the rock cavern around them extended into a large cave enclosed on three sides by the dripping gray mountain shale with a curtain of white water crashing down over the opening. The water was freezing and splashed in their faces as he squinted below them. The rocks declined toward the bottom of the cave where a pool gathered. The water was stirred by the falls above it, and he saw a small dock cut into the stone, a river barge tied to a rock piling.

Their escape.

Pulling Rosalie after him, they scrambled down the loose rocks that had been rounded and smoothed by the crashing water, followed by the refugees.

He helped Rosalie on when they reached the boat, then turned to meet another refugee. The older woman's face was scarred from what looked like a burn, and she clutched a child to her chest, tucked against her in a shawl that covered the toddler in a tight weave and allowed the mother to use her arms. Malcolm took her hand and helped her over the gunwale.

There were four more and their guide, a young man, ears pierced with silver charms and the mark of the dove in a motif along his arm, one large bird in the center of his forearm, surrounded by a myriad of others in various stages of flight that looked like a jagged collage of what could have been random shapes unless one knew where to look. Malcolm didn't recognize him from the Vagari clan, but there were many who roamed about on missions and were rarely with their caravan. The man's aquiline nose and sharp eyes were distinctive, but the build and hair were all Rusalkan.

He nodded to Malcolm, using his hands to swing his legs aboard the boat and dash to the front, where he reached for the rope that tethered the front to the dock while Malcolm untied the one at the back. Duncan joined them on the boat, and Alexander took a pole that leaned against the wall, bracing it against the front of the vessel and using it to push the boat away from the dock and shove it toward the edge of the curtain of crashing water.

Duncan thumped his chest with his fist and nodded to his little brother, who nodded back, steel in their spines and a set look on their faces. They knew these mountains like the back of their hands, and the way they had built their life meant they knew how to use it to defend themselves and their home.

Just the same, Malcolm clutched a trembling Rosalie to his side, holding her close, helping her cover herself with the oilcloth the others were using to stave off the water. His hand covered her head as prayers for protection filled his heart. She still shook beside him, but over the thundering of the falls, he caught a few of the words that fell from her lips, joining with his own voice.

For better or for worse, their journey was resumed, and it wouldn't be much longer before they reached their object. While he trusted Duncan to know the best way through and out of this mess without detection, dread fingered the back of his neck. Perhaps it was just a chill, but there was something that shrank inside of him as their boat broke into the daylight from behind the curtain of water, the light waning in the west now that the sun was nearing the horizon.

He hoped it was nothing more than a foreboding, but the rest of the journey would be the hardest part with nothing more than barren, jagged cliffs to guide them home and far too much open terrain, abandoned mines, and desolation.

He squeezed Rosalie's shoulder before reaching for one of the poles to join Duncan in his attempt to guide the boat safely down the flowing river. The thunder of the falls receded in the background, and he steeled himself for the passage ahead. Fourteen years would not go to waste; he would see her home.

At long last, Lord helping him, the heir would return to Elira.

"Get under cover! The nets! Quick!" Duncan suddenly hissed, throwing a panicked look over his shoulder that sent Malcolm diving into action.

The rescues ducked their heads, and Malcolm shoved Rosalie's head beneath an oilcloth that covered the nets without a second thought, assisting the guide with the rest of the rescues and ensuring that they were bundled beneath the nets, then covered by the oilcloth, lashing it to the side and leaving room for him and the Vagari guide to crawl under.

The wound in his shoulder screamed when he pulled the ropes taught before exchanging one last look with Duncan, who whistled the signal to hurry before Malcolm hit the deck and slid beneath the tarp to join the others.

He could hear the refugees' frenzied breath. He felt for Rosalie and found her groping, cold hand. Gripping it in his own and squeezing, he offered a comfort he didn't feel himself. But there was an assurance with her grip. She was trembling, but she squeezed back and in that gesture. Something that calmed his nearly exploding heart and allowed his mind to focus on one thing.

Listening.

Duncan's staff scraped against the edge of the boat in time with his steering, and Malcolm strained his ear to hear anything else beyond.

He picked up horses' hooves pounding into the dirt on the side of the river, and he squeezed Rosalie's hand again, pulling it harder against the deck of the boat in a gesture to pull her into hiding even more. The reality was that no matter who was riding up beside them, they had to trust the Lord and whatever escape He would provide. There was nowhere else to hide.

"Halt! Stop your barge by order of the king."

The voice was Rusalkan, and a chill ran down his spine. *Lord, hide us.*

"Sir." Duncan acquiesced, and the boat slowed, turning in the current as he planted his guide staff in the river bed and the boat turned around it. There was a tight formality to his tone, and Malcolm could hear the prayer hidden in his silence.

"We'll have to search your cargo. We're on the lookout for escaped slaves by order of Zuko, King of Rusalka. Throw us the anchor rope!"

Twenty-Nine

CHANGING PLANS

ELGON, THREE YEARS AGO...

Elgon swung Tamaska over his head, smiling to himself before his own chuckle rumbled from his chest. He settled her on his shoulders and held onto her feet while she twisted her hands into his hair. Marcus grinned at them both from his seat on the doorstep, a large trough of herbs in his lap that he was bundling for hanging.

Elgon trotted over to join his friend in order to give Tamaska as bouncy a ride as possible while she squealed and kicked her feet against his hands. He could hear her brothers chasing one another across the yard with shouts and wooden swords in their hands, striking them against one another. His gift to them.

He flopped to his knees beside the doorstep, allowing Tamaska to climb down from his shoulders and reach up with curious hands for some of the herbs her father was working with. "You have a rich and beautiful life, Marcus."

His brother nodded, a smile mixed with melancholy in his eyes as he pushed Tamaska away gently but handed her a small bundle of the herbs to play with on her own. She started laying them out side by side in a perfect row on the step at Marcus's feet. "I do indeed. I'm grateful you took the time to come out and share a small bit of it with us."

"I couldn't do less with all that you and Dilara have been able to do with the refugees. I needed to see for myself how they were doing. Padsley was a perfect place for many of them." His eyes followed his thoughts to where Dilara and the women under her and Marcus's care tended a massive garden that stretched to the back of their plot and was filled to overflowing with more vegetables than he could name or count, thriving under the many watchful and tender ministrations of those who had been set free to pursue something they could choose to do rather than what was required of them.

"How are they doing?" Elgon quirked a brow at Marcus.

The first batch of slaves Everard had rescued had been offered the choice of staying in the city, or finding their fortune without. Serve the king for wages, find employment with a craft they may have once done, or travel to the countryside where people like Marcus, Dilara, Fendrel, or Rensen and Keitha would see to their needs, integrating them back into society and a life they could love instead of hate.

Dilara's past had opened up a place in her heart to serve the women who found themselves without a family, without a husband, some with children, some having lost them. What

Marcus had shared with him about her life clearly had given her a compassionate and redemptive ability to bring healing to hearts alongside her husband who ministered to the body.

Elgon rested his hand on Tamaska's head. She didn't seem to notice and kept playing. "You and Dilara are truly a perfect match for each other."

Marcus smiled and tied a bundle of sage with twine. "Aye. The Lord saw to that." He paused, resting his hands and glancing up to catch his wife's eye. She smiled and waved before turning back to the pole beans she was coaxing to climb a tripod, angling her body awkwardly when she bent to allow space for her swollen stomach. "He turns even the evil for our good and His glory."

Elgon sighed. "I try to remember that on the hardest of days, though I confess, it's not easy to see."

"Time doesn't make it better, does it?"

Elgon shook his head, his throat closing up around the emotion that still rested there.

"A false approach, that one. Time only heals wounds when the master Healer Himself touches them first. Truth is, time doesn't heal wounds. It only makes them worse unless they've been properly tended to. But even wounds can turn into scars, and those never go away."

Elgon reached into the trough and pulled out a bundle of the herbs, taking the piece of cut twine that Marcus handed him, following his friends actions and making his own bundle. He understood that Marcus's pointed words weren't just for the sake of speaking, but were speaking truth to his soul, no matter how seemingly irrelevant a commentary they might be.

"How's Fendrel getting on? Enjoying his new duties?"

Marcus grinned. "More than he'll let on. He misses the day-to-day healing, but he still gets to do that, even if it is much less now that he's seeing to his duties as representative. He enjoys the opportunity to converse with his patients on more than just wound care. I heard that last week a woman giving birth snapped at him to hold the politics till after the baby had been born."

Elgon chuckled. Fendrel was nothing if not passionate, but his compassion was what made him a truly great representative of his people. There was nothing that he did for himself when his people needed him.

"Has there been any news?" Marcus's voice was hesitant, almost as if he was unsure of asking.

"Just rumors, but even those have ceased to bring me more than a small hope that they could possibly be true. I wonder how much of the rumors and news that make it back to me are planted by Zuko to keep me waiting, guessing, hoping. How much of it is a sick game he plays, and how much of it has truth in it?"

Marcus sighed. "The Lord didn't tell you to hold onto hope that they would return if there wasn't a reason for it. He doesn't ask us to do things to tease us."

"I know. But when the evidence doesn't speak to that, it's hard to wonder who holds the reins and is giving me a run about."

"Only the enemy does that."

"I know. I'm just trying to remember that He's still moving, even when I can't see it."

Hooves clattered in the distance on the cobblestones that

paved the way to Marcus's front door. Marcus turned his head, glancing in through the open back door to the open front. He tried to stand with the trough in hand, but pitched forward with the movement, his bad leg not fully under him.

Elgon leapt to his feet, nearly tripping over Tamaska who bumped into his knee as he steadied Marcus with one hand and the wooden trough with the other. Her dramatic wail made his heart lurch, and he set the trough down and handed Marcus his cane. The medicinal was now clinging to the doorframe and already apologizing when Elgon scooped up Tamaska and tried to comfort her.

"Don't worry, Marcus. It was nothing. There, little one, all's well." He jostled her on his hip, holding her hand and shaking it to distract her.

Marcus limped across the house and toward the front, much faster on his cane these days than in times past. A rider pulled up near the doorway and flung himself from the saddle.

"What is it?" Elgon heard Marcus's words as he distracted himself by handing Tamaska her mangled herbs and letting her pull the leaves apart in her little pudgy hands.

"Fendrel said I'd find the king here."

Elgon's hands froze, and he stepped through the doorway. "Kenton? What are you doing here? What's happened?"

Kenton brushed his hair out of his sweaty face and strode forward, hand on the hilt of his sword to keep it swinging against his leg as he walked. "It's Everard. He's reached Wood River and the training grounds, and he told me to send for you. He has news, but he would not tell any of us what it was."

Elgon felt the room swirl around him, and he leaned back

to balance with the child in his arms. He held steady, and Marcus's hand was on his shoulder as Tamaska wiggled from his locked arms, whining against his tight grip.

What news could Everard have that needed to be delivered personally?

ROSALIE, PRESENT DAY...

Rosalie clung to Malcolm's hand like it was a lifeline. The pressure he returned gave her an assurance that even if the worst were to happen, she was not alone. Could never be alone. The man who held her hand had been sent by a God who dwelt in and with her in every single moment, and despite the terror coursing through her veins, she also felt a peace that blanketed it all and snuffed out the panic that had threatened to overwhelm her at the sound of a Rusalkan accent.

"I'll need to check your cargo. There's been talk of slave smugglers in these parts."

"There are slave traders all over these mountains. What's new about that?" Duncan's voice was compliant, but there was a note of urgency in it that made Rosalie wince.

"These slaves were not for sale and were stolen from the king himself." The words were spoken with a dry and sullen menace. "Those harboring said stolen slaves will forfeit their life."

There was a breath of silence, and Rosalie held hers, her heart hammering loudly in her ears.

"Search away, captain, though you'll want to keep your distance. I'm carrying the bodies of my sick kindred down the mountain for burial away from anywhere that could taint our water. The pox has been about in these parts, and we lost too many this time. I'll not have the bodies infecting the rest." This time, Duncan's inflection and delivery were perfectly balanced.

Curses were flung back and a sword was drawn, the curved blade distinctive in its sound as it had to be removed at an angle from its sheath. "If they're dead, they won't mind being impaled."

Malcolm's hand crushed hers, but neither of them moved. Nothing under the tarp dared utter a breath as footsteps drew near, and the sound of a sword point slicing through fabric and hitting the deck with a dull thud made her want to shiver.

The hiss and thud came again and again while her mind jumbled poured forth a silent stream. Hiss and thud. Hiss, thud. Wouldn't it make a different sound if it were striking human flesh? The sound drew closer, the blade poking into the nets and the canvas at intervals down the length of the boat.

The blade came down beside her shoulder, and she heard the sound before she felt the sudden sting on her skin.

She didn't so much as flinch.

Silence.

Curses.

"Be on your way. Bury your dead. Make sure you do it far enough from the river so it's not poisoned." The commander's voice was gruff, commanding.

The sound of tack creaking and then hoofbeats disappeared into the distance.

The scrape of the guide staff shoving the boat back into the current and the movement of the water beneath them filled her senses.

"They're gone, but don't get up yet," Duncan hissed, as if he wasn't moving his lips. The boat jostled and turned in the current, the water choppier than before, the staff scraping against the side as Duncan steered and pulled them through the flow of the river.

Rosalie could no longer feel her hand, Malcolm's having squeezed any circulation from it.

The boat started rocking to and fro in a manner that was far more turbulent than before, and Rosalie felt the biting sting in her shoulder as her stomach lurched at the movements. The inability to see their direction as they were shrouded in the canvas made her ill. She sucked in air through her nose, whistling it out through pursed lips as she fought to keep her focus off the swaying and on something she could control. Scripture floated into her mind, a myriad of thoughts and prayers woven into a tapestry of hope that calmed her nerves.

The staff struck the side of the boat, and it turned sharply.

"The coast is clear. Ye can come out, but stay low. I don't know how many spies are set along the river. The boys should be after us soon enough, and we'll know for sure. Please tell me ye're all right." Duncan was breathless and more agitated than Rosalie had ever heard the giant man.

Malcolm released her hand, and her fingers tingled as the blood returned and the canvas was tipped away from over her head. Malcolm was on his knees beside her, looking her over, concern in every line of his features. He paused at the scratch on her shoulder, but as she caught a glimpse in the light, she drew a breath of relief and touched the single drop of blood with her forefinger. It was no worse than a thorn scratch.

Malcolm immediately turned to the others. Not a one was hurt. Their eyes were wide, and the guide with the ink sleeve of doves splashed across his arm fell against the side of the boat and collapsed to a reclined position.

The man started chuckling, and he shook his head with awe. "I don't wish to repeat that experience, but wouldn't I just like to see the commander's face if he knew that his sword had the opportunity to pierce the flesh of six living escapees and instead it spared every single one."

There was a smile on Malcolm's face, and a few of the others also laughed with relief, except for the mother who clutched her young child to her chest and kept her eyes focused on the opposite end of the boat, staring at nothing while rocking back and forth.

Rosalie felt her heart go out to the woman. There was something about her that drew her in, the burn on her face not the least of them as she wondered what could have happened to her.

Rosalie shuddered, turning her eyes away and letting Malcolm blot the blood from her cut and tie a strip of fabric around her sleeve to keep the wound clean. She had always been spared anything that would mar her skin or deem her unworthy. She hadn't understood as a child, but as her teen years came upon her and Zuko visited with more frequency, his eyes casting over her in a manner that brought her confusion and fear, she had started to understand her role.

The hair on her arms stood on end, and she shook again, remembering the way he had chastised her captors when they had dared to slap her across the face where she could scar.

She wrapped her hands around her stomach and looked

away when Malcolm sent her a questioning glance.

"Are you all right?"

She nodded, rubbing the skin to bring some warmth back to her chilled body.

He turned and sank to a seat beside her, resting his back against the low side of the boat. "The time to climb will come soon enough. Enjoy the rest."

She nodded again, swallowing against the lump in her throat and trying to relax against the curved side of the boat. The close shave had brought the peace she had experienced with the Highland family crashing down around her ears, and the understanding that her last haven of rest was behind her and she hadn't even had the chance to say goodbye filled her with so much pain it felt a bit like a dagger to the heart. She hugged herself, feeling tears suddenly well into her eyes and a sob clutch at the back of her throat.

A hand landed on her shoulder, and she let herself collapse against Malcolm's side as he hugged her gently.

He brushed her hair's tangled and tossed curls away from her forehead with a hesitant hand, and she let the tears fall.

"I didn't get to say goodbye. I didn't get to thank them." The words came out broken, strangled.

She felt him nod, and his hand rested comfortingly on her head. "They know."

But she didn't think they did. There was no way they could fully understand the weight of what they had given her. They had provided freedom to one who had little understanding of what that was. They had given family to a child who knew of no such love and provision. They had offered protection to one who had desperately needed it their entire life. They had been the hands and feet of Jesus to a child who had lived without that earthly expression her entire time on this earth.

And she hadn't even been afforded the opportunity to whisper her love and gratitude or to hold them to her and experience the weight of their goodbye like a promise given and kept in the future, yet unseen.

She raised her bleary eyes to catch their surroundings. The river seemed to cut through cliffs that towered above them. No longer hills, but jagged rocks, stretching toward the sky like the arm of a drowning man. Fog coated their edges, softening and hiding the sky from her view and coating the trees with a softness that was safe and mysterious all at once. The trees themselves looked like they were drowning. The boat had picked up speed, and Duncan drew in his staff, settling it along the boat's flooring and striding to the stern where the tiller was tethered straight, his large steps set wide as he needed more stability and balance. He untied the tiller and pulled it, directing the vessel farther out into the middle of the river which had grown wider and faster.

Malcolm glanced aft where the refugees and their guide were situated, and he jerked the tip of his head toward the back of the boat when he caught the guide's eye. The young man nodded in return, slipping away from his wards and nearly crawling toward Malcolm and Rosalie at their position near the back of the boat, keeping his head low and protected.

"I need to ensure the safety of my rescue." Malcolm's voice was low, but the tightening of his arm around Rosalie's shoulder made her wince as he touched the cut on her arm.

"Ye cannae split up now. There's only one path to go. Ye're all headed in the same direction, and any other path is too dangerous now that we know they're looking for ye." Duncan's eyes were on the river ahead, his shoulders straight.

The young Vagari guide stroked the thin and trimmed beard on his chin, his eyes thoughtful. "But will it slow you down?" he asked Malcolm.

Malcolm's jaw clicked and he squinted. "If there's no help for it, there's none. But we'll need to keep moving. The faster we can get to the border, the better chance they all have. If the canyons and caves are the only way, there may be more safety in numbers."

The man nodded, continuing to stroke his chin before he glanced at Rosalie. "She the one?" His eyes jumped to Malcolm's face.

Rosalie shrank into Malcolm's shoulder as he hesitated, studying the man with sharp eyes before he answered. "Aye."

The Vagari drew in a breath, letting out a nearly silent whistle through his teeth. Then he grinned at Rosalie. "S'bout time. Name's Benaiah. You can call me Ben." He stretched out a hand, a ring on his small finger hammered from metal and displaying the stamp of a dove.

Hesitating, she took his hand and caught his eyes. She froze. There was something there that reminded her of Nim. Something like an inner light that sparkled like the moon reflecting off a dark pond and shining back into the world. She couldn't help but smile back. The Vagari people held a gift inside them that instantly set her at ease.

"I'll get ye as far down as we dare. Hopefully the boys'll meet us there with the horses to haul the boat back. If they don't..." Duncan's voice trailed off, and he lowered his head, clenching his jaw.

"They'll have to be there. Your family has lived in the highlands for generations. They can't arrest you simply for living and letting live." Malcolm spoke reassuringly, though Rosalie caught a note of unsurety in his tone.

Duncan nodded, steering around a rock in the middle of the river. "Aye. That's what one would think, but Rusalks rarely ask for permission or need a reason to do their dirty work."

Rosalie swallowed, feeling a bit sick. The idea of the highland family being at risk because they had taken care of her made her stomach roil as badly as it had when she'd hidden under the nets.

"Ye'll have to take the slag canyons down the waterways and find the right caves. Swinging north, there are three, marked with an olive branch carved into the stone. Ye'll follow through them till you reach the mines and go from there into the border. Should take you five days if you can keep things moving." Duncan spoke as he guided the boat even farther toward the right side of the river, the water clattering over the rocks now and bouncing the boat back and forth as they went. "Just past the rapids, I'll put you off, and ye'll find the first trail marked with an arrow of shale."

Rosalie felt Malcolm tense with readiness, and she drew in a shuddering breath.

"Rest. We'll be there soon, and there will be little time for it after," he breathed in her ear as Ben sidled toward the front of the boat, most likely to inform the rescues of the plans for the future of their journey.

If only rest was so easy.

ENGUERRAND, THREE YEARS AGO...

Slamming the door, Enguerrand strode into his hall, his cloak billowing over his shoulder and his hand on the dagger at his waist. Swords were heavy, deft as hammers, and for those who sought to lord it over others rather than make use of the subtle, slyness of a small hidden blade, its curve making it easy to conceal and twice as deadly as a straight one.

"You come bearing a message." It was a statement rather than a question as he strode into the room and folded his arms, attempting to look and sound unbothered when internally he was seething.

The messenger was late.

The young man, his hair black as raven's feathers and his skin windblown and callused, bowed before him and straightened quickly. There was an arrogance and a strength on the man's face that would have irritated Enguerrand if it hadn't impressed him. Anyone who could stand their ground in his presence automatically earned a small bit of his respect, even if he was still just as willing to sacrifice them on the altar of his desires to stay on top. Arrogance could be useful if it were directionable, but it was dangerous if it started to take on a will of its own.

"My lord, the Eris representative said they could take on more slaves than you had sent previously. They're ready to pay accordingly for such."

Enguerrand nodded, sweeping his hands behind his back and pacing away from him. "Is that all?"

"No sir. That's not all." The nerve of the lad, to come with such a tone and attitude into his master's hall.

Enguerrand spun, nailing the man with a gaze that had

withered lesser mortals. "Spit it out or you'll be without a job and possibly your life faster than you can comprehend. There are more than a few men who would be happy to take your place."

The man's eyes sparked with a flame that meant business, and his hands clenched at his sides. Good. He was on edge and angry. Angry men did rash things.

"They want to open up another trade date. They have more ships. They see no reason why waiting for only one shipment a month is worth it to them when they can broaden trade and increase shipments at the same time."

Enguerrand felt his blood boiling within him. How dare they demand more of him? Didn't they know he was managing more than just the supply, which in and of itself had been dwindling as half a dozen slaves went missing by the day? It was hard enough getting his hands on supply, but to take the risk of unveiling themselves further, of increasing traffic through the tunnels under Niran in such a fashion, was foolhardy.

He cursed and paced faster. If he offended the Eris traders, it was likely they could find business elsewhere, but he was the only one who had given them access beneath Niran. The only one who had opened up a trade route under the very noses of Elgon and his stupid kingdom of ingrates who couldn't stand the thought of making some extra coin off a few deserving, ignorant people who were better suited to labor overseas.

Truly, he did them a service. Why anyone would want to live in this frigid, desolate country was beyond him. He hadn't eaten a good meal that wasn't meat since his arrival here, everything having to be carted in over the mountains or gone without. Elgon was far too prideful even to dare trade with Rusalka.

But Enguerrand was between a rock and a hard place. The lure of more gold to add to his coffers, the ability to vie for more authority and perhaps even a throne was something he never spoke of, but turned over in his mind like a shiny rock in the hands of a child who was obsessed with his treasure.

Zuko thought he knew all, was aware of everything. But what he did not know was that the vassal he had spurned and thrown to the abandoned castle deep in the mountains was fast becoming wealthier than he and using it to buy back his authority.

He needed that coin. It called to him like a siren from the deep, singing the song of freedom, power, and the ability to make his own decisions once again.

"Fine." He turned suddenly, stopping in front of the man who did little to hide the look of annoyance on his face. "Tell them they'll get their second shipment date. We'll double the trade, but for the price we agreed upon formerly *and* a surcharge for the extra risk and to cover my expenses. Let them know that the figures we agreed upon will need to be tripled, not doubled, if they want more than one shipment a month. I'll arrange it and send them the dates when it's at the ready. You may go, but send in the boys on your way out. I'll need them to spread the word to the traders so they can get their quotas up." He nearly spat the words and turned away from the man who hesitated before skulking out.

Enguerrand settled on his pedestal, and he stretched his neck to try to ward off the tightness that seemed to grip his muscles.

He didn't just have Elgon and the Niran guard to worry about. He could get past them. His men knew the waterway like the back of their hands; they would just need to choose the right time, as always. But more than one journey a month put them at more risk of being found out.

And Zuko. It was getting harder to keep this from him. He had started asking questions. The acolytes who seemed to find ways of making their slaves go missing were getting bolder, and even Zuko had started to question who in his kingdom could be responsible for such disappearances. Zuko's temper would not be assuaged forever if he discovered that his slaves weren't just being stolen by acolytes, but by the vassal who pretended that his barren mountain home provided him little in the way of taxable produce.

He clapped his hands for the slave to bring him his mead. Wine. He missed drinking the wine that came over the sea. He smiled. It wouldn't be long though. And perhaps, if he played his cards right, he'd have two thrones for the price of one.

Thirty

COLLAPSE AND CAPTURE

ROSALIE, PRESENT DAY...

Rosalie jolted awake with the dry scraping and thud on the bottom of the boat. It was dim, the light blanketed and cushioned by the fog and the cloudy skies. She shivered and drew her cloak around her, pulling it down toward her feet as she pulled her knees into her chest and tried to get some of her body heat back. There was nothing but empty space beside her, and with a start, she looked right and left for where Malcolm could be.

Her heart calmed as she caught sight of him, partially hidden by the fog, helping Duncan tie off the boat at the front. A sound off the starboard side of the barge echoed out through the invisible canyon, and she froze and tried not to shiver, straining her ears for another sound and holding her breath. Had the dark knights circled back to find her? Was she going to be taken back? After coming this far and escaping their stabbing search earlier, how on earth had they found them in this fog?

Duncan cupped his mouth with his hands and released an owl call, a hoot with vibrations that echoed back over the chasm and made her blood run cold.

Silence met her ear until another call in response made her muscles sag, weak against the side of the boat, and she sucked in a breath of relief. She had almost held her breath for long enough to see stars.

"The boys are here." Duncan nodded, turning back to the rest of the passengers and helping them over the lowered transom that met an outcropping of rock like two pieces of a bridge.

Malcolm was suddenly at her side, helping her up by her elbow and giving her a side-eyed glance. "You all right?"

She swallowed hard against the dryness in her throat but nodded.

He seemed not to fully believe her, but he took her hand in his and drew her off the boat, the pressure of his fingers around her own bringing her a comfort that settled her nerves and reminded her that she was not alone, no matter how terrifying things could be.

Horses' hooves clattered, and falling stones blended with the sound. She shrank against Malcolm, feeling a bit of the fear and confusion from her first few days with him returning. So unsure, so worried about what was to come. There was nothing for her to hold onto, nothing with any reference for the life she was living, the journey she was on.

She didn't quite know what to do with it. By nature, despite feeling a part of something bigger, it was so ethereal, so distant and lacking foundation in her understanding of her world that there was little she could do to place herself in it.

She was a princess—what of that? What did that even mean in the grand scheme of the world? What power did it give her? As her feet slipped about on the loose rocks, her boots struggling to find purchase as they stepped up the incline and away from the flowing water that had carried them thus far, she felt an emptiness deep inside of her. A place that didn't know where to place her foot, where to belong and to whom.

The horses slid to a stop, and broken shale clattered down the stone face in front of them. Tears of relief rose to her eyes. Alex and Cameron. Their faces were welcome sights, and she stumbled forward to envelop Alex in a hug as he came off his horse, but she froze. Did she have the right to do so?

He gave her a look, his green eyes probing, questioning, as if reading her heart on her face. The hard set of his jaw softened nearly imperceptibly, and he stepped forward into the waiting space between them, falling to one knee and crushing her to his chest. She let the tears fall, hidden in his cloak as she hugged him with the desperation of a lonely soul looking for a place to belong, only to find it and then have it ripped from her grasp again.

It was almost as if he understood, had sensed her pain as he held her, his chin resting on the top of her head. "There are brighter days ahead, wee one. Ye'll find ye're home. Because it's here." He pulled away from her and tapped a finger to the place just below her collarbone and over her heart. "The True

King lives here. And where His spirit is, there is freedom. No matter where ye be in body." His words were soft, spoken only for her, his warm breath blowing soft and foggy around her in the icy cold near the river.

Her chin quivered, and a few tears ran down her face before she could stop them. "Thank you. For everything. For…" Her voice broke, and she saw the moisture start to his eyes. There was so much she wanted to say, but somehow, she had no words to say it.

"I know, wee one. I know." He laid his massive hand on her head, his goodbye silent, but feeling like a benediction and a blessing all at once. He stood.

Cameron gave her a smile and shook her hand, giving her a little bow with his head before he tied his horse to the boat to pull it back upstream.

Duncan's embrace was just as crushing as his brother's, and his massive hands rested on either side of her face, swallowing it up and giving her a solid place of comfort between them. A place that was so strong and able to harm, but so gentle and safe. "A rose blooms amongst thorns. Never forget it, wee one. A heart that blossoms amidst adversity has the beauty and grace to change the world. God go with ye." He kissed her forehead before clasping forearms with Malcolm and climbing astride his horse.

"May the Lord protect and guide ye all and give ye great success on your journey." His voice was strong and commanding, and his tone gave her a hope that she drew up from the depths of her soul. He smiled softly and clicked his tongue, his horse disappearing into the mist, following his brothers.

Even though it felt as though something had been taken from her, again…the highlanders had given her something too. A hope, a peace, and the love of family in a place that had been desolate and broken.

But now her hands were empty.

Until a large, warm one slid into her palm and gripped it. "Let's go, Rosie. You've people waiting for you."

Hope ripped through her heart like a busted seam, sending something new and fresh and bright across the scars and pain. There was someone waiting for her at the end of this journey. But would it be everything she had hoped and prayed for? Or would everything that had been her dream and desire be met with merely a life that she didn't know…and that didn't know her?

It had been three days. Three days of walking, of climbing, and of slowly dying of thirst. The highland family had given them as many victuals as they could carry, even those that were their own. Water skins were heavier, but there was less to go around.

Natural water sources were fewer and farther between as the rocks were drier and their path was harder to traverse. The rocky trail was not like the moss-covered stones of her previous journey or the forest laden cliffs with leaves to cushion any fall. Rosalie's feet were covered in blisters from the constant rubbing of her boots, and her hands ripped on the palms from clambering over the sharp shale and down the other side. Her wool dress was covered in snags and small tears from where it had caught on the jagged rock.

Malcolm gripped her waist from behind as she slid down another incline and let him help her down. She tried to hide her hands, but he gave her a look this time. She'd thought she'd hidden them all this way, but he had apparently noticed. He turned to help the woman with the burned face down after her. Motle, she said her name was. The woman reached up after she was solidly on her own two feet to help the others, but Malcolm softly pushed her aside, assisting Ben down the slope. He had Motle's baby, Freuda, tied in a bundle on his back.

Last came Adrian, a boy younger than Rosalie with sad blue eyes and tousled hair that would have been golden if it were clean, and then Lena. She shuddered when Malcolm's hands met her waist, and he released her as soon as she was on solid ground, raising his hands in a gesture so that she knew he meant her no harm. She pulled her cloak tighter around herself and shivered, avoiding his gaze and passing them on the trail.

Motle gripped Adrian's hand and pulled him after her, Ben following as he gently adjusted the precious bundle on his back, the baby fast asleep and unaware of their perilous journey.

Rosalie moved to follow them, but Malcolm's hand on her shoulder stopped her. "Here," was all he said as he ripped the cuff from his sleeve on each side and used the fabric to wrap her palms. Using a bit of leather string that he pulled from a pocket, he fastened it over top to hold it over her skin. She tried not to wince when he touched one of the cuts on her hand, the shale having worn jagged scrapes into them.

He rested his hand on her head as he started them back down the path, using his other to heft the pack higher on his back. "We should be nearing the second cave by now."

Rosalie swallowed against the dryness in her throat. They hadn't seen another stream cutting through the mountain rock since last night, and her body was begging for water, but she wasn't going to be the one to ask. If the rest of them were fine without, she would be too.

Trying not to show her disappointment at the announcement that they were still not even halfway through these mountain crags and caves, she followed Malcolm down the trail after the others.

A whistle from up ahead was Ben signaling them, and Malcolm took her forearm in his hand, avoiding the bandages and cuts and pulling her with him as they picked up their pace to meet the others. Ben had found something.

As they came around a corner, she tried not to gasp at the mouth of darkness that cut through the fog and met her eyes, its yawning blackness stretching over her head. The opening was about Malcolm's height all around, and it was so dark. Without thinking about it, she caught herself shrinking away, the inky shroud pulling at past memories and reminding her of the last cave walk. She shook just thinking about it. And that cave had been one where she could see the exit the entire time. No light pierced the darkness of this one, and instead her heart trembled as images of being swallowed up by a monster, drowning in hidden waterways, and falling into an unknown abyss filled her head.

Malcolm glanced back at her a moment before leaving her to join Ben at the mouth of the cave, splaying his hand over an olive branch with two leaves carved into the rock on the right.

"This is it." Malcolm nodded in agreement, helping Ben pull an unlit torch from the pack that rested below the baby, attempting not to wake her. Pulling flint from his pocket, he struck it till the torch sparked, the tinder and fabric wrapped around the top catching fire and slowly burning all the way around as Ben turned it, pulling the flame upward.

"You can lead the way?" Malcolm asked.

Ben nodded. "We can't stop now; we have to get to water. We're running low. There's supposed to be a spring in this cave."

Malcolm nodded again, letting the others follow Ben ahead of him.

Rosalie watched as Ben's light cut a swath through the darkness, but it pressed in around them anyway, closing off the light and hiding the others from view as they disappeared into the cave's mouth. The light did little but flicker a spark in the yawning hole, and she shrank back, her shoulder blades bumping into a rock outcrop that made her jump and catch her breath.

"Rosalie."

She started. Malcolm had snuck back to her, standing close now. He cocked his head to the side, trying to bring a bit of a smile to his face, but the lines were too heavy and thick, painted in creases of worry and sorrow for far too long.

She shook her head, sucking in another gulp of air. The air here was thin, reminding her further of her prison home and making it hard to catch her breath. "I-I can't see the other side."

He didn't move. "It's only dark for a while. Light always comes, Rosie."

Her chin quivered and she trembled. "Not always," she whispered, the pain of years of a tower life, lost to the past, lost to the pain, and living forgotten and alone, rushing back.

He knelt in front of her, taking her freezing hand in his tenderly, avoiding the wounds. His palm was warm, and she let him keep her hand as she stared straight ahead at the cave that promised to swallow her in darkness and take her back to the freezing dungeon room that never ceased to be a memory of pain.

"Listen to me. You can survive the darkness. Not because it's not terrifying. Not because it's safe or because it's all right. I won't lie to you and tell you that it's going to be all right. But you can survive it because you carry a light. Not like the torch that Ben and I wield but something bright and hopeful and alive inside of you, brighter than any man made lantern. A light you would see even if you were blind and your eyes were tied shut." He rested his other hand on her shoulder. "No matter what happens, that light will never leave you. Do you trust it to stay? Do you remember all the times it was there, no matter how dark?"

Tears fell down her cheeks, and she felt the grip of the fear lessen at the words he spoke.

"Just remember the light. I'll be with you the whole way through."

She sucked in a deep breath. Then nodded. Holding tight to his hand, no matter how much it hurt. He returned her grip, then let go long enough to light his own torch. Ben's had already disappeared into the void, and she squeezed her eyes shut, letting Malcolm lead her.

All the while, she remembered the light. Remembered the moments where comfort had come to her curled on a stone floor, freezing cold. Remembered the love and tenderness of Zehra and the life-giving words she had helped her memorize as a tiny child. Remembered the open door that brought with it a light she couldn't live without.

She remembered the golden fires of the Vagari camp, the whirling dervish of their dancing feet and skirts, the light and love in a camp that lived surrendered to the King.

She remembered the flicker in Vieggo's eyes. The twinkle that came with a smile and a wink.

She remembered the love wrapped in tender care and truthful words from Mother Hobbs.

The hug around the waist and delighted talkativeness of Bogden and Izabella. The soft hand of a caress and hair brush through her long locks from Immanuella.

She saw the light of the family love of the highlanders like a glow strong enough to set a forest ablaze. The chatter, the teasing, the gentleness in the faces and hands of giants. The glow of Jennie's red locks reflecting the firelight as she smoothed Rosalie's hair and helped her tend to Malcolm.

They glowed around her like an army of torches, burning bright with a light they carried within. The same light Malcolm said she carried. A love and longing for a King in heaven that could not be put out.

They weren't the light. They carried the light. Held it aloft and let it rule their lives, speaking truth and comfort and bringing freedom to captives and hope to the broken.

She saw them all, their faces bright, filled with something she knew she had inside of her. The King lived in her, as assuredly as He lived in them. They lit her path, their faces like torches spread before her, a people, alive and living in the presence of a King and the power of a Savior.

She didn't feel so alone anymore. Those memories of the pain, the cold, the dark were crowded out by something infinitely more beautiful than anything she had ever experienced before. They were crowded out by the light and love of dozens of faces. And she clung to that light, letting it warm her from the inside out, filling her with the hope that goodbye was not forever and that she would see them again.

The ground rocked under her feet, and she gripped Malcom's hand tighter, the pain from the cuts stinging as she stumbled into his arm.

"Steady." His voice was laced with a worry she didn't understand. She opened her eyes and saw the golden flame of his torch and blinked at the brightness of it. She squinted into the dimness ahead and caught sight of Ben's torch, heard his whistled call to ensure that they were together or close enough to be heard.

Malcolm answered, and a roar from inside the cave echoed back at them with a burst of air that swept past like a breeze. The air of the cave had been clammy and stale, unmoving till that moment.

Something didn't feel right.

A second roar thundered, nearer than before, and the ground rocked beneath her feet, dust falling from above. A sudden movement shoved her towards the right as the world came crashing down like a waterfall collapsing to a river below.

The torch died. The world went black.

ELGON, TWO YEARS AGO...

Elgon ran through the castle hallways like mountain lions nipped at his heels, driving him forward. Aching, haunting memories of the last time he'd been summoned to the castle while away rose like a phantom before him.

Kenton had been reticent to say anything, had sworn he knew nothing of the reason Elgon had been called for, but his face was filled with a dread and worry that Elgon couldn't see beyond.

All Kenton knew was that Everard had returned and he had news.

The long ride to Niran had exhausted Elgon, but adrenaline kept him running faster than he should've been able to.

Terror claimed his insides as its playground, tighfisting his heart and his lungs at the same time. He had made this mad dash before. The news had been staggering. The horror greater than his wildest imaginings. *God, please don't let it be again. Don't let my hope have been for nothing.*

He hit the stairs running, huffing for breath as he heaved his body over them, praying that the news was good but preparing his heart for the worst all at the same time. Malcolm met him at the top of the stairs and grabbed his arm, pulling him from his sprint into a more subdued trot as he kept pace alongside him.

"Everard is waiting for you in the meeting room. Breathe."

Malcolm's hand on his arm and his voice in his ear gave Elgon a sense of surety that he wasn't in this alone—but it didn't quell the panic.

Sucking in air, trying to fill his aching lungs with it, he turned the next corner, skidding on the stones beneath his feet, and nearly bowled over Tobias who stood at the door, ready and waiting to open it. The lad bounced out of the way after throwing open the entrance, and Elgon dashed through it, halting only once he'd set eyes on Everard.

The large man turned, and there was something in his face that sent Elgon to his knees, no longer able to support his own weight. He tried to say something, anything, but nothing came out.

Malcolm was on the ground beside him, his arm underneath his shoulder in support.

Everard finally spoke. Words as precious as hoarded gold. "There's a child. She's alive."

Emotion pounded him like a wave upon the shore, and his eyes filled with tears, spilling out as a sob escaped his cramping insides with the force of a storm.

"She's alive."

His child. A daughter, like he'd thought. All that hope. All those years. Those prayers. Those sleepless nights and aching days. She was alive. *His* daughter. His princess. The heir to his heart and his throne.

He sank to his hands, feeling the cold stone beneath him as he let the devastation and sickness of hope deferred empty from within himself. The tears—salty, aching, like a torrent— flooded his vision and fell in a puddle on the floor in front of him.

And then his heart stopped again, frozen in that place inside his ribs where it was tethered to a connection outside of himself. Tethered to the woman he called wife. He tried to sit up, but his hands shook beneath him, and he was afraid to move.

"Vi?" he asked, almost afraid to say her name lest it ruin him.

Everard kneeled before him. Elgon felt the man's hands on his shoulders as he lifted him with his strength. Dirt was still streaked across Everard's face, exhaustion in every line, circles under his eyes as if he hadn't slept in a week. But there was also a hidden fear, a worry that hung somewhere in his expressive eyes.

"There was no news of her. Only the child was found. We do not know yet that she is gone. We have not confirmed it. But—" His voice broke, tears in his eyes and shining like diamonds on his lower lashes. "They could find no indication of her presence."

Elgon's sob rent the air like a whip cracking, wounding him anew. Air escaped his lungs, but there was no sound before he was crushed into Everard's shoulder, and he wound his hands into fists in his friend's cloak that smelled of pine and sawdust.

She couldn't be dead. Could she?

But something in the silence of all these years. The unanswered messages to Zuko, a lack of evidence supporting her existence... Zuko would have said something—would have lorded it over him. Would have used her as a pawn if he had her. The world swam around him as something in him broke. Some tie to a world he had held onto for so long and now had been ripped from his grasp like an anchor line cut and washed into the waves of the sea.

She was gone.

Something deep in his heart knew. That line had been severed. The thing that held him to a hope outside himself had left, sunk to the bottom of the ocean.

He knew she was gone.

"I have to go." He shoved himself to his feet, reaching for the sword at his side to ensure it still rested where it should. His legs trembled, and he caught himself on the meeting table with a heavy hand, his elbow hitting the wood as his entire weight came to bear on it. His vision blurred. He couldn't fully see where he was going, but he pushed past the arms that tried to hold him.

He pushed through the door, straight past Tobias's wide open eyes that were filled with their own tears and into the hall. He stumbled, catching himself against the wall and bashing that same elbow. He tried to stand, to ignore the voices behind him.

"You can't go. My lord—" Malcolm clung to his arm, trying to pull him back, but he wrested it from his friend's grip, the world's sound fading in and out around him as he staggered toward the end of the hall.

"I have to go to her. You can't stop me. I must get my daughter." He fought against the hands that gripped him on every side. He needed to see her, needed to find his daughter. She had been left all alone. Alone somewhere in a castle ruled by a demon.

"Elgon." The name thundered in the hall and snapped him back, the heavy hand on his shoulder spinning him around.

Elgon caught himself against the wall, his back sliding down the stones.

The voices echoed distantly as his vision wavered.

"Tobias, fetch a glass of water—quick now."

"He'll be all right in a minute. I've more news, but I don't want to further burden him."

"It can't be helped."

"The lords should be called. They'll need to be informed."

"I'll see to it."

A glass of water was pressed to his lips, the metal cold and clanking against his teeth. The water was cool as it slid down his throat, but it welled back up and he turned, heaving, nothing but the small swallow of water he had taken in burning up his throat.

"Breathe." The voice was low, and the large hand resting on his head, cool to the touch, felt like a benediction, words of peace and comfort flowing over him as he sagged against the wall, letting his eyes squeeze shut against the light that shone into his present darkness.

The words were indiscernible, but they brought peace nonetheless, breathed over him in prayer.

He swallowed against the back of his throat, letting his mind wander to the words that were being whispered to him in his pain and hollowness. Letting the emptiness within be filled even as he begged for it to be taken from him.

"I heal the brokenhearted and bind up their wounds. I am near to the brokenhearted and I make Myself known to those who are crushed in spirit. Breathe, my son. I have not finished my story. I am not done writing it. I did not give up on your legacy. I hear the cries of your heart, and I am with you in

your pain. I feel your sorrow as keenly as My own. You are not the only one who weeps. I am here with you. I am here with you in the shattered now. I suffer as you suffer, and still I hold you and bind up the wounds you carry."

Elgon sucked in clean air, letting it fill the places in his chest that ached as though they had been pierced through.

He opened his eyes and saw Everard standing there, tear stains marked in the dirt on his face. He didn't need to say anything, but the eyes with which he met Elgon's spoke of his own sorrow, a heart cry of pain and compassion that mingled together in the broken shards of his gaze.

Malcolm was there next, his hand gripping Elgon's, and the king turned to him then, his voice breaking. "You must get her, my brother. If anyone is to rescue my daughter, I beg of you, let it be you."

MALCOLM, PRESENT DAY...

The darkness was more than he could bear. It weighed on him, pressing into his chest like it was trying to steal his very lifeblood. He could barely draw in air. The tiny bit that did reach his lungs caught, and he coughed, the pain of it sending lightning bolts through his vision.

He focused on just dragging in one breath. Just one. Then another.

He tried to move his hand to shove off whatever oppressively heavy object was sitting on his chest and the pain that followed sliced through him like a blade, spiraling him into the stars, reaching for the flashes and pin-dots of light that were afforded to him.

Don't move. That was the only way to avoid pain.

But if he couldn't move and he couldn't breathe, he would have to surrender to the darkness.

And Malcolm would not surrender.

He tried to blink the dust from his vision. The grit in his eyes would have been something he would have loved to use his hands to remove, but his arms were pinned to the cold, biting stone beneath him.

He coughed again at his next intake of oxygen.

Rosalie.

He tried to speak, but nothing came out. Perhaps more air? He pressed once more against the weight on his chest, heaving, every bit of his strength poured into a single movement. It did little else but send blinding hot pain slicing up his left arm and into his neck. He stilled, limp and cold.

He could only think her name.

Voices reached his ears. Were they voices or just the imaginings of his mind desperate to breathe? There they were again. Deeper, nearer, but somehow floating in the ether that swirled above his head.

"Leave him. He's dead. No one can survive that."

"Take the others. We'll make it back to camp by nightfall and to the tunnels in the morning."

"What about their wounds?"

"Dress them and pretend they don't exist. This makes our quota and then some, so now we won't have to put up with the pittance of pay they give us."

"Shift it. I want to make it to camp long enough for a good supper. It's been long enough since we've eaten venison."

The words drifted off, and a high pitched whining rang in

his ears. Was that screaming? He wondered how on earth to make any sense of the sounds. His mind seemed to float somewhere outside of his body, as if he couldn't connect the words, couldn't think straight, couldn't sort through anything he had heard.

Rosalie.

Where was she? Was she being taken by those voices? Were they here to drag her back into the hell he had rescued her from?

Panic rose in him. The desperate plea for air screaming to a crescendo in his brain.

Must.

Get.

Out.

Sucking in as much as he dared into his lungs, he threw all of his strength against the weight that rested on top of him, but lightning seared through every limb and fiber of his being, wrenching a groan from his lips and dragging him deep into the recesses of the darkest lake he'd ever seen in his life. And somewhere deep inside the vortex of blackness that sucked him in, the thought floated to the surface like one last air bubble escaping the lips of a drowning man.

This too, was all his fault.

Thirty-One

LETTING GO

ROSALIE, PRESENT DAY...

He's dead.

It's all my fault.

He's dead.

The words echoed in her mind, taunting her, filling her with horror that made her fall to her knees and wretch for the third time as visions filled her mind of blood coating the cave floor and his hand poking out from beneath a rock, blue, like it didn't belong to him at all.

A kick to the back of her legs and a pull on the rope sent her stumbling back to her feet, her wrists caught in the knots just like Lena in front of her and Benaiah behind.

"Get on with you! Quit ye're falling and flopping about! We've got a camp to get to." The words were harsh, bitten out on a rasping voice, and she swallowed back the bitter taste in her mouth, letting her feet stumble forward, trying to ignore the sharp pain that stabbed up her legs and into her back.

The loud thundering sound they had heard had sent the roof of the cave crashing in on them. Her worst nightmare come to life. Malcolm had flung her against the wall, her back slamming into the rock and leaving her limp and breathless for she knew not how long.

She hadn't been able to move. Hadn't been able to open her eyes till she finally snatched a breath into her lungs. It was still pitch black. She didn't know how long she laid there till the torches came. And with them the angry, harsh voices that reminded her of her life before. They had pulled her from the rubble, tied her while she watched them declare him dead. Then they dragged her away, her screams echoing against the rock and into her ears.

She just left him. His body crushed and mangled under the rocks. The pool of blood beneath his nearly blackened blue hand where it rested, drained of all strength and life, there on the cave floor. She shuddered, and her stomach would have heaved again if there had been anything left inside.

Ben bumped into her from behind, and she turned her head to see his sorrowful but compassionate gaze on her, the gash on his forehead still spilling blood down the side of his face, though most of it had dried on his cheek and down his shoulder and arm.

She knew he was trying to offer comfort, and she nodded, turning forward again as the rope jerked her tethered hands, making her stumble over a rock in the path.

All this way, only to be taken by slavers on their route to

sell their wares. She sucked in another breath as she stumbled over another stone. She dared not speak, dared not even breathe in their direction lest they take her for the missing girl who was stolen from Zuko's castle.

All this way to watch the only friend she had ever known—the one who had rescued her, set her free, and brought her nearly home—die in front of her. Die in the act of saving her. Die for the very cause he had sworn to give his life.

Silent sobs shook her shoulders as tears burned hot trails down her cheeks. She looked ahead to see Lena, then Adrian, then Motle, her child slung across her front, and only one hand tied so she could keep the child in her tight grip. It wasn't terror written in every line of their faces and the sagging of their shoulders—it was defeat.

They too had tasted freedom, had felt the coolness of it like a breeze. Felt it like water to one dying of thirst, flowing over tongues and throats parched for it. Let it wash over their souls like the blood of their Savior, setting them free to a world they had never known.

One with hope, with a desire for more, and with the gift of a life that they thought never could be theirs.

They had all tasted of it. Seen its goodness. Even in the fear that pervaded a journey through Rusalka, the fact that they had yet to experience the true goodness of a place of freedom, they still had hope. They still tasted something that was theirs, but was too far away to be believed for.

The substance of things hoped for and the evidence of things not yet seen...

They had all tasted and seen of the goodness of the Lord. Be it in the face of a stranger showing kindness, protection, and hospitality to them, in the breaking of chains, or in the love that came in the form of an arm to help them over a rough way.

He dwelt among them, because He lived *in* them.

She choked on another sob. She would go back. She would be sold across the sea. They could take her anywhere and do anything to her, but her soul would remain untouched. The King had placed a light inside of her, a light that could never be put out, and a love that would grow no matter the thorns to bloom into something beautiful for His glory.

Just like the cloud of witnesses that had seen her along this way.

The light inside her wouldn't go out. It couldn't.

Because what the Lord had set ablaze could never be tamped out.

ELGON, ONE YEAR AGO...

While the capital city of Niran was teeming with those who had come from near and far to see their queen off, though the markets clattered with the sound of people and even here, on the ramparts, he heard the noise of their voices and their feet, Elgon felt so utterly alone.

Alone, yet not alone as the nearness of the Holy Spirit drew him closer, holding him together in a world that felt so broken he wanted to let himself fall apart.

It was one day. One day in the public eye. One day to give his people the chance they deserved to say goodbye. One day to let their condolences, sorrowful eyes, and painful memories choke him till he could no longer breathe. One day to be theirs, and then he could mourn in peace, pray for his daughter, and try to string together the fallen thread of his hope that had scattered about the floor like beads torn from their place.

His eyes were dry. His face set like stone. The sun was setting, and one last pyre would be sent. One last boat laden with the scent of a thousand violets. One last arrow of flame sent flying over the sea to find its place in the ship that bore the memory of his wife to the setting sun.

He drew in a shuddering breath. He hated that this day was for more than just himself and his people. He felt the knife twist in his gut at the thought that this day was more than just a remembrance and honoring of Violet. Today was also for optics for the kingdom that held his daughter captive as much as it was for him and his people to mourn.

The pyre of fire would be a signal to the king across the mountain that Elgon Indulf of Elira had given up hope. That his heart had wavered, and he no longer waited, no longer sent messengers, no longer yearned for the day when his wife and child would be returned to him.

He had asked that today, instead of receiving guests, that they would be able to leave their wishes, prayers, and condolences in note form at the throne while he was elsewhere.

Not without Violet. Not on his own.

Something of the last thirteen years had been the understanding that every single moment he spent on the dais without her by his side was a reminder that she would be there again one day. That her presence would return, her heart would beat near his own once more. Every time he took that throne, he glanced at the empty one beside it, prayed for her return, and consoled himself with the thought that she would fill it again one day.

But now that throne was empty forever, void of her presence, the ready smile on her lips, the teasing tone and words, and the heart that beat for himself and in service to her people like no one he had ever met.

He wasn't ready to stand at his place again, alone. Not yet.

A throat was cleared behind him, and he turned to see Kenton, his hands folded in front of him and his head bowed in respect. "Sir, it's time."

Elgon nodded, drawing in a breath of air, the scent of violets wafting up from the garden and bringing back memories that mended the tears in his soul.

He followed Kenton out to the alure that looked down upon the Sirene Sea. Each footstep sent a picture riveting through his mind, nailed there with the passion and love of a generation.

Violet, her face glowing with sweat and her hair glowing in a golden mane tied back with a scarf, her wispy curls, always escaping, pressed against her face with the perspiration.

Her first timid smile, the one that set his soul ablaze and made him question his place in the world all at once.

The worry lines of her brow as she tended him in their first days together, the fear and trembling that weighed her shoulders down with every breath and made him want to lift it from her with every fiber of his being.

Her face on their wedding day, the hymn of the King's love and nearness echoing through Raintamount forest, and her eyes shining like stars as they stared straight into his.

The smile the wind tried to snatch away, the whipping of

her skirt against him, and the feel of her in his arms when she told him that he would be a father.

It was so real it was almost as if she was there, in front of him, her hair thrashing about in wild abandon, the sea air tangling with her skirts and tossing them about in the wind.

She turned to look at him, and he froze, his feet tied to the ground, his heart refusing to beat any rhythm in his chest. He tried to breathe, but air had fled from his lungs.

She smiled at him, the joy and abandon of her discovery of her unborn child overshadowed with a soft sadness and compassion as she laid a hand over her abdomen.

She's yours, my love. I serve at the behest of a higher kingdom now. Tend the Rose.

He couldn't blink, couldn't move; he gasped for air and she was gone. Her shadow no longer falling across the alure, the dying sun throwing golden light and shadows across the sea and over his face. The warmth of it caressed his skin amidst the chilled sea breeze.

The pounding of the waves below, the hushed voices floating up over the wall and singing, the words of the hymn landing like a healing balm on his heart.

Your love remains,
Your promise is sure.
Even though the darkness falls
Your heart toward us is pure.

ZUKO, ONE YEAR AGO...

"They've given up at last, Rebus. Not much longer now and we'll make our ploy for the throne." Zuko stroked the hair on his chin, letting his fingers steeple beneath his beard, and allowed himself a small smile as the body of the last remaining foil to his plans was carried from the room.

Rebus was pale and sullen as he stood beside his father, the looks of his mother the only thing marring his icy and cold stare, so much like Zuko's own. But there was still insubordination in his face. The lad, though growing up under his roof as his son, still had no true understanding of the immovable mountain of a man he was up against. He would yield in time. Though he may need to experience pain before that were to occur.

Pain was the only thing men understood. He could tell a man something, but it was only when he had twisted his threats into reality that they truly understood.

"I don't understand why you had to kill him. He brought us more revenue in a year than any other vassal on this god-forsaken land."

Rebus would learn that one did not speak out of turn with such vehemence, especially to the king. Curling his hand into a fist, Zuko backhanded the boy, his rings slicing into skin and splattering blood. He wiped the drops that had splattered on his fingers onto his robe, staring straight ahead and not at the son who now held his face, shock and pain mixed with anger and—ah, there it was—a touch of fear.

"I'll explain it to you this time, since I see I cannot expect you to learn. Enguerrand was a sly one, one who sought to steal not just the Eliran throne, but this one as well. He thought I didn't notice, but his trade was made known to me more than a few years ago. I let it play out till he took a step too far, and then of course he paid—with his life. And no, I know you are thinking it, but he was of no more use to us. My spies had infiltrated his own service and taken over communication with Eris and the others we sell to. His trade, his riches, his wealth, and his secrets are mine. And as you see, he no longer has need of them."

Rebus clenched his jaw and shifted on his seat, well aware that to leave without permission would gain him more pain.

"But now we merely wait, with no obstacle in our way. She'll be old enough to wed in just a few years time—young, yes, but old enough to bear a child. You two will be Rusalka's bid for the throne. An heir worthy of swaying an entire nation. And all without one drop of blood spilled unnecessarily."

Rebus swallowed, shifting again, blood still dripping from a gash above the eyebrow.

Zuko rolled his eyes. "Aye, you can go see your wounds tended."

His son scuttled from the room without a backward glance, holding a sleeve to his forehead.

Let the boy run. He'd be tethered to life as a king soon enough.

If only he knew just how easy his simple life was and how much his father had done to make it so.

Zuko stood, stretching like a cat waking from its nap, and flung his cloak out of the way and over his shoulder. Perhaps a bit of air would do him good.

Striding from the room, he moved past the dark pool of blood on the floor, his boots leaving footprints across the polished stone floors like fallen petals from a rose.

MALCOLM, PRESENT DAY...

The light pierced his eyes, sharp and so bright he could almost taste it.

He gasped, the weight on his chest still there even after all this time.

How long had he been asleep? He couldn't feel his fingers, his arms…not even his legs. It was almost as though he floated somewhere above it all, but then there was that pinching feeling at the base of his neck. He wouldn't feel that if he were dead and floating around the ceiling of the cave like a ghost.

Why was there light in a cave?

Blinking, he tried to let his eyes get used to the brightness, but it shone even through his squinting and then closed eyelids.

Rosalie.

Dear God.

He turned his head, a groan ripping from his chest at the movement. He couldn't see her. Straining against the weight on him, he twisted his head around, peering into the darkness of the cave. Rocks surrounded him, pinning him to the ground. He couldn't find her.

The hole in the roof of the cave was positioned just so to let the light of the sun shine directly in his face.

Why had there been a cave in? What was the rumbling he had heard before? He sucked in another breath, his mind frozen in time, unable to fully think, to fully understand what had transpired.

"Rosalie." It was barely a whisper against his dry, raspy throat.

"Rosalie!" He tried again. Louder this time. Dust clogged

his nostrils.

"Rosalie!" He screamed it.

Nothing.

Panting, fear overcame him, and his breath came short and fast. He coughed, the pressure on his lungs growing even fiercer. Every breath a reminder, a dagger to the ribs, with accusations on the edge.

Failure.

Danger.

Broken.

Lost.

Failure.

Worthless.

He was the wrong choice for this mission from the start. He should have said no that day when Elgon's eyes had drilled into his heart with the pain of his sorrow and his desperation. He should have listened to the voice that murmured deep inside that he was the wrong choice, that his failure would come back to haunt him and he would—undoubtedly—fail again.

He should have refused to be the one who was sent.

He had just made it worse.

Rosalie was gone, headed for a worse fate than before. Deep in his heart, he knew. He knew she had been found, taken back to her prison in the mountains, like a bird in a cage. And even if she wasn't yet, she soon would be. Those dark knights were far too close, and everything that they had worked for, these fourteen years of praying, hoping, pleading with the King of the universe to give them the answer, the recompense that they sought… All of it had been for nothing.

Nothing at all.

He let his head fall to the side, avoiding the light that pierced him through.

He deserved to die. Everything in him could see no way forward.

He wished the light would go away. He felt naked. Alone. Vulnerable. His heart bare to the mountain air and blasted with the spotlight of terror at being seen for who he truly was.

The failure he knew himself to be.

"Hello?"

He opened his eyes. His arm was pinned beneath a rock. His entire body was. But he saw his hand. Tried to move it. It was nearly black with bruises, completely blue and purple.

"Hello? Anyone there?"

He had thought it a trick of his imagination—but no, it was a voice. The pain ebbed over him, the black around the edges of his vision gathering again.

He tried to speak, but nothing came out except a cough.

"Ah, I found you."

He opened his eyes again, squinting at the figure of a man standing over him, his shadow cast over Malcolm's form and backlit by the blinding sun.

Either this stranger was an enemy and Malcolm was about to meet his end...

Or he might just be his salvation.

PRISON OR FREE?

MALCOLM, PRESENT DAY...

"If you're going to kill me—just do it now," he wheezed, his words barely above a whisper.

"Well, that would be a perfect waste, now wouldn't it?" The stranger sank down to his knees beside Malcolm, glancing over the rocks that covered him and pressed him into the earth. "You do look like you're in a spot of trouble, brother. Let's get you out of this mess."

"A girl—did you see a girl? Please, leave me and find her. I owe my life for hers."

"All in good time." The stranger grunted, shoving at a rock and heaving it off of Malcolm's torso.

Malcolm cried out as the pressure released. "No, please," he rasped. "I mean it. She is more important. I need to know

535

she is safe." He was almost sobbing, his breath coming shallow over the crushed feeling of his ribs.

"Oh, she's just fine. Just fine indeed." The stranger grunted again, heaving another rock, his tone cheerful.

Malcom bit back a curse. This man was either dense or useless—both, perhaps. "Please!" he begged, his cry nearly a scream like a strangled mountain lion. "I beg you. She is worth more to me than my own life. Please, find her." Tears leaked out the corners of his eyes, falling into his ears. "Find her. Find Rosalie."

"A rose is nothing without the hedge that protects its delicate petals." Another grunt and another piece of space opened up on Malcolm's body, meeting the cold air. Why couldn't he move?

"Please." His words were weak, and suddenly the pain came thundering back, the numbness gone like a flood slowly leaving his body. He was suddenly chilled, every rock that was pressing into his back from where he lay perfectly clear and apparent to him.

His nerve endings screamed with the horror of it. He moaned, bucking the pain and nearly thrashing with it.

"Shh, the King's not done with you yet." The stranger paused, whistling through his teeth. "Panu." Whirling to look at him, he took Malcolm's face in his hands. "Lad, you'll have to bear with this one. It can't be helped. He will give you grace to bear it. But it won't be easy."

"What—?" Malcolm swallowed back the bitter taste in his mouth as he turned his head to watch. The man pulled his belt from around his jerkin.

He watched, almost as if he were completely set apart,

hovering in a world between alive and dead. Why was his hand black and blue? Why couldn't he feel it? There was a rock in the way and he couldn't turn his head enough to see where the rock ended near his shoulder and now the stranger was blocking his view of what he was doing with his hands.

He was about to die, wasn't he? He squeezed his eyes shut and turned his head. *Lord, I deserve it.*

The stranger babbled, his words making no sense, but his tone a plea.

The man wrapped the belt around Malcolm's arm just below the shoulder and above where the rock still lay, crushing his arm. As he pulled it tight, Malcolm gasped, unable to breathe anymore, his breath frozen in his lungs.

Nothing came from him until the words snuck past parched lips.

"Let me die!"

"I said the King's not done with you yet. You forget that whatever evil you perceive you've done is of no account. The ledger is clean. His is at the very least. Yours needs some work."

Blackness took him for a breath, and then a puff of air made its way into his lungs.

"Breathe, man. Breathe."

Malcolm gasped, his eyes flying open and dragging air into his lungs. Cold, pure, mountain air. The rock no longer rested on his arm.

"You're not going to die. Not if I have anything to say about it. There's someone out there, a few actually, who desperately need you."

Malcolm focused on the owner of the voice. His face was

covered with a beard. The light had started to wane, the hole in the ceiling no longer positioned right below the sun. He tried to blink. To feel his arm.

"Here, drink this. You'll need it." He lifted Malcolm's head and held a cup to his lips. It was wine. He swallowed it, a bit of life coming back into him just from the moisture, but then he felt a warmth flowing through his veins, around his chest, the weight lifting. He dragged air into his lungs, taking deep breaths between each swallow. The stranger rested Malcolm's head on his knee.

"Look, I have something to say, and it's not going to be easy. You've made it through a rough piece, there's no mistaking that, but you'll have to make it through the next without much help from your arm, I'm afraid."

It took a few moments and a few more swallows for the words he had heard to catch up in his mind, and he turned quickly, a stab of pain lacing up his arm and around his neck. His right arm below the man's belt that was wrapped tightly around his bicep was completely black and blue. The flesh looked…dead.

The wine tried to burn its way back up his throat, but he swallowed it back, squeezing his eyes shut and dragging in lungfuls of air. There was a crackling around his ribs when he took in so much air, but the pain it brought lessened the pain of the realization. He was no longer a whole man.

"You're whole. More whole than you think you are."

His eyes sprang open. There was a mirth in the man's eyes. But it wasn't a painful jab. There was so much compassion dwelling there on his face that it only came across with an understanding that he was trying to lighten the mood.

"How did—" He broke off, words hard.

"Drink." He held the wineskin to Malcolm's lips again and let him swallow. "It's not hard to hear the aching of a heart that's been screaming the same thing for fourteen years."

Malcolm froze. Who was this stranger?

"Aye." he sighed. There was a sorrow in the strangers face, pain, and his shoulders sagged as if the weight of the burden was nearly too much for him to bear. "You've listened to lies a long time, Malcolm, son of Killian."

Malcolm started, his hair standing on end, and he tried to rise.

He was restrained with a hand to the shoulder. "Not yet. You have need of your rest. You have a piece to travel yet. Your journey is not yet over."

"How?"

"I know more than you could ever possibly understand. I know the way you decry yourself, the words you speak over yourself in the darkness when nobody hears. I know the pain you bear, the cross you carry, but you don't understand, my son. He already carried it for you."

Malcolm could barely move. Barely breathe.

"I know. You think you've hidden it. You think because it lives in your mind and your mind alone that no one could possibly know. But you have to understand. Your part of the story was not finished. Is still not. Your journey only began that day. Your pain became your passion. Your heart broken open was all the more ready to serve the glory of the King. Your sorrow became your strength. Don't you see? Who else could I have sent across mountain, river, and through the very fire to set her free?"

Malcolm could barely see for the tears, his heart hearing words his mind could not comprehend. A dagger of truth pierced his heart, stabbing the very essence of the constant refrain that had been his life for the last fourteen years.

"Do you not see that His ways are higher? His plans greater? And His path so much more widespread and winding into every conceivable circumstance? Your failure has been His triumph. Not because of anything that you did. Or anything that you did not do.

"But because He is in the business of taking broken things and making them whole again. He is in the business of setting captives free. And because one was taken, two even, hundreds have been set free. Not just from their chains, but from their sin.

"His gospel became a light, a path in the darkness, a country turned inside out with the very truth they are afraid of. The very truth and heart that they seek to crush. It has come about that their country is bursting with light and love and holiness at the very seams. All because of your perceived failure."

Malcolm sucked in another breath, his lungs feeling lighter, freer, the pain of the wound to his heart lessening as the knife plunged deeper.

"You see," the stranger bent forward, whispering in Malcolm's ear, a softness and tenderness in the hand that rested on his forehead. "You *are* worthy to Him. You are *worthy*. Not because of what you've done or not done. He bore all of that. His burden was the brokenness you carry. His heart was rent in two that you might live in life and abundant truth. He came for you as assuredly as He came for the rest. Guilt and shame have no place here, not in the life of one bought by the blood of Jesus Christ."

The last vestiges of the horror and darkness within him clamored to the surface, every name he had ever called himself, every last, broken piece. And the knife dug deeper.

"You are free because He set you free, and whom the Son sets free is free indeed!" The man's voice was a shout, echoing off the walls of the cavern with a power that made the stones and pebbles tremble.

"Now go. Remember who He calls you and no one else. Go. Your journey is not yet done. Your path not complete. Come. We must fly."

The stranger hauled Malcolm to his feet, and somehow the pain was gone, hovering, waiting to pounce, but removed from his shoulders.

His mind wavered, his vision fading, but his feet were moving. His arm resting solidly on the shoulder of the one beside him. The arm around his waist was firm like the bough of an oak.

He could barely see where he was going, but his heart was lighter, and he was able to move at a pace he did not understand.

The ground was a blur, rocks tumbling and bouncing out of his way on the path, his very feet flying with a speed he had not thought himself capable of.

The sun had hidden behind the mountain peaks, and his vision blurred from gray, to black, to white hot, then gray again. Sometimes he saw the mountains, sometimes all he saw was the trees. But he moved, something beyond himself dragging him farther.

"Don't forget."

His hand touched rough bark, his good shoulder leaning against the pine that scratched his face, sap sticky beneath his fingers. He blinked. The treeline was up ahead. A line.

Was that a wall? Stones, waist high, covered in moss and pine needles.

Voices were nearby. He tried to move toward them, his feet stumbling, his weight falling forward, but his feet moving just enough to catch himself, one foot, then the other.

He fell against the fence, the pain in his ribs flaring to life again. Breathing hurt, and the air he swallowed broke the fog that clung to him.

The voices were louder as he used his good hand to prop himself up while he lifted one leg, then the other.

Losing his balance, he slipped from the wall and fell to his good side, rolling onto his back and staring at the blue sky overhead. White clouds floated across his vision, an orange hue to the side of them. The sun must be setting. He felt a breath of wind, and he rolled, pulling himself to his knees, then his feet.

The voices drew nearer still, and he staggered to his feet, stumbling towards them and the foggy outlines of cabins and a wooden fence. He blinked, trying to make them clearer. He did not know if he were entering the territory of friend or foe, but something moved his feet along, even when he could not think to do so.

"Who goes there?" The words were faint, echoing in the back of his mind like an empty cave.

"Help," was all he said, and the black, fuzzy shapes drew nearer.

He pitched forward, his foot catching, and the strength he

had carried suddenly draining from his feet like a barrel tipped on end. He landed in someone's arms as they gently lowered him to the ground.

He blinked away the grayness that swept in.

"Malcolm? God alive, man." The face spoke, the blonde shock of hair falling in front of the green eyes speaking of home, and…life. "Someone get me a stretcher!" He shouted past Malcolm, the sound reverberating in his head.

"Kenton? We need help."

"We? Who is with you?" Kenton looked about, his muscles tensing and holding Malcolm closer, adjusting him so that he lay more comfortably against his knee.

"The man. He pulled me out."

"Out of what? What man? Malcolm? Stay with me! Hurry it up!" He shouted again, and Malcolm blinked, turning his head.

An empty field leading to the wall blocking off the forest was all that met his gaze before his eyes lowered shut and he let the black claim him.

ROSALIE, PRESENT DAY...

Hands still bound, Rosalie stumbled on after the line of the others. They had spent the night by the fire, eating barely anything, while the men who had captured them and the others that they had joined had feasted on venison stew, the smell enough to make her faint with hunger.

The children were crying; there were far too many little ones. Her blood boiled. There were about thirty people in all, the group larger than the seven ringleaders could have managed on their own had most of the captives not been so weak, sickly, or small.

They'd been made to walk all day, two lines of slaves, tethered to each other with both of their hands tied, the men forced to carry packs like mules while the leaders rode and jerked the line anytime someone stumbled or fell to their knees from exhaustion. The children cried silently from hunger, and the men kicked them from their positions on their saddle whenever any of them got too loud, promising them that they would eat when they reached their destination.

Wherever that was.

Motle sobbed quietly in front of her. Her baby had cried all day and had gone silent, either asleep or too exhausted to cry anymore. With both her hands now tied in front of her just like the others, Motle couldn't even tend to her unless they stopped.

Rosalie looked behind her at Adrian who was floundering along and nodded for him to move forward. If only she could take the baby off of Motle's back and give her a break, carrying the wee one for a little of the way at least.

Adrian nodded, his small face serious and understanding, strong for such a small boy and filled with intelligence that lit up his black eyes. He trotted just a bit, slackening the line between them, and at a smooth point in the path, Rosalie stepped faster, gaining ground on Motle and scooping her tied hands under the baby and lifting, releasing some of the pressure off Motle's shoulders.

The woman sniffed, half turning, the dark circles under her eyes brimmed with tears. Rosalie motioned with her head. Motle untied the shawl that held the baby against her back and slowly let the child slide till Rosalie had her cradled in her arms, using her tethered hands to jostle the child till Freuda's head was resting on her shoulder.

The baby mewled softly, her voice broken and weary. Rosalie adjusted the baby till she was fit snugly in the open place between her hands and her chest, her arms wrapping around the child. She walked carefully, avoiding stones and ridges that would trip her up, and glanced ahead at Motle.

The woman was rolling her neck as if to relieve the tension, and she sent a grateful look over her shoulder. Rosalie smiled softly back.

"It's going to be all right. Jesus won't let us falter. He'll be our strength, no matter what's ahead," she whispered, looking past Motle to the next slave driver along the train of captives. She knew from her limited experience that they would not appreciate any of the slaves talking.

Silence was their greatest desire.

Motle sent her a quizzical look and then rubbed her elbow against her side, rolling up her sleeve and lifting her hands to show Rosalie her wrist over her shoulder. A small dove was painted in ink on the rounded bone that protruded on the outside of her arm.

Rosalie dipped her head in acknowledgement, bouncing the baby when she stirred as she walked.

Motle heaved a sigh and nodded back. Sisters, even in the silence. Kindred spirits carrying a hope that would outlive and outlast any abuse.

Rosalie's arms grew weary, but she shifted the weight of the baby as the walk wound on. The daylight waning in the west as the sun set and the shadows of the trees lengthened, the massive pines stretching forth their dark shadows like hands reaching to swallow the earth.

The golden rays of the sun were cold as the shadows claimed them, the heat, short-lived at this altitude, cooling quickly and sending a shiver down Rosalie's spine. A captive slipped and fell ahead, skidding down the hill a few steps and heaving the line with them. Rosalie caught herself and kept her balance as the entire line swayed with the movement. They would have to break for the night soon or someone would get hurt.

Freuda stirred, waking with a cry so weak and languid that Rosalie's heart nearly broke. The child had to be starving. Motle's own sobs joined in with her child's, and Rosalie bounced the mite in her arms, sore from carrying her this whole way.

How horrible a thing to have tasted freedom and then have it ripped back from your grasp.

They were kept tied, allowed to sit while the men made a fire, and were given a small morsel of stale flatbread that had been left over from the previous day. Even though her stomach cramped from hunger, she held Freuda in her lap while Motle ate and drank, giving the mother the rest she needed.

Something akin to hope beat in Rosalie's breast. The understanding that this was not the end of her story. Something about either being sold or brought back to Zuko didn't fit within her understanding of what was to come. Perhaps it was a false hope, but it was hope nonetheless.

I am not finished yet.

She had already been through the worst things she could

imagine, and the concept of all of it being for nothing seemed so wrong in her heart that her mind had started to believe it.

Malcolm's sacrifice could not be for nothing. The journey here, every soul they had encountered who had helped them and shown them the way, their sacrifice would not be for nothing.

She looked around at the faces of those that were with her, compassion and understanding welling within her. These were her family, her brothers and sisters. They had experienced their life being stolen from them. What they had loved, they had lost. Their freedom had been something that had been given, and then it had been taken away. And yet they stood.

If only they knew the hope that was afforded them. The heart of Christ that could be theirs for the asking. If only they knew the depths of faith and joy He could give even in the darkest of nights. If only they knew of the sacrifice He had given so that they might be free in their hearts if not in their body.

She needed to tell them. She whispered the words of her King into the ears of the child that slept in her lap, the sing-song pattern of her voice filling her own exhausted, weary heart with courage.

"My soul waits on the Lord, for my expectation is from him. He only is my rock and my salvation, my defense, I shall not be moved. In God is my salvation and my glory, the rock of my strength and my refuge is in Him. Trust Him at all times. Pour out your heart before Him. God is a refuge for us."

Motle's tears had dried, and she leaned in closer to Rosalie. She noticed that Motle and a few of the others were listening.

She let her voice grow in volume, while still keeping it soft enough that their captors would not hear.

"To you, O Lord, I lift up my soul. O my God, in you I trust. Let me not be put to shame. Let not my enemies exult over me. Indeed, none who wait for you shall be put to shame. They shall be ashamed who are wantonly treacherous.

"Make me to know your ways, O Lord, Teach me your paths. Lead me in your truth and teach me. For you are the God of my salvation, for you I wait all the day long."

Those around her had stilled, almost as if listening on bated breath, waiting for her words to reach their weary souls like one dying from thirst and waiting for a drop of water.

"You have come to set the captives free, to preach the good news to the poor, to bring sight to the blind, to deliver those who are oppressed. You have brought us this far; you will not forsake us now."

A few breathed a whispered amen. One of the Rusalkan captors wandered over, the guard pressing the slaves away from each other, and she stilled her voice, waiting for him to pass as he ensured that those who were talking were silenced.

"Get some sleep. You lot will need it. We don't have time to waste, and we don't plan on taking it easy. We'll reach the waterways tomorrow one way or another. If you can't walk there, you'll be dragged."

Rosalie helped Motle take her baby to nurse, allowing her to lie down without tangling the rope that still bound them together. She pulled her feet close to her body, hugging her knees to her chest and resting her chin on top of them.

She caught Ben's eye from across the way where he sat with the few men who were double tied and held closer to the captors as they were perceived as more likely to escape.

He gave her a nod, a certain spark in his eyes. He was planning something, she could tell. He seemed totally at peace and resting in his captivity, as if waiting for just the right moment to spring. Ready and waiting for whatever was ahead.

"I haven't heard those words spoken out loud in some time."

Rosalie turned. A middle-aged woman, her gray and dirty blonde hair tied back in a dingy scarf, lifted her skirt and crept toward her, adjusting the rope around her wrists so that she didn't wake or disturb those she was tied to.

Rosalie pulled her cloak closer. "I've forgotten to speak them out loud."

The woman smiled, her eyes shining in the golden light of the fire as she settled next to and slightly behind Rosalie. "We all do. But you've reminded us of something that we might have lost, and spoken something that others have found a hope where they had none before. Even those who do not believe will have heard your words and wondered at them. The scriptures have that power, don't they?"

Rosalie nodded.

"Where do you come from, that you know such words by heart, child?"

"I've come from the interior, near Izevel mountain."

"The king's castle? What did you do to deserve being sold down for the ships? A pretty young thing like you?" Her voice held surprise that Rosalie didn't know how to answer. Did she dare tell this woman how she had escaped and been recaptured?

"I wasn't sold." She was too afraid to say more.

"Ah. Taken then? Ah, were you one of those that escaped and were re-taken? That rarely happens, but when those that are once set free are retaken, the masters rarely look upon that kindly."

"Is any slave looked upon kindly?" Rosalie asked, her heart breaking for the people gathered around her.

She had no idea that slavers worked so closely to the Eliran border. And that they sought to trade their captives off near here. What waterways did the slaver drivers speak of?

"Rarely." The old woman's wrinkled brow dipped. "Though, you might be. Those that are young and pretty stand a much better chance than those that are simply seen as a back for heavy labor."

Rosalie felt a chill run down her spine.

The woman leaned in over her shoulder. "But one who takes truth with her as her weapon will be free even though her hands are bound."

Rosalie turned to look the woman in the face. There was a smile on her lips, and she nodded, raising her hand to touch Rosalie's shoulder, but it was held back by her bindings. She sighed, her eyes filling with tears. "Though the Lord may have other plans for your future."

The words resonated with something so deep in Rosalie's heart it felt like a well springing forth from dry and frozen places. *I have a different end for your story. This is not the end of my glory in your life.*

"Your mother would be so proud of you. I see His spirit in you and His courage in your face," the woman whispered, a soft sadness in her tone that Rosalie couldn't quite understand.

As the woman turned to curl up for sleep, Rosalie felt her heart swell within her. She had never known her mother. Had lost any chance to be with her, learn from her, glean of her wisdom. Malcolm had told her little, but what she did know, she admired. But something about the soft way this stranger had told her such an observation increased the faith in her heart that knew she was not meant to continue on to slavery.

She would return to Elira, she was sure of it. But there she would not stay. Elira would be her home, but Rusalka was her calling. The people here would need to know the depths of their heavenly King's love for them, the freedom He had paid for that would set them free. The peace He had wrought that would give them courage, and the wounds He had born that theirs would be made clean.

And she would not leave them to suffer a fate she had survived by the grace of a God who had given her the hope to live it through. She looked at the exhausted, weary faces around her before she curled up on her cloak. She wouldn't leave them here. If God had a story for her to live, she would use it to bring freedom to those like her.

ELGON, PRESENT DAY...

"Majesty!" Tobias panted into the room, his feet pattering over the stones, interrupting the servant who was speaking to Elgon and nearly tripping over the man's feet as he dashed up to them.

Elgon gripped the young man's shoulder, using his hand to hold him steady and keep him from plummeting to the floor face first. "What on earth is it, lad? Take a deep breath."

"There's—no—time—for a deep—breath." He gasped for air, his lungs heaving and his hand pressed to his side, the expression on his face full of frustration.

"There is always time for a deep breath. Come now, you really are going to wear yourself out."

"Malcolm's back!" Tobias blurted, gasping again and running his hands through his disheveled hair that stood nearly on end.

Elgon froze as he remembered that Tobias had been with Kenton.

At the Wood River outpost and training grounds.

And now he was here.

Malcolm.

His tongue was frozen even as a torrent of adrenaline coursed through his veins, his skin growing hot as his muscles tightened like springs ready to fly.

"What do you mean Malcolm is back?" Elgon waved the servant from the room, dismissing him from the meeting that would no longer continue. He bent slightly and took Tobias by the shoulders so he could get a better view of his face.

"He stumbled from the woods this morning. On the border near the outpost." Tobias lifted a hand to his chest, trying to suck in oxygen, his eyes nearly too wide for his small face.

Elgon swallowed back the lump in his throat. "And he was alone?"

Tobias nodded, probably grateful for a question he didn't have to verbally respond to.

"Where is he now?" Elgon stood, his hands rolling into fists at his side. He needed to get there.

"Being tended to by the outpost medicinal. He came in injured."

Elgon's heart stilled in his chest. His child. His brother. *Lord, help.*

"Come, we must go to him." He strode from the room, trying to keep himself from running, but his massive steps ate up the ground anyway on his way to the stables.

So close yet so far away. Malcolm had finally made it back to Eliran soil, but his ward was nowhere to be found? What had happened? What had brought them this far only to separate them? And what had wounded Malcolm?

His heart beat in time with his steps and pounded in his ears while he saddled Sigeric with all speed. The old boy was getting on in years, but still had a spring in his step and life in his eyes as he tossed his head and pranced sideways, touching his nose to Elgon's hip as if sensing his distress.

Putting his foot in the stirrup, he threw his leg over the saddle and trotted out after Tobias, already ahead on his horse. Sigeric's hooves echoed hollowly as they struck the cobblestones on his way out of the city.

He tried to still the horror that filled his heart at the running of his mind. *Lord, where is my child? Keep her safe. Protect her.*

And bring her home to me.

Thirty-Three

COURAGE AND STUBBORNNESS

MALCOLM...

Malcolm swallowed hard, trying to avoid looking at the stump that was now all that remained of his right arm. His sword arm.

"He said he couldn't save it. It had been without blood flow for too long." Kenton stood over him, his arms folded and his leg bouncing with covert anxiety.

"Help me up." Malcolm tried to heave himself to a sitting position and swing his legs over the edge of the bed. Gray clouded his vision, but he made it nonetheless.

"Are you insane? The medicinal said you shouldn't be moved!" Kenton reacted and threw his arms out as if to catch Malcolm. As if he had need of such assistance.

"I don't care what he says. I'm going with you." Malcolm stood, his feet steadier than he had dared hope for. He pulled his shirt back on over his head, what remained of his lost arm wrapped in thick bandages and tied to his chest in a sling. It still throbbed, but the draught the medicinal had given him had not only lessened the pain, but given him hope that he could return to Rosalie and rescue her from the clutches of those who had taken her.

Kenton huffed and let an innocent curse fly. "You are hardly fit for any sort of travel, let alone on a raiding party into enemy territory!" His face was red, and his hands balled up in fists at his side.

"I don't really give a care for what you have to say. I'm going, and that's final. Don't make me pull rank."

"You lost your arm!"

Malcolm whirled, hoping that he hid the slight bout of dizziness that swept over him at the sudden movement. "You don't think I know that?"

Kenton might as well have had steam coming from his ears as his jaw tensed from clenching his teeth. "You can't even hold a sword," he murmured.

"Well, it's a good thing you're coming along then, isn't it?" Malcolm turned and ducked under the tent flap, beckoning with his good hand to a squire who stood to the side.

His only hand.

He swallowed. "You there. Fetch me a horse along with one for your commander." The boy ran off, and Malcolm turned once more to Kenton, who had followed him from the tent. "How many do you wish to take with us? I'll let you manage your men since you are far more acquainted with them than I."

Kenton grumbled, still glaring, then whistled around two

fingers. A young knight trotted up and listened to his directions before he dashed off, presumably to fetch those that would make up their posse.

"I wish you'd reconsider." Kenton's arms were folded across his leather armor.

"You could stop wasting your time on such a fruitless measure and instead pray that we can find the princess and return her safely to her father."

"But—"

"For the King's sake Kenton, I've waited fourteen long years and prayed for this moment, along with the rest of the kingdom. There is no time to waste on useless arguing, and I can certainly rest later. Please, dear friend." The anger fled from his voice, and he dropped his tone. "Please, help me in this. I can't look him in the face till I see this mission done. He doesn't deserve this. And neither does she. She's all alone out there, and I can't let them take her. Not when we are this close."

"I know." Kenton rested his hand on Malcolm's good shoulder, his eyes meeting his friend's. "I know that, but I worry for you, no matter what you say. I wouldn't dare let her wander alone out there another second. We'll get her. I promise."

Malcolm gathered himself. The words from the stranger who had dressed his wound and helped him to the border echoed in his spirit like some loud voice off the caverns of a cave.

"Don't forget."

He drew a sharp breath. If God could forgive a man like him, then He was certainly capable of giving him the strength he needed to see this mission through.

He hadn't made it this far to fail now.

A group of soldiers rode up, the reins of extra horses in their hands, their leather armor laced and buckled up, swords at their hips. The horses pranced, sensing the energy of their owners and snuffling, throwing their heads and stamping their feet.

Kenton offered his shoulder and his hands in a stirrup which Malcolm used as leverage to climb aboard the saddle. His legs shook at the effort. He sat straight while Kenton mounted, then urged his steed forward with his legs, posting and wincing as the pain of the trot that turned into a canter twinged in his lost arm.

He retraced his steps through the forest, finding the tracks, and happy to see that he hadn't been imagining a stranger's assistance. There were two sets of footsteps dragging through these woods. It took them a few hours to trace their way up the mountain and back to the collapsed cave. Swallowing the bitter taste that rose in the back of his throat at seeing where he had nearly died, he instead remained atop his mount while Kenton perused the area to pick up any signs of Rosalie, Benaiah, and the rest of their party who had been taken, most likely by slavers.

A sharp whistle pierced the cliffs and crevices, and he prodded his horse over the rocks and around the fallen stone. Kenton was remounting his own horse and threw a hand over his head in a wave Malcolm's direction. "I found the trail! A group of them went this way!"

Malcolm pulse was racing, and it made him weak, his arm throbbing. He could still feel a phantom cramp of his missing wrist and hand, and a chill ran up his spine. Swallowing back the nausea in his throat, he focused on breathing in and out with the hoofbeats. Whatever draught the medicinal had given him was wearing off, and some of the exhaustion was setting in. Even though he had been unconscious all night and slept through till noon before they had started on this venture, his body seemed to be running out of energy and the ability to work through the pain.

He did his best to keep up with Kenton. He needed to be coherent and have enough strength and energy to make it through the ordeal ahead. Most slavers were not going to give up their slaves easily, and he knew they might not get Rosalie back without bloodshed. But why was the trail headed toward Elira? Why not back into Rusalka and the direction they had come?

The hours dragged on as the trail pitched up, then down, while steadily making its way toward Wood River and the waterways that cut through the abandoned mines on the way to Niran. Where on earth were these slavers headed? There was no one up this far north to whom they could sell any slaves. Perhaps they knew that they were trapped and were simply trying to escape into the mountains or the mines till the Kingsmen left them alone and they could safely escape back east.

The hair on the back of his neck prickled. Years ago, those who had taken Violet had disappeared into these very mountains, without a trace of a trail…

A soft whistle pierced the air as the sun beat down on his head, the air cold, but the sun hot on his skin. He pulled up his horse behind Kenton, who had lifted a hand to shoulder height, which he then tightened into a fist as a signal to stop and hold.

Malcolm's heart paused in his chest before thundering on. They had to be close now.

Urging his steed forward so that he was near Kenton and rising in his stirrups, he glanced over the layer of trees below them. The trail on the cliff face below was filled with slaves, tethered one after the other in two long lines, bound at the wrist and walking as quickly as they could. He could hear the shouts of the captors as they urged the slaves onward. The leaders seemed to be in a hurry.

"I'll send a group forward and a group behind," Kenton whispered to Malcolm. "We'll trail them. How do you want to play this?" The knight strained his neck to glimpse the group below around the trees.

"Can you see her?" Malcolm whispered back, trying to see around the triangle tops of the pines, but unable to make out Rosalie's figure in the group below.

"Brown hair, brown cloak? You really did disguise her well. I'd never be able to tell her apart. There's only a few down there that match her height and age, but it's hard to know which one she is."

"We can't just ride in there, swords raised, and hope to get to her. We'll need to negotiate."

Kenton nodded. "We want to keep as many of them safe as possible."

"How about all of them?"

Kenton whistled through his teeth with a shake of the head. "It will take some doing, but we'll see how it goes. If they make a move at the captives, we'll have no choice but to ride in and overtake them as best we can."

"They might as well be holding all of them as hostages. They could easily try to harm one of them to ensure that we don't ride in with swords swinging."

Kenton looked thoughtful. But he shook his head. "Nothing for it. We'll need to see it done, regardless. Either we rescue as many as we can, or we rescue none at all. I've only seen about six of the traders, so as long as the men in the slave group join our side, we should be able to take them. Rusalks aren't necessarily known for their fighting prowess."

"You forget Everard and the dark knights."

Kenton nodded. "True. But these are no warriors—they're slavers. Lord favor us, we'll see it done. I'll split the group. You follow them along this ridge, and I'll signal when we're ready to arrest their movements."

Malcolm nodded, urging his horse backward to avoid the lightheaded feeling that suddenly overtook him at the dizzying view of the path below.

Kenton turned his mount, signaled to his men, and they split into two groups. Three went back down the trail to circle around, coming up on the rear of the slave group, while three rode past Malcolm to overtake the front. They moved silently, their horses' hooves shod with leather to ensure a better grip on the rocks and as silent a step as possible to avoid detection.

Kenton rejoined Malcolm, and they waited for the signal.

A hawk's cry—the signal—echoed up the chasm, and they moved toward the front of the group below. The rear guard was in place. Joining their men who stood with swords drawn, the lone bowman had an arrow nocked on the string and ready to be pulled back and let fly at a moment's notice. They took up positions on either side, flanking the rest of their comrades. Kenton drew his sword, and Malcolm went to do the same. His molars clicked as his jaw tensed, sharp pain shooting up his arm with the movement and the realization that his hand no longer existed.

Kenton nodded, giving him the go ahead.

Malcolm cupped his hand around his mouth, his muscles tense at the uncertainty of the moment. "Halloo, halt! We have you surrounded!"

His voice ricocheted off the cliff sides and stone that surrounded them, the location of his voice somewhat disguised by the echoes.

The slavers froze in their steps, hands going to swords at their sides and their heads turning, searching for the source of the shout.

"We demand you set your prisoners free and we will let you go, unharmed," Malcolm shouted. It was taking more effort than he was used to, and it left him feeling weak and lightheaded. He braced himself against the pommel of his saddle.

Confusion reigned on the path. The captives were murmuring and shuffling about, questioning one another and turning this way and that to see if they could find the source of the words that extended a hope of freedom to them.

Another shout echoed behind the group, and this seemed to stir them to a frenzy. Malcolm from his vantage point in the trees gasped when one of the leaders grabbed a woman, her long blonde hair swinging over her shoulder and tangling in her face as he held her to him, his blade at her throat. Kenton tensed beside him, and his horse hopped sideways.

"Stop right there or I'll hurt them!" the man who must've been the leader shouted. The woman in his grasp couldn't speak, but she winced as the rest of the captives either cried out or milled away from their captors in fear.

A few of the children started to cry, and the sound sent shivers of fear and panic up Malcolm's back.

"We do not wish to harm any of you. We outnumber you two to one and will not harm you, we swear it. Only let the captives go or your lives will be forfeit!" Malcolm felt a bit as though he were spinning. Why on earth was shouting requiring so much effort?

"It seems we are at an impasse!" The captor bellowed, turning and pulling the woman with him. "You come down upon us and I'll slit her throat, and hers will only be the first!"

Malcolm's horse shifted on his feet, belying the feelings of worry and concern beating in his own heart. He glanced at Kenton who stared back for a moment. Then he nodded. With a few fingers in the air, he motioned to the archer, who shot his arrow at the man's feet.

"You think we are bluffing, but you would be wrong! Our archers have arrows trained on your men, and should any of your captives come to harm, you'll be dropped dead where you stand!" Kenton's shout echoed through the forest, and the man's face turned red.

Something shifted, and the rest of the captors each grabbed a slave as a body shield, their knives at their throats. Malcolm strained forward as the sound of terrified cries and broken pleas calling for help filled the air.

Another arrow flew, this time without the command to do so, and chaos broke out. Malcolm surged forward, his horse moving swiftly down the incline. The woman the leader had been holding fell to the ground, her eyes wide and her hands at her throat, covered in blood. A young girl rushed toward her.

Rosalie.

Benaiah jumped one of the captors, using the rope that bound his hands to wrap around the man's throat. The slaver's face turned purple before he dropped his blade to reach for the rope at his neck. One of the other men joined suit as Kenton's call for the rest of the kingsmen to attack filled the forest.

Malcolm rode toward Rosalie, but the captives got in his way, their movements without any purpose or forethought aside from the panicked desire to get away from those that sought them harm. A baby's cry pierced the air, and the hair on the back of his neck rose. He couldn't reach the princess; he couldn't risk trampling a woman or child on their disordered attempt at escape.

There was another call in the chasm—his worst nightmare. Hoofbeats thundered through the woods. Dark capes broke the treeline and fluttered into the foray.

The dark knights had found them.

ROSALIE...

Her mind froze everything but the panic when she saw the woman go down. Flinging herself against the rope line, not caring who she pulled with her, she strained toward her, the woman's green eyes round in her face, her mouth open as if gasping for air as blood poured through her fingers that were gripped around her neck.

"No!" Rosalie screamed, pressing her hands over the wound while simultaneously trying to see the damage. The woman's eyes found hers, and she removed one of her hands, resting it on Rosalie's shoulder with a look in her eyes that sent shivers through every limb. Her lips moved but no sound came out.

Please.

The captive's eyes flickered, her lids fluttering, and Rosalie pulled the corner of her cloak, balling it up and using it in an attempt to stop the bleeding as the sound of a melee broke out around her. The chaos faded as she focused on one thing and one thing only. This woman could not die.

Rosalie watched as her eyes fluttered again, their green dimming like a forest in winter, the brightness gone. Instead of pulling Rosalie toward her, the hand shoved at her shoulder, feebly, though her face still begged for help.

But perhaps it wasn't for help for herself.

Please. She mouthed again and glanced over Rosalie's shoulder. Rosalie's chest felt like a weight was sitting upon it as she tried to take a breath, the chill causing the skin on her arms to prickle as she followed the woman's gaze over her shoulder and saw Motle with Frueda clutched in her arms, terror on her face as she tried to keep from being trampled by horses' hooves and avoid the grip of one of their captors.

When Rosalie turned back to the woman, her eyes were nearly closed, but she shoved at Rosalie's shoulder one more time.

Gulping back a sob, horror filling every fiber of her being, Rosalie turned, her eyes searching for an escape, a way to get to Motle. One of the captors was fighting off one of the slaves—and a soldier unlike she had ever seen before. He looked…more like her than any of the Rusalkans ever had. His hair was lighter, his build slimmer and a bit shorter.

Staying low as an arrow flew overhead, she scurried toward the Rusalkan from behind and reached for the hunting knife at his belt. He whipped around, and his elbow struck her on the chin before his blade swept down. The blade caught her extended arm and she nearly fell, clutching it to her chest. The blood already on her hands mingled with the new wound, and she gritted her teeth.

Sucking in a breath to steady herself, she reached again for the knife and this time pulled it from his belt. She dropped and rolled, keeping the knife away from her body as she did so, and then she was back to her feet to move in the direction of Motle. Slicing the rope from around her own hands, she gripped Motle's shoulder, spinning her toward herself and using the knife to also slice her free. Frueda was screaming, her tiny arms flailing as the swaddle that held her was tangled and falling from around her small frame.

Rosalie ignored the burning feeling in her arm and flipped her cloak off over her head in a swift motion, nearly crawling away from the clash of weapons, grunts of men, and the screams of the slaves, wrapping Freuda in her cloak and handing her back to Motle.

An owl cry like those that the Highlanders had used in their communication with each other screeched above the rest of the chaos, and she spun, her legs trembling, and she half fell against one of the trees for support. Her eyes searched the crush of bodies for anything familiar.

A man on horseback caught her gaze.

The chaotic noise faded, and the frantic movements that flashed before her eyes slowed.

Malcolm?

He nudged his horse forward, and she dodged a flying body on her way to meet him. Shouting filled the air, but she could barely hear it as he reached his arm for her as he neared. Lifting her foot, she caught the top of his as it rested in the stirrup and gripped his lowered arm, hurtling herself upward and throwing a leg over the horse. She gripped his waist and felt his body convulse, falling nearly over the saddle from her momentum, and she realized that his right arm was tucked inside his sleeve.

Missing.

Nausea rose in her throat and she reached lower to avoid the sling and bandage that wrapped around his chest, hauling backward to help balance him on the saddle. He sagged against her grip as more shouting and a piercing whistle echoed in the stillness. She looked back—more horsemen. Those that matched the soldier she had first noticed separated themselves from the Rusalks, disentangling their horses from the chaos and trotting after another man who looked like a much younger and cleaner cut version of Malcolm, only blond.

Malcolm prodded the horse into the trees. Rosalie glanced back, her heart tied by some invisible strings to the chaos behind them and caught sight of the crumpled body of the fair-haired woman on the ground, her eyes closed, her face white, and then she lost the view in the trees.

She didn't realize that she was crying till the wind hit her face, cold and icy, tangling and tossing the loose locks of her long hair as it spilled messily from its braid.

Malcolm sagged forward again, and her body moved with his and threw them off balance. The horse beneath them slowed from a canter to a trot as the rest of the horsemen that surrounded them surged ahead. Several of them had slaves clinging to their riders backs, but there were too few. She recognized Lena, but there were so many left behind. Her heart surged in the opposite direction, pulling her back to where the sound of shouting still echoed through the trees.

"Malcolm!" The younger blond soldier turned his horse and swung alongside them, his green cloak billowing with the movement of his mount. Rosalie gripped the front of Malcolm's shirt and tried to support him back into a fully upright position. He was heavy, a dead weight on her arm that stung, blood dripping from the cut she had forgotten about.

"I'm fine." She felt Malcolm's muscles convulse beneath her hand as the horses slowed even more.

It was then that she heard hoofbeats behind. Turning, she saw dark knights in their wake, their black capes billowing behind them. Terror squeezed her chest in its icy grip like a hand crushing the very life from her body.

"Take her." Malcolm gasped, trying to turn to use his arm to help Rosalie switch mounts.

Strength, stupid or otherwise, rose in her head, and clarity cut straight through the confusion, pain, and chaos of her mind. "No! I won't leave you," she demanded, her tone echoing as she clasped hands around his chest and steadied him, kicking her heels into the horse's sides and keeping her seat as they surged forward.

An arrow glanced off a tree to their right and the young man moved his mount behind them, covering them with his own body as they made for the trail above and galloped ahead of the group that pursued them. Once broken from the trees, the Elirans surged ahead. The horses in front avoided the cliff trails towards the mines and instead pursued flatter land at the base of the hill they careened down. Rosalie caught sight of forested meadows spotted with trees, the forest growing less sparse by the second.

"Leave me!" Malcolm shouted against the wind, trying to pull up on the reins.

Stubbornness filled her, their horse dropping back behind the rest of the men who rode ahead, captives still clinging to their backs. "I won't! Keep moving!"

She kicked her feet against the horse's side again, Malcolm falling forward again, folded over their mount's neck, his skin pale and dripping with sweat.

"My lady, let me take you ahead." The young man's horse was beside theirs, the animal's head straining against his reins at her hip.

"No! I will not leave Malcolm behind!"

The young soldier glanced back over his shoulder, his face growing pale as he drew his sword and dropped behind their mount again.

Rosalie looked back once, the sound of hoofbeats following them through the trees. The dark knights were in fast pursuit and gaining on them as the weight of Malcolm's slumping body and her own slowed down their mount. The animal's head was now rocking in an effort to keep them moving as foam flew from his mouth.

Dear Jesus, please, she begged, words beyond utterance

filling her mind and spirit and drowning out the hoofbeats. An arrow flew past her in the opposite direction, then another. Glancing around Malcolm's form, she saw that two of the soldiers had turned in their saddles, bows in their hands as they reached for another arrow each.

She could almost make out the tree line, the rays of the setting sun flooding across the forest floor in an almost horizontal line, the shadows long and flashing before her eyes.

The sound of metal clanging rang in her ears, and she whipped her head back. The young soldier's blade locked with a curved one as they fought for supremacy, the dark knight ducking under both blades to reach for the Eliran's reins to tangle them up and pull them to a stop.

Rosalie's and Malcolm's horse stumbled over a branch, and they both surged forward, her hands torn violently from Malcolm's waist, her body suddenly flying through the air over his.

ELGON...

The sound of pounding hooves met his ear, and Elgon turned just as the first horsemen broke through the treeline, three of their spent mounts hurtling themselves over the waist-high stone wall, the other two balking last minute and turning sharply to avoid it, their heads shaking as they trotted in a circle.

His men were being pursued—by dark knights. He threw himself into Sigeric's saddle.

"Mount up! Ready!" He called out, drawing his sword from

its sheath and turning his horse's head with a flick of the reins, moving Sigeric toward the wall. "With me!" he shouted over his shoulder to the rest of the kingsmen who had waited in readiness at his command upon learning that Kenton and Malcolm had ridden back into the forest with a small troupe to find his daughter.

The mounted men followed him as he rode straight for the two kingsmen and the rescues they were assisting over the wall. He saw the fluttering dark capes and heard the clash of metal beyond, deeper into the woods. Kenton and Malcolm were still not within sight. *Dear God, protect them. Keep them safe.*

The memory of other times, other battles, the skirmish years ago near Kaira and then the aftermath in Pavlin, filled his mind with gruesome stories. The thought of his daughter, so close to home, so near to the father that had sought and prayed for her all of her life, left in the hands of such dark warriors filled his soul with terror and anger in equal measure.

His heels to Sigeric's side, Elgon's body was tense as he pulled his arms close just before his mount surged over the wall. He brought his body up off his horse and moved with him to keep his balance as they soared over and into the forest. He glanced back, and others followed, a few dismounting to help the kingsmen and their wards back to the safety of the encampment and the training grounds.

His chest was heaving, his heart pounding in rhythm with Sigeric's hooves as his steed swerved around trees with ease. He searched the forest for Malcolm or his daughter, but all he saw were dark knights, the esteemed Rusalk warriors, their black cloaks flying in the wind, their curved blades raised seconds before they clashed with the kingsmen. Elgon's sword glanced off the metal of one and swung back around to strike the rider from behind, his sword finding purchase in the leather armor the man wore before the dark knight plummeted to the ground, the enemy's horse screaming and half-rearing in fright.

Elgon's muscle memory took over, and his mind barely registered what was occurring as his sword crossed blades with a Rusalk warrior again and again. He caught sight of Kenton, no longer mounted, his blade crashing into a Rusalk warrior's as he spun, then plummeted to a knee, sliding his blade in under the Rusalk's defenses and taking him down before leaping to avoid another's blade.

There had to be three dozen of the warriors, though fewer remained now as their blades met their match in the kingsmen. Elgon dodged another sword as it swung for his head, moving low and catching the warrior in the gut, the force of his blade pulling him from Sigeric's back. He let go of his sword as it nearly jerked his shoulder from its socket as he tucked in preparation to hit the ground, the groans of another soul hitting his ear just before he felt the impact.

Dear God, keep my daughter safe.

Thirty-Four

LOST...AND FOUND

ROSALIE...

Rosalie's arms shook as she peeled herself off the ground, still trying to suck a breath into her frozen lungs, dirt clinging to her face and hair as it fell in a matted mask over her face.

Air. Jesus, air.

The spasm in her gut finally released, and she sucked in a gasp, too little, choking on it and coughing as her cramping lungs tried to drag in another. Turning, she coughed again, looking frantically for Malcolm. They both had flown from the horse and were tangled in the tall grass that grew beneath the trees.

There.

Crawling across the ground, pinecones and branches dug

573

into her knees as she reached his side. He wasn't moving.

And there was blood staining his shirt where his right arm should have been.

"Malcolm!" she called, the sound of blades, shouting, and general chaos drowning out the sound of her own thoughts and stealing her voice. She grunted, gripping his good shoulder and flipping him over to his back. He was a dead weight, her muscles screaming at the effort after her fall.

Then the young soldier was beside her, blood and dirt staining his face as he fell to one knee beside her, dropping fingers over Malcolm's neck below his ear. "Jesus," he pleaded, leaping back to his feet. He tucked his hands under Malcolm's shoulders and began to drag him. "Come on!" He shouted to her, and she gripped Malcolm's hand in hers, her ribs aching with every movement as they pulled him toward the low stone wall she could now see around the trees.

At the barrier, he grunted, heaving Malcolm's shoulders higher and trying to clamber backward over the wall at the same time. She stooped, ducking under Malcolm and lifting with her shoulders, helping leverage him over the wall. The soldier nearly fell in his efforts, but he staggered, catching himself, and she helped lift Malcolm's legs over it. Laying Malcolm down, he reached over, gripping her under the shoulders and heaving. She jumped for momentum, and he pulled her over and helped her to her feet.

He stooped again, and she followed suit, gripping Malcolm beneath the armpits, and she tried to hold onto his shoulder rather than the stump she could feel beneath the sling, cringing at the thought of how much pain he must have been in.

But she was just grateful to see him alive.

A piercing whistle made her jump, and Kenton waved an arm over his head at the soldier that had heard him and was now running toward them, two others following close behind with a stretcher.

When the soldiers reached them, the stretcher was laid in front of Malcolm, and Rosalie watched as they lay the unconscious knight upon it.

"Take him to the medicinal tent. He needs to be tended immediately," the blond ordered.

Rosalie watched as Malcolm was trotted off by the two other soldiers dressed just like the rest in green tunics and leather armor. She was shaking, and suddenly her knees gave way, and she blinked as they hit the ground.

An arm was suddenly around her waist, another under her elbow. "Let's get you to the medical tent as well. That's a nasty gash." The young soldier hauled her to her feet and moved quickly after the pair that carried the stretcher. Her feet barely touched the ground as he took her weight, propelling her forward. She winced at the pain in her ribs that suddenly pinched.

"The name's Kenton, by the way." He had a pleasant voice, and though it dripped with exhaustion, she sensed a strength and a surety behind it.

"Won't they come after us?" She tried to turn and glance over her shoulder at the sound of fighting still ringing in her ears, echoing so deep within her bones that she shuddered and quaked.

"This is Eliran soil, my lady. You're safe here."

She no longer made any pretense of holding herself upright or moving her feet as all feeling left her body.

She was home.

His word had not returned void.

ELGON...

"Where is she?" Elgon turned to one soldier, then another as they tended to the refugees outside the tents. He used his sleeve to stem the blood that trickled down his face from a gash above his brow. They had hunted the Rusalks deep into the forest, sent them packing, and found the remaining captives under guard, about to be ushered into the mines and taken somewhere only God knew. They were now all being tended to by the medicinals and their assistants.

"Someone should tend to that, majesty."

"I'm fine!" His voice came out much louder—more of a shout—than he had intended, but the feeling of utter exhaustion made it hard to focus. Being unable to find the one thing his soul most longed to see filled him with more of a panic than every Rusalkan blade coming at him at once. "Please, have you seen Malcolm? Have you seen the young girl he came with? Where is Kenton?"

"They were taken to Niran, majesty." A lone voice, panting, full of excitement rushed up to him, and he turned to see Tobias at his elbow. The lad was unscathed and Elgon drew a breath of relief, such as he could. Then his heart flew into his throat.

"Niran?" He trembled. The adrenaline had left him incapable of taking a deep breath, and now that it had dipped and surged again, he was struggling. Tobias's eyes widened, and without hesitation, he took Elgon's hand in his, leading him away from the medicinal tent where the refugees were being tended to.

"Malcolm was hurt badly. He needed more care than the medicinal could give him here, and she would not be parted from him."

Elgon's throat felt like a hand was squeezing it shut.

She.

His daughter was with Malcolm.

She had made it to Elira. He nearly came to a halt, but Tobias pulled him onward. A horse had been made ready for him, and he mounted shakily, taking the reins and turning his steed back to the capital city. The walls and parapets of Niran rose out of the moors, the mist from the sea gathering in a cloud behind it, pierced by the sun's golden rays as it reached for the horizon. He spurred his horse onto greater speed.

After all this time. All these years. She had come to his doorstep, and he wasn't even there to greet her.

He thought of Violet, her green eyes swimming with tears looking like Raintamount during a storm when she said goodbye to him. He still trembled, his face wet and cold as the wind from his movement hit him in the face. He was unsure if it was wet with blood or tears.

He hardly noticed Tobias riding beside him as Niran grew in front of him. The castle walls and the city sprawled at the bottom of the hill stretched out of the moor and up the side of the mountain, Illias Pass towering over and behind it. It was nearing sunset, the clouds over the sea casting shadows that chased each other across the moor as the sky deepened in color to a glowing yellow and orange.

The gates were thrown open as he approached, and he urged

his horse even faster, the animal stretching out its neck, his hooves sounding hollow as they struck the cobblestones, then rode over the wooden bridges and up into the city, winding and turning in the maze-like streets, wending his way to the top and the castle entrance.

He was almost there. He could sense the urgency and the trepidation of this moment gathering in his gut like a ball of yarn Violet used to wind.

Finally, the castle stables. The wooden door was again held for him, the watchmen aware of his approach. The horse had not even stopped when he slid from his back, his feet nearly giving way when they struck the stones, but he gathered himself and pushed on.

Entering through the kingsman entrance, he jogged his way up the stairs and turned a corner. One of the maids was on her way to the kitchen with an armful of linen, and they almost ran into each other headlong. She didn't say a word, but only pointed toward the medicinal hall, understanding on her face, a smile laced with tears.

His heart beat in his chest like the thunder of a hurricane with each stride as his trot turned into a run through the castle halls, his boots echoing off stone walls that had felt so empty and lonely for far too long.

Another servant was exiting the medicinal hall when Elgon reached the door, bloody linens over her arms, and she nearly dove out of his way as he charged through.

He pulled up in the massive ward room with its towering ceiling, looking in every bed, searching, seeking for a face he had never seen but that he knew would be familiar.

A curtain at the far right corner reminded him of that awful moment when he had realized that Violet was gone, and his knees almost gave way. He stumbled forward, the residents of the room silent.

The curtain was pulled aside, and Raphart caught his eye before he moved over, pushing the curtain against the wall and revealing a small figure sitting beside a bed with Malcolm's hand in hers. Tangled brown hair cascaded down her back.

His body seemed to freeze of its own accord, though he fell another step or two forward.

And then she turned.

He gasped for breath.

She had her mother's eyes.

She stood, hesitancy on her face, but her eyes were probing, questioning, hope flickering in them as if she wanted to believe something but was too afraid to even dare.

She took a few steps toward him, her own feet stumbling over the cobblestones. Her eyes were begging, tears filling them, wide in her small, dirty face that was covered in freckles.

"F-father?"

He could only nod, his shoulders already heaving with sobs when he held his arms open, and with a sudden release of any hesitation, she ran to him, her arms flying around him and her head landing solidly in the place over his heart.

It was then that his knees gave way and he sank to the floor.

Something real, vibrant, breathing was in his arms at last. Whole. Alive.

His.

Fourteen years. Hope lost, found again, and held onto with every single ounce of strength and some he did not possess.

Finally come to rest in his arms.

He cupped her head in his hand, his heart pounding against her, his shoulders heaving as she shook, sobs wracking her small frame as her arms tightened around his chest. He kissed her hair, his tears leaving their wet trails in her riotous locks.

"Thank you. Thank you, God," he breathed, and her arms tightened their grip. "You're safe. Safe at last. My daughter. My child."

She sagged against him, and he held her even tighter, kissing her head, then pulling her away and cupping his hands around her face to look into those beautiful eyes of hers. So like her mother, so filled with her own strength and a light and personality he couldn't wait to get to know.

"What is your name?" he breathed, his heart still slamming against his ribs.

"She named me Rosalie," she whispered. His breath caught.

"Welcome home, my flower."

MALCOLM...

Malcolm drew a shallow breath, pain flashing through his arm, shoulder, and side as he tried to draw in air. Every tiny particle of energy and strength felt completely drained from his body as if he were a dry well, devoid of any water or life.

His vision was hazy, blurry in the faint light that steamed in through the windows and the golden glow from the candle chandeliers that were suspended overhead. They flickered, their flames burning bright, and he squinted.

He was at Niran. In the castle medicinal hall.

He tried to swallow, but his throat was dry, and he turned

his head. He could barely see, his vision fading in and out, but he blinked against it. The fuzzy figure on the ground a stone's throw away was hard to make out.

He tried to draw more air into his lungs, but they complained at his attempt, throbbing with pain. He blinked again and the image took shape.

Elgon was holding his child.

He sank deeper into his pillow, closing his eyes and letting his head roll back against the sheets. It felt so heavy, too heavy to keep upright.

They had made it home. His mission was complete. His heart's cry and desperate attempt to bring the heiress back to the throne of Elira was accomplished. After all they had been through, every trial, struggle, and fear along the way. Every nightmare, every throbbing pain, every frantic escape… All of it had finally come to bring the answer to many long awaited prayers.

Thank you. His heart was too full, his mind and spirit too weak to think of much else to say.

Well done, my son.

Epilogue

HER HAIR CASCADED down her back, the front pieces braided away from her face, and her arm rested in a sling beneath the red and gold trimmed cloak that she wore over her dress. She had apparently broken a few ribs in her fall from the horse a few weeks ago. She hoped that Raphart would allow her to go without the sling today for the ceremony. Cream linen, soft and fine like the Vagari wove, was covered in golden embroidery and beads, flowers intermixed with birds in flight, bright colors gimmering with the threads of gold. Her tapestry bodice matched the colors and was something so fine, she had never seen the like in her life.

Today was coronation day. A day of celebration for the entire kingdom, and she would get to experience for the first time the life of the Eliran court that was her birthright. Today she was crowned as princess, the heir to the throne, by the father she had finally met.

She had longed for a family her entire life. Every piece of her hoping, wishing, dreaming of the day when she would be loved and held by those who would do anything for her and she them.

Her taste of that throughout the journey here was something that had given her so much joy, but also great pain. For in knowing another's heart, there inevitably came a farewell, and there a piece of mourning for something so soon taken away.

She touched her hair, the curls soft and pristine, fully clean for the first time in longer than she could remember. Her heart pattered in her chest, and she swallowed back a bit of the nervousness that tried to work its way up her throat. A child with no home and no family would stand before an entire country that had prayed for her and cherished her thought and memory as their own. A young girl with no one had become a princess with an entire nation at her doorstep, simply grateful that she was alive.

This room was a testament to her change of circumstances. The arched ceilings, the wrought iron windows overlooking Niran and the sea. A bed so comfortable she had lost herself in it the first night, its posts draped by beautiful red tapestry curtains. The room's stone walls held memories of a time in captivity turned on its head, for now her room was her own, and she could come and go as she pleased.

A knock at the door sounded, and she turned, her voice catching in her throat and unable to answer. She swallowed. "Come in!"

The arched wooden door swung open, and her father

stepped in, his ceremonial emerald cloak billowing behind him with matching gold trim on the edges. The crown that rested on his head took her breath away, the lions wrought into the metal interspersed with emeralds.

"Are you ready, my child?" the king asked. His brown eyes, shining in the light streaming through the windows, glistened with moisture as his steps were arrested at the sight of her. He let out a slow, shaky breath. "You are stunning. You look so like your mother."

Rosalie gripped the edge of her cloak and twirled it around her, holding it out for his better view. "I shall never grow tired of hearing that."

His face slipped into that look that had already grown familiar to her, one of pensive memory, like shadows across a face torn between joy and sorrow. He held out his arms to her, and she ducked into them. A place that felt so safe and where she drew so much comfort.

A place she belonged.

They held each other for a few moments, and she listened to his heartbeat echoing solidly in her ear.

He rested his chin on her head and kissed her hair. "Are you ready?"

She nodded and took his offered arm as he led her from the room.

"I hope you don't mind, but I've arranged for a private meeting with a few who wish to see you."

The nerves making her tremble, she nodded again, happy to do anything that brought him joy.

"These people knew and loved your mother even before I did."

She caught her breath as they entered a room, large with windows that faced out toward the sea that stirred her heart like a stoked fire.

"Everard!" She dashed forward into his arms which he opened for the purpose. His eyes were filled with unshed moisture, and she ducked into his embrace, so grateful that he had not just survived but had made his way back home. Like many of the friends she had made over her journey, she had worried that she would never see him again. He held her for a moment then let her step back, dropping to one knee so that his towering height wasn't quite so overpowering. He reached into a pocket, his movements sure and purposeful as he pulled something from within it and held it out to her on the palm of his hand.

She drew in a breath. A silver locket, a bouquet of a violet and a rose wrought in detail, hung from a tiny chain. She touched it where it rested in his palm, the metal cool to her touch. She glanced from it to him, and he didn't have to say a word for her to understand what this meant for him to give to her.

He lifted it, looping it around her neck and fastening it there while she held her hair out of the way. Spinning back to face him, she touched it with a reverent finger. "Thank you."

He nodded, the look on his face one of joy, gratefulness, and understanding. He touched her shoulder before she turned away to the others who were waiting. "Your mother would be proud."

Her eyes filled with tears at his words, and she nodded gratefully.

Her father introduced her to a man about his own age, hair

blond and defying all attempts at combing it down, his eyes so blue they danced like flowers in his face. His wife, who had the gentleness and softness and assurance of one who does not need to be loud or bold to be seen or understood, squeezed her hand in her own with a motherly smile. "Marcus and Dilara are your godparents, and they are the ones who have taken in many of the women and children who were rescued on the day you returned to us."

She placed her hand over her hammering heart. She was constantly reminded again and again by the wealth of family that she now had.

An old man, more than a bit gray and using a cane to move, held her face between his somewhat wizened hands and stared into her eyes with his two silver ones. "May the God who was everything to your mother be everything to you." She smiled under the benediction and nodded at the name her father gave. Fendrel, one of the lords on the council he had told her about. "Raphart informed me you were ready to have your sling removed." He winked at her, a life and vibrance in his eyes that was brighter than she would have expected of one so old.

Her father drew her from the room and leaving the sweetness and knowing between old friends made her nerves kick in again, and she tried to swallow against the dry feeling in her throat. Wide-eyed and trembling, she allowed her father to lead her by way of a hallway to the door of the throne room. Music played as the massive wooden doors swung open. He drew her into the cavernous room that glowed with light shining in from the many windows. Shadows like tree trunks fell across the polished wooden floor from the columns that sprouted upward to meet the arches of the ceiling, flying high overhead.

A hush came over the room full of people, some in beautiful clothing and ceremonial cloaks like hers and her father's, others dressed in more day-to-day uniforms, the kingsmen lining the walls at attention with their hands on the hilts of their swords.

Her heart hammered so hard she thought everyone could hear it, and her mouth went bone dry again as she stepped one foot after the other, slowly toward the two thrones that rested on the dais at the front of the room. She caught Malcolm's eye from his place beside the throne, full Kingsman regalia on, and the only thing marring his distinguished look the missing arm and pale weariness about his face.

She couldn't even remember the words that her father said as he helped her up the step and lifted a crown from the emerald cushion it rested on in the hands of a gangly teen a bit younger than her. He held it above her head, and then slowly dipped it, resting it on top of her curls. The weight was subtle, but something shifted in that moment.

No longer was she lost, waiting to be found. No longer was she a stranger in a foreign land, a captive to a power that wished only for her evil.

As a cheer went up from the crowd, and it echoed about the room, the ceiling holding in an abundance of joy and noise, she felt a rush of emotion run through her, and she turned toward the crowd.

These were her people. Her family. Her home. Finally, the lost rose had returned.

She held tightly to her father's hand as they wound their way down the steps, the golden light thin at the end of the day. A bunch of violets were gripped in her hand, and she held them against her face, breathing in the barely-there scent of spring mingling with the sea air that tickled her nose with its salt.

He helped her over any harsh steps, his hand firmly encasing hers. The tenderness but safety of feeling her hand in his strong one filled her with a gratitude she was far from being able to express, even after these few weeks. Her white embroidered coronation dress escaped the stiffness of the afternoon's ceremony and tangled in the wind, billowing against her legs and behind her as they walked.

Her foot hit the sand, and she stared with wonder out over the sea, the roar and crash of the waves echoing as they struck the shore beneath her feet. She drew a breath, letting the riotous freedom of it lift her spirit to fly high like one of the birds that adorned her dress. Her hair billowed with her skirts, both of them performing a dance to the song of the wind and waves.

A small raft waited on the beach, far enough away from the reach of the crashing waves. Standing before it, the king wrapped his arm around her shoulder, pulling her into his side. She barely heard his voice as it rumbled beside her till it picked up volume and the words reached her ear over the wind.

> "Never let our hope die out,
> For surely as the sun will rise,
> Our faith must waver not,
> Through flood or drought.
> Your love remains,
> Your promise is sure.
> Even though the darkness falls
> Your heart toward us is pure."

Tears flooded her eyes as the words of hope and promise filled her very soul. A weight rested within her as she poured out her praise beside him, unable to use any but words and utterances that only the spirit knew, communing with the God of the universe that was the maker and holder of all that she saw before her, but somehow dwelt within her in all that power.

Her father turned to her, holding out his hand which she took as they walked toward the raft. She lifted the petals and leaves that smelled of fresh spring air to her nose one last time, breathing in the scent before placing it on the small raft beside the bouquet her father laid there. He held her shoulders as a kingsman stepped forward with a torch and a bow and arrow. Handing the items to her father, he pushed the raft out into the water and stepped away again, giving them the moment alone.

Her father handed her the torch, and the golden warmth touched her face, melting the cold feeling from the wind. He nocked an arrow, keeping the bowstring slack as he waited for the raft to catch the outgoing tide and slip further from shore.

Raising the bow, he held it out to her so she could light the wrapped tip with the torch.

"Wait." She caught her breath, unsure, yet desperate for the chance at the same time. "May I?" She glanced up at his face, ready for a dismissal and half expecting a rebuff, but the tears in his eyes fell to the smile on his lips.

He nodded, taking the torch and handing it to the kingsman whom he beckoned forward. Taking the bow when he offered it, she positioned her hands just as the Highlanders had taught her and adjusted her fingers on the bow string. She swallowed, suddenly nervous that she would miss.

"Would you like me to help?" His voice was soft, reading her hesitation and filled with a gentle offer instead of any kind of remonstrance.

She nodded, and he stepped behind her, his hand gripping hers on the bow and touching the fingers that held the bow string. "We'll do it together then."

He nodded to the kingsman, who lit the arrow, and together they sighted the raft bobbing about on the waves.

"For Violet," he whispered in her ear, almost as if speaking to the sea rather than to her. She drew back the arrow, and he helped her balance the bow as well as aim. "Let go in three, two…fire."

The soft *thwang* of the bow sent the arrow flying straight for its mark, and a flash of flames sent the raft alight.

She let the bow drop, her eyes captivated by the sight, and he wrapped his arms around her from behind.

Lord, let me be even a small bit like my mother. The parts of her that were like Jesus.

She touched her hand to her father's hands that were clasped over her shoulder.

"You know the verse that flitted into my mind just now? It's the very one I said to myself, over and over, every day that I begged the Lord to return you to me. 'Now faith is the evidence of what we hope for, the assurance of what we do not see.' Though we can't see your mother here on this earth, we have hope that we will meet again, one day, in heavenly places. We shall praise the King together, and there will be no more sorrow, or tears, or pain. In that hope, I trust."

She rested her head back on his chest, the wind caressing her face as the flame burned farther away.

I can't wait for that day.

And she smiled.

THE END

WANT MORE CLEAN READ RECOMMENDATIONS TO FILL YOUR LIBRARY?

Use the QR code below to sign up to receive a FREE copy of the Clean Readers Guide to the universe!
Includes:

- over 100+ book recommendations sorted by genre so that there is something for everyone.
- a clear definition of spice and smut.
- targeted information outlining the dangers and effects of spice and smut on the brain.
- resources for how to vet books in future and find more recommendations.
- And more!

Sign up here!

ACKNOWLEDGEMENTS

This book was a journey and one that I couldn't have completed if it weren't for so many helping hands.

Livy – thank you for being the big sister I always longed for and the bestest of best friends a girl could ask for. Being able to walk in prayer and grow together has been something that has filled me with so much joy and thankfulness at the mercy and gifts of our King.

To the Instagram and TikTok community God has so richly blessed me with. . . You are so precious to me. The friendships that have grown over these last few years and the excitement that you have over this series has given me motivation and joy to continue on, knowing that if at least one of you enjoy this story and find yourself encouraged in your walk with Christ, every hard day will be worth it.

Erin – I'm so thankful for the way the Lord brought us together. Having a sister walking through this season with me and heading in the same direction has given me so much joy and encouraged me in seasons where I felt lonely and alone.

Micaiah, sweet sis. Thank you for all of your hard work, your fangirl comments and the way that you simply live life. You inspire me. Thank you for letting me adopt you as honorary sister. I love you so much and am so proud of you and excited to see what God does in your life.

Abigayle, thank you for your edits, your invaluable ability to be a cheerful critique! I love working with you and am so grateful I got to be on the receiving end of your incredible gift for editing! You are a treasure and your sisterhood and encouragement, and sass brighten my days.

Rebecca, thank you for being the bookish sister, for your encouragement and excitement for me and these books and for all of the ways you selflessly serve and step into this space to support me. It blesses me more than you know.

To my family. God is good. And I know His plan is perfect. I love you all so terribly much.

To my King. I serve You and no other. I pray I set captives free, heal the sick, and speak life and hope to the brokenhearted. I serve at the behest of your kingdom.

Till next time,

Victoria Lynn

JOIN THE ABOLITION MOVEMENT:

Human trafficking is the most prevalent form of slavery that we know today. While William Wilberforce abolished the slave trade in England, and it was abolished in our nation during the civil war, this new kind of slavery is more pervasive than you could imagine.

What is frightening is that Rosalie's and the other captive's stories are being played out over and over and over again on the world's stage every single day. But there is a way you can help…

Some quick stats:

- 25 million people are trapped worldwide in forced labor or sex work according to the International Labor Organization.

- Forced sex and labor generates annual profits of around $150 billion USD yearly.s

- Much like Dilara's early entrance into slavery, Nearly 20 percent of trafficking victims worldwide are children.

- This evil happens in our nation and most likely has a foothold in your neighborhood and city.

- The US is one of the top three nations of origin for human trafficking victims (US State Dept.)

- Traffickers often find victims through social media, schools, or in their own neighborhoods.

This evil is heartbreaking. But I believe we can end Modern Day Slavery in our lifetime! Let's set the captives free! Here are ways you can help!

- PRAY: Prayer is still the most powerful weapon we have and one that every single one of us can do, no matter our circumstances. Pray for this evil to come to light, for captives to be set free, for mindsets and trauma to be healed, and for not just the rescue, but also the healing of those who have been slaves.
- EDUCATE: Don't turn a blind eye! The more people who are aware of what goes on, the easier it is to spot, stand up, and speak out! This is happening in your neighborhoods, towns, and schools! Ministries like Women At Risk International, A21 and others offer training and resources on how to spot trafficking and what to do about it!
- DONATE: Rescue missions, after-care, home and job placement all take money that most victims don't have. Donating to a ministry or organization that you trust can be a huge way to make an impact!
- SERVE: If you are feeling called to be what I call a 'boots on the ground' emissary of the gospel, do some research and get plugged in with a local resource center, after-care facility or ministry and offer to be the physical hands and feet of Jesus!

Ministries and Organizations that I personally trust and recommend:

- **Exodus Cry:** Exodus Cry is committed to abolishing sex trafficking and breaking the cycle of commercial sexual exploitation while assisting and empowering its victims. *https://exoduscry.com/*
- **Women At Risk International:** unites and educates to create circles of protection around those at risk through culturally sensitive, value-added intervention projects. *https://warinternational.org/*
- **International Justice Mission:** is a global organization that protects people in poverty from violence. They partner with local authorities in 29 program offices in 17 countries to combat trafficking and slavery, violence against women and children and police abuse of power. *https://www.ijm.org/*
- **A21:** is driven by a radical hope that the cycle of human trafficking can be broken and are committed to Reaching, Rescuing, and Restoring those in danger of trafficking or imprisoned by it. *https://www.a21.org/*
- **Operation Underground Railroad:** has made a significant impact in the fight to end sex trafficking and sexual exploitation by assisting in rescuing and supporting thousands of survivors in almost 40 countries and 50 U.S. states. Our approach is adapted to geographical location, the needs of survivors, and best practices in the field. *https://www.ourrescue.org/*
- **Polaris:** Founded in 2002, Polaris is named for the North Star, which people held in slavery in the United States used as a guide to navigate their way to freedom. Today we are filling in the roadmap for that

journey and lighting the path ahead. One of their goals is targeting the systems that make human trafficking possible. *https://polarisproject.org/*

- **Troy Brewer Ministries:** is actively working with orphans and vulnerable children in Mexico, India, Colombia, Belize, Uganda and Southeast Asia. Troy and Leanna have traveled the globe establishing villages in some of the most remote, dark corners of the world. Through SPARK Worldwide, the ministry Leanna founded to Serve Protect And Raise Kids at their SPARK orphanages, Troy and his partners bring hope and the Gospel of Jesus by helping Leanna build schools, churches, medical clinics, water wells and orphanages for the poorest of the poor. *https://troybrewer.com/sex-trafficking-qa/*

SECRET VAULT

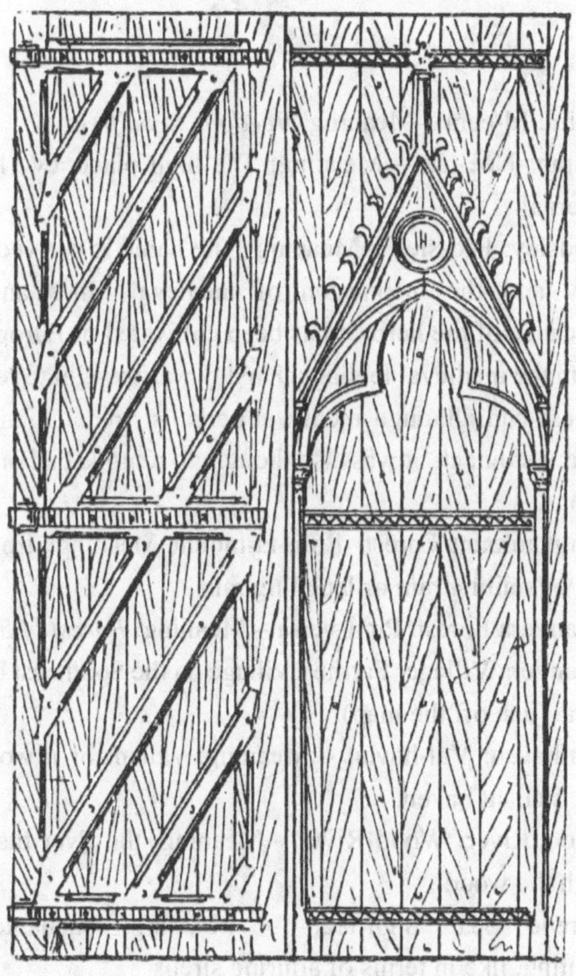

Do not open until you have finished the book.
Spoilers inside.

LOCATION GLOSSARY:

Elira: El-eera – Meaning: *freedom, to be free.*

Niran: Nee-ran – Meaning: The high place, everlasting and eternal.

Padsley: Pad-slee – Meaning: The name is derived from Parsley and the inspiration of medieval times and the significance of the herb. It has been cultivated in Europe and fits with the medieval feelings. Parsley was thought to remove bitterness and although medieval herbalists recommended it for a sour stomach, it was also thought to remove bad or bitter emotions.

Raintamount Forest: Rain-ta-mount Meaning: from the mount of smiling rain or laughing rain

Pranvera Forest: Pran-ver-a – Meaning: *Forest of Spring*

Pranvera Village: Farthest village on the Southeast border of Elira. (just off the map)

Valhaven: Val-haven – Meaning: valiant or a worth of haven. Valiant haven.

WoodRiver: Wood-River – Meaning: the river that cuts through the wood.

Sirene Sea: Sigh-rean – Meaning: enchanter or enchanting, like in terms of alluring sirens

Illias Pass: Ill-ee-as – Meaning: *Yahweh is God/the Lord is my God*

Rusalka: Roo-sawl-kaw – Meaning: Infested with demons and water filled with evil.

Izevel Mountains: Eye-za-vel – Meaning: Hebrew origin,to exalt or to dwell. Usually in the context of exalting evil.

Pavlin: Pav-lynn – Meaning: Small or humble. Of little consequence.

Kaira Mountains: Kie-rah – Meaning: God guides me and Between the rivers.

Vagari Plateau: Vag-arie –Mountain pass where the Vagari originally came into Rusalka and where they reside during certain seasons of the year.

Wraith Foresth: forest north of Vagari Plateau purported to be filled with the ghosts of stolen slaves and lost Rusalkans.

The Highlands: Family home of the Highland family who dwell far north and are one of the final stops on the underground escape to Elira.

Elgon Indulf: The prince and true heir to the throne. Name meaning: *noble or white, worshiper of the Most High. High minded.*

Violet Frell-Indulf: A farmer in the south country near Padsley. Name meaning: *Purple flower of royal valor. Frell means Free or freedman.*

Rosalie Indulf - Princess of Elira, Elgon and Violet's daughter

Malcolm: First knight to the king. Name meaning: *follower of peace, dove*

Richard Frell: Violet's deceased father. Name meaning: *powerful or brave valor*

Miran Frell: Violet's deceased mother. Name meaning: *worthy of admiration and peaceful one.*

Obed: The Kingsman that Violet takes in. Name meaning: *servant of God*

Enguerrand: The Chancellor and usurper of the throne. Name meaning: *Raven. Ravens are intelligent creatures, often solving complex problems with ease. Plotting and calculating. Will prey on baby animals of other species. Ravenous for power. Hungry for control.*

Marcus -Dilara
Tavish: Their oldest
Tristan: mountain - second born son
Tamaska: youngest daughter

Dracul: Head of the dungeon/torture chambers of Zuko
Zuko: King of the mountains
Rebus: Zuko's son
Merlin: one of Rosalie's guards
Talon: one of Rosalie's guards
Kenton: Was a boy and squire to the king, then an apprentice knight, and is now captain of the guard under Malcolm and Elgon.
Vieggo: derived from Vigo, meaning to fight, or war) Rensen's brother who owns a tavern in Rusalka which is the gateway for the underground railroad of Rusalka.
Commander Montcalme: Head of the calvary that took two battalions to Pavlin.
Lord Milton: An older lord of Pavlin
Huxley: Kingsman medic
Zehra: Violet's maid also taken captive to Rusalka
Raphart: head castle healer
Everard: spy for Elira and guide for captives.
Baird and Stephen: Violet's personal guards.
Azriel: The captain of two battalions
Fiona Hobbs: Mother Hobbs
Motle: the mother with the baby, Freude, who travels with them in the latter part of the journey
Lena: the young woman, rescued from a bolero
Adrian: young boy who was with them.

THE VAGARI:

Garridan: helper, secret keeper, guard and guide
Nim: Romanik's daughter. Young widow whose husband was killed on a rescue mission.
Rominick: head of the Vagari caravan, magician and warrior
Imanuella: Rominick's wife.
Izabela: their daughter
Bogden: their son.
Benaiah: Ben, Young Vagari messenger and guide to captives. Nim's younger brother-in-law.

THE HIGHLANDERS:

Mac and Nessa - patriarch and matriarch of the family.

Duncan and Carlissa first son and his wife
Their children
Levi
Song
Jaelinne
Jubilee
Jude

Knox - Rowan Second son and his wife
Their children
Liam

Cameron: third son
Jennie: Mac and Nessa's only daughter
Alexander: fourth and tallest son
Gavan: fifth son
Ian: sixth son

THE COUNSEL:

Lord Milton from Pavlin
Malcolm - Head of the military
Raphart - chief medical officer
Lord Rowan - representative of Niran and distant cousin to the king
Fendrel - representative from Padsley
Rensen - representative from Pranvera
Lord Josua - representative from Valhaven
Lord Loucas representative from Wood River
Elgon - King of Elira

VAGARI TRANSLATIONS:

Kochanie - my love
Mlody: young one
Gołąb: dove
Chwała Panu: Praise the Lord
Rano: morning
Pokój: Peace
Śniadanie: breakfast
Ciepły: Warm draught

RECIPES:

MAM NESSA'S SOURDOUGH BREAD

INGREDIENTS:

Ingredients

- 1 cup (227g) ripe (fed) sourdough starter
- 1 1/2 cups (340g) water, lukewarm
- 5 cups (600g) of Unbleached All Purpose flour divided
- 2 1/2 teaspoons table salt

INSTRUCTIONS:

1. **To make the dough:** In a large bowl or the bowl of a stand mixer, stir together the starter, water, and 3 cups (360g) of the flour using the flat beater attachment. Beat vigorously for 1 minute.
2. Cover and let rest at room temperature for 4 hours. Refrigerate overnight, or for about 12 hours. The dough will have expanded in size and become more relaxed after its overnight rest.
3. Add the remaining 2 cups (240g) flour and the salt. Stir to thoroughly combine, then knead (by hand, or with a stand mixer equipped with the dough hook) to form a smooth dough.

4. Allow the dough to rise in a covered bowl until it's light and airy, with visible gas bubbles. Depending on the vigor of your starter and the temperature of your kitchen, this may take up to 5 hours (or even longer). For best results, gently deflate the dough once an hour by turning it out onto a lightly floured or lightly greased work surface; stretching and folding the edges into the center; turning it over, then returning it to the bowl. Adding these folds will help strengthen the dough's structure, and allow you to feel how it's progressing over time.

5. **To preshape:** Transfer the dough to lightly floured or lightly greased work surface. Gently divide it in half.

6. Gently pat the dough to deflate it slightly and remove any large air bubbles. To make a loose round, stretch the outside edge of the dough away from itself and then fold it back toward the center, pressing it down to seal. Repeat this process five or six times, working your way around the dough until all the edges are gathered in the center. Turn the dough over so the seam is facing down, cover, and repeat with the other piece of dough. Let the dough rest, covered, for about 10 minutes.

To shape into bâtards:

7. Place the preshaped dough on a lightly floured surface and stretch it gently from the top and bottom, elongating it into an oval. Gently pat the dough to remove any lingering bubbles.

8. Fold the top third of the dough down toward the center, as if folding a letter. Press with the heel of your hand to seal. Then fold the left and right top corners toward the center at 45° angles, pressing

to seal. Repeat this process a second time. Then fold the dough in half, bringing the top edge to meet the bottom. Seal the seam with the heel of your hand, pressing firmly where the two edges meet.

9. Turn the dough over so the seam is facing down. With cupped hands, gently roll the dough back and forth; your fingertips should be lightly touching its surface as you roll. Move your hands from the center out toward the edges, rounding the dough and tapering the ends very slightly by using more pressure.

10. Place the bâtards on a lightly greased or parchment-lined baking sheet.

11. Cover and let rise until very puffy, about 2 to 4 hours (or longer; give them sufficient time to become noticeably puffy). Don't worry if the loaves spread more than they rise; they'll pick up once they hit the oven's heat. Toward the end of the rising time, preheat the oven to 425°F.

12. Spray the bâtards with lukewarm water; this will help them rise in the oven by keeping their crust soft and pliable initially. For an extra-crusty crust add steam to your oven: see details in "tips," below.

13. Slash the bâtards. Try one slash down the length of the loaf, two diagonal slashes, or another symmetrical pattern of your choice. Make the slashes fairly deep; a serrated bread knife, wielded firmly, works well here.

14. Bake the bâtards for 25 to 30 minutes, until they're a very deep golden brown. Remove them from the oven and cool on a rack.

15. Store bâtards, loosely wrapped, for several days at room temperature; freeze for longer storage.

VIEGO'S DRAUGHT

INGREDIENTS:

1 Tblsp of Organic Apple Cider Vinegar

1.5 tsp – organic ginger powder

1 Tblsp. Of local honey or maple syrup(or to taste)

1 cup of boiling water

INSTRUCTIONS:

Add all ingredients to a saucepan over medium heat and bring to a simmer. Pour into your mug of choice and enjoy! You can add more ginger or vinegar to make a stronger flavor!

VAGARI CHAI CIEPŁY

INGREDIENTS:

1 teaspoon of Vagari Chai Blend

1 cup of boiling water

1 teaspoon of honey or maple syrup

¼ cup of steamed milk

Sprinkle of cinnamon and ginger for extra spice

INSTRUCTIONS:

• Steep tea for five minutes.

• Steam milk with other ingredients

• Pour together

• Enjoy!

VICTORIA LYNN has an insatiable desire for truth, light, and beauty and has always sought to find them in story. Joining the Indie Author scene at the age of 18 with her debut novel, she has been writing and publishing ever since.

She seeks to bring the life-giving words of the Savior to a dark and broken world that desperately needs to know of His sacrifice.

A writing and publishing coach, best-selling author, seamstress and creator, she loves spending her spare time traveling deep into the mountains and forests, surfing the ocean waves, spending time with her family, turning her 2 acre plot into a homestead, or sewing gowns fit for a princess. She thinks perhaps she was once a woodland fairy and her current greatest desire is to own a mini-cow.

VIOLET lives her quiet life in her sleepy village, trying to remain as dead to the politics that are threatening their world as possible. She follows the rules, stays out of trouble and does her best to remain out of sight from the dreaded and overbearing Kingsmen.

With the new regent on the throne till the prince comes of age, the country has been thrown into a turmoil. Unlike the kindly king before him, the new ruler is overbearing, frightening and tyrannical in his rule. Taxes are bleeding the people dry and without the money or goods to pay, they have been forced into penal servitude and imprisonment by the Kingsmen, who show no mercy. The despair and fear that has taken over their lives has ruled out any level of hope.

When Violet stumbles upon an unconscious and injured Kingsman in the woods, despite the consequences, she is compelled to take care of the injured man. When he wakes and has no memory of his identity or past, she takes the only precaution that will keep her and her grandmother safe; she destroys the evidence of his past life.

If Violet's lowly Kingsman regains his memory, will she survive the consequences? And will the Kingsman be able to live with his past life? Who will fight to free Elira?

BOOK TWO:

MARCUS is tired of losing those he loves. The last shred of his childhood has been uprooted, and he feels alone… again. When the ruler's new policies take effect, the anger of the Rusalkan mountain king is unleashed upon the borderlands. With refugees streaming into Elira by the hundreds, the stories from the wall are horrific.

Marcus joins a convoy to lend his medical skills to those in need at the Eliran border. What he finds there requires him to face his own deformities. Will he be able to overcome them? Or will his life forever be marked by suffering and sacrifice?

Dilara's life as a slave in Rusalka was anything but idealistic. Consumed by a system designed to use, abuse, and discard the likes of her, she has been taken through the very depths. Carrying a traumatic secret and wounded in her frenzied escape, she finds herself with an unlikely protector and an even more confusing relationship. Can she traverse the waters of this new life of hers and make it her own?

Enjoy these other works by Victoria Lynn!

London in the Dark

With a sudden death in the family throwing a brother and sister together, there is bound to be some conflict when one is the leading detective in London. When a string of thefts suddenly seems tied to their family legacy, can Cyril and Olivia find the answers to their questions? And their struggling relationship?

Bound

When two children escaping abusive families encounter each other at the same lonely train station in the middle of the night, throwing their lot in together seems to be the best option for them both. But when injury lands them in the hands of their worst nightmare - foster care - will they be encountered with the love of God or dragged back into their broken lives?

When Beauty Blooms

Marjorie Kirk is a woman with no fortune, no prospects, no family, and no skills. She is awkward, shy, and the farthest thing from any semblance of a society lady. The new minister keeps turning up in the most awkward of places and she can't help but feel that her life is doomed to one of embarrassment.

A story of a young woman with social anxiety and how she learned to bloom.

What is Glory Writers Press?

What started with a dream for a community that stood for light in a world of darkness, turned into a vision for a Hybrid publishing house. One that supports authors, gives them a platform, and provides the knowledge, advice, and expert service needed to get them selling books that honor Christ and His sacrifice.

Because we are tired of compromise. It has crept into every nook and cranny of the publishing industry, and we believe as followers of the one true God that:

- We hold the answer to all of life's problems - Christ Himself.
- We should be sharing the Gospel message to this hungry world.
- Standing strong in our faith and convictions is a powerful way to draw others into His Kingdom, while also encouraging the Church higher.
- We do not need to pander to society to sell books, nor should we.
- As Kingdom creators, we have the mandate (and the ability) to shape culture according to His Kingdom; speaking truth over a generation that has fallen prey to confusion and deceit.

And one of the most powerful ways to do that is through a story.

What does Glory Writers Press publish?

Glory Writers Press is dedicated to providing Christian Fiction that:

- has a unique voice, intriguing storyline, and out-of-the-box storytelling skills with biblically sound faith.
- Clean fiction with no smut, sexual content, or glorification of lust. No cussing, or gratuitous violence. Think PG-13 max rating.
- Books that seek to glorify God, all while encouraging and edifying its readers.
- Christian Middle Grade, YA, and New Adult for a market that is saturated with bad fiction
- Books with mission driven storytelling and execution

Where Can I Find Out More?

Follow the journey and stay in the know on our Instagram account below!

https://www.instagram.com/theglorywriterspress/